The
Magic
Touch

Rachel Simon

The

Magic

Touch

Viking

VIKING
Published by the Penguin Group
Penguin Books USA Inc., 375 Hudson Street, New York, New York 10014, U.S.A.
Penguin Books Ltd, 27 Wrights Lane, London W8 5TZ, England
Penguin Books Australia Ltd, Ringwood, Victoria, Australia
Penguin Books Canada Ltd, 10 Alcorn Avenue, Toronto, Ontario, Canada M4V 3B2
Penguin Books (N.Z.) Ltd, 182–190 Wairau Road, Auckland 10, New Zealand

Penguin Books Ltd, Registered Offices: Harmondsworth, Middlesex, England

First published in 1994 by Viking Penguin,
a division of Penguin Books USA Inc.

1 3 5 7 9 10 8 6 4 2

This book was written with the assistance of a grant from the
Pennsylvania Council on the Arts.

Grateful acknowledgment is made for permission to reprint excerpts
from the following copyrighted works:
"The Name Game" by Lincoln Chase and Shirley Elliston. Copyright ©
1964 (renewed 1992) by Music Sales Corporation and Al Gallico Music, c/o
EMI Music Publishing. International copyright secured. All rights
reserved. Reprinted by permission of Music Sales Corporation (ASCAP),
New York, NY and CPP/Belwin, Inc., Miami, FL.
"Aquarius" by James Rado, Gerome Ragni and Galt MacDermot. Copyright
© 1966, 1967, 1968, 1970 James Rado, Gerome Ragni, Galt MacDermot and
Nat Shapiro c/o EMI U Catalog Inc. Reprinted by permission of
CPP/Belwin, Inc., Miami, FL. All rights reserved.

ISBN 0–670–85262–7
CIP data available

Printed in the United States of America
Set in Bodoni Book
Designed by Brian Mulligan

Contents

Prologue

A man tap-dances in the shadow of a church, click-clacking off the minutes as he waits in the sticky night air. Except for the metal taps on his feet and the organ inside the church, this section of Washington, D.C., is pin-drop quiet. The people who live here are bolted into their apartments, where they whisper behind dark windows and try to hide themselves from a killer.

On the steps of the church, the man thinks of the people at the service—*wireworms and beetlebores!*—and strokes the blade of his bowie knife. When he sat at the feet of the Gacy Guru, he learned how important it is to be sure everything is in order. He checks again: rain clouds are gone; bowie knife is concealed. Good. Luck is bound to be ripe. He pauses in his dance and shakes a cigarette from a pack.

The church organ strikes up a hymn, and the man lights a match. Soon the faithful will crawl into the street, eager to help a weeping man/a man with a broken arm/a man lost in the city—whatever he wants to be. Thrill shudders through him. In his suit, he looks harmless as a game show emcee. That is, if you don't notice the perspiration swimming down his face.

He cups his hands around the match flame, listening as the

faithful begin their trudge through the lyrics. Hymns make the hairs on his body stand ready as spears. He laughs out loud and draws the lit match toward his cigarette, but then his eyes fix on his wrists and he drops the fire; his shirt cuffs are red! How could that be? He'd rinsed his clothes! He'd done it right! *Cold water for blood,* his mother used to scream. As if he couldn't get it straight. What, did she think he was stupid? He'd fed his grandfather medicine every night. He'd washed out his grandfather's sheets every morning. He'd mastered time steps and shuffle ball changes by the age of nine, and the first man he killed was the director who told him tap was passé. And if that's not smart, how about this: he hasn't been caught yet.

He tugs his sleeves beneath his jacket until the cuffs don't show. He wears a button-down shirt and a double-breasted suit, and he looks the man. *Over here,* Epicure *magazine, roll out your red carpet for me.* In his wallet he carries cellophane photo holders containing hair and fingernail clippings, four different kinds from this summer alone. They produce a lovely crinkle when he sits on them, a sound that reminds him of applause, makes him feel like he's in a theater, tapping his way into eternity.

He leans against the handrail and relights his cigarette.

At the intersection up the street, a cab stops and a female gets out of the front passenger seat. Short. Long black hair. Not like the others he's scoped out around here, with their furs and pearls and pet poodles named Foo-foo. This one wears jeans and a sweater and lots of rings. Just like the only girlfriend he ever had. She's even laughing—sharing a joke with the driver.

Lucky break. As the Gacy Guru used to say with a shrug: *Of course, sometimes you* nths *won't need to plan; they'll come to you on a silver platter.*

• • •

The woman peers through the window, smiling bye to the cabbie. He'd wanted to stay with her afterward, so she'd spent longer with him than usual. He asked how she came to have this gift. She started to say—but then stopped herself, and instead, to distract him, she began to sing softly. It was a lullaby he'd been taught in his childhood; same dialect, even. He hadn't heard it in so long, the tune brought tears to his eyes.

The cab speeds away. In front of her, the wet street reflects the mercury in the lamps overhead, and gasoline puddles ooze along the tar. She steps off the curb. She could have asked for a ride to her Dodge, which waits down by the train tracks, hiding itself in a clutch of weeds. But she knows she'll probably find someone else if she travels there on foot.

As she crosses the street toward an old stone church, the bell begins to toll the hour. She looks up. The stained-glass windows are lit from inside and depict stories of the Bible: Eve and the serpent, Abraham and the sacrifice of Isaac, Job and his test of faith. She turns her gaze back to the ground.

A lone man stands before her, smoking a cigarette. She doesn't smell the exhaust from a bus, doesn't hear the echo of his footsteps. So he must have been there awhile.

He pretends he doesn't see her. She knows he does.

This female has tits that could make buttons work overtime, but her sweater's knitted up tight, so there's no handy little peephole here. And she's done something to her hair: purple highlights flash through the curls, then shift to blue, then green. Some wacky dye? Must be the stained glass, picking her out like a spotlight. Obviously this was meant to be.

She slinks toward the church. *Hang it up, pissant, the church doesn't like blowflies pollinating their pews.* Besides, the bell is dong-ing already; the faithful only have to do their fare-thee-wells before the church delivers them into the night.

He hurls his cigarette into the gutter. The papers printed his most recent MO, so he left his arm cast in his room. But big deal; every day he gives lip to the snidest drivers at his freeway tollbooth: he can think well on his feet. So what will it be—the *I need bus fare, my car broke down* routine? Or the *Would you like an escort? I'm on Town Watch* one?

He clears his throat and turns toward the female.

She is looking at him.

"Would you like to go for a walk?" she asks.

She lets him lead. He is jumpy. She usually talks first, to seduce them into it. But she and this man are already five blocks from the church and it still feels like Twenty Questions. He won't even relax into her jokes. If that's what he wants, fine. He won't be able to say later that he didn't have a chance.

Another block. They leave the affluent neighborhood with its historic church and head for streets where the row houses are small and rickety. The eyes of six different inhabitants peer through blinds to watch. She registers their presence, but he doesn't realize what she's seen. He is an *nth;* the Gacy Guru trained him to do a lot, but not how to read shadows.

She knew he'd prefer the dark. Most of them do. Habit, she figures. Though it's easier for her as well; sometimes, when she watches their faces during, she still feels angry. With some of them—with *this* one, she knows—it will be easier not to look.

She hadn't mentioned money! Now that was blind trust. The church faithful were trusting, but that came from sucking up all those hymns. But this is his first streetwalker, and his mind shim-shams at the thought that she's stupider than the on-my-knees-raise-my-spirit-up-Amen crowd. It's those female germs. Female disease. Gives them disgusting smells and blood. Burns out the lights in their brains.

Well, he's not bringing up money till she does.

All she brings up are questions about *him.* She pokes like a census taker. He answers in grunts. *What gives, pissant?* Her eyes creep him out; their blue throws off his footing the way an icy sidewalk does. Finally, end of the fourth block, he blurts, "Give me a break, will you? I'm the silent type." She shuts up.

Ahead of them, a weedy field slopes down to train tracks. But he prefers the street to their right. Down there are empty factories and a deep alley. He's done two others there already.

She glides along as he turns onto a side street. No need to let him think she is concerned about where. If she alarms him, he might run. He glances over, expecting her to be flustered. Instead, she smiles.

The side street is lined with old brick buildings. Rats devour trash as she and the man walk down the block. Hanging across the street is a faded sign: BAKER'S CHOCOLATE AND SWEETS. Beside her, painted on the bricks: TACKS & HARNESSES, WILL SHOE FOR FREE. A house at the far corner tilts as if it is sinking like a ship into the earth. It is empty. The whole block is empty. Even someone unlike her would realize this.

Between the house and the factory is an alley, a place where prostitutes take clients. But this doesn't bother her. It is hardly the first time a man has made that mistake.

Maybe she'll balk at the last minute. Numbers Two and Four had, reared up when he pummeled their noses open, and to this day their eye fragments shine with revelation, though a lot of good it does them six feet under.

He nears the alley, the bowie in his jacket caressing his chest. *She's a hooker, deedle-dee-dee, not a churchy, deedle-dee-doe.* When the cops find her, it'll smash their theories to smithereens. What a ticklishly sweet thought! The Gacy Guru couldn't have choreographed it better! What more could an *nth* ask for? *Ha!* A little laugh slips out. "Ha!"

She smiles and says, "It gets me giddy sometimes too."

He glances to her, aheming to fight a sneer. His gaze skips up her sweater, over her chin and lips, up to meet those coy little baby bl—

Her eyes—weren't they just blue? They're brown now! Wait, hold on, it's got to be the mist. Or bad memory. That's it. Corroded memory. *But he's got a great memory! He remembers every step Shirley Temple ever—* Then it's the streetlights, okay? Electric company ran out of mercury and used . . . iron, okay? *Get a grip, dungbug. Eyes don't do costume changes.*

He inhales to clear his head. *Plaster on that smile. And don't forget your manners.* Nodding as genteelly as an usher, he holds out his hand in a ladies-first gesture. She steps into the alley, and pigeons flap away.

He is breathing heavily when they stop at the far end of the alley. "You're so eager," she says, laughing. She comes close and skims her hands inside his jacket. As she twines them up his back, her wrist bumps the knife in his pocket.

His breathing falls off track.

"Relax," she says.

She gently loosens the jacket. It falls to the asphalt. The knife is well muffled by the cloth. It doesn't make a sound.

• • •

Who cares about the knife. Fists start the show anyway. You get the faithful alone and down and open their legs and disinfect them, and then you let your fists do the dancing.

She unbuttons his shirt. It's too easy to be true.

"Oh, you're sweating." She tosses his shirt onto his jacket and slithers behind him. He jolts when her tongue touches his back. He lets her continue and practices making fists.

She inches down, licking, wriggling out of her jeans. His back is slick with perspiration. She yanks her sweater over her head. Then, on her knees, she turns him around, and her fingers brush his zipper. He is very ready.

The female's hands fly, stripping away his belt, hauling down pants and briefs. She's naked, he can see clearly; suddenly the alley's lit up like day. *Who turned on the houselights?* He looks up. No lights. Looks to the street. No lights. Back to her. The light's around *her!* Like it's beaming out of her body! He gasps. "You're so excited," she says, hands on his thighs. "Just the kind of man I like." *Don't you know it.* She's bare as an audition stage, so small he could grind her under his feet. She reaches up—*her skin's just white, that's all it is*—and as she begins to stroke him, his worries ease away.

She wraps her hands around his cock—*ummm*—and then those damn colors flash again in her hair. Whoosh! Like stained glass streaking through her curls. *What the hell is with her hair?*

She lies back on her clothes and pulls him on top of her.

• • •

PROLOGUE

He is inside. He releases a shot of breath. *Triumph.* She is under him. *Yes.* He starts moving. She follows his lead. She follows his breathing. *Going along. The act. Just like a whore.* "That's right," she says. His sweat pours onto her.

But what's happening? He's too worked up. Like a boy. *Savor it.* Like a baby. *Get your control.* He can't. "You need so much love," she says. She feels him rising. He is too close to coming. She shifts into slower gear. *What's she doing?* He hears music. A radio must be nearby. *It—is—too—*

He feels more naked than naked.

Her eyes are closed. Her mouth is open. He is so close. *Now.* He draws himself off her stomach. *Now.* He pulls his arms up from her sides. She wears a smile. *Smile, germ!* His fists form hard. Her breathing picks up speed. He is so close. He raises his arms above her head. Sweat beads on her face. He is almost there. She thrusts even harder. "Yeah," she says. *Yeah.* He is on the top stair. He is at the edge of his breath.

He begins the downward arc of his arms—

And she is on top of him.

What?

He is looking up into her face.

How—

Her eyes open, and she is driving *him.*

He tries to raise his fists, but they are pinned. He looks to his sides. Inexplicably, bizarrely, her tiny hands are clamping his thick wrists to the ground.

"Bitch!" he spits.

"It's okay," she replies. She keeps her voice calm.

His breathing shakes, and fright shivers out of him, and he has to close his eyes, but even then he sees the light.

"What're you doing to me?" he screams, gulping for air.

"You'll feel better when it's over," she says.

Strange smells suddenly surround them—*baby powder, milk, and . . . quinine!* He hasn't smelled quinine since his grandfather was dying! He jerks his head back, trying to get away from the smell. But the blowfly weighs him down. He tries to buck her off. She strengthens her hold. He squeezes his eyes shut and belts out a roar: "Mrraugh!"

. . . But as his eyes close, he hears himself cry "Mama!" He's not in the alley—he's in a crib! He is banging on his wall and his diapers are wet and no one is coming! "Ma*ma!*" Above him spins a Humpty Dumpty mobile, on a shelf sits a bottle of milk. And what's that smell? Quinine! Coming from the room next door. Right—he can hear them, his mother sobbing and his grandfather coughing. On the other side of the wall. In there, Grandpa is dying and Mama is wailing, and all he has in his crib is dumb old Humpty Dumpty to take care of him—

He pushes his eyes open. He is back in the alley, panting. The black-haired female is fucking him, and he has no energy left to resist.

It is almost impossible to speak. He opens his mouth and, using all the will that remains, forces the words out.

"Who . . . are you?" But as soon as he says it, he knows.

"Shhh," she whispers. Her voice is sweet. Her body is warm. The colors flare through her curls.

It no longer feels like sex. It feels like something he's never felt before.

PROLOGUE

He is losing himself. He is slipping away. He squirms and struggles and tries to hold on.

"Let go," she says.

He has no choice.

"I'll help you," she says.

He lets go.

Author's
Note

The basic story of Celeste Kipplebaum Runetoon Kelly is so well known, many people have asked why I bothered writing this book. After all, the impact she had on human history was, to put it mildly, cataclysmic. But there was much more to her rise and climax than most people realize, and that's what I wanted to chronicle here.

The first clue that I should devote years to putting this book together came, not coincidentally, from my home, when I encountered certain fragments of writing, one of which I've published here as the Prologue. It took much longer than I'd like to admit to understand these fragments (so strong was the curse of the Gacy Guru), but once I'd cracked the code, I dug through them all and discovered "The Story of the Sea." Thus I finally made sense of the central event in Celeste's life, an event most readers don't know about—an event for which Celeste herself was not even present. As one of her friends used to say, Ain't life grand?

Many people allowed me to incorporate their words and experiences in this book. To them, my ever-loving gratitude. Thanks also to Celeste's publisher for making Celeste's writings available to me. Finally—and most importantly—a million kisses to my better half, who gave me a clue. I cherish you as my muse, my guide, my companion, and, of course, my typist.

—*The Author*

The
Magic
Touch

A Promise Fulfilled

Celeste's mother had been dead two days when Celeste was born.

If, during those two days, Celeste could have looked down the long road of the birth canal and seen the life that waited for her, she might instead have backed away, chosen to remain in the womb, slowing her own heartbeat and suckling death, growing blue and quiet, until she and her mother were covered by sheets, laid in a coffin by people she would never know, wept and mourned over, lowered into the ground. There she could have drifted into darkness and silence. There she could have savored oblivion.

Sure. And if you believe that, I have a bridge to sell you. Place your bid before midnight and I'll throw in some mystic secrets for free.

Truth is, if the birth canal had been a periscope into Celeste's life, and her ears had been open, she might instead have felt her grandmother Edwina Kipplebaum Runetoon Kelly babbling through her like blood, and the words might have snapped the child to attention, seized her with the responsibility of what she had to live. "Celeste! Celeste!" her grandmother would have exhorted her. "Those lucky enough to know themselves have an obligation to the world. Think of the many people who never know who they are: squatting openhanded, waiting for life to give them identities, certain they can do nothing of importance. Or worse yet—my dear, are you listening? are you looking?—worse yet are those people who know themselves but can't do anything about it. This could happen to anyone—even someone with a gift as wondrous as yours! Imagine: Einstein in a country where math is laughed at when it goes beyond fingers and toes; Dickinson in a house where Dad paddles anyone who scribbles a poem. Often, those whom the Powers That Be don't want to speak lose the ability to hear themselves. Oh, such a tragedy, to feel like the scraps left over after life snipped away the true creation. But you, Celeste, are lucky; you are a promise fulfilled. You know who you are, you have room to grow—*and* you have a gift so special, so tailored for its era, that the world doesn't just need you; the world *must have* you. So stop diddle-dallying. You should come out already, don't you think?"

Think? Good golly, Miss Kelly, how could Celeste have thought it through? Even if she could have heard your sales pitch. How could she have understood the birth canal and the corpse? Let alone the life that lay in wait after that day in the delivery room.

Sunbeams angled between the blinds, lining the delivery room with long fingers of light. The unborn Celeste and her dead mother lay on a bed. Around them stood nurses and Miss Kelly's children, their feet sore from the weight of their two-day vigil.

The three nurses knitted their brows. Among them was fifty years experience, yet they trembled at what they'd never seen before. Sweat outlined the underwear beneath their gowns: slips for the two women, a T-shirt for the man. The male nurse stood off by himself, his brown skin a sharp contrast to the paleness of the patient in front of him. His eyes flitted to the other nurses, to the children, to the sun stripes, but the place where his gaze kept coming to roost was the body of the dead woman.

Clustered among the nurses stood Miss Kelly's children. Tall and short, boys and girls, post-diaper to post-puberty, they wore a hodgepodge of clothes that broke every fashion barrier: mod, macramé, greaser, mini, rock star, migrant, Maoist, hoot-a-ninny, haute couturist, cardigan allurist, black leather purist, American tourist, spandexed, cross-sexed, Tex-Mex, and jeans. But despite the diverse attire, in the delivery room they all seemed to look alike; every face was equally strained with worry.

The pregnant woman lay on the bed, her brown hair loose down the pillow. When she was alive, the sun's rays had dived into her hair and lit up the red curls like stashes of buried rubies. But death stole all her color. Her red strands sank deep into brown. Her pink fingernails flooded with blue. Her skin looked like frosted glass on which no life had been written.

Only two days earlier, the nurses had thought the woman seemed ageless. That was not what she told Nurse Molly Bee when she admitted herself—"Seventeen," she answered on the forms—but Nurse Bee, cocking an eyebrow beneath her supersprayed, foot-high coif, felt that the patient carried herself closer to middle age. The girl seemed so *serious,* dressed to the zeros in a plaid maternity dress and clogs, her curls twisting free of a braid, her fingers clutching a knapsack that the nurses later learned was full of students' tests. Her gray eyes seemed haunted, as if layers of ghosts lived inside her. And when she spoke, it was in the calm words of someone seasoned enough to tuck pain into a back pocket. "I think I'm ready for my baby," she said.

Molly Bee had never seen this girl before, despite having worked in the clinic for years. People in more populated areas could go to hospitals, but the small mining town of Fossilfink Falls, Pennsylvania, down on its luck since the bust in coal, was too poor and remote to have a hospital. The clinic was it. Located in a converted farmhouse, with gadgets more state of the hobby than state of the art, it was overseen by a single doctor, who trudged into this black valley only once every three days.

Molly Bee sat at the receiving desk, studying the girl. Plump yet perpetually famished, Nurse Bee stuffed her soul with newspaper gossip and fantasized about becoming a celebrity columnist: blissful access to the pantheon of the famous! joyful nirvana of the A-list! muscled hunks licking her every crevice in exchange for a smidgen of bold print!

But instead she was stuck in this boondock that had long ago been strip-mined down to infertility, and all she could gossip about were people as trapped as she. So she scrutinized this girl, and— *aha!*—homed in on a naked ring finger. "Your husband," Nurse Bee asked casually, "know you've made your way here? We can call and tell him."

The patient smiled politely. "I'm not married."

The thrill propelled Nurse Bee backward in her chair. She composed herself, adjusting her uniform and her lacquered hairdo. "You've been seeing Dr. Twitcox at another clinic? It'll take him a while to get to us, but I can track him down."

The girl shrugged. "I've been doing my own doctoring. I'll just see him when he comes in."

Nurse Bee regarded the young woman. No doctor! But she didn't *look* poor. "All right," Bee said, struggling to remain efficient. "You need to fill out forms. You *are* insured, hmmm?"

"I have money." The girl reached for a pen, and Nurse Bee mentally paparazzied every detail—no jewelry, no cosmetics—so she could broadcast this story later to any ear within drooling distance. It would provide the local entertainment for at least a week; Nurse Bee had friends all over the valley.

Little did she know how widespread her audience would eventually be.

People still ask me if I can remember my birth. I guess they figure that since it made such headlines for a while, it should somehow be imprinted on my mind. But of course I can't.

I wish I *could.* Was I scared in my mother's womb? Sad? Or too preoccupied with myself to notice she'd died? I hate to think so, but I've been intimate with lots of people, and I've learned that when we're caught up in our own mess, we don't often think of others. No one is above this. Despite what your readers might believe, not even me.

—Interview with Celeste, *SNM Today*

Nurse Bee's eyes shifted focus. After all, the girl was breathing normally, so once Bee freeze-framed the visual highlights, she didn't need to concentrate on the here and now. It was more important to get going on speculation: to spin herself a hypothesis that might encompass this girl's life story.

Maybe . . . she'd come from a city. Yes. That's it. Erie or Scranton . . . in a car listed on a college ride board . . . Lacking family support and the love of the . . . *rogue* who dumped her, this girl came anonymous to these dismal Pennsylvania coal hills. Right. She'd be challenged but would maintain her dignity. She'd battle the odds, resist poverty, struggle against the uncertainties of a life lived without a man . . .

Papers piled up on the desk. Nurse Bee glanced at one, and her engine gagged: the address was not some city but the old school outside town. It *had been* a school, Bee corrected herself, but closed ages ago, after the Fink Coal Company went bankrupt and families packed up in search of work and the remaining kids got bused down the single road out of town to a school an hour away. For years, the old place sat forgotten, with weeds of every nastiness growing high.

Then the property was bought by a stranger, Edwina Kipplebaum Runetoon Kelly, a wealthy eccentric from New York City, who imported her utopian ideas to Fossilfink Falls and turned the school into an orphanage. She called it, natch, the Kelly Home. Children came from all over the country, not only the truly orphaned but also kids whose parents had other places to be or other people to love. Now pink and set behind an iron gate, the orphanage was known as a place where kids ran about unsweetened, unfiltered, and unpreserved, free of additives, religion, and television. They were educated—in fact, the older kids taught the younger. But they were also allowed—no, emboldened—to create themselves: to pick their own names, develop their own talents. And how outlandish were the talents they developed, or so went the rumors: kids who could understand the language of animals, or catch a piece of sky in a jar, or turn other people into trees.

To what end these "talents" were to be developed no one knew. Speculation bubbled up from time to time but always simmered back to the stock understanding that these *were* just rumors, possibly even generated by Edwina Kelly herself—who was, as far as the locals were concerned, a little cuckoo. After all, this was the lady who'd installed an iron gate across her drive that declared: TO KNOW ONESELF AND BE A SQUIRE, TO SERVE THE WORLD AND BE A KNIGHT. You have to be kind of flaky to do that.

Locals had always steered clear of the orphanage. Though not just because of Edwina Kelly. When the place first opened, years ago, Edwina Kelly had marched the children into town one morning, a ragtag menagerie dressed in oddball clothes. As they crossed the town green, Gluper Flugel, who was working off his usual morning blur at the coffee shop, peered out the window and proclaimed that they looked like a circus from hell. "They give me a fear," he told everyone. "Best stay away from them." The few who witnessed subsequent dawn marches agreed with Glupe, but after only a month,

Miss Kelly and her orphans ceased the walks. Thereafter they rarely came to town except to go to the clinic, and Gluper's pronouncement held sway.

Nurse Bee, however, wasn't sure she concurred with Glupe. To her eyes, the orphans seemed like decent kids. A little rambunctious and sacrilegious, maybe. But they never displayed any of the rumored weirdo talents, and though they were rather fast, at least they used birth control.

Until now, that is.

Nurse Bee squinted at the girl's face. "You're not one of the orphans we've seen before," she said. "You new out there?"

"I'm not *in* the orphanage," the girl said. "I live *at* the orphanage. My name is Marina Kelly. My mother is the director."

Nurse Bee blinked, and floated an image of Edwina Kelly on the girl's face. The old double exposure trick; most effective genetic test ever devised by gossipkind.

Well, what do you know: same rounded nose, same arched cheekbones, same thick lips. The girl spoke the truth. Bee's bangs fell flaccid at the sight. She licked her fingers and swept them into place. "I didn't know Miss Kelly had a child!"

"It's not exactly new news."

"Shouldn't she be here with you?"

"She's got a class to teach."

"A class! This is more important than a class!"

"The hospital will take care of me."

"Does she even know you're here?"

"I left her a note."

"You're about to have a baby!"

"A note should take care of things."

"Where did you leave it? How are you sure she'll see it?"

Marina set her hand flat on the desk. "I have been her assistant for ten years. I know where she keeps her messages."

Nurse Bee said nothing, but her mind ticked off each person she'd call, who would then call someone else, the news spreading across the valley like the lighting of a giant Christmas tree.

"Okay?" Marina said. "Now can you show me to my room?"

Marina had spent her whole ninth month in the office, rushing to finish work before the baby came. But in the Kelly Home, anything was cool, even being a grind. Besides, she did one thing that was viewed with awe. She had these incredible dreams, complete sagas of whole countries, intricate tales from other times. She could spend hours describing them, stories about Chinese peasants and Mexican farmers and people from the Revolutionary War. We loved listening to them. But then when she got pregnant, she stopped the dream telling to concentrate on office work. This was a great disappointment! Some of us tried to coax her out of work mode, but the only success was this boy who knew how to sculpt bread. He made her sourdough flutes, and even though she'd never been musical, she took to those flutes like Bach to the organ. So no dream talk, but good tunes, which made losing the dreams okay. You know, I'd forgotten about those flutes till now. And I still can't remember the sculptor's name. I don't believe it. This is going to drive me crazy.

—Iambia Teneye, as told to author

Nurse Regina Patchett, long of nose and long of legs, escorted Marina down the hall of the second floor of the clinic toward the birthing room. Light blazed with unusual passion through the open doors. "Oh my, look at the sun!" she said to Marina, about whom the nurse knew nothing. Not that it would have mattered; Patchett's experiences at the clinic stayed corralled in her mind. She was married to the local minister and never disclosed the slightest detail from the hospital to him, even when she knew it would provide the perfect embellishment for his sermons. She thought of her mind as a secretary-style desk, where every event got its own pigeonhole. As she later explained, she had no interest in being a messenger for scandal; she was only interested in being a messenger for God.

"Your baby picked a lovely day to come," Patchett said, fanning her arms outward. "The sun is so strong, I feel like I could touch it."

Marina's face lit, then darkened, lit, then darkened, as she passed in front of successive doorways. "I hope it doesn't take too long," she said, and then paused. "What's normal?"

"That depends on a number of things," Nurse Patchett said. "How close together are your contractions?"

The girl stopped. "My what?"

Nurse Patchett, a step ahead, turned. "Your contractions." When that got no response, she added, "The things that feel like cramps." Marina peered at the floor. "When was the last cramp?"

Eyes still down: "When I signed in downstairs."

"How long have you been having them?"

The girl's eyes ran back and forth, as if reading her recent past in the floor. "I had one after dinner, and then I felt nauseous all night. The second cramp came this morning." She looked up. "That's why I figured it was time, so I walked here."

"And you didn't have problems walking? That's four miles!"

"I did feel a little tight in my chest."

"Your chest is not where you'd feel it. That was probably because you hadn't walked in a while. Any more cramps?"

"Not yet."

The nurse smiled. "I think you might be early. But you can relax in your room while we wait. We have a TV."

"Do you have a calculator?"

"I said we have a TV."

"I heard you."

"It's color. We've even got remote control."

"I've never watched TV."

Nurse Patchett's voice retreated before her mouth could grab on. Her trachea gave chase, finally rooting it out from the pigeonhole labeled "Deprived," where it cowered beneath *Life* magazine images of starving children. "Well, maybe it's time you did," she said, locking her voice back into its box. "Let's get you settled in."

Marina continued down the hall. She sighed quietly and, as if speaking to herself, mumbled, "At least it's during the day."

Patchett considered that the girl might be scared by the dark. After all, their exchange so far indicated she was more sheltered— more a child—than Patchett had expected. "Does the dark make you uncomfortable?" Nurse Patchett asked.

"No," Marina said. "The fall term ends in a few days, and night is the best time to tally up grades—"

A choke cut the sentence short. Marina's eyes grew wide, and she clamped a hand on her chest.

"What's wrong?" the nurse asked.

The girl bent forward. "I—can't—br . . ." She sucked in air with a heavy wheeze. "Uh! Uh!" Her face wrinkled in pain.

Nurse Patchett shot a look up the corridor for help. All she saw was the sunlight.

Marina let go of her knapsack. "Oh, no," she wailed. She grabbed for the wall and leaned into it and gasped.

The nurse bolted to a room. "Urgent on two!" she buzzed into the intercom. The sun was blasting onto her face. She shielded her eyes—decided not to wait for a response—dropped the speaker— whirled back.

Less than five seconds had passed.

There, in the doorway, sprawled the pregnant girl, both hands on her chest. She gasped wildly as panic stormed across her eyes, like a drowning victim fighting for air.

"Inside you is growing a magic girl,"
Sang a man in my dream to me.
"Hurray! Hurrah! That's great!" I said.
"Let's hope," sang the man. "We'll see."

—Marina Kelly (Original in code)

The first to come running was Nurse Sammy Samson, who had been lingering over his Marvel comic and morning coffee in the kitchen when he heard the SOS. He screeched back from the table and flew up the servants' stairway. "Labor?" he called out to Patchett as he tore down the hall, the light flashing strobelike against the earthy color of his skin, the mossy fuzz of his woolly hair, the sunflower height of his body.

"She was barely contracting! She just collapsed—"

He dropped to his knees and felt the girl's neck. No pulse. "Jesus!" he cried. "Get help!" But even as he spit out the words, he knew it was pointless: Dr. Twitcox wasn't due until tonight, and when he showed up, he'd be crocked. Doctors in Anthracite County earned chicken feed. All the clinic ever had were failures, drunks, and frauds. Dr. Twitcox was no exception.

Samson spun the girl onto her back, grabbed for her wrist. Pulse gone. Shit! He tilted the head back, clamped nostrils closed, dropped his mouth onto hers. Somewhere at the edge of his consciousness, feet pattered down the hall and voices droned. He blew inside her. Again. Again. Felt her carotid arteries, but the beat was playing hooky. Christ! Pregnant women do not go like this! He pushed—fifteen times—and again: two breaths, fifteen compressions, two breaths . . . and as he worked, his mind spiraled out from under him: *Who the hell is this girl?*

Nurse Samson had gone to the same schools as everyone in

Anthracite County, and in his youth lived a life of loose pants, so he recognized all the ladies around—he'd never fussed over color —and sometime he would have seen this one, wouldn't he? No doubt about it, with hair like that. What about her eyes? He opened his eyes—one compression—looked at hers—five, six; her eyes were closed—twelve, thirteen. Pulse still flat! He pounded at her chest, dropped his mouth down again. *Stay professional!*

"How many rounds?" It was Bee. Samson held up five fingers and continued. A moment later, he felt Bee's varnished bangs rake against his arm and realized she was crouching beside him. "Come here," Bee said, and then he felt Patchett there too.

Samson exhaled and gazed at the girl's face. *Dammit, dammit, dammit!* He could see it—the pale tide of death rolling in, staining her red lips blue, her red hair brown. One more time. Maybe . . . *Maybe!* He covered her mouth—she was so cold he jumped. He pressed on anyway, trying Dr. Twitcox's imaging techniques—if you visualize life, you'll get life: *cherry blossoms, thawing mud, the spring Burpee catalog,* following the rhythm to the end of the cycle. But with each breath there seemed further to go to grab onto warmth. He breathed harder, clawing toward hope—*newly hatched chicks! freshly pressed forty-fives! or even . . . piss-poor cover versions of the rockingest record I want my jockey to play!*—but the warmth kept receding until finally . . . finally . . . it was gone. Even with his scope trained on the most distant horizon, he could not locate the faintest sign.

He threw himself against the wall and turned to the others.

But they had lowered their ears to the belly.

"I can't get her!" Samson moaned. "She won't come back." He pounded the floor. The sunlight that had skittered so brightly had faded, as if all the doors had just been closed.

On the edge of his mind he heard Patchett. "S-S-Sam?"

And then he felt Bee's palm on his shoulder, steering him toward the body. "What are you doing?" he asked, following her lead as she pressed his head below the navel. "I *know* she's pregnant!" But when his ear touched the cold curve and Bee released him and said, "Listen"—then, he stopped resisting.

He cupped his hands on the belly. "Hear it?" they asked.

He pulled his ear away and then lowered it again. He shifted to the chest, then returned to that spot.

He sat up and met the nurses' gaze. "It can't be," he said.

"We know," Bee replied.

But there it was. They all heard it. In the body of a dead woman pulsed the heart of a living child.

What made her come the way that she did?
What kept her breathing?
Gave us this kid?
Entombed
In the womb
Cocooned
Wrapped in gloom.
Five, six, seven, eight—
You better come out before it's too late.

—Jump rope song (Author unknown)

Above the clinic, a gang of storm clouds thundered across the tops of the mountains. The powder puff cumulus that had been sunning themselves cringed at the sight, and when the storm clouds began shooting off ions, the powder puffs turned tail and scrammed out of town. Swaggering triumphantly, the storm clouds took over the entire sky. Then, pleased and bloated, they let loose in an orgy of rain.

As the first drops fell, Marina was moved to the room called intensive care. This meant it had monitors, but otherwise it was as pitifully equipped as the other rooms. Nurse Samson sat beside Marina, scrutinizing medical journals and sipping caffeine. Every few minutes he checked through his stethoscope and, unfailingly: in her chest, silence. Then, lower, to the baby: a beat that could give Edgar Allan Poe a run for his money.

Sam's logical faculties pshawed it. But over and over he listened, and had the other nurses listen, and paced the floor, and listened again. The rain pounded harder, the sky grew darker; while inside the dead woman, the stubborn little beat drummed on.

Nurse Bee called the Kelly Home but was unable to reach Miss Kelly. "She's in class," an orphan named Kit told her, and he took the message that Marina was "very, very sick" and Miss Kelly should get to the clinic at once. Bee then tried to reach Dr. Twitcox at home, only to be told the doctor was on the road, which could mean he was visiting another clinic, or was sitting in a bar, or was simply driving, his only companions some self-help tapes and his ten-gallon feet. "Maybe he's sleeping out the storm under a bridge," Nurse Patchett suggested, drawing the blinds. Nurse Bee dialed her finger sore trying to get help, but the doctors she reached cut her short before she'd finished pleading; they were paid by the county, and county salaries were not worth the risk of flash floods or falling trees. And the one helicopter within flying range was in the shop. Bee bandaged her phone finger and conferred with Patchett and Samson. But with malpractice lawyers poised to snatch the last pennies off a dying town's eyes, the nurses wouldn't dare attempt a C-section themselves. They had nothing to do but wait.

At about three, Samson left Marina with Nurse Patchett and went to the kitchen. There he flipped up a few pancakes and ate and, beneath the roar of the rain, wondered about the dead girl.

She was not married, he and Nurse Patchett had learned from Nurse Bee. She was the daughter of the famous but seldom encountered Edwina Kelly. She was supposedly seventeen.

All the facts he could believe except the last. That she was unmarried, no big deal—it wasn't as if a contract was needed to grease the faucet of sexuality. He laughed; he knew this better than anyone. Well, his born-to-be-wild phase had ended long ago, no need to dwell on it now; that was why he'd become a nurse: to save himself by saving others.

As for the second fact, that Marina was Edwina Kelly's kid, no big deal again. Sure, Edwina Kelly could be as susceptible as anyone else to sensual pleasure. Clearly, she once had been. He could see some of her in Marina: their feet and hands were both small. Though Marina was average height and slim, Edwina short and stout and oh so *solid*.

Occasionally, when Miss Kelly brought an orphan to the clinic, Nurse Samson had tried to picture the woman in her youth. Through his mental View-Master he'd imagined he could see her as she'd been in New York: descending a grand stairway toward an elegant foyer, making her entrance to some social gathering. A ball, perhaps. Edwina would be in white, with bones so fine, guests would have trouble distinguishing her arms from the slender spindles on the banister— No. Not Edwina Kelly, not with her stiff-legged stride and stiff-faced demeanor. Chuck *that* image. Samson dropped in a new and improved disk. Now, in successive slides, Edwina emerged again, but this time wearing her standard gray dress and work boots; stop-started her rigid legs down the stairs; and, at the elegant foyer, stiffened right outside the front door, in search of diversions more in keeping with her tastes than a silly and pretentious *ball*.

He wondered how friendly she had been in those days, and how dogmatic. It was hard to imagine her other than the way she was now: severe as a general, coming out of the Kelly Home only to accompany a child to the clinic or attend the firehouse auction. She came every year, loaded pots and shoes and blankets into her jeep, and sped the used necessities to the Home. A few times, however, she stunned people by dropping wads on frivolous items: beaded gloves, pogo sticks, music boxes, marionettes, an oversize teddy bear, an undersize carousel, a fleet of unicycles, seven geriatric cars. Each time that happened, the town's collective gasp hovered until someone remembered that the firehouse had spiked the punch again. You could almost hear the gasp melt into a *Whew!* once folks chalked up the aberration to that.

I wear no jewelry
Don't own any silk
Walk stiff and fast
And drink only milk.

They say that I'm plain
Call my face poker
Think I can't feel
Like a dancer or joker.

But I know my self.
When I want to, I grin
When I see a gift grow
See a knight's work begin.

—Nursery rhyme, recalled by Kelly Home orphans in
We Are Here Together: Life at the Kelly Home

Now, when it came to the third fact, the fact of seventeen, *that* made Nurse Samson shudder. Seventeen, pregnant—not so hard to believe. They'd had girls that age before. But dead? *Finis? Kaput? Right in the goddamn clinic? Before their eyes? With pills and know-how and Sam's own Please* please! *aching to the bottom of his mis-*

sion? No. That could not happen. Not in America. Not in this time. *Seventeen!* His own mother'd been older than that!

The pounding of the rain hit rock concert decibel. He shoveled in a soggy pancake. It tasted like silt.

He sloshed the sustenance around his mouth and peered out the window. Already the parking lot was laking up. Beyond it, ribbons of rivers writhed down Route 55, which was the single road that led past the clinic, out of town, across Heecheemonkee Creek, and into the treeless hills, where, miles away, it joined another two-lane wonder, which was probably just as flooded.

Fog spread-eagled across the valley. Samson squinted through the glass, trying to make out the center of Fossilfink Falls—once a town and now more accurately a village. Misted over were the steeple of the church; the peaked roof of the firehouse; the five-and-ten; the grocery; the coffee shop; the houses. Though he couldn't see them, he knew almost every one of the houses was empty. Most had been abandoned when the mine closed, and now they sat, their windows dark, glaring at a town that could no longer feed them families, vacant except for the birds huddling under the eaves— blackbirds, the only kind of fowl in town. And above the buildings, on both sides of the valley, towered mountains coated with so much coal dust that not a single blade of grass could grow. In fact, Sam had stopped thinking of them as mountains. To him, they were simply enormous black dunes.

He swallowed his silt and was pivoting away from the window, when he spied something moving across the parking lot. No—several somethings. A corps of soldiers, it looked like. Marching beneath umbrellas.

Sam rubbed his eyes and stepped closer to the glass. He could not hear them. They were not chanting. And their feet, even as they struck the asphalt, did not make a sound.

But how could they? These soldiers were wearing sneakers.

"It's the Kelly kids!" he said, and bounded down the hall.

In the living room, he found Bee clucking into the phone. She shooed him off—"I'm busy!"—and clapped a hand over her ear.

Sam continued past her to the window. The marchers were closer now. He could make out the boy who broke his nose last month, the girl he once treated for sunburn.

And that had to be Edwina Kelly in the lead. There they were, the famous stiff legs of the head of the Kelly Home. Kids in Sam's school used to imitate her. To do an Edwina Kelly, one's knees should bend as little as possible, the arms should hang straight, even in the swing.

Orphans followed in formation. Samson counted: five across, four deep. Was twenty the total? No one knew. The orphans weren't enrolled in school and never attended church. Once, the nurses had counted up fourteen, but here were already more. Who knew how many existed? Like other locals, Sam had never been to the Home. But not for Gluper Flugel's reasons. It stung Sam just to give the place thought; he winced when he realized how many children could go unwanted.

Most of us were proud of growing up in the Home. Miss Kelly gave us lots of attention. She wanted to raise us to be what she called "Knights of the World": people who went into the world—which she referred to as a battlefield—to do good turns for others. To be a knight, you had to master two things. One was the traditionally chivalrous qualities: courtesy, charity, valor, respect, self-sacrifice, etc. The other was battle skills—but not *traditional* battle skills; our weapons, Miss Kelly taught us, are ourselves. In other words, the harder we strove to develop ourselves, the more effective we'd be on the battlefield. Which meant, practically speaking, that we had a freedom other kids would trade their best toys for. I don't mean Miss Kelly was never judgmental. It just wasn't in a way that restricted us. Her judgments came only when we restricted ourselves.

"What are you doing?" I remember her asking once. Rick had stolen some Disney coloring books from the five-and-ten. We froze, thinking, *Oh no, now we'll have to do time in the store.*

Miss Kelly strode down the living room, eyeing us. We all held our breath. At the far end, she said, "Coloring books are for people who want walls. Do you want walls?" Rick said no. "Do *you?*" she asked me. I said no too. One by one, we all did. Then she snatched the books away and stacked them in her arms.

"Ach," she said, flipping the top one over so she wouldn't see the front. "Disney? Maybe *his* crew was creative, but that doesn't mean you should take on his ideas as your own. You are all you, not anyone else." She sighed at us. We were sweating in our seats. "Get up," she said, motioning with her chin. We rose, slouched and scared.

"Are you a Xerox machine?" she bellowed.

"No," we replied in unison.

"Well," she said, hitching the coloring books under her arm. "Then stop acting like one."

She turned and marched out.

—Bop Mooney, letter to the editor, *Vanity Fair*

Nurse Samson watched until the phalanx disappeared under the front awning, then he scrambled into the vestibule. The sneakers padded up the marble steps like forty wet whispers, and when Samson reached them, Miss Kelly was standing by the front door. Her gray coat was wet, her gray hair curling, her face set hard.

"Edwina Kelly?" he said. "I'm one of the nurses involved with your daughter's case. Please, may I have a word with you?"

Miss Kelly looked Samson over and then glanced at the orphans under the awning. "You stay here," she told them.

Sam held the door for her. "I've just relieved the nurse on duty," he said, his head down, afraid his bloodshot eyes would betray his fib. Though they'd met before, their conversation had been rather limited. ("Bactine," went the typical exchange.) Now, as she crossed the welcome mat, her face was tight as a clenched fist and about as friendly as one. "You do know your daughter is very ill," he said. Also a shading—really, a complete blackening—of the truth.

"Yes." They stood in the front hall.

"And you know that she is . . ."

"In the family way?"

"Yes. You know this?"

"Do you take me for blind?"

"No, no—I didn't mean any offense, Miss Kelly. But things are a little nutty here today, and I just got on shift—"

"So you said."

"And your daughter is . . . in intensive care now. Were you informed of this?"

"That's why we're here. To be with Marina."

"Ma'am, not many people are allowed into intensive care."

"Then we'll take turns. We need to give her our strength."

"I don't know if that'll be possible."

"I'll just have to clear that with the doctor, then."

Samson looked at his feet. "There's no doctor here yet."

Miss Kelly glared at him. Then she glanced away, and for a moment Samson thought he saw her eyes widen, as if she'd just remembered something, and a kind of darkness unfurl across her face. But then she blinked away whatever she was feeling and looked back at him. "If no doctor's around, and we're ready to care for her, I don't see how there could be any problem."

"I—"

"Why don't you show me the way?"

"Ma'am, I think there's something I should tell you," he said, and before Miss Kelly replied, he thought he saw the darkness again. It seemed to shudder up from deep within and to pass beneath her skin like a tremor.

But then it was gone. And it stayed gone as he led Miss Kelly into the alcove off the living room, where he cracked his knuckles and faced her. It stayed gone as he explained, as best he could, what had happened that day. And it stayed gone after he finished and stood waiting to hear her grief. All he saw was a slow nodding of her head. All he heard was her silence.

"Miss Kelly called us into the clinic living room and told us about Marina, and we all just wailed our guts out. Except Miss Kelly. She never cried in front of strangers. Or laughed. She was totally non-nonsense, until you knew her. But her mouth was pulled into a tight frown, and she kept wringing her hands, so even the nurses caught on she was in agony. She told us there was hope for the baby, but it still took us a while to calm down."

"Around five, we went into the room and stood around the bed. The only sound was that baby monitor beeping. There was a male nurse looking over Marina. Samson, of course. I thought he looked as sad as any of us. Suddenly—maybe it was from being around nurses—I felt embarrassed we'd come empty-handed. I told Kit we should have brought her something—"

"And Samson must have overheard, because he gave us this look. At first we thought he was pissed at us for talking, but then he nodded slow, like he was mulling it over."

"Then later he ran home and brought back a tray of miniature roses. Gorgeous red roses, with petals as small as fingernails. He called us to the living room. He'd put pins through the stems so we could wear them. We asked where he'd gotten them—a flower store? He said, 'That'll be the day. Bouquets from florists hose you into catatonia. I'm a nurse; I know. But these babies just tickle the nasal passages. See?' We took a whiff, and he was right; their fragrance was much less sweet. He explained: He'd been breeding flowers for years, and these were his own special genetic mix. I asked how come they smelled so different from other roses. Was it because of their size?"

"Miss Kelly was pinning a rose to Bop's collar just then, and she looked up to listen."

"And Sam said, 'These roses are further down the odor spectrum. Didn't anyone ever tell you about the odor spectrum?' He caught Miss Kelly watching and winked at her. 'It's like the light spectrum, but for the nose.' We got a good giggle, and Miss Kelly smiled just enough to show he had won her respect."

—Kit Lincoln and Caboodle Davis, two home residents,
as interviewed on *Lifeline*

At midnight, seven hours late, Dr. Twitcox docked at the clinic. Dr. Twitcox was a bald sack of a man whose belly lopped like a swollen abscess over the tourniquet of his belt, and who had such prominent furrows in his brow, he seemed to have worms tunneling across his forehead. In from the rain he shuffled his six-foot-four self, prepared to do no more than culture a strep or bandage an arm. He was therefore quite unprepared for what awaited: fifteen children sprawled around the living room, and Nurse Bee, she of the daytime shift, drooping blearily behind the front desk. But the doctor had no time to process; his appearance in the vestibule jump-started Nurse Bee immediately.

"You're *here!*" she gushed. Children roused themselves as she effervesced around the desk to meet him. "We've got an amazing situation, Doctor, I can't even begin to describe it, you've got to see it, I mean her, I mean *them*, come, this way."

"Hold on, woman," Dr. Twitcox said, but Nurse Bee tugged him like a barge into the hallway. This was not exclusively due to reluctance; Dr. Twitcox always moved as if his feet were made of cement. The only off-the-shelf footwear that fit such mammoth feet was acrobat slippers, which is what he wore, but Dr. Twitcox did not handspring gracefully across the gymnasium of life; he lumbered, he stumbled, he brooded, he sat. The only acrobatics he did were in his mind, where he looped through slogans he had learned on self-help tapes, meditations designed to combat a world he believed was conniving to do him in.

Twitcox shuffled his Frankensteinian feet toward intensive care as Nurse Bee flapped her jaws. "She walked in, young girl all ready to have a baby, well, not exactly ready but would be soon, and when we were moving her upstairs, she just collapsed onto the floor, and we tried to resuscitate, but it looks like heart failure, massive heart failure, and Doctor, Doctor, the fetus held on, you can make out the heartbeat clear as—"

"You can *what?*" Dr. Twitcox said. He couldn't have heard that right, of course not; his ears were playing tricks on him. Couldn't she give him a minute to clear the storm out of his auditory nerves so he could *hear?* He'd been drinking in his car with rain pounding and it was still pounding and he couldn't even picture what she was saying— *Small miracle you ever got through medical school, can't so much as find the last fifth in your own back seat let alone make sense of a medical emergen—* What was he doing! *Stop right now and repeat after me: You are Dr. Fig Newton Twitcox, the son of a doctor, upright and sincere slayer of sickness, hero of the helpless, keeper of the American way.*

"Let me make sure I'm grasping this amazing situation." *You dodge a crisis artfully.* "How old is the mother?"

"Seventeen. And was. She didn't make it."

You—"Was! Do you know what you're suggesting?"

"Yes! The girl had no history of heart trouble, no family precedent. And now she's dead and the baby alive. It's very strange. Mystifying. We moved her here—"

Nurse Bee pushed a door open. Inside stood five children, a squat middle-aged lady, and Nurses Patchett and Samson, and every last one of them was wearing a miniature rose.

"What's this?" Dr. Twitcox said—*You bandage chaos, lance fear, seize the bull by the horns*—and then, looking back to Nurse Bee: "Are these people sick?"

"No, no, they're family—well, sort of family."

Dr. Twitcox's gaze hopped from one pair of expectant eyes to the next as the fetal monitor beep-beeped like a bouncing ball— *You bribed your way through med school, and the whole time they laughed at you, moron, punybrain*—and tried to employ some positive visualization, but the only imaging he could squeeze out of his constipated mind was the AMA glowering at him with hands planted firmly on its hips.

He hooked his finger inside his collar and shaved off a film of sweat. Then he inserted "Advanced Self-Help" into his thoughts and cranked up the volume—*You are the pooh-pooher of snickering, the paragon of placidity*—and finally, back in control, prescribed, "Remove these people."

The stout matron waved to the children, and the intruders departed, closing the door behind them.

Dr. Twitcox turned to the nurses. "Now," he said, baritone coursing authoritatively through his blood. "Explain."

Nurse Samson took a deep breath. "We can't. But the fetus is alive—you can see for yourself." He motioned toward the monitor.

"The umbilical cord ceases operating postmortem," Twitcox said. "Evidently your machine has malfunctioned."

"But we—"

"They do teach the umbilical cord in nursing school, yes?"

Nurse Samson held out a stethoscope. "Listen," he said.

Twitcox had never liked tests. Besides, he was tired from driving and couldn't concentrate with all that damn rain, and was the fifth in the back seat or had he finished it in Coalbelch— *Assess the situation.* Right. *You can do it, you can come out on top, best defense is a good—*

"Here, sir," Samson said, waving the stethoscope.

Twitcox reached for the limp instrument, fit it around his neck, and clamped in the eartips. Then he dragged his feet to the patient and pressed the stethoscope to the woman's abdomen.

He sighed, and tapped his foot, and was about to roll his eyes, when he heard it: Pump, pump. He picked up the instrument and landed it again. Pump, pump. He glanced at the nurses. They were smirking. He moved the stethoscope to the mother's chest. Flat sound of death. It could not be! *Remain calm at all times—* "This is some kind of trick," he said.

"It's not," "*It's not,*" he heard. He closed his eyes and popped in "Super Self-Help," but with the pulse coming through the eartips and those voices pelting him, he could barely hear— *You bandage . . . ch . . . aos, lance fear, seize . . . the boot by the corn—* He sped it up—*YouareDr.FigNewtonTwitcoxsonofadoctor,* blasted the volume, UPRIGHT AND SINCERE, SLAYER OF SICKNESS—but when he opened his eyes and faced the screaming nurses, the tape snapped and spun out of control—CREAM OF THE CROOKS, KING OF THE KONG—

He threw down the stethoscope. "Don't do this to me!"

"It's not us," the male nurse said, and the lady nurses spat at him—"It's true!"—and their tongues lashed out at him, their eyebrows vibrated like cilia—"The baby's alive!"

Accusations! Lies! Fabrications of a situation that's an impersonation of truth! Their voices swarmed around him like wasps. Just like in medical school! *Duncecap and dodo.* A vivisection of his role! A bleeding of his soul!

"Get away!" he shouted, flinging up his arms for a shield.

They lunged at him, talons out. "Wait!" they cried.

"It's not possible!" He backed up.

They ran after him, shouting. *The conspiracy strikes! The coup d'etat succeeds!*

"Not possible!" He whirled around and dived for the door.

The doctor wasn't the only one who couldn't believe it, but at least we didn't take off like him. A grown man crashing into kids to get down a hallway! Last we saw of him was his car squealing into the rain. Great, we thought. A hysterical Hippocratic. And people wondered why we scoffed at authority.

—Broomcorn Jerry, as told to author

Nurse Bee buzzed back to phone duty, but with the storm peeling plywood loose from windows and swatting cars into creeks like tin cans, the few doctors she reached—she only bothered with well-paid ones this time—had their hands full. "I got people stuck in cars, swept away by rivers, screaming with broken legs—and you expect me to give a shit about some *dead woman?*"

Meanwhile, the vigil persisted in shifts. Over the night, faces became attached to names. Bee taught some kids her no-fail approach to memorizing numbers (phone numbers were her specialty, but she worked on times tables with them). Patchett taught the lankier girls how to double-helix their legs when they sat ("We tall ladies must take extra care to keep our knees together"). All Samson did was stay with Marina.

As for the baby, it seemed to be in no hurry. When Marina had shown up at the clinic that sunny morning, she thought her baby was primed for its grand debut, but with death and rain, the child had ducked back into the dressing room.

And so orphans and nurses waited. Feet fell asleep, tears watered the miniature flowers, hands were held, voices consoled. When the orphans weren't near, Bee gabbled with her phone pals on one line, while Patchett, on another, cooed velvet nothings to her husband. When the nurses weren't near, the orphans distracted each other with parlor tricks. Nobeline expertly folded herself into invisibility; Catnip twisted her body into the most difficult of contortions; Bronto wrestled color out of the carpet and then massaged it back in.

But the orphans had seen all these tricks before, and their attentiveness soon dissolved into yawns. Something had to happen.

Finally, in late afternoon of the second day, the rain broke off. It stopped as suddenly as if a sheriff had banged at the door to the storm clouds' orgy: the clouds hauled on their skirts and zipped up their flies, threw their amplifiers and light show into suitcases, and skedaddled out of town, leaving a clear sky to the homecoming strut of the radiant and victorious sunlight.

The end of the storm startled the orphans, who'd lived with the black noise for two days; they peeked outside and reeled from the sun. "Open the blinds," Samson said, and Kit and Caboodle screwed the window wands until light stripes whiplashed the room.

And as the sun struck Marina, the baby decided to come.

The first sign was the quickening of the beep on the heart monitor. *Blip . . . blip . . . beep! beep! beep!* Samson tore down the hallway, alerting everyone. A stampede returned to intensive care. Instructions were dispensed hastily, and the nurses, shot through with adrenaline, wheeled the bed near new monitors and set up Marina for delivery. Patchett and Samson stood between the legs. Bee planted herself at the monitors. All around waited orphans, hands washed and ready.

"Now?" someone asked.

"Now," Sam said.

And wasting no time, he slipped his fingers into the cold inside Marina's body. It was soft still, but so very icy. He felt his way up the birth canal, his marvel at what was happening fading beneath the demands of the moment. When he came to her dilated cervix, he felt the infant's head. "I've got it!" he said, and then worried how to get it *out*. She's dead, she's dead: the thought stopped all logic. But before he could ask for ideas, he felt the child, without benefit of contractions, without the nudge of modern medicine, without even a pair of forceps knocking at the front door, begin to creep out. "What the—" Sam began, and then trailed off: because coming into his hands he could feel the head. He cradled the tiny bulge and then felt the neck surge forward. How was this happening? But he had no time to think; this kid wasn't crawling out—this kid was going for the six-inch dash! Sam backed down the birth canal as the infant tore pell-mell for the finish line, then he yanked his hands into the room to clear the way, and then, before he could blink, before he could breathe, into his arms and the light of the room splashed the child: the head, bearing a regular prune face; the body, small and slippery and red; the legs, skinny and new; the feet. And when the last toe was out and she lay fully in his hands, this child from a dead woman let loose a piercing scream.

He swung the howling infant up for all to see.

"It's a girl!" Bee said. Her hair had flopped into her eyes, and she forgot to brush it off.

They all grabbed each other, laughing inside their crying inside their laughing. Orphans and nurses flushed shades of red that to this day have not been appropriated by valentine cards. Even Miss Kelly, revealing to the nurses that she was not as mono-expressional as they had thought, let herself go and wept.

In the midst of all the hoopla and whoopee, Nurse Patchett wiped her tears and held out her hands. "I'll clean her."

"Not yet," Samson said. The child was bawling like all newborns, and in every way—size, appearance, gestures—she was just like a newborn, except for one thing: she did not have a living mother. And for some reason that Sammy Samson could not understand at that moment, logic and medical training absconded for parts unknown, and, abandoned by them, all he had left was his heart, and he said to Nurse Patchett, "Let her touch her mother. Just this once."

The child still in his hands, Sam backed away from the stirrups. He threaded himself through the orphans, who quieted as he passed, and Miss Kelly, who watched, wiping her eyes. The orphans parted to let him reach the bed, and by the time he stood before Marina, there was barely a stray snuffle in the room.

On the bed lay Marina, motionless and white, eyes closed forever. He held the child so the newborn faced her mother. The baby wiggled. Sam tightened his grasp on the tiny waist and whispered, "This is your mother." Then he brought the child down and pressed her between the mother's breasts.

And when the child's skin touched the skin of the dead woman—when the body of this new person came down on the corpse of the old—that's when it happened. The moment that's since become a requisite dot on history-book time lines. The moment we all think about when we hear the name Fossilfink Falls. The moment that kicked off the very reason you're reading this book.

The baby stopped thrashing. The room grew completely quiet. And as everyone froze—nurses gripping instruments, children hugging each other, Sam's hands holding the child's waist—Marina's eyes began to flicker.

"What's that?" Patchett said, and the group moved closer. Marina's eyes fluttered clearly, and while the nurses stood spellbound, their patient drew a breath.

Color rose into the white face, and the room burst into shouting and tears. Marina inhaled a second time, and a third. Her heart monitor began beeping. Sweat bloomed on her forehead, and Samson rushed forward to pat it away.

"It's a miracle! It's a miracle!" he cried, looking into Marina's beautiful gray eyes.

So the child was named Celeste, to signify the heavenly wonder of the moment. And that is how she became known by the world.

The Story of the Sea
Day One   Morning

At a dock in New York City, on a glorious sapphire morning, an ocean liner hauls up its gangplank. The all aboard siren bellows one last time, and the band on deck strikes up a rollicking tune. On the ground, people wave handkerchiefs to their departing loved ones. "Lucky stiffs," grumble the well-wishers, aching to flee their daily grind and join the color and gaiety on the ship. Up on deck, the lucky stiffs have forgotten their daily grind. Wives in full skirts and broad-brimmed hats clasp husbands to their lips; men in freshly shined oxfords and double-breasted suits pinch lovers on their behinds. Sunlight bathes the deck. The passengers rejoice at the three days ahead, which seem as magical and full of hope as the glittering ocean around them.

But one passenger does not rejoice. To her, hope is just a four-letter word, a word that makes her wince because it seems such a lie. Her name is Edwina Kipplebaum Runetoon Kelly. She is thirty-eight, married, childless, and tired. She came on this cruise with her husband, but John Kelly is nowhere to be found among the white gloves and lipsticked smiles. He can't be bothered with formalities like affection; champagne in the cabin is too much for him. No, as the crew reels up the anchor and the ship pulls out to sea, John Kelly cavorts on a lower deck, cha-cha-ing his fingers up the silk stockings of a ship attendant. All around Edwina, people feed their passions. Edwina, alone at the railing, feeds a seagull circling above.

It is the first vacation she has had in years. She pushed for it in desperation, bribing John Kelly away from his office with the promise of paid tickets. "I'll use the rest of my inheritance," she told him, since every penny she earned at the factory got sucked up by necessities. It will be worth it, she reasoned. Finally, she might get rid of the empty feeling that life is no more than a garment factory with green paint over the windows and bosses who talk to her breasts (when they talk to her at all) and a home with two well-worn depressions on opposite sides of the mattress.

Well, dream on. Because here she is, sitting out the party once again. In front of her, lovers toast the sea in joy, children hold up pinwheels to the breeze, and Edwina realizes that the only thing this trip will get rid of is her bank account.

If she were one to pray, she would.

But Edwina doesn't believe in God. For that matter, she doesn't believe in the Devil. To Edwina, God is a pacifier, a story created to steam the wrinkles out of nightmares. The Devil is a backup system; if the desire for comfort doesn't control you, perhaps the fear of evil will. They are real only in movies and the minds of the devout. Not in Edwina Kelly. She believes in them no more than she believes in hope.

But this day, as she watches the ocean ahead, monotonously flat for miles until it slams against the sky, she thinks how much the sea looks like her future.

And how she'd give anything to change that.

Cloud
Lady

Nurse Samson was right. The birth of Celeste and the resurrection of her mother *were* miracles. But it's one thing to bring a person back from the dead. It's another thing altogether to bring her back so the death experience is no more than a hiccup in the otherwise smooth flow of a life.

Death is not forty winks, not a stroll around a supermarket, not a romantic repose in a gondola, not a slow dance at the prom. Death does not dream, or glide, or caress, or whisper. Death stomps and thunders. It makes mincemeat of time. It is where nouns and verbs become One. These were some of the thoughts the orphans had about death. Though Miss Kelly abhorred organized religion, she encouraged the orphans to air their ideas on mystical matters: "so *you* can decide how you feel, without anyone shoving beliefs down your throat." And many ideas were bounced around the Home, but the orphans, like most people, were never sure whether they were even in the vicinity of the basket, much less whether they'd scored a theological slam dunk.

All they were sure of was that when Marina awoke from her two days—two days when the invisibility experts among them did not see her floating beatifically above her body, and the aspiring psychics among them got only static when they dialed their Ouija boards—Marina was nowhere near what she had been before.

At first, during the celebrations, everyone was too giddy to notice. They just figured that, as with any new mom, Marina's behavior could be attributed to exhaustion. After all, Celeste showed no signs of having been birthed through death. She was average length and weight, displayed no unusual markings, no extra fingers or toes. Ordinary black hair whorled on her head, porcelain-white skin covered her body.

Samson was the first to consider that Marina might have spent too much time in the court of the Grim Reaper. As everyone tossed miniature roses pom-pom-like in the air, Marina did not speak. As orphans clinked glasses of apple juice festively beside the bed, Marina did not smile. Her eyes focused inward. A mass orphan migration to the cleaner pastures of the living room provoked no reaction, either. Even when the nurses washed her, it triggered no giggle, no darting glance, no Snow Whitishly cinematic *Where am I?*

After Nurse Patchett hustled the infant away to lullabyland in the nursery, Nurses Bee and Samson wheeled Marina into the recovery room. There they examined her and found vital signs up and running. They also found she could understand rudimentary instructions—"Scrunch over here, honey"—but seemed to have left her ability to interact somewhere in the great hereafter. "Can you see me?" A portrait would have made better eye contact. "Is your name Marina?" A statue would have been more likely to nod.

"It could simply be shock," Nurse Bee said.

Sam pondered. "Maybe we can interest her in something."

So they rolled Marina's bed to face the window. A violet sunset spread royally over the sky. Shadows advanced like a tide across the yard. A rainbow bent over backward in the west. But Marina seemed to focus only on the inside of her head.

"Let's think about this," Sam said. Nurse Bee tried but promptly fell asleep. While Hollywood fairies danced in Bee's dreams, Samson dredged up memories of nursing school exams, hoping to recollect something relevant to this dilemma.

Nurse Bee burst awake just as Sam hit on a promising possibility. "But the county doesn't pay overtime!" she screamed, and then opened her eyes and put a dainty hand to her mouth. "Did I say something?"

"I think you need a rest," Samson said.

Bee paused just long enough for the specter of Florence Nightingale to float through her mind. *Oh, you wouldn't* dream *of making him work this out by him*self, Florence was saying. Yes I *would,* Bee told Florence, and, in her most nursy voice, said to Sam, "I'll save a wink for you," and tra-la-la-ed out the door.

Alone (blessedly), Sam went to the window. This was his plan: Maybe he could somehow direct Marina's gaze. And maybe, if he did that, he could direct her back to the world.

He looked outside. The sun had sunk below the horizon, and night had slipped over the rainbow. He couldn't imagine what might get her attention. But he had to start somewhere.

"Quite a few stars out tonight," he ad-libbed. "You know any constellations?" No response. "And the moon . . . uh, no moon; too bad: we get a great view from here. But what's that over there?" He leaned closer. "Will you look at that. More clouds."

Marina blinked extra hard. Samson piggybacked her path of vision; she seemed to be focusing on the clouds, a small cluster along the horizon. "Think we'll have more rain?" he asked.

She didn't answer, but her face changed for the first time since her rebirth. Her eyebrows pinched low, her lips grew tight and droopy. It was an expression Sam could only read as sad.

Okay, that was progress, even if was rainphobia. Maybe if he pruned back her fear, her words would have room to grow. "Don't worry," he said. "I think the storm's over."

No acknowledgment. Could she be afraid to talk? He *was* a stranger, after all. "I'm a nurse. My name is Sam. You know, 'Sam I am'?"

Marina peered at him. He hadn't scored a laugh, but he had gotten her eyes to locate his face. "Do you know what's happened?" he asked.

She opened her mouth and he thought: *Yeah!*

But instead of speaking, Marina made a fist and drew it toward her face.

"Careful," he said.

She continued moving her hand, slowly pulling the thumb away from the other fingers as if hitchhiking into herself. Then she pushed the thumb between her lips, slid it all the way in to the second joint, and sucked. She gazed up at Samson, sucking so hard that slurping sounds filled the room, and he came to see what they were in for.

By car, there was only one way between the Home and the town of Fossilfink Falls. That was funereal Route 55, which crested and dipped over black hills, passed boarded-up houses, skin-of-their-teeth farms, neglected cemeteries. Two miles and a hairpin curve later, the handyman specials gave way to fields—fields once brimming with corn and now with mutant plants too vulgar to warrant Latin names. For two more miles the road cruised past these weeds, scurrying beneath the overhang of vampire vines, skirting the edge of zombie grass, provoking drivers to wish they carried garlic or a silver trowel—until it reached the stone wall and iron gate that marked the entrance to the Kelly Home.

Fortunately, pedestrians had a second option.

Years before, electric cables had been strung across the state, and steel-truss towers—or "giants," as the orphans called them—transmitted high-voltage current to areas as remote as Fossilfink Falls. The giants intersected towns, woods, and fields as they marched up and down the hillsides, creating back paths that stretched for miles. Four such miles linked Fossilfink Falls and the Home—four miles cut through lush, dense woods. Plants shied away from the constant *bzzzt!* the power lines emitted, allowing a continual twenty-foot-wide swath of unobstructed passage. The path could not have been prettier, easier to walk on, more private. The only open space in the woods besides the path was a quarry, which had gone belly-up shortly after the mine died. But for years it remained secluded too, as the road that had led there from Route 55 had long since disappeared.

It was along the giant path that Miss Kelly and her troop had marched two days earlier, taking the high ground when they discovered the jeep couldn't slosh its way through the flooded road.

And it was along this path that Miss Kelly sent Kit and Caboodle the night Celeste was born. "Please go fetch the jeep. Marina still needs us, but tomorrow I want to get the baby home."

Kit Lincoln and Caboodle Davis, boyfriend and girlfriend, both cowlicked and leather-jacketed and enamored of bric-a-brac bola ties, did backup work for the Home. Kit drove Miss Kelly to and fro when her legs hurt too much for her to walk or drive. He was the perfect chauffeur. Kit treasured cars the way people treasure pets and was, in fact, trying to synthesize a fuel from everyday elements that would propel his cars at least partway into life. Likewise, when it came to office chores, Caboodle was the perfect choice. She could carbon-date old letters by the faintness of the type, match up scattered papers by the staple holes.

When the request for the jeep came, Kit and Caboodle tucked umbrellas beneath their arms and went outside. Parking lot lamps lit the way around mud puddles, helping the orphans pinpoint the two oaks that marked the beginning of the path.

"Sure is hot out tonight," Caboodle said.

They looked up. A swarm of clouds churned in the sky. Kit said, "Maybe it'll—"

"Rain again," Caboodle completed.

But the clouds were odd. They seemed lit from within, like lantern glass around a glowing candle.

"Couldn't be the moon lighting them up," Kit noted.

"There's no moon out tonight," Caboodle agreed.

Soon things got even stranger. The clouds began spinning and spinning, the way cotton candy gets pulled onto a stick.

Mesmerized, the two orphans sprinted onto the path, while above them the clouds wound into a tight pillar. Then the pillar sprouted two shafts from its sides, two others from its bottom. Some of the cloud receded, some pressed forward, until at last the vision fleshed out with familiar kinds of curves.

Fifteen or so of us were in the clinic living room when Kit and Caboodle screeched up in the jeep and told us to run outside. We scrambled to the parking lot, looked up, and just froze. It wasn't like we hadn't seen nudity before—the Home encouraged total, you know, self-expression—it's just that we'd never seen a naked lady in the sky. A lady made out of clouds. Only she was more than just some bizarre centerfold. Because as I stood gawking in the parking lot, I started to feel like she was touching me. Like a heat was coming from the cloud and the whole sky was caressing me. Like I was being made love to by the air.

Eventually I broke my gaze. And though the world around me looked the same, I felt different. Not more like a man—which I know is what you want to hear. No. Some other way. Something I've only ever been able to describe as climbing out of a bath.

—Leo Macaroni, *Epicure* magazine

• • •

Iambia Teneye was among those in the parking lot. Unlike Leo and many of the boys, Iambia and many of the girls felt that the lady reminded them of a mother, or what they thought a mother would feel like: warm and embracing. But Iambia was a Watergateologist, who lived in trench coats and low-brimmed hats, so when she broke *her* gaze, screw the warm embrace; she just wanted to get some higher-up in on the know.

Her objective was consummated when she burst into Marina's room and found Miss Kelly and Samson watching the new mother. Marina lay in bed, wiggling her fingers like jellyfish tentacles.

"Miss Kelly!" Iambia blurted out. "You should see this thing going on outside!" She ran to the window, babbling, pointing, until Miss Kelly left her daughter's side and hobbled over to the glass. Iambia parted the blinds, Miss Kelly tilted her chin. "See?" Iambia asked.

"Yes," Miss Kelly mumbled.

In a daze, she stepped aside, and Sam rose and *great balls of fire!* In the sky *was* a lady—a voluptuous, three-dimensional lady! Thick hair tumbled down the front, generous breasts hung pendulously, as real breasts do (this was not a pornographic cloud, where all breasts are created perky). The face had big eyes, high cheekbones, thick lips; the body, a round tummy, wide hips, thighs that touched at the top. Slim arms, small hands, short legs, tiny feet. The image was so clear, he could make out the pubic hair. "I got to start getting more sleep," he said.

It was years before we learned of that cloud. The Matrix had only a single student Monitoring the Fossilfink Falls area at that time, and it so happened that he was otherwise occupied during the event. Only much later did he hear about it and inform us at the Temporary Zero-Zero. Had he been more on the ball, we might have understood this to be the opening salvo and could have gone to work much sooner than we did. But all has not been wasted; we have gotten much effort out of this student, as he strives to atone for this negligence.

—Gacy Guru, videotaped memoir,
And You Thought It Was Just Paranoia

Nurse Patchett had spent the hours since the birth sitting beside the newborn's crib, her legs coiled around each other, since otherwise they were too long to squeeze between the chair and the floor. She preferred sitting to standing; with her six-foot-six-inch body, plank-shaped nurse uniform, and scroll-like hairdo, she worried that if she stood she might be mistaken for a column. For those moments when she had to stand, Patchett wore foam pads in her bra and panties to force the illusion of shape. She also always carried a hankie, with which she dabbed her frequently dripping nose. Her husband, a minister, once joked that she ought to hire a plumber to fix her leak. Patchett, who could not bear to be compared to a pipe, told him the only leak she wanted to fix was between his head and his mouth. And she did, by knitting her legs together for five full days after that, the longest break she and he had ever taken, surpassing the four days at the Prayer-A-Thon, which had involved logistical impediments they simply could not overcome.

At the sound of the children outside, Nurse Patchett peered through the blinds. The Cloud Lady hovered in the sky. Patchett looked at the infant, and thoughts of the disciple Peter skipped like a rock across the normally placid surface of her mind. Peter had been one of the first people to recognize that Jesus was the Messiah, and Patchett wondered suddenly if this kid might be the sequel and if Patchett herself was supposed to play the part of Peter. The birth was certainly strange, and Celeste *had* brought her mother back from death, just as Jesus revived Lazarus. . . . But the kid had no halo, and Patchett was not a wise man, and the Second Coming wouldn't begin in this pathetic town in northern Pennsylvania, at least not when it could just as easily—and more poetically—be in the lovely southern Pennsylvania town of Bethlehem or Nazareth. Besides, what about the signs predicted in Revelation? Or the fact that the child was female?

Patchett bent over the crib, cradled Celeste in her arms, and examined the little face. The infant shifted and opened her eyes and, with a grace well beyond her age, gazed at Patchett.

"Impossible," Patchett whispered; as an experienced nurse, she knew babies can't make eye contact for weeks after birth. But there it was. Celeste blinked at Patchett, and something about the child reminded Patchett of the vibrating bed she and her husband had bought for their anniversary. Though Celeste was not quivering. No, Patchett realized; she herself was quivering. She set the child down and backed away from the crib. She had never told her husband anything about the clinic, but this time she would make an exception.

FADE IN:

Fossilfink Falls—Shots of town and Route 55

MR. HAMELIN (*voice over*)

The town of Fossilfink Falls seems best suited to black-and-white TV. The only color is the occasional roof or flag. Otherwise, it's as dreary as bankruptcy.

Kelly Home property—Rolling down driveway

MR. HAMELIN (*voice over*)

But once you enter the gates of the Kelly Home, all that changes. Exotic flowers splash across the garden, turning the front lawn into a virtual Alice in Wonderland cornucopia.

Birds of every hue soar from flower to tree. A dinosaur carousel sits in one corner of the yard, a collection of mint-
condition automobiles in another. But of course, the center
of the action is the building. Originally a mundane yellow,
Miss Kelly and her orphans repainted it pink, making the
Kelly Home roughly the color of bubble gum.

Building—Following with Mr. Hamelin

MR. HAMELIN

A side entrance leads to the office, a rear door to the private
Kelly apartment. But enter here, through the front, and it's
like walking into a homemade F.A.O. Schwarz. Stuffed with
secondhand furniture and handcrafted playthings of every
kind, vast as the school auditorium it once was, this gigantic
living room encompasses almost the entire first floor.

(*Pan electric train, cloth mountain, living trees*)

On the second floor are classrooms, where the older orphans
taught the younger, and on the third, bedrooms. But it was
in the living room that the orphans spent most of their time.
This was the heart of the home, both where the mystery
began and where I guess you could say it ended.

—Piper Hamelin of UBC, *Lifeline*

The day after the birth, we tried to get back to normal, but it was
very weird. Marina was still at the clinic, and there was this new
baby, and Miss Kelly was trying to keep it together. I remember our
first lunch. We filed without a peep into the living room—we didn't
want to give her anything more to deal with.

Instead—big joke on *us*—she gave *us* something to deal with.
She stood up while we were eating and said, "I have two matters to
discuss. The first concerns school. Classes will resume after lunch.
Students, make sure you're prepared. Teachers, see me if you need
tips on the jitters.

"The second concerns the baby. Marina was tight-lipped about the pregnancy. If you are or know the father, I would appreciate hearing from you. An anonymous note will suffice."

That's how she told us. Then she started flipping through her grade book. My friends and I looked at each other. We'd speculated on the father for months, and I'd asked some guys outright, but they denied it. And no one spoke up then, either. Marina was the only person who knew the dad's identity, and she couldn't talk, so it looked like something we'd just never know.

—Rick Shuffling Buffalo, as told to author

Miss Kelly had raised the orphans without much exposure to or love of the media. The purity of the Home was at stake, she taught. She believed she'd been shackled by what society told her to be, so she and the Home shunned television and radio and church and trips to cities and anything else she thought likely to pollute them. She called these things Halls of Mirrors. "They give the illusion they are aiding you on your path," she said, "while they steer you higgledy-piggledy on a path of their own. What's worse, they make the illusion so much fun, you don't even notice you've lost your way." She didn't want that to happen. She wanted the orphans to develop into their own selves.

And lo and behold—they did. Some gravitated toward worldly activities: history, math, carpentry. Others levitated toward the more arcane: speaking the language of leaves, harnessing moonlight for pen ink, animating automobiles. As Miss Kelly put it, "Your life should fit your core self like a glove. The more *you* you are, the stronger knight you will be. And the smarter too; you will know where you belong on the battlefield—whether you should entertain the sad, educate the lost, house the homeless, raise a happy family, or do some deed of which I cannot even dream. You will know what to do when you know yourself. Remember: as the world is in a grain of sand, so is the salvation of humanity in the spirit of each person."

Many experiments merely run their subjects in circles; few achieve the climax of an unequivocal *Eureka!* But Miss Kelly's experiment succeeded. In orphan after orphan, isolation and noninterference worked. Orphans *were* their own selves. Wondrous abilities flourished. An upbeat mood permeated the atmosphere in the Home; they had seen Utopia, and it was them.

So the orphans never questioned Miss Kelly's media obsession. Not only did it make complete sense to them; it worked.

Which is why no one at the Home was aware of the tabloids until they arrived at the door.

A few days after the birth, the mayor of Fossilfink Falls, Gravely Beaks, stopped by the Home. This dwarf, a third-generation Fink, had never been to the Home before, but that morning, spiffed up in his white gloves and green velvet suit, Gravely Beaks Cadillaced right up to Miss Kelly's apartment door. Miss Kelly opened it to find a little man standing in her shadow. "Mayorrr Grrravely Beaks, at yourrr serrrvice," he said.

She reached down and shook his pudgy gloved hand.

"Sorry to disturrrb, but I thought I ought to check on you. Perrrhaps you need some assistance?"

"We are fine."

"Therrre is nothing? I am, afterrr all, the mayorrr."

"No. Nice to meet you." She made to close the door.

"And you have, afterrr all, just made the headlines." He whipped out a small stack of papers.

She released the door and took the papers.

DEAD WOMAN GIVES BIRTH—BABY MAKES MAMA LIVE AGAIN! bleated *World of Today*.

NEWLY ALIVE MAMA BORED—I WANT TO GO HOME! SHE SAYS, squawked *Scrutiny*.

RESURRECTED MAMA BRAIN-DEAD, honked *True World*.

The color left Miss Kelly's face. She shoved the tabloids back at the mayor, and he said, "I could help keep away rrreporrrterrrs, if you would like."

"That would be desirable."

"It's a snap!" Mayor Beaks tried to demonstrate, but his gloves acted as a silencer. "Just a matterrr of securrrity. I'll instrrruct everrryone in town to keep mum about yourrr location, and we will barrr them frrrom the clinic."

"Thank you."

"But herrre at the Home itself you could have a prrroblem."

"We have the stone walls, the gate."

"Yes, but no lock. The five-and-ten has many in stock. Orrr I can brrring one. In fact, ho ho! I just happen to have one in my carrr."

With Miss Kelly's consent, the mayor then helped the orphans rig up the gate, and as he drove off with a smile and a wave, the orphans took it several steps further. Caboodle unlisted the phone number, Porkaluna Montezuma strung electrified wire over the top of the fence, Kit went to the nearest SPCA and brought back a dozen hounds.

But everyone, even Miss Kelly, knew that reporters weren't likely to come by anyway; the tabloids had already proved they didn't give a virgin's tushie about truth.

For while it was true that Celeste *had* made Mama live again, it wasn't even a half-truth that Marina was talking. And it was far, far off the truth—in an entirely different country from truth—that she was brain-dead. Much evidence existed to support the fact of her brain *life*—she made eye contact now, she flashed a shallow smile during baths. But the big whopper of evidence, the genuine Exhibit A, was how she acted when she saw her daughter. Any jughead—yes, folks, even reporters—would know that if you act like this, you've got to have more brain than a rutabaga.

"We drove Miss Kelly to the clinic the first time she took Celeste to visit Marina. It was a nice day. Everything seemed like it would be fine."

"When we got there, Samson was in the room, spoon-feeding Marina. She didn't seem to recognize Miss Kelly or us. So we were pretty surprised with what happened."

"Miss Kelly laid Celeste down in Marina's lap. Celeste peered up at her mother, and Marina down at her daughter. Miss Kelly started explaining to Marina who this was, but before she got very far, Marina seemed to look inward—"

"And burst into tears. She threw her hands up and kicked and kicked. Miss Kelly grabbed Celeste and sped her to another part of the room. Samson tried to calm Marina down, but she wouldn't quit bawling. Finally, Miss Kelly had us take Celeste to the car. The crying stopped as soon as we left the room."

"Miss Kelly brought Celeste to the clinic after that, but every time, same thing. Marina crying. Marina falling back on whatever progress she'd made. Miss Kelly said she might have to stop Celeste's visits. After a few more months, she did."

—Kit Lincoln and Caboodle Davis, *Lifeline*

Celeste was an infant and so didn't take the rejection personally. As for Marina, she wasn't exactly at a loss for company. Miss Kelly came to visit often. And soon after the birth, Samson pretty much moved into the clinic.

This new development occurred one evening when Miss Kelly was waiting for Kit to pick her up. Samson ambled outside and took a deep breath and looked Miss Kelly in the eye.

"Miss Kelly," he said, "I've been thinking. Marina needs twenty-four-hour care. She needs someone to feed her, teach her, be there in case she begins to talk."

"Are you suggesting we bring her home?" Miss Kelly asked.

"No; I think she should be overseen by medical personnel."

"You want to send her to a bigger hospital?"

"Well, actually . . ."

"Speak up! What are you suggesting?"

"I . . ." Kit pulled up in the jeep. *How could he say it?* Sam wondered. He had no business asking for such exceptions! He had no special skills. *How presumptuous to ask! How ludicrous! How—* And then he looked away and remembered the old positive visualization technique. He closed his eyes. The jeep engine idled. Samson took a deep breath and drew up an image of . . . *Marina.*

He looked back at Miss Kelly. "No. She should stay here. I'd like to watch her myself."

Miss Kelly eyed him. "Oh? Do you have a reason?"

Samson paused. He *could* spill out his life. He *could* tell Miss Kelly about growing up without a mother, about how he'd been raised by his father, a piano tuner who spent less time adjusting tuning pins inside pianos than he did vibrating himself inside female customers. He could tell her about finding out as a teenager that his mother had died during childbirth and that Dad had been too busy wetting his wick to know she was even in the hospital. Or how, after Sam learned this, he had raged against his father—and ended up diddling around the county too, a replay of his dad in a minor key. It was the classic paradox of genes: the harder you run, the tighter they pull. He could go into how one day he woke up, and stopped running, and planted himself in celibacy, and started growing flowers. In his mind then, pussies blossomed into petals, semen dried into pollen, and the only sexual organs he let himself fondle were pistils and stamens. But botanical breeding didn't pay the bills around here. Nursing did—and was a way to heal himself by healing others. And now, at the age of thirty, he'd been given an opportunity to nurse a new mother back from the dead. The cycle would be complete.

But Samson didn't like parading his life before people. So he recited his other reasons. "I delivered the baby. I placed her on Marina's body. Marina's recovery is, short of Celeste's birth, the most amazing thing I've ever seen. I want to make it even more amazing. I want to help Marina get better."

Miss Kelly sized him up as if she were pulling leaf after leaf off a cabbage. It was said Miss Kelly could tell, just by looking, if a person was being true to himself. Kit, watching from the jeep, saw her making this appraisal, and now he braced himself for her to say, You are not meant to care for people but to be an assembly line worker or a veterinarian.

But instead her eyes softened, the way they did whenever she encountered self-honesty, and she said, "Well, Nurse Samson. I think that would be just fine."

Dear Marina Kelly,

You must get better for your miracle baby. I myself have recovered from a bad household accident when I slipped on the kitchen floor and fell onto my open dishwasher and forks stabbed me all over. It was not fun. But I have five children and for them I got better. So keep trying. You can do it!

A friend

Miracle Child—

You think you are so special being born into the papers without working a day ever. Well don't get a big head. Bad things happen to everyone and could happen to *you* too.

(unsigned)

Dear Baby,

I just got my eye out! I want a new eye. Please get one for me.
I will believe in whatever you preach then.

Lester

Dear Edwina,

I dig this might be way out, but you and I could be cousins. I
was born in Brooklyn, my grandpa's name was Kipplebaum, and I
remember him yapping about the Runetoon branch once at some
family chowfest. Could you be my coz? If so I'd be real into seeing
you. My old lady and I live in New Jersey, just a hop, skip, and a
busride away.

Mo Wolfly

In their nonfactual articles, the tabloids never gave more of an
address than Pennsylvania, as if this twelfth of the original thirteen
was no larger than Betsy Ross's flag. But "Miracle Child, Pennsylvania" seemed to be all the U.S. postal system needed. And so,
though the orphans never saw the tabloids, they sure did see the
fallout.

Once a week, Kit carried a pouch of mail in from town—a hundred a pop the first few times. He would dump letters across the
floor and sort by category: well-wisher, ass-kisser, god-fisher, rem-
iniscer, soothsayer, doomsdayer, hip-hip-hoorayer, creep. Public
readings were then performed by Bop Mooney. "Everyone seated?"
Bop would begin, and launch into invented accents and gestures for
each writer.

In her pre-biped days, when the most Celeste could muster was
a crawl, she lay in a cradle during these performances, doing a slow
gurgle as Bop mugged to a full house. At one year old, when she
recapitulated evolution and pulled herself to two feet, Celeste wandered around ba-ba-ba-ing as Bop preened and pattered to a handful

of diehards. At the threshold of toilet expertise, when she was a single credit short of her degree in Personal Hygiene, Celeste pumped up and down in a living room swing as Bop did his verbal flatulation to anyone who wandered past.

By then the letters had dwindled to one or two a month—a lot, really, since tabloid references had long since sputtered out to clues in crossword puzzles. The dreaded rash of unwelcome visitors never materialized; aside from barking at the perennially unannounced Mayor Beaks when he pulled up to the gate, the watchdogs had nothing better to do than breed.

Throughout these early years, Celeste had little awareness of her mother but, given that she was in an orphanage, didn't feel the lack. Occasionally, Miss Kelly had mentioned Celeste to Marina, but even that prompted tears in the child-woman, despite the many trips she and Sam took to see specialists, despite her growing abilities to finger paint and to play yo-yo and tiddlywinks. So at home Miss Kelly didn't volunteer information about Marina, and for the most part Celeste didn't ask. Celeste simply told herself that she, like the few kids in the Home who were pseudo-orphans, had a mother who was "not capable of being a parent," as they described their dysfunctional progenitors. But she did have a grandma who sang her to sleep from time to time and always praised her accomplishments, and that's plenty, for someone living in an orphanage.

Except for the mother stuff, Celeste was an ordinary and happy child, who matured at an ordinary and comfortable pace. Actually, at the Home, where extraordinary development was so common that Dr. Spock himself would have been thrown into a tizzy, Celeste's ordinariness was what people noted. She was not remarkably attractive or repulsively ugly. She did not hurtle through the alphabet or catapult to algebra. Her first words were not in quantum mechanics or astrology but were closer to the gutter: "schlong," "wazoo," "machu pee-pee," "tit."

The orphans wondered what specialty Celeste might have and

when she'd reveal it. Her third birthday passed, then her fourth. Celeste played with dolls and crayons and cars. Okay, she was disdainful of clothing, often wearing nothing more than fingerfuls of plain silver rings, and she was a fussy eater, allowing only peaches and cashew nuts to pass between her lips, and she was a masterful tickler (and eager ticklee), giggles spilling out like tumbling dice, but these quirks were hardly considered exceptional. Maybe one day she'd be able to spin wool into gold, but for a long time Celeste showed no particular inclination toward any skill, let alone anything unusual.

This changed shortly after her fifth birthday. From infancy on, Celeste's eyes had been black, the same color as her long, curly hair. But one morning when she arrived for breakfast, her eyes were *green.* M&M, Kool-Aid, AstroTurf green.

"Celeste!" Nobeline said, dropping her spoon. "What happened to your eyes?"

Celeste looked baffled. "What do you mean?"

Nobeline steered Celeste to a bathroom mirror, where Celeste blinked at her reflection. "How'd you do that?" Nobeline asked.

"I don't know."

"You didn't have any control over it?"

"I don't think so."

"Well, I'll be," Nobeline said.

"Is this normal?"

"No. But so what? They're cool."

"They're wild," Bop said when Celeste returned to breakfast.

"They're lovely," Miss Kelly said when the orphans called her over from the office.

That night, Kit, who'd been out all day getting supplies, went to Miss Kelly's apartment to see these transformed irises.

Only, the thing was, now they were blue.

"Blue?" Celeste asked. Kit held up a hand mirror.

Yessir, they were blue. As blue as a morning glory. As blue as an ice pop. As blue as chlorine. "Blue?" Caboodle fumbled when Kit called her into the apartment. Celeste was peering into the mirror at her new-again eyes. She gazed at the orphans. "Do you think something's wrong with me?" she said.

"No-ho," Caboodle laughed, but out of the corner of her mouth added to Kit, "You better go get Miss Kelly."

When Miss Kelly limped into the bedroom, she took Celeste's face in her hands and examined the eyes. "I have never seen this before," she told Celeste.

Celeste's face tensed with fear. "Is it okay?"

Miss Kelly drew the child toward her and kissed both her cheeks. "It is wonderful," she said. "If you ever worry that you are not special, just look in the mirror, and you will know."

"But I don't need to be special," Celeste said.

"Nonsense! Everyone needs to be special."

"Maybe you'll be able to *see* special too," Caboodle piped up from the corner.

Celeste blinked. How could she know if she was seeing any differently from anyone else? How could she know if their blue was her blue?

Did everyone see a rainbow after rain?

Did everyone see flashing webs inside shadows?

What if they didn't?

"I don't want to see special," Celeste said.

"How do you know?" Kit asked.

Celeste stared back into the mirror. In the reflection, she could see her own shadow, flickering against the wall. She knew it so well. And her colors, her webs—they weren't so different from the orphans' shadows. It was just her edges that were different. They were fuzzy, not well defined. As if she almost didn't *have* edges. As if she diffused into the air.

But that was it. That was all that was different.

"I'm like everyone else," she said defiantly.

Miss Kelly drew a breath. "I love you no matter what color your eyes are," she said, and she took the mirror away.

Her eyes were like a kaleidoscope after that. The next morning, they were amber with flecks of orange. By noon, coffee brown. After dinner, cherry red. By bedtime, purple. She had as many different colors of eyes as she had rings on her fingers.

At first, Celeste seemed scared by it. "Ooh, they're pink now," someone would say, and Celeste would run off. When people asked how she did it, she'd snap, "I don't *know!*" She kept her eyes downcast a lot. She started to wear clothes. Eventually, we stopped saying anything, and she lifted her eyes back up from the ground, but she never ran around naked again.

—Iambia Teneye, as told to author

At the end of Celeste's sixth year, a virulent flu ravaged the Home. It began as a twang in the belly, so slight it felt like no more than a bowel getting ready to roll. But within minutes, the twang progressed into a tweak, the tweak into a twitch, the twitch into a twotch. The victim would then buckle in half and scramble at a right angle to the lavatory, where a complete evacuation occurred at both ends of the alimentary canal. This was followed by a week of aches that felt like you'd been drilled for oil, sinus blockage that felt like you'd been stuffed by a taxidermist, and a feverish intimacy with your bed.

The flu began one night and tornadoed through the Home, felling many while leaving a handful untouched. Classes were stopped. A samovar full of chicken soup simmered day and night in the stairwell. Nurse Samson came by with medicine and a warning: those who hadn't gotten the flu should keep to themselves. This illness was like a bungee jump toward death: you stopped only an inch before impact. The sick should be treated by the recovered. The healthy should stay away.

During this time, something happened to Celeste, something that historians have sparred over for years. One side maintains that this flu was like Helen Keller's childhood fever: it was an illness that gave birth to a new life. On the contrary, you ignorami, retort their opponents, citing the skeletons that later came spilling out of Celeste's closet; it was a kick in the pants, something that punted her more rapidly into her destiny than if she'd stumbled there simply by herself.

Well, break it up, guys. We can blow both theories out of the water: Celeste never got the flu.

She had survived the initiation rites of mumps, measles, and chicken pox. She had suffered poison ivy, sunburn, earaches. But when Celeste didn't contract the flu immediately, Miss Kelly prudently followed Sam's advice and told her to stay away from anyone contagious. Which wasn't the easiest advice to follow, with Celeste living right in the eye of the storm.

The nadir of the flu happened to come on a Sunday. The entire third floor of the Home was filled with casualties, waiting for their fevers to break. A symphony of groans, honks, and sneezes drifted down the corridor.

It being a Sunday, Miss Kelly was off for her weekly visit to Marina. Kit, who was still healthy, had gone out to get more chicken for the soup. The only others feeling well were Iambia and Celeste, who occupied themselves in the living room. Celeste had promised Miss Kelly to stay put, and Iambia had promised to watch Celeste.

Iambia's earlier fascination with Watergate had blossomed into a fascination with tape recorders. Not, like Dick Milhous, so she could alleviate the heebie-jeebies (she didn't *have* heebie-jeebies). But for history—and for *fun*. To Iambia, happiness was a warm reel-to-reel. The problem was, her prized recorder, which she had built herself and which had immortalized so many jump rope songs and nursery rhymes, had recently fast-forwarded to a stop. So that Sunday morning, while Celeste drew pictures in her favorite living room swing, Iambia pulled the tape player apart in an attempt to correct the disorder.

Everything was copacetic until Iambia remembered that her toolbox was stashed in Miss Kelly's apartment. She stared at the mess. Kit was due back at noon, and it was almost noon, and he was never tardy, given how cooperative his cars were. And Celeste was preoccupied with her drawings. What would be the harm in a quick jaunt to retrieve some essentials? Underline *quick*. "I'm going to the apartment real fast," Iambia said. "Do you swear you'll stay here?"

"Yeah," Celeste said, and Iambia ran off.

But at twelve-oh-one, when Kit came in, Celeste was missing.

He flung open the door to Miss Kelly's apartment and found Iambia, who knew from the look in Kit's eyes that she needed to bypass explanation and go directly to action.

They flew through the living room, topsy-turvying tables, sweeping away stuffed animals, pulverizing pagodas of cards, uprooting blankets and balloons. They dashed outside and scrambled around the grounds. "Celeste! Where are you?" Their blood pounded, and they cringed at the scolding they'd get if Celeste had gone upstairs.

Finally—*no choice!*—they ran up the stairs themselves. Poke, pull, stomp—but the classrooms on the second floor were empty, and the baths and the closets; and—*shit!*—up to the third floor: the sick ward. "She better not have gone into any rooms!"

Third floor. The corridor was as bare as Mother Hubbard's pantry. Bathrooms? So deserted they expected tumbleweeds. Iambia had just slammed the linen closet closed and moaned, "She must have entered the quarantine!" when Kit noticed a door ajar. "Caboodle's room!" They scrambled inside.

In bed lay a sweating Caboodle, eyes closed, and over her leaned Celeste. The child was resting her ringed fingers just below Caboodle's collarbone and seemed deep in concentration.

Kit whispered, "Come back downstairs!"

Celeste looked up.

"You could have woken her," Iambia snapped. She padded in and grabbed Celeste, who let go without a word. Iambia shot Celeste a glare and marched the girl out the door.

But just as they closed the door behind them—

"Wait," they heard.

They peeked back inside.

Caboodle was sitting up in bed, her hand on her forehead.

Kit said, "See, Celeste? You woke her up."

Caboodle threw off her blanket.

"What are you doing?" Iambia asked, opening the door wider.

"Celeste," Caboodle said, lowering her hand from her brow, "did you do something to my flu?"

Celeste nodded.

Caboodle glanced at Kit and then back at Celeste.

Caboodle asked, "What did you do?"

"I took it."

"Well, where did you take it?"

Celeste looked around, wondering if she could find it. Her eyes passed over the desk with its peeling varnish; the bed with its balled-up pillow; the window with its braids of dust.

Then she examined Caboodle's shadow, stretching across the bed and floor. Within the dark shape, colors blinked on and off. Celeste scrutinized the pulsations, the dappled emeralds and cobalts and fuchsias and crimsons, the delicate webs that held the colors together. The brown and gray Celeste had seen before she touched

Caboodle had receded, and the webs crisscrossed normally once again. Not a trace of flu remained.

And then Celeste glanced at her own shadow. It was the shadow of health. Nothing had changed. Not even her hazy edges.

Celeste looked back at the orphans, and when she spoke, she sounded as astonished as they felt. "It's *gone*," she said.

The Story of the Sea

Day One   Dinnertime

At five o'clock in the evening, the ocean liner steams through calm water. Land has long since disappeared, and to most passengers, real life seems like no more than a miserable dream.

As the dinner gong sounds, John Kelly swaggers up a circular staircase to the sundeck. There Edwina Kelly, ruddy-faced from a day feeding seagulls, glowers at him. She almost asks if he had fun, rolling in the berth with a ship attendant. But she knows nothing she can say will dent his conscience; it's like trying to do alterations on a stone. So she holds her tongue, as usual.

John Kelly, who believes he resembles Michelangelo's <u>David</u> but is actually swaybacked and pockmarked, strides along the deck, pausing by curvaceous sunbathers. John also believes he is most dashing when he fully controls his image, so he punctuates every few steps with a pose, as if debating whether he is a real person or a billboard advertisement for one. His favorite poses come from statues. He keeps a handbook on classical sculpture at home, but is not above appropriating more modern material.

"Coming to dinner, Eddie?" he calls. His smile is empty and his gaze glassy, like a mannequin he saw at a Castle of Values.

Edwina shuffles in his direction. As she nears, John Kelly stoops like <u>The Discus Thrower</u> to pick up a sunbather's runaway napkin. He debonairly returns the napkin, then marches staccato back toward the stairs. He walks this way all the time, even at work, though he is only a draftsman. <u>Senior</u> draftsman, he always reminds her. He reminds her of everything, from how to shop for rhubarb to how to thread a bobbin. He even reminds her to deposit her paycheck from her factory job, where she stitches costly dresses that fit no one but the lucky.

The humid ocean air makes the wood in her legs feel heavy.

"The meal will be moldy before we get there," he sighs.

At home, he wants his dinner at a certain time, in a certain way. Since the accident with her legs, he has thrown a couple of punches on the few occasions when the stew was overcooked.

Her family is dead.

He never wanted children.

Every drop of learning she ever absorbed said that a woman stays with her man: through thick and thin, through love and sin.

"You test my patience," he likes to tell her.

He struts down the circular staircase and out of sight. She hurries after, and just as she reaches the railing, a stranger emerges from the top step.

"He should not talk to you that way," the stranger says.

She stops, startled. The stranger wears a long coat and a head of unruly hair. His eyes are pitch black. Around him is a strong but pleasing scent, which smells like a hug in winter.

"Excuse me?" she asks.

He glances down the staircase. Then he looks at her, and examines her body. "So you're Edwina," he says slowly.

Edwina takes a step back. "Who are you?"

He places a finger against his lips. "Shhh," he says. "I'll find you again."

He steps down the stairs, out of sight.

She scrambles after him, round and round. The man is nowhere on the stairs, though his scent remains to the bottom.

"Finally," John Kelly says. He is sitting on a deck chair, pondering a menu like The Thinker. Edwina limps toward him. She almost mentions the stranger but then decides John has whole harems of secrets; maybe it's time she kept one for herself.

The
Secrets
of
Shadows

From jack-offs to jack-in-the-boxes, Kit hated any surprise delivered before its time. So when he went to pick up Miss Kelly from her visit with Marina, he kept his mouth shut about Caboodle's revival. Miss Kelly's first clue that something momentous had occurred was the sight of Caboodle executing a cheerleader-style split in the driveway.

Miss Kelly climbed out of the car. "I thought you felt ill."

Caboodle sprang from the horizontal to the vertical. "I did! But listen!" And she poured out the story of her healing.

Miss Kelly kept nodding, then held her hand to Caboodle's forehead. These knuckles that had estimated so many Fahrenheits almost beeped with exactitude on this: "Ninety-eight point six." Miss Kelly removed her hand and, expanding her depth of hearing, cocked her head toward the building, from which emanated not the deathly quiet of the past week but the ear-splittin' louden-boomer of an exceptionally hyperactive day.

She opened the front door.

The living room positively percolated. Orphans skipped rope, batted balls, hula-hooped, raced trains, do-re-mi-ed, belly danced, tooted bugles, talked Duck. And nowhere, not even on the most sedentary rump, was a swatch of flannel to be seen. In fact, at that very moment, the washer was cachunka-chunking away, busily agitating sweat out of the orphans' flu-drenched pajamas.

The door banged shut. Heads spun her way—and Slinkies fell slack, books flipped closed, and the orphans hustled over to Miss Kelly, their stories of sudden recovery elbowing each other for attention. Miss Kelly peered through the pandemonium, searching for her granddaughter. Finally, she spied Celeste in the corner of the room, pumping back and forth on a swing.

The yackety-yak might have gone all day. But at some point, as though a TOTAL sign had rung up on her cognitive register, Miss Kelly raised her hand. "Enough. I must speak with Celeste."

Then Miss Kelly commenced her trudge across the living room, and as she did, the orphans detected a smile rising onto her countenance. With each step, it chinnied up higher—her lips dawning, her eyes misting, her cheeks cock-a-doodle-doodling—until her face was a dazzle of joy. The orphans grabbed each other in awe. Not because Miss Kelly was smiling—she did that occasionally around them. But because of the smile's complexity. Look what her granddaughter brought out: a beam of affection, tinted with the sad and sweet wisp of relief.

In the sunlight, Celeste swung back and forth, the ropes *squeak-squawking* as she kicked up and down. The orphans shushed each other to hear the ensuing exchange, and Iambia, thinking fast, darted to her recorder and flipped the power to On.

"Oh, my little peanut—you're a healer! A rock-em-sock-em-ologist, a threat to the threats, a twenty-four-carat M.D.! O frabjous day! Callooh! Callay! But how did you know what to *do?*"

"I don't know."

"No one told you?"

(*Squeak*-squawk) "The shadows told me."

"The *shadows*?"

"Yeah."

"What do you mean?"

"You know. The shadows. How they look. They looked sick in the red parts. That's how I knew."

"You see colors in shadows?"

"Uh . . ." (*Squeak*-squawk) "Yeah?"

"Yes or no?"

"Yes. I mean, is that all ri—"

"Right? It is grandio—" (*Ahem*) "Stop swinging now. I have something to tell you."

(*Celeste slows her arc to a fixed point.*) "Celeste, the good you give to the world is determined by *you*. I can teach you knightly qualities, but you must hear in yourself who you are."

"What do you mean?"

"Be very quiet. If you settle into yourself, settle like flour in a sack, you will hear yourself."

"What does that sound like?"

"It might sound like a lion roaring you are an opera diva. It might sound like a dove cooing you are a diplomat. It might sound like those shadows whispering—"

"They don't whisper, Grandma! They're quiet!"

"They are? Well, do they speak inside you?"

"Huh?"

"Do you hear your life told in the whoosh of fleeing fevers and the hiss of scabs fading, the hush of bones fusing and the pitter-patter of healthy hearts?"

"I don't understand."

"You have to *listen*. Listen to your*self*. It is trying to get you to hear. And once you do hear, the you inside will be stronger and clearer, until it orchestrates your every move."

"You mean it'll take over?"

"No. It *is* you. Do you understand now?"

"Not really."

"Well, what do you hear inside you?"

"I don't hear anything, Grandma."

"Nothing?"

"Nope."

"You really don't?"

"No!"

"Well, then. Go back to your play now. There's no more for us to talk about today."

—Tape recording

Miss Kelly corked her catechism and departed, and the orphans scrambled across the sunny room, milking a big fat HOW.

"You look for changes," Celeste explained. "Shadows are like a huge dance floor, but instead of dancers there are colors, and each color moves to its own beat. The colors are in groups, and each group has *its* own beat too. And then sometimes all the beats come together, like they suddenly got . . ." She faltered.

"Synchronized," Iambia filled in.

"Yeah. So there are tiny patterns and medium patterns and one jumbo-sized pattern. And you look for changes in the patterns and colors. Oh, and also in the webs. See, webs tie every group together. Also they're between groups. It looks kind of like dragonfly wings. Only more so."

The orphans inhaled, tasting this new idea.

"Is it like," Porkaluna asked, "you read shadows the way fortune-tellers read palms?"

"I don't see any fortunes. Just what is now."

"Like if you're sick."

"And what you're feeling, and what you're up to."

64

"So you're saying," Olga surmised, "shadows tell the truth."

"Right."

Having ingested this weirdness, the orphans exhaled and asked the next—and most important—question: "Will you teach us?"

"Sure," Celeste said, though she wasn't sure she *could*. It didn't happen if you squinted extra hard. Nor would yoga positions or ginseng popsicles or 3-D sunglasses coax it into being. Maybe—maybe all they had to do was practice. "The one thing you have to have is light," she said, and as luck would have it, in the room there was light. "Then just look."

The orphans sprawled on the sofas and chairs and peered at the floor. The sun blasting through the windows made everyone's shadow beautifully well defined. They inched their fannies apart so the darknesses wouldn't overlap. "Now watch for colors."

Leo fixed on his glasses. Nobeline rubbed her eyes. The clock ticked in the stairwell. The wind blew outside.

"I see something!" Grace said. They all cranked their heads in that direction, and a few thought they duplicated her results. But it was just a sliver of cellophane someone had left on the rug.

Back to the drawing board. They focused on the floor again.

In Matrix seminars, the first lesson of Shadow Reading is that beginners should never look directly at a shadow. It is like looking at the sun; if you are not an expert, it will make your shadow vision blind, and all you will see is black. No student ever learned Shadow Reading until he could first see his own darkness within.

It sounds difficult, but it is not. Indeed, what politician or CEO worth his salt does not read shadows? As anyone in the Matrix can tell you, that is how they *became* worth their salt.

At the time when Celeste first revealed her ability to read shadows, the Matrix was quite extensive—and so clandestine that the occasional whistle blower who tried to warn outsiders was summarily carted off to an asylum. But aside from the unusualness of Celeste's birth, we had no reason to Monitor her. Student Beaks had been assigned to check on the Home and report to the Temporary Zero-Zero, but fool that he was, he did not know about the healing, nor that she could read shadows, nor even about that cloud. Had he been more astute, we would have been tipped off sooner and been saved a great deal of trouble now.

—Gacy Guru, videotaped memoir,
And You Thought It Was Just Paranoia

For Celeste, healing seemed to encompass anything physical. She set broken bones, calmed menstrual cramps, adjusted vision to 20/20, cured the common cold, cleared up acne, melted cancer, soothed jock itch, and made dental decay cry uncle.

At first, healing did for Celeste what *Drink me* did for Alice. Celeste grew and grew. She left 6X in the dust and galloped through sizes. Hemlines that had been perfect one week were nerdily short the next. With her socks flashing a big white *We surrender!* from the ever-widening gully between her shoes and her jeans, she would have been ostracized as a Fashion Don't in most communities. But the orphans didn't care. Her growth spurt jizzled on for months, finally petering out around Celeste's eighth birthday, when she hit five feet—her final adult height.

Healing also did for Celeste what artificial stimulants did for entire generations of Americans. It gave her a rush. Hands on the sufferer's chest, she could feel the illness rise up from the body, feel it lock in on her presence, feel it charge her at the speed of light. It shot into her like a sudden dream, like a glass-shattering scream, like 10 cc's of sensation. She would close her eyes as it entered and remove her hands. It would splash inside, triumphant, plotting its way to pain—but suddenly realize something was wrong. It couldn't go forward. It was trapped. And then it would begin flailing about, a fish gasping desperately for water. But there was no escape. The more it writhed, the quicker it broke apart, until it thrashed itself into its own destruction.

Throughout the process, Celeste wouldn't feel the toothache, suffer the cold. She wouldn't feel sick at all. She would feel like soda after you shake it up. She would feel like fireworks at their climax. She would feel her senses go erect.

In short, she would feel *great.*

This also, of course, influenced her adult life.

She tried to teach the orphans to read shadows so they could heal. How she tried! She offered a class. She drew diagrams on overlapping sheets of plastic the way encyclopedias use see-through pages to map the body. She drafted a periodic table that charted the rhythmic patterns. She compiled a textbook of equations. *(Gray in lower left quadrant + brown in lower right red circle = nose clog.)*

But it didn't matter. The orphans just couldn't grasp the fundamentals. They did their homework and followed her instructions, but they always ended up staring themselves into a nap. And one day, after Roberto referred to the lessons as a planned siesta, Celeste put an end to shadow class.

"She was not an effective teacher. That was not her forte."

"She sucked as a student too. History, levitating—you name it. We figured she'd improve. But year after year, the same."

"We watched, believe us. She was a little kid when Kit and I graduated, but we were—what should we call it—"

"*Shy—*"

"Thanks—about going into the real world, so we stayed around the Home for years. Besides, Miss Kelly couldn't drive comfortably with her leg problems, and with Kit at the Home, she always had a driver or, once he perfected his fuel, cars that could do the driving for themselves. As for me, I knew my way around the office, and with Marina out to lunch, someone had to fill in. So for years we witnessed Celeste's progress in class."

"To be fair, she wasn't a *total* bomb. She did all right at becoming invisible. And in some language classes, she was good—particularly when it came to speaking Bird, Leaf, and Bodies of Water. Also she did fine in Voice Disguise class."

"Don't whitewash it. Remember all those F's? And how we kept wishing she could take a test in healing, just so she'd get an A? But since she was the only healer, no one could test her."

"Though you could say she did get tested anyway. Pretty early on. But don't ask us the grade. This test was in the classroom of life. They don't give out grades there."

—Kit Lincoln and Caboodle Davis, *Lifeline*

Kit's Dodge Royal, aka Loretta, was a platinum-blond convertible with chrome trim, tail fins, fuel injection, four on the floor, and overly sensitive feelings. Forget to tell Loretta she looked beautiful, and she'd launch a hot cigarette lighter into your lap. Cuss her out, and she'd spin the odometer like a slot machine. Moon over another car, and she'd wrench the emergency brake suddenly upright—her equivalent of flipping the bird. But treat her with respect, and she was putty in your hands. All you needed to feed her was Kit's breakfast of champions: K-Y jelly, sugar, paint thinner, coffee, Jack Daniel's, spermicide, honey, and Coca-Cola. When she got low on oil, hold the 10W 40; the only oil Loretta liked was Oil of Olay. And you didn't need a key to turn her on: stroke her in the right place, with the right rhythm, and soon her vents would sigh, her body shudder, and if you moved quick—slipped into the seat while she was still trembling and popped the clutch—you could hit sixty in five seconds and cruise off into the sunset.

One Sunday soon after Celeste had begun healing, Loretta drove Miss Kelly to the clinic. Kit being busy, Miss Kelly had to use one of the animated cars. She chose Loretta arbitrarily, but it was a moment the Dodge would never forget. "It was my new hood ornament," she purred years later in her husky voice. "It gleamed like a Liz Taylor diamond." Although Loretta played no part but observer, that day put a skid mark on her memory: "It was the first time I ever felt that *je ne sais quoi* with Celeste." (Much to the Dodge's chagrin, however, Celeste wouldn't respond for a long time to come.)

Needless to say, Miss Kelly's concern was not with introducing a girl to a car. Miss Kelly had healing on her mind.

Figure this: If Celeste could cure everything from hangnails to heart murmurs, maybe she could cure Marina. It was a long shot; Celeste had been able to diagnose Kit's Chevy but not fix it, nor had she been able to fix Miss Kelly's legs. But then again, the Chevy was a machine, and Miss Kelly's legs—that is, the bones inside— were wood. Marina was completely alive.

At least, in her body. The specialists *said* her brain showed activity, and she *had* become quite skilled in origami. But Marina still hadn't so much as nodded since the birth.

For years, Celeste's name was the single straw that could break the back of Marina's recovery, so Miss Kelly had long ago ruled out any references to the child. But when Celeste began healing, Miss Kelly considered repealing.

"I've decided we should go somewhere this morning," Miss Kelly told Marina the day Loretta delivered the gray-haired matron to the clinic. "I want you to see the Home, where I live. There's someone there who might make you better. Sam says he'll come too. We'll have you back here by tonight."

She whistled to Loretta to pull up to the door. "And all the way there," the Dodge reminisced years later, "Marina held Sam's hand. It was *tres* romantic. Didn't let go till I parked."

I was eating cashews in the living room today when Grandma came in and asked if I remembered hearing about my mother. I said yes, she's the lady that lives in the hospital. Grandma said she'd just brought my mother home. Her name is Marina and she's with a friend who's a nurse. Nurse Sam. I saw Sam when we had the flu. So I went out and Marina was sitting in the garden with Sam. When she saw me she backed off like I had cooties. I thought she was going to cry and I ran behind Loretta to hide but then Sam talked to Marina and she got calm. He said to come out. So I came out and said hello. Marina looked at me but didn't speak. Grandma said Marina was sick and asked me to check out her shadow. She said, Look hard now, do you think you can heal her? But I didn't have to look hard. The shadow was like a baby shadow. I told Grandma that. She said she knew that but could I fix it anyway? I said no. That was the way Marina was. Grandma got all sad but then I told her about the other shadows inside Marina. The ones that are all piled up inside hers. I said, There are other ones that she can hear. Or not hear but *be*, sort of. Only she doesn't know it. What are you talking about? Nurse Sam asked. I said, Like the way Loretta's shadow looks when people sit inside her. Can you read these other shadows? he asked. No, I told him. Are they why Marina can't speak? he asked. I'm not sure, I said. He said, Well you would help us a lot if you would heal them out of her. I can't, I said. That's the way she is. There is nothing I can do.

—*The Diary of Celeste*, volume I

• • •

Sure, it was a grave disappointment, but like Newton failing to get his nap only to score the consolation prize of discovering gravity, Marina failed to get healthy but scored the consolation prize of discovering the Home. After Celeste had returned to the living room, and Samson and Miss Kelly had gaped over the enigma for an appropriate period of time, Samson said, "Well, let's give her a nice visit anyway," and walked Marina through the garden.

"This is a violet," he said, and—*be-bop-a-lula!*—Marina reached out and stroked the petals! A seed of hope winked hello inside him. "Come over here," he continued. "Check out the hyacinths." She leaned over the bell-shaped flowers—and took in a full-fledged, rootin'-tootin', normal reflex *sssnnifff!*

"M-Miss K-Kelly?" Sam stammered, and Miss Kelly looked over. "This is the biggest fuss she's made since I've known her!"

And then, to Marina, he asked, "You like this place?"

Marina responded with her shallow smile—and then she kicked off her clogs and skipped-to-her-Lou through the garden, tiptoeing through tulips, squirting honeysuckle juice on her tongue, showering lilac petals on her head, rubbing mimosa leaves over her cheeks. Samson followed behind, his hope sprouting buds—no, blossoms—no, *prom-sized corsages complete with baby's breath and ribbons!* He giggled like a boy climbing into a back seat his first time.

At one point, when Marina squatted to study a spiderweb, Miss Kelly made her way over and lowered herself until her eyes were level with Marina's. She brushed her daughter's rubyesque hair behind an ear and asked, "Do you remember this place?"

Marina peered at Miss Kelly, then glanced up at Samson.

"Is it familiar to you?" Sam asked. "Do you recognize it?"

Slowly, almost imperceptibly, Marina shook her head no.

"Oh!" Miss Kelly cried. "She can communicate! Oh!" She reached forward and kissed Marina's face.

Samson knelt down. "Do you like it here?" he asked Marina.

Marina flashed her shallow smile and nodded a quick and definitive *yes.*

They moved in then. Marina took the spare bed in Celeste's room, and Samson moved into Miss Kelly's extra bedroom. He decided he wanted just to care for Marina, so he quit his job at the clinic and went to work in our garden. And he fit right in at the Home. He bred lilies that smelled like pizza, juniper shaped like trousers, weeds that played music if you danced on them.

But the only thing that really seemed to matter to him was Marina. They were always together. If he was planting a tree, she was there. If she went for a walk, he joined her. All she could do was nod yes or no, but they seemed so connected. Like they understood each other without words. In a way they were a funny pair, not doing what the rest of the Home couples did whenever we could. But there was something between them that went deeper than the body. Love, you might say.

—Broomcorn Jerry, as told to author

"What are you doing?" the eleven-year-old Celeste asked Roberto and Anabolic June. The teenagers were naked on a blanket in the woods off the path, Roberto on top of Anabolic June.

The couple ceased their rhythm and lay still, their deep-sea breathing suddenly crashing into land. Anabolic June tipped her head back to see Celeste. The little girl had been told certain activities went on in the woods, but she always did seem a bit naive. Obviously this was her first illustration of the truth behind the birds and the bees.

"Celeste," Roberto said, seizing the corners of the blanket and wrapping it around them, "leave us alone."

Celeste didn't budge. "What are you doing?"

Roberto rolled his eyes. "You know what we were doing."

"Were you sleeping?"

"No."

"Were you kissing?"

"Yes. And more."

"You were doing the fuck, weren't you?"

Roberto smirked. "Right."

" 'Were' is the correct word," Anabolic June sighed.

"Now," Roberto said, "see you late—"

"What's it feel like?"

"Let's talk about it some other time, okay?"

"I want to know now."

"We don't want to tell you now."

"Does it feel like . . ." Celeste trailed off.

"It feels like nothing else."

"I *know*," Celeste said. "But it looks so . . ."

"So what?" Roberto asked.

"So different than what I thought," she said, and ran away.

The orphans shared a good laugh and went back at it, but they wouldn't have laughed if they had known why she asked.

Today in the woods Roberto and Anabolic June were naked and doing the fuck like in that dream I had last week.

The dream was on a big beach. I was standing naked on the sand and a monster came out of the ocean. Only it wasn't really a monster. It was a giant shadow. I couldn't read it. There was too much inside it. Like the way the layers in Marina's shadow look. And it had a fuzzy outline like mine too.

The monster came over to me. He said Lie down. He was breathing loud and he lay down on top of me and he was very hot.

Then I felt something touch me in that place between my legs, and I was so confused but it felt so good. I looked at the monster but all I could see was colors. He moved and I did too, and then he gurgled hard and I felt something go inside me.

Then he was gone. I got up and I was all wet and the wet fell onto the sand. I looked down and right under me baby plants were growing. They were pretty. They hadn't been there before.

—*The Diary of Celeste,* volume I

The seasons rotated. Old orphans departed to serve the world, new orphans arrived, and time shuffled Celeste's monster dream to the bottom of the deck.

As for Marina, time dealt her—well, not a winning hand, but a change of face. Her shallow smile millimetered up to full, and occasionally she even laughed. Tears, which had accompanied her for so long, went away except for the infrequent nightly visit.

Marina still did not speak.

Marina played. In addition to her earlier passions, she immersed herself in the sensual pleasures of finger painting. Her fingers, gooey with color from aqua to marine, sailed purposefully across reams of paper. Out of the colorful chaos, she created exotic landscapes, chock-full of skyscrapers and taxis and people. Geography whizzes would yank dry paintings from the clothesline and one-up each other on the locations. "New York!" "Rome!" "Shanghai!" "Berlin!" "Istanbul!"

All places where Marina had never been.

All with stonework and street signs and clothing and jewelry, so detailed it seemed she must have been there.

All as richly tapestried as the way she used to describe her dreams.

The only exception was the paintings that were simply a spuming swirl. They looked the way Niagara Falls would look from a barrel. They looked like a Jackson Pollock painting done in beer head and semen. They were what she painted most often.

"Does this have anything to do with the shadows inside you?" Sam would ask. No answer. "Are these images from your dreams?" Still, nothing. He would go to Celeste and repeat his queries. But Celeste, expert shadow reader though she was, merely shrugged. The shadows were too layered to make sense to her.

Sometimes, Marina and Celeste played together. Under Sam's attentive gaze, they strung flower necklaces and caught frogs and went swimming at the quarry. Celeste had fun but, truth be told, no more fun than she had with anyone else. She knew their relationship was special biologically, but it wasn't really special otherwise. Certainly, when she sought parental wisdom, Celeste never went to Marina. Celeste went to Miss Kelly.

"Grandma, can you tell me about my father?"

"I'm afraid that was your mother's secret."

"Can you tell me about Marina's father?"

"I'm afraid that is *my* secret."

"Gee. Well, can you tell me about God?"

"God is His own secret."

"Then how do you know He's a he?"

"It's just a verbal convention. Most everything that has been written about God says He's a he."

"What do you think?"

"I hate to speculate."

"What about the Devil. Can you tell me about the Devil?"

"He's as much a secret to me as God."

"You mean they're like each other?"

"They're not supposed to be, but from what I can tell, they're both equally unreliable. Any more questions? And try something I can answer this time."

"Okay. When am I going to start to menstruate?"

(*Pause*) "Any day now, I'm sure."

—Tape recording

What else could she say? Though Celeste knew enough about mechanics to pen an entry in *Encyclopedia Genitalia,* by fifteen her body had not yet wised up. She could make out a slight fuzz in her nether regions, and her nipples protruded like candy kisses, but she had none of the sweat and lust and goo that help little girls slide into adulthood. Except for the incident in the woods, she administered no sexual inquisitions. And except for the monster, she experienced no tubular dreams. She didn't pant after anyone. Her hormones seemed stuck in traffic.

But Celeste didn't mope over this. She didn't mope over anything. Because she was not only physically, but emotionally, on the south side of adolescence. Teenage angst was as unfamiliar to her as TV. She healed, she danced, she chirped in Bird, she cackled in Leaf. She stopped wearing shoes. She dressed up in different clothes once or twice a week (even removing her rings!), and for that day made believe she was some character invented out of thin air, disguised voice and all. She kept her room a mess. Her pale face beamed a man-in-the-moon grin, her black, cascading ringlets made her seem like a weaver of giggles. *What, me worry?* her whole being seemed to exude, despite her developmental delay.

Samson examined her and found nothing amiss. "Fifteen is no big deal. She must be a late bloomer." But he offered to run some lab tests anyway, just to weed out all loitering concern.

So one fateful afternoon, he donned nurse duds and jeeped to the clinic. Alas for the lass, it was his first visit in years.

"We *thought* you were still doing nursing!" Bee exploded upon his arrival. "Need more free samples?" (She'd been forwarding him free samples.) "What are you out of—cortisone? condoms?"

"Well, we can *always* use condoms," he replied as Patchett anteloped over, "but actually I've slacked off on the nurse gig."

"Oh?" Patchett said. "It's been so long since we've seen any orphans here, we simply assumed you were handling them all."

"I do take care of Marina, but aside from that I mostly tend to photosynthesis. My nursing services are unnecessary."

"Why is that?"

He *should* have shoved a prophylactic on the truth. He *should* have said the free samples did the trick just fine, thank you.

But he didn't.

The truth gushed out. "Well, because Celeste is a healer."

"What?" Patchett pealed. "You mean the resurrection of her mother was not an anomaly?"

An *oops!* immediately inseminated Sam's cerebral cortex, but its journey to the lips was slow, and Sam's mouth kept grinding away. "That was the only resuscitation—we've buried a lot of dogs she couldn't revive. No, she doesn't do any more death-to-life stuff. She just heals what we medical folk can heal."

"Uh *huh.*" Patchett and Bee nodded, and at the second syllable, Sam's awareness of his boo-boo finally reached his mouth. His lips closed as quickly as a hooker's legs after *Time's up.* With a mumbled "Got some lab work," he made tracks down the hall.

The test results were normal. Sam bade adieu to the nurses and went home, his confidence about Celeste unshaken.

The nurses waved cheery bye-byes, but as far as they were concerned, there was a whole lot of shaking going on.

Maybe you're one of us.

Maybe you tried religion but felt it was too rigid. You want your individualness celebrated.

Or maybe you tried a self-awareness group but felt it was too vague. You want to *know* who this "Higher Power" is.

Maybe.

Maybe you're one of us.

—Direct-mail appeal, Spiritual Nudity Movement

Most of the orphans never went into town, and with one exception, town never came to them. But that exception was a doozy. Actually, that exception was a dwarf. A white-gloved, green-suited, two-term (and counting) dwarf. The mayor of Fossilfink Falls, His Lowness the Honorable Gravely Beaks.

For years, Mayor Beaks had dropped in on the Home at random intervals. He prepared for his visits the same way he prepared for visits to any constituents. He'd part his gray hair in the middle, check his teeth for loose food particles, and button up his green velvet suit. Then he'd hop into his Cadillac, slip on the white gloves that ensured warm handshakes, and tool off to the Home. But the barking of the dogs—*who were not supposed to be there; he'd only suggested a lock, not maximum security!*—always alerted the Home to his arrival, and before he had shifted into Park, an Unwelcoming Committee of orphans and Miss Kelly would be heading for the gate. They would tell Beaks, once again, that things were fine and then send him on his way.

His drop-bys were sporadic, so no one caught on that he always came in midafternoon—the time of day when shadows are at their sharpest. But not even Sherlock Holmes would have presumed that Mayor Beaks was capable of understanding shadows.

Or, indeed, that he had a yellow belt in Shadow Reading. A yellow belt. Which was only one belt away from the coveted white. Which meant that when he wanted to observe his constituents, he knew how to be pretty frigging discreet about it.

Every day, Beaks rejoiced in belonging to the Matrix, but never so much as he did on his jaunts to the Home. *Thanks to the grrrace of Gacy,* he'd sigh as he reached the iron gate, *Shadow Rrreading's the only way to get a handle on this loony bin.*

Little did he know that the handle was a mirage. Although Celeste had approached the gate many times over the years, Beaks had always been shooed away too fast to read her shadow. He was literally in the dark about her abilities. And his ignorance might have gone on forever—and you might be nuzzling your snookums now instead of reading this book—had it not been for a minnow-sized comment he snared during shots of tequila. A comment flung out casually by the local minister, Mahoney Patchett.

The Reverend Mahoney Patchett presided over The Only Church in Town, which was housed in his gas station. A decrepit marquee above the Esso sign invited motorists to PRAY WHILE YOU PUMP, though there were regular parishioners too. Mahoney wore gas station duds, boots, and a hunting cap, and looked like the kind of guy who'd chew tobacco, but his wife, the columnar Regina Patchett, hated that habit, so Mahoney chewed bullets. Actually, he sucked them. Their shape reminded him of a clitoris; he'd wedge a full metal jacket between his teeth and suck and swirl and practice his tongue flick. The only times he'd spit it out were when he got up on the pulpit and when he went down on his wife. Then he added the bullet to the stash in his pockets, which he fingered like loose change, which is what people thought it was.

Beaks had long wondered why Patchett wasn't in the Matrix. He seemed to have the fixings of a Matricist. His full-service station allowed him to straddle two worlds—the pious and the profane—and be confessor and eavesdropper in each. He also knew the difference between a fifteen-shot magazine and *Reader's Digest*—in fact, he subscribed to more mercenary rags than Beaks had ever seen. The Gacy Guru said candidates for the Matrix should have *the stomach to watch laws and sausages being made—and the ability to sneer throughout.* Beaks didn't know about any sneering, but Patchett sure witnessed a lot of human slush. Plus, his shadow revealed a streak of untapped materialism. Dangle financial rewards before his eyes, and you might find a real go-getter. Maybe his omission had been an oversight. After all, it was up to current Matricists to recruit new students, and Beaks was the lone Matricist in town. Maybe Mahoney deserved recruitment.

Beaks tried to find out. One deer season, he invited Patchett to go hunting. It looked quite promising at first. Patchett owned a .30-06 caliber rifle (good), quoted from *Hunting with Harold* on UBC-TV (even better), muttered about wishing he could afford a Pocono getaway to enact marital fantasies (almost grand slam), kept his cool when a whitetail bounded into his crosshairs, shot precisely through the neck where it met the spine, strode confidently toward the crumpled animal. Grrreat! Grrreat! Beaks followed along, debating how to introduce the idea of the Matrix. They reached the fallen deer. The moment was ripe. Patchett flipped the buck over. All they had to do was remove the entrails. Beaks opened his mouth—

And Patchett sat back on his heels. "Forgive me, Lord."

Being a dwarf, Beaks could look right into the eye of a seated man. He peered at Patchett. "I beg yourrr parrrdon?"

"It's just . . . ," Patchett mumbled. He spit something out of his mouth (*a bullet?*), pulled a handkerchief from his pocket, and honked. "It's just so *upsetting.*"

Beaks examined the kill. The shot was perfect. "What is?"

"That he has to *die*."

Mayor Beaks paused a minute. "I thought that was the point. You kill them, you take them home, you eat them."

"I *can't* eat them," Patchett groaned. "I'm a *vegetarian!*"

"Then why arrre you shooting them?"

"Be-be-because"—Patchett sniffed—"God needs the deer population down. So he gave men this desire to *shoot*. I know it's silly to get upset, I know it's natural—I *like* shooting, it's like nothing else—but it makes me feel so . . . so *guilty*."

"Ho ho," Beaks said, "I get it." Though he didn't get it at all. He helped Patchett dig a grave and participated in the blessing over the body, but Beaks had to admit that the Matrix was best off without the lunk; Patchett couldn't *be* a Monitor—he needed too much Monitoring *himself*.

So Mayor Beaks made himself available to the minister. Subtly. Together they hunted antlered ruminants, guzzled the fine nectar of Methylyn Monroe, drooled at the knockers of televised floozies. Patchett came to think of Beaks as his chum.

Which was why Beaks was around one night doing shots of tequila when the babble bubbled over to the subject of the Home. "My wife'd love to hire that girl," Patchett mused.

"What girrrl?" Beaks asked, and Patchett filled Beaks in on what he'd heard about Celeste's healing, adding, "Regina thinks Celeste might have a direct line to the Almighty. And Regina might have a point. Remember the birth? And that cloud?"

"Cloud? What cloud?"

"You know, that naked cloud. I mean, I know strange when I see strange, and fifteen years ain't enough to make me forget."

Beaks nodded nonchalantly as Patchett spoke. Knowing this cloud business needed some serious investigating too (a naked cloud? Shit!), he thought to himself: *What if the girrrl* IS *a dirrrect link between this dump and the Pearrrly Gates? What if?*

What if, indeed. "Messiah" was high on the Gacy Guru's list of things to watch for. If Gravely Beaks, called a squirt in grade school, squirted with water guns in high school, forced to eat dog poop in college, avoided by all women except whores and then humiliated by their giggles over the size of his pecker, spied on by nieces and nephews who thought it funny—*funny!*—that he had to stand on a stool to pee in the toilet . . . if *he*, Gravely Beaks, was the first in the Matrix to lock in on a so-called Messiah's coordinates, ho ho! Such a discovery might lead to his big break; next thing he knew, he could be in D.C. or the U.N. or—dare he think it?—sitting right beside the Gacy Guru, traveling in opulence and bloated authority in the center of the whole goddamn shebang: the Temporary Zero-Zero.

You may wonderrr: do I believe in the Almighty myself? Oh, I think it's a good trrrick to get so many suckerrrs to buy into it. But having been shorrrt-changed when I bought my own genes at the Divine Shopping Centerrr, I rrroll my rrr's at the verrry idea. Besides, I think the whole notion of God leaves much morrre unanswerrred than it answerrrs, especially with so many testaments and trrranslations and denominations.

I ask you: What the hell kind of God doesn't answerrr questions? Not to mention, crrreates the likes of me.

—Gravely Beaks in Broadway production
The Baffle or the Bust

So when Beaks beefed up his surveillance to include Celeste, theological curiosity played no part. He simply wanted to go AWOL on this shithole and move on to bigger and better things.

However, he needed new tactics. Previously, he had been thwarted in every effort to Monitor the Home. In addition to getting stopped at the gate, the back path had proved useless because dogs patrolled the nearby woods. One inch closer than the quarry, and they were upon you. But until he could evaluate her, he'd have nothing to report to the Gacy Guru.

He launched a new campaign. *Lurrre herrr out.* He stopped by with raffle tickets and free pony rides and box seats to see the Phillies. She didn't even come outside. He drove a video game over. A large-screen TV. But the orphans turned him away.

It all looked very bleak until Christmas. Then, in a moment of stunning brilliance, Beaks decided to dress up as Santa. To the Home he would come, bearing gifts, and when Celeste emerged to get hers, he would speed-read her shadow. So what that Celeste was a teen, he figured; Santa is, along with E.T., Big Bird, and Ronald McDonald, one of the few symbols of righteousness that haven't been slingshotted off the American Mount Olympus. What kid could resist a visit from an icon? Even if teenage cynicism had already descended on the little darling, she'd have to come out just to laugh —and to get her mitts on her share of the booty.

He stocked up on presents. Thirty, he guessed, would cover the whole litter of brats. He ordered a kid-sized Santa suit and added one more ho to his normal pair of ho's. He stayed up all night, watching TV to bone up on his Shadow Reading. At dawn, he threw on the red suit and white whiskers. Then he heaved the bundle of presents over his shoulder and stepped onto his porch.

But *curses!* Extensive cloud cover strikes again! For hours, not the shadow of a shadow lay on the ground. He bit his nails while he paced his front porch. Finally, in late afternoon, a splinter of sun pricked through the nimbus, and around him shadows bled into view. He dived into his Cadillac and peeled out.

Dogs charged the gate at the sound of his car. "Ho ho ho!" he bellowed, getting out. "Merrrrrry Chrrristmas!"

You have to pity the deluded dwarf. For the orphans, who had more ideas of God than Crayola has colors, Christmas was just another day. When Beaks arrived, they were busy with all kinds of activities, but none concerned Jesus. Some orphans unicycled in the living room, some levitated in bed, some volleyballed on the drive. One was on the path, playing her favorite game: bandito in the hills. Unfortunately for Mayor Beaks, that one was Celeste.

The orphans came over, curious about this squat Santa at the gate. They had read about Santa. "Herrre you go, cutie," Beaks said, handing gifts through the iron bars. "One forrr everrryone." While a few orphans refused his offerings, most accepted. But all were so bewildered, they neglected to notice Beaks's eyes, which were flickering toward their shadows.

Finally, as he neared the bottom of his sack, Mayor Beaks asked if everyone was present, "Even, mmmm, the little Celeste?"

"She's out on the path," some orphan replied.

Beaks vamoosed out of there as soon as he could. *Chrrristmas comes but once a yearrr* . . . And she was *alone*. On the *path*. If he was lucky, far enough down the path to be off the patrol dogs' radar screen. Then it would be just her and him—and her shadow.

He screeched into the clinic parking lot. Years had passed since he'd tried the path, but he remembered well the gnarly trees that marked the opening. *Good!* But *bad:* shadows were getting long; dusk had already begun her foreplay. No time to remove his suit. If only he had flying reindeer! He whipped off the whiskers and hit the ground with the speed of Road Runner. *At last, you slipperrry sneak, you and I will get to meet!*

He panted through the woods, trees looming over him, their shadows reclining like Cleopatra waiting for Mark Antony. Soon the shadows of the mountains would conquer everything in their path, and night would come. But even if Celeste was shadowless when he found her, he could always interrogate her the old-fashioned way: he could speak to her.

The *bzzzt!* of the power lines filled the air. He huffed and puffed through fallen leaves, listening. At one moment he saw a flash— *was it . . . ?*—but it was just the sky sparkling on Heecheemonkee Creek, which snaked beyond a bank off the path.

He scampered up a steep hill, his respiratory system begging for mercy. With a whoop of joy, he noticed a full moon—a second chance—*if* she was still there, *if* the clouds sat out this dance.

He scuttled down the hill to the quarry. He couldn't go any farther than this; those damn dogs would be over the next rise. In the dusk, the quarry pond water was black, and the last flecks of sunlight were skating over the dark surface. He surveyed the rock garden of the quarry. But no girl romped anywhere. *Shit!*

Maybe—maybe if he was lucky—he'd missed her, and she'd still have to pass by. *Gacy willing!* He sat on a boulder, hoping, looking, patting his forehead dry with his gloved hands.

Above him, the sky was the teal and magenta that shadows become when people are sexually excited, which is why twilight summons loneliness, why women smell wet as dusk when they're aroused. He heaved, trying to reclaim lost air. *How had he missed her?* If he didn't see her here, his whole scheme would go kaput. *Never forget a backup plan,* teaches the Gacy Guru, but Beaks didn't have a backup plan—*Fucking fool!*—and you can't get to the Temporary Zero-Zero without evaluating your prey thorou—

"Hold it right there." A male voice cracked out of the dark.

Beaks spun around. The clouds had moved over the moon. He couldn't see a single shadow—just the silhouettes of rocks.

"Stand up and put your hands in the air."

Beaks peered into the night. "Who's that?"

"I said stand up."

He rose to his feet.

"Put them *up!*"

His white-gloved hands shot high in the air.

"What are you doing here?" the voice said, and a tumble of rocks nearby made clear that the man was moving.

"I was out for a walk—"

"Don't give me that. Toss your weapon on the ground."

"I don't have a weapon."

The shuffle of feet continued. Beaks tried to find the source. His arms were tired, and he hated how his white gloves—only a political prop, after all—gave his captor a beacon to find him. He knew the world was full of trigger-happy screwballs and convicts on the lam, but he'd always assumed he'd never meet one. They haunt cities and turnpike rest stops—not towns like Fossilfink Falls. Still, he should have brought his .38, but the Santa suit had no pockets. What was he supposed to do—put it in the sack of toys? Which was in the car anyway. And what about—

Scrunch! went the soil nearby.

He scanned the area but couldn't see anyone. "Come out!"

"I'll make the demands. What are you doing here?"

"I'm—I was out for a walk." *Keep him talking.*

"Sure. Bet you work for the FBI."

"FBI? Why would I—"

"Don't try to con me."

Behind! To the left!

Beaks spun around.

Maybe ten feet away stood a girl with waist-length hair. She was about five feet tall and wore pants and a fringed jacket or vest. In the dark, he couldn't see her face. Also, because of the clouds, he had no clue about her shadow. But *maybe* . . .

"Arrre you Celeste Kelly?" he asked.

"Wait a—," said the girl. "Who are you?"

"I'm Mayorrr Beaks."

"Mayor Beaks! I thought you were one of the guys from the Home! In the dark you look like a kid. Oops. Sorry, I don't mean to be rude."

"That's all rrright," he said through gritted teeth, and then asked casually, "Um, who's that with you? The man I heard."

"Man? Oh, that was me. Just disguising my voice."

That Kelly Home sure did raise one brood of weird kids.

"And . . . wherrre's yourrr gun?"

"It's no gun. It was my *hand.*" She giggled, and he cringed at how absolutely, positively mortifying it would be if the Gacy Guru ever discovered that Gravely Beaks had been snagged by a forefinger and a thumb.

Well, at least that meant he didn't have to worry.

"So you'rrre Miss Celeste Kelly," he said. *Rats! No light yet!* "How forrrtuitous. I'd been hoping to meet you. You know, it's not smarrrt to play alone in the darrrk."

"I was just on my way home."

"Good. Now come a little closerrr, so I can say I saw you."

She began to step forward, but as she lifted her foot some instinct kicked in. Maybe it was just the old don't-talk-to-virtual-strangers response. Or maybe some Danger sensor going off inside her. All she knew was, she'd better proceed with caution.

"Come on," he prodded. "I'd like to see you betterrr."

She set her foot back down. "How come?"

"Sweethearrrt"—he inched closer—"I'm not going to hurrrt you. I just want to get to know you."

"Why?"

"Because you'rrre a special little girrrl in these parrrts."

"What do you mean?"

"You know what I mean. You'rrre a healerrr."

How did he know *that*? she wondered. And why did it *matter*? Something felt very creepy here. She tried to size him up but in the diffuse moonlight could make out only his eyes. They were a squint, irises ticking back and forth, calculating like some kind of optic adding machine, seeking.

But *what*, she wondered, was he seeking?

Just then the clouds slipped away from the moon. Light poured down, and Gravely Beaks jerked his gaze toward her feet.

Had he lost something? Celeste peered in the same direction. No stray cuff link glittered up from the ground, no newly sprung button. Nothing lay near her feet at all—nothing, of course, except her shadow, with its vibrant health and nebulous perimeter. So what was he looking for? What did he need? She glanced up to his eyes—

He was reading her shadow! He was looking for her!

She gasped and was just about to dive down to investigate *his* shadow, when he mumbled, "What the hell's with herrr edges? Check the face!" and blasted up to find her waiting stare—And the two adversaries locked their eyes together.

He had started to dissect her shadow, she realized.

He would want to finish the job, she knew.

She had not even thought to look at his.

But at that moment in the December chill, the only sound the echoes of their breath, her only focus his slitted gaze, it was not this missed opportunity that concerned her. It was what she was seeing. Because as they faced each other in the moonlight, neither moving, neither speaking, the glint in his eyes sent a shudder into her, tripped an understanding encoded in her genes, and made her feel for the first time in her life that she was seeing—and she took a deep breath and stood up taller, admitting it to herself, loud and clear—that in those eyes before her at that very moment in the quarry, she was seeing not love, which she was used to, nor friend-liness, which she might have expected, but the steely, selfish gleam of *evil.* An acrid taste splashed through her mouth, as if she had just bitten into a piece of rancid fruit.

Swiftly—she'd have only a second before he realized she was shadow literate too—she ripped her gaze from his and swept her eyes across his shadow. No time to take note of color or rhythms.

Time only to see what he was after, how much he was after—no, cut to the quick—*why* he was after.

But she managed to get only the barest of glimpses before—

"You can rrread *my* shadow!" he blurted.

She looked to his face. Confusion was puckering his nose. Shock was wrinkling his mouth. Questions were storming his eyes.

He reached his white gloves toward her—

And she bolted. Up the rocks—go! Her hair streamed behind her. She scrambled across boulders. Run. Run! Oh, no—look: the moon! Bright as a spotlight. He'd see her shadow from behind; he'd learn her intended route, her desires, her fears—whatever it was he wanted! And suddenly, cresting the rise of the quarry, stumbling onto the path, she could feel what would happen if he found what he wanted, feel it with a certainty that surged through her veins, that hardened her bones; that scared her as much as death. She veered off the path, tore into the shadows of the trees. Oak shadows lay on top of hers, hiding hers. Keep moving. Keep going. She tried to make herself invisible but couldn't concentrate. Almost crashed into a maple. Zigzagged and tangled in a bush. She couldn't see in the dark. But she *could* hear. Listen: birds were calling to her. Birds were trying to help. *Oo-oo-oo!* (Swerve right!) *Tchack!* (Swerve left!) She let them guide her—over hills, logs, stumps. Thank you, thank you. She'd get away, she'd tell Miss Kelly. She whirled around— No! He was trudging behind, still following. *How?* Oh, the leaves! They were crackling beneath her feet! "Please," she begged in Leaf, "be quiet!" *Spoilsport,* whined the leaves. But they shushed, let her haul her ass in silence. If only the dark would hold! He might pass her, and then she could run home and— *But he'd come looking for her there! He knew where she lived!*

She had no time to think, though, because at that very moment the clouds shifted again, and the moonlight angled around, and she saw with horror that there were no trees directly over her head.

"Therrre you arrre!" Beaks cried from the adjacent rise, and picked up speed. She scanned the view. All around were trees— and, down a steep bank, the creek. She could keep running, but what if she couldn't shake him? She couldn't let him *get to know her.* Not now. Not ever.

The clouds drifted back. A dark second to make a decision. Trees might have shade, but the creek had depth.

She babbled in Creek, "You deep enough for me?"

Certainly, the creek replied.

In Bird, she shrieked, "Cover for me!" and as mockingbirds and owls exploded in a barrage of sound, Celeste raced to the edge of the bank and leaped.

A clean arc in the air. She braced herself for impact—

And the creek caught her like an open hand.

With a *splunk!* that was muffled by the ornithological cacophony, the surface closed over her body.

Sweet seagirl, ease your fears, snuggle in here, soothe your tears. Water plants stroked her body as she sank to the cold bottom. She grabbed onto rocks to keep herself down.

Glug, glug, settled some air bubbles. Above her, she could hear the birds, calling. *He runs still,* they squawked.

She opened her eyes. A school of fish goggled at her face. She let out tiny beads of air. The beads bugged the fish. The fish took a recess. The water was muddy. The water was cold. She had to breathe. What if he was outside? Her blood vessels were contracting. Her lungs screamed her name. Black scubaed across her vision. Her heart reached for its *Gone Fishin'* sign.

She shoved her head above water.

Ahhh. Air in.

She listened.

No steps. No rustle of hiding in the bushes.

Wooo. Air out.

She whispered in Leaf, "Where is he?"

The leaves laughed. *The runt's already halfway back to town.*
She heaved herself onto the bank and tore off for the Home.

Miss Kelly was in her apartment when a soaking Celeste burst in, chattering so hard her teeth could have sent telegrams.

"What happened?!" Miss Kelly said, rising from her desk.

"The mayor!" Celeste gasped as Miss Kelly wrapped a shawl around her. "He can read shadows, just like me! I was at the quarry, and he came after me!"

"Do you mean he tried to molest you?"

"No! He wanted to read me. Read every beat and color in my shadow. So he could . . ."

"Could what? Could what!"

"So he could see everything in me—even things *I* can't see. But he couldn't read the whole shadow. He didn't have enough time— I got away!"

"But why did he want to? Can he heal, like you?"

"No. He wants to *use* me, Grandma! Like a tool. Or—no—like *gold.* Like he wants to use me to buy himself something."

"But what could he possibly—"

"I don't know! I just know I can't let him finish reading my shadow. Because if he does, the result will be— I don't know how, or why; I just know that if he succeeds, it'll take . . . it'll take"— and she swallowed to force down what she knew to be true—"it'll take my life away from me."

Miss Kelly closed her eyes. "No," she whispered.

Celeste reached for her grandmother's hands, and as their fingers touched, the moment caromed back through her. She'd been at the rise before the Home, running, panting, she could already hear the dogs, already smell dinner, and there, in the dark, her childhood had seemed to unzip itself and fall off like tattered clothes, and suddenly she just *knew* what she had to do.

"Grandma," she said with sad resolve, "I need to go away."

Miss Kelly's eyes shot open.

"Please," Celeste said, squeezing their hands together. "I need your help. Send me somewhere far away from here. Send me to a place where he can't find me."

Sorrow washed over Miss Kelly's face. Celeste wanted to say more but had no words, and her mouth felt as dry as dust.

The Story of the Sea

Day Two Dawn

Morning sun scrubs the ocean sky yellow. While groggy passengers jab at poached eggs in the dining hall, Edwina sits on the deck, a plaid blanket around her crippled legs, and reads a newspaper. She is alone. John Kelly passed up her invitation to watch the sunrise; he wanted to go down to the game room and shoot pool. She has doubts about his cue stick, pretty sure it's not angling toward any side pocket.

The ocean is not good for her legs. The wet air makes the wood expand.

She snaps the paper up higher and turns to the funnies. But since the ship won't dock again until the end of the three-day cruise, all the comic strips are yesterday's. She sighs and glances up.

The stranger is sitting in a lifeboat that is strung above the deck. He wears exactly what he wore yesterday, and the same huglike smell wafts toward her.

He salutes, singing, "Hello, my baby, hello, my darling."

She laughs. A white-haired couple strolling by smiles at her. "The funnies are my favorite part of the news too," the lady says to Edwina.

"Oh," Edwina says, fumbling with the paper. "No, I was laughing at him." She points to the lifeboat.

The couple pivots. In the lifeboat, the stranger dances the Charleston.

The couple turns back. "Who?" they ask.

She can see him over their shoulders, winking at her. "That porter who just walked by," Edwina lies.

"Porter?" the stranger mouths. He reaches into his coat, extracts a bottle of malt liquor, and balances it on top of his head.

Edwina, afraid she'll laugh again, forces her eyes back to the paper.

The couple lingers at the railing, watching the ocean. Edwina reads and rereads <u>Dick Tracy,</u> then notices the stranger is speaking the same words she is seeing. She switches to the crossword puzzle. "Did you ever wonder what's in the black squares?" the stranger calls out. She flips the page. Birth announcements sit cheek by jowl with obituaries. She scans them all, trying to ignore the stranger's medley of "Yessir, That's My Baby" and "Dem Dry Bones."

Finally, the couple shuffles away. Edwina lowers her paper and peers up.

The lifeboat rocks gently on its cables, but the stranger who sat in it is gone.

Lickalinney

A compass with its legs spread wide, one bearing down on the stain on the map that is Manhattan, the other swinging into the smudge that is Philadelphia, has to pass through the New Jersey town of Lickalinney. Two hours from the city of new wealth, two hours from the city of old, Lickalinney dozes away in the northwest corner of the state, a small town with but one reason to merit mapification. Not the view; it is not nestled amid purple mountain majesties. Nor the history; it crowned no good with brotherhood. And except for a hot dog factory long since relocated to Mexico, God shed no grace over its economy.

Lickalinney rated because of the famous Sleeping Beauty. Legend had it that after a reckless night of indeterminate intoxicants, this teenage girl kicked the brain wave habit and woke up in a coma. Groundbreaking court battles then raged over her right to die. She won, but the joke was on the victors; although the respirator was unplugged, the girl, reneging on the deal, stayed alive. Cake bake fund-raisers helped the broke family for a while, but soon even that feat failed them. So the enterprising town came to the rescue. They bought a split-level house, moved the girl into a bedroom, erected a glass wall across her doorway, set up in the other rooms monitors that played videos of OD'd rock stars, piped in music by live repentant rock stars, induced a major cola company to sponsor them—and named the place the Just Say No Museum. "See What Can Happen to YOU," read the brochure. Schools bused popeyed kids from as far away as Ohio to chug cans of carbonated sugar and follow arrows on the floor past Jimi and Janis and Brian and all the rest, until they climaxed at the shrine, the centerpiece, the laziest Susan of them all: the Sleeping Beauty. Though, given the sideshow of the other rooms, most visitors gawked only momentarily at her. And once comfy chairs were placed by the videos, and pizza and doughnut franchises signed on, dust formed on the girl's glass where previously there had been foggy ooohs, and kids lounged in the video rooms, bloated and burping.

Which was often a great blow to teachers, especially since bus drivers usually pissed away half the trip trying to find the damn place. Lickalinney was an octopus of swirling subdivisions, each one a maze of curves and cul-de-sacs with such inspired addresses as "Milk" and "Lawn." Plus, each development had only a single model of house. The museum was in Poppy Fields, where locals plotted the ways in and out by the colors of the shutters. But visitors had no such clue, until officials, forced to take charge of the situation, finally blanketed the town with maps.

And so orange Plexiglas *You Are Here*'s spawned along the highway, proliferated down the secondary roads, and virtually copulated like Day-Glo rabbits into the subdivisions, where they were far more abundant than real rabbits, or even trees. Indeed, any road that had been arboreal was shaved bare to make way for them. A few folks circulated a petition to halt the bulldozers, but their neighbors, confessing a long-standing hatred of raking, refused to poise their pens. The trees went down, the signs went up. From highway to shining byway, the town was a denuded plain.

With one exception. Along one secondary road was a lake, and since it was fenced off, a patch of woods was allowed to stay within its borders. In summer, passersby who explored beyond the chain link were rewarded with water and foliage. In winter, passersby—well, passed by; the fence was padlocked tight.

It is across the street from this lake that we resume our story. For there, in a small red house along a treeless road, lived Edwina Kelly's long-lost kin Mo Wolfly.

Fifteen years before, Mo Wolfly, bank teller during the week, drum for hire on weekends, had been buying cassettes at a Castle of Values when he glanced at a tabloid and saw a Miracle Baby story, and in it the name Runetoon. He sent a missive to Miss Kelly, who replied that yes, her family *was* from Brooklyn, and ever since, they had exchanged annual touch-base cards. So when Celeste wanted to evacuate Fossilfink Falls, Miss Kelly called Mo and explained her plight to him.

Her white lie of a plight, that is. She and Celeste felt that the less others knew about the situation, the more likely Beaks would be foiled (how convenient, they agreed, that Miss Kelly's cards had been too lightweight to mention Celeste's funky eyes or healing skills). So for the plight, Miss Kelly offered that old, all-purpose standby: Celeste had been unhappy at home, and now there'd been a crisis, and it'd be better for all if—

"No sweat," Mo interrupted. "She can crash at our pad." Hey, he couldn't let his coz down, could he? Even though, over the years, he'd spaced on mentioning Celeste to his wife—Mo and Didi did communication even less than they did fornication—he'd just lay it on her later. Didi'd be cool. She always was.

"It would not be a burden?"

"You kidding? Look, put her on a bus in Scranton. Send her down. We'll make her one of the family. She'll have a gas."

I'm scared, Grandma, I told her at the bus stop.

She held my face in her hands. He won't find you, she said.

I started crying. She hugged me and said, Take heart, you are very well hidden. Even Mo will not guess about your eyes.

She is right. My eyes are one color—Sam found some brown contacts in his free samples last night. I look normal.

But I don't think I was crying over hiding. I think it was over leaving her. When I was packing, and we were both so sad, she said I could take anything of hers. So I took some clothes—they have her smell. They will remind me of her. Now she pressed her hands on mine. I will always be with you, she said.

Then I remembered Iambia's tape recorder. I asked Grandma if she could tape our phone calls and send them to me. So I could hear her voice anytime I want. So I could play back all the smart things she says. So I could feel like we're still together.

See? she said. You *think*. You will be all right.

The bus door opened. I got on and waved, and we pulled away. She was standing beside other people, and I could see how small she was, but she will always seem big to me.

—The Diary of Celeste, volume II

Mo Wolfly was a fortysomething man with a fortysomething gut. When he was at the bank, playing teller to fat cat patrons, he wore a tie, rubber finger caps to count cash, rubber ponytail holders to Barry Manilowize his Jerry Garcia hair. When he was at his drums, playing hail-fellow-well-met to any band with bread, he wore whatever they asked, from polka dot to bloodshot. He used slang that no longer scored. He often went to bed late.

His wife, Didi, wasn't sure she liked going to sleep alone, but Didi wore a perpetual smile and pink sweaters and spoke in a girlish and teeny tiny voice, and far be it from her to know what she liked. Though Chanel made her sneeze, Didi peddled perfume at a local store, spritzing *eau de achoo* on female shoppers. Though books put ideas in her head that made her uneasy, she kept up with the best-sellers. She had many acquaintances. She adored the color pink. She owned a chatty pet parrot named Michener.

The Wolfly evenings were set like concrete. Mo spent them in the basement, clubbing his sheepskins along to CDs, hitting Stop only to toss down some sweets. He dug Pop-Tarts and Cracker Jacks and Oreos. At dinner, though, he picked and pecked; it was more a time to read than to eat. *Musician, Minstrel Pop!,* sheet music—anything. After, he descended again and clamped on headphones (his one concession to the missus) until the wee hours, or until he'd delivered all his goodies to his paunch.

When Didi first got home, Michener flew to her shoulder, and the two meandered nuzzlingly to the kitchen. There she tuned the TV to her favorite game show, sat him in his high chair, and went to the bath; she needed three showers to rid herself of perfume odor. Back in the kitchen, hair turbaned in a towel, Didi cooked dinner as Michener regurgitated *Hide and Go for the Gold!* It was a good system, though during dinner he babbled the next program. This made it hard to talk, so like Mo, Didi read. After, she and Michener retired to the bedroom, where she got into bed with her paperbacks and read him a few chapters aloud.

Into the midst of all this fine social interaction came Celeste. Celeste was put in the spare room: the attic. Where boxes staged a be-in. Where a jukebox grayed in the corner. Where crates of records waited for their pensions to roll in.

Celeste lowered her suitcase to the floor. Then she walked to the window and pulled off her boots—Miss Kelly's brown proletarian calf-highs—and sat on the bed. Webs cobbed in the rafters. A bare bulb dangled from the peak. Boxes towered hauntingly. "Just your garden-variety mementos," Mo had explained. "From my days as a roadie. You'll think they're a drag—just leave 'em alone." Celeste opened a lid anyway. Books. Reeking of mold. Never having been much of a reader, she didn't bother to check their spines; she just closed the box back up.

Then she popped open the window shade. Light trumpeted into the room. Outside stretched the map-lined road and rusty chain-link fence and, beyond, the scalloped edge of the lake. She shoved the window open. The lake sibilated, geese ronked, leaves oodly-oodly-ooed. "I'm so glad you're here," Celeste squealed in their languages. "Tell me, what is this place like?"

Oh, you poor sap, the leaves moaned, and when she asked what they meant, they replied: *It ain't no Sunday romp on the lawn.*

SCENE: *Celeste's First Meal in Lickalinney. Seated around table.*
(Note: Actors should read parts simultaneously.)

DIDI	MO	CELESTE	MICHENER
"Oh, I'm so happy to meet you! Mo didn't fill me in. Mo *never* fills me in. What grade are you in?"	Sighs		"Welcome to *Exes*! I'm your host, Bob Diaperine! Please meet Amy, a lovely CPA. Behind this curtain are her 3 exes—
"How lovely. That was one of my best years. I had a very wonderful friend, Lila —her mom was on *The Price Is Right*! But she lost, and Lila took it hard, though not as hard as her brother; he was a soccer star. Lila had lipstick that tasted like *candy*! And we used to . . ."	"I told you that." Yawns. Opens book and reads.	"10th."	guys who might be any-one from her first kiss to her last husband! She doesn't know who's there! Amy's going to ask them questions—she can ask anything! If she guesses all 3 identities, she wins a free car! But not if they can help it! Ready, Amy? Okay. Ex Number One . . ."

—Script for Broadway production
The Baffle or the Bust

● ● ●

Throughout dinner, Celeste watched Mo's and Didi's shadows. Wishy-washy colors drowsed stagnantly. Anorexic webs splintered and floated off. Sluggish rhythms dragged through sloppy cycles.

She'd never seen such symptoms. Their shadows were like a taco without jalapeños. A kangaroo without a spring.

In other words, functional, but completely lacking in oomph.

The problem was not physical—Celeste could tell that in a flash. But it also wasn't emotional; emotion didn't do this. The problem was another beast altogether. Something she had never seen at the Home and didn't understand now.

She couldn't ask the Wolflys about it; they didn't know she could read shadows. So she bided the puzzle till after dinner, at which time Didi took a one more for good measure shower, Mo descended to his cavern, and Celeste turned to Michener.

The yellow-naped Amazon eyed Celeste from his high chair. She was more fluent in domestic than foreign Bird, but gave it her best shot. "Can you clue me in?" she pirated in Parrot.

"Can you clue me in?" he echoed in English.

She paused. "Don't you know Parrot?"

"Don't you know Parrot?"

Maybe he'd hung out with other birds in the store. She tried to remember handy phrases from her Foreign Bird Language class. "Do you understand me?" she fruit-looped in Toucan.

"Do you understand me?"

"Is all you do repeat?" she tuxedoed in Penguin.

"Is all you do repeat?"

"I need a friend, and what do I get? A tape recorder."

"Have a cracker," Michener replied, and when Celeste brightened, he blinked dumbly at her. "Polly."

She climbed the stairs to the attic. She opened the window and whispered in Leaf, "I see what you mean."

Hey, if you think this is bad, the leaves cackled back, *just wait until you begin school.*

Rah rah
Siss boom bah
You want to win?
We say ha.
We creamed Celeste
We know the score
So lick our cleats
And hear us roar.

—Lickalinney football cheer

Celeste, the fifteen-year-old who looked ten, who had no eelie-feelie dreams, no dick-in-the-dark delusions of passion, whose hands had never set forth on self-exploration, whose games had never included Doctor, whose chivalry had never been tested in the world: Celeste went to school.

On a winter morning, she strode her T-and-A-less body down the road in Miss Kelly's trademark work boots, shin-skimming gray dress, and leather jacket, and, of course, Celeste's own assortment of plain silver rings. At the top of the rise, she gazed down. Lick-alinney High sat in a shallow valley, a plume of smoke rising from its roof, yellow school buses circling the building. The wind whipped her hair around her. She thrust her hands into her pockets and continued on down.

As Celeste approached the front doors, teens high-topped and knapsacked and baseball-capped inside. She funneled in with them, scanning shadows around her. She could barely believe it: almost every shadow seemed bruised or shattered or sleepy. She stepped out of the hallway flow and gaped at the floor. Every shadow was different—but with few exceptions, every shadow was off. Off in the same way Mo's and Didi's were. What did it mean? What could be so pervasively wrong? Is this what Miss Kelly meant about the world? Is this why she was raising knights?

Eventually, Celeste found her homeroom, a cinder-block cell with several circular tables. Four or five students sat around each table, talking low. Along the front wall, behind a rectangular desk, a mustached teacher polished his eyeglasses. Celeste approached him, shooting a look at his shadow. It was meek, shriveled, as if in the throes of a drought. Another variation of the same problem.

"I was told to expect a Celeste Wolfly today," the teacher squeaked, like a saloon door. He fit on his spectacles and squinted down at Celeste. "Are you her little sister?"

Celeste's face reddened. "I *am* Celeste," she said, folding her arms over her flat chest.

Peals of guffaws and desk slapping from the back. Celeste turned around. At the table with the uproar, a gang of boys traded Torturers & Terrorists cards. The boys wore elephantine pants and wedge haircuts and T-shirts that said such things as OUT OF MY FACE and SO BLOW ME. Adam's apples stood prominent as fists in their necks. Shadows festered like open sewers around their athletically clad feet.

"I beg your pardon," the teacher creaked. "There's an empty table there. Take a seat; you can have it to yourself. . . ."

As bad luck would have it, Celeste's designated table was a mere six feet from where the card studs were camped. She sat down. No one in the room sent a tender glance her way or even cocked a tepid smile, so she lowered her eyes until the teacher began to call roll. "Butane. Butane. Butane," he began, addressing the boys behind her. It seemed that everyone at the table was a Butane: brothers held back so many times, there was now a bulge of them in a single

103

homeroom. And the one with the most septic shadow was Billy. Billy Butane. Evidently the leader, Billy made *Goochy-goochy-goo* and *Waaah!* noises when Celeste's name was called, then elbowed his brothers, who hopped on the bandwagon. A moment later, he dropped the sounds in favor of blowing kisses. Celeste cringed in a hail of acid smooches.

Not until the intercom came on did the bandwagon shut up. "All rise," Principal Fleece intoned disembodiedly, "and pledge to the flag." Celeste had never pledged to any flag, so she rose and listened. Around her, voices somnambulated through the words, blurring the meaning with their soporific cadence. A song ensued. Celeste strained to follow the lyrics. She'd just begun to wonder about the rockets' red glare when something landed on her back and fishtailed down her spine. She whipped around.

Billy Butane was licking his finger with a smirk.

"Not even a training bra," he said. "Tsk, tsk. This is high school, douchebitch. *High*"—and with each hand he cupped invisible melons over his pectorals—"school." He turned to his brothers. "Let's find a station with a real babe."

The gang tittered. Celeste's face burned. The teacher glanced over, then began wiping his glasses again. Billy reached to his belt and drew a weapon: a remote control. He aimed it at Celeste, grinned, and made a practiced and resounding *click*.

Be careful you
Walk lightly.
They are scared of you
Most rightly.
Don't let them see
Don't let them know

Don't get in the way
Of their favorite TV show.

—Placard outside jail after Celeste's arrest

No, those youngsters weren't in the Matrix. Nor were they *nths*. But you have to commend them. They appropriated some of our techniques without even knowing we existed. If only Matrix students were as clever as those Butanes. How unfortunate we did not have them on our side at the time.

—Gacy Guru, videotaped memoir,
And You Thought It Was Just Paranoia

Though Lickalinney High was the happy hunting ground of the Butanes, many equally benevolent cliques had staked out turf as well; the school was a patchwork of territories, each bordered by rivers of rage. The Jailbusters stomped on the Trekbrains, who thumbscrewed the Rappers, who shouted out the Straight Edges, who water-pistoled the Hip Boppers, who vandalized the Trophy Boys, who kissed-'n'-told on the Prom Queens, who rumor-whipped the Jailbusters. And the Butane Gang oppressed all around, all around, the Butane Gang oppressed all around.

Now, Celeste, having pricked Billy's ire her first day, had what you might call a peer-acceptance problem. That is, she was instantly bar-coded as generic dork. And each day, as her out-of-itness became more obvious, her value got slashed even more.

Let's face it—Celeste had a streak of stubborn. She wore those gray dresses and work boots and Rapunzelishly long hair and unadorned silver rings, despite the fact that during those fifteen minutes of history, such a look was a distinct no-no. She knew shit about the important things in life—current music? nada; TV? zilch; movies? ditto—and didn't aspire to learn. And though it wasn't a

matter of choice, while everyone around her was bumping their uglies from dinner to curfew every night (because *there's nothing else
to do around hee-yer*), Celeste still hadn't gotten her hands on a
ticket to the Hormonal Sweepstakes.

You may wonder if her face contributed to her difficulties. After
all, it's hardly classified info that Celeste was not fairest-of-them-all
beautiful: her nose was a trifle crooked, and she had a slight gap
between her two front teeth. But she was not ugly, either: her eyes,
even with contact lenses, were deep and large as the most kohl-
lined Hindu maiden's; her smile could generate enough warmth to
heat a small Bulgarian village; and beneath her marble-white skin,
blue veins skittered faintly as an underground Venice. Put the exotic
in a let's-not-rush-to-Hollywood face, and you got a girl who seemed
unthreatening and innocent, yet mysterious, as if the enigma of the
Mona Lisa smile had swept across an entire countenance. And so
it's possible that in a school where mystery and innocence were
greeted with open harm, her face may indeed have made her stand
out. Like a wart.

And oh, how they loved to pick on her. Billy Butane's gang
spattered Celeste with haw-haws whenever she spoke in class. The
Prom Queens squealed "Tacky!" at Celeste's undershirt in the
locker room. In gym, Trophy Boys kicked balls into her chest. In
the halls, Rappers dispensed shoves from behind. Before health
class, she would find used condoms on her seat. On her locker she
would find Colorform figures in obscene poses.

Sure, there was the occasional wimp who peered at her with
empathy. But when Celeste tried to lock eyes with said misfit, he or
she scuttled away, lest his or her own life become worse.

So Celeste bit the bullet. But it was not easy.

And home, alas, was no haven. Mo and Didi had spent so many
years fine-tuning their isolation that even ninety-pound, sixty-
trillion-celled, raven-haired blips did not register on their screens.
Actually, that's not entirely true. She registered once a day, during

dinner, because that was the one time they could not distract themselves from her increasingly melancholy face. Didi did her best to help; she spent the meal talking about her own super-duper happy days in school. Mo tried too—"If you're feeling low, come hang out"— but the few times Celeste took him up on the offer and tried to talk to him, his response was, "Yeah, school's a downer. Want a Pop-Tart?"

So she spent her nonschool hours with the window open in the attic, talking to her friends at the lake. "Can you explain humans to me?" she would beseech them.

You're asking us? she would get back.

They twistee us away in plastic leaf bags.

They defile our luscious depths with sewage.

They mash us flat with their cars.

She did a lot of sighing and crying. If this was what it took to become a knight, she wasn't so sure she'd succeed.

"Almost all the shadows here are way off, Grandma. I think these people are sick—but not physically. I don't understand."

"Welcome to the world, my little acorn shell."

"What do you mean?"

"You are seeing the most widespread ailment of all. Much more common than the cold. I call it 'spiritual illness.' "

"But in the Home we were raised without religion, and no one had this problem in their shadow."

"Not religious spirit. *Life* spirit."

"I don't get it."

"You see, we are all born complete, fresh, ready to roll. That is your true self. At the Home we cultivate children's true selves, so the shadows are clean; no snafus. But often, out in the world, don'ts and cruelties and freeze-outs and my-problems-are-more-equal-than-your-problems make our true selves clam up and hide. We erect scaffolds of false selves, selves that cower or attack or in one of a myriad of ways dump unto others as we had dumped unto us. This is so routine, so much the pattern from which people are cut, that humanity has become one long march of the Wronged Wronging the Wronged, one large battlefield where the wounded wound the wounded. So you see why I created the Home? Because humanity has had enough lances, enough gunpowder and blood. It is time for the field to get green. And so there I made the Home: a place where children study their true selves and leave to be that self in the service of the world. As for you, with school—with anything—you must ask yourself what you can do to right the wrongs there. *You.* With *your* special gift."

"You mean how I could heal them?"

"That does seem to be your gift."

"But I can only heal physical illness."

"Do you know that for certain?"

"Yeah."

"Absolute, bet-your-booties, no-snippet-of-doubt certainty?"

"Well . . ."

"If you are sure—if you *know* the solution exceeds your abilities—then leave, move on; the battlefield covers the globe. But if you are *not* sure, then you might be just as lost in the next place."

"I don't know. (*Sigh*) I wish you could tell me, Grandma."

"It is hardly for me to know. Besides, how could I?"

"You're saying I have to figure it out myself."

"That is correct. To be a knight of the world, first turn your heart to you. Then the truth will make itself known, and you will know just what to do."

—Tape recording

• • •

Celeste listened, but her heart just wasn't speaking loud enough. So she wrote in her diary, did her homework, talked to her lake pals from the attic window, stared at the boxes.

And toughed it out until June.

Finally came the last day of school. Yahoo! So yahoo, in fact, that tradition at Lickalinney High was to cancel afternoon classes and in their place hold the famous Summer Spree. This was an outdoor blowout, ostensibly featuring an air-guitar competition; a dunk booth starring bewigged academic despots; the presenting of yearbooks and class rings; a smorgasbord of Lickin' Good hot dogs, cotton candy, cola; and baking sun. But the real attraction was the bods, those barreling-toward-melanoma bags of pheromones and secretions that promenaded around the school property in shorts and T's, boobs howdy-doing, butts babalooing, dicks buckerooing, clits playing hard to git. It was an *Attention, shoppers,* end-of-the-season special, look hard and pant now—next clearance sale's a long way off; no credit allowed.

The Spree kicked off at noon with a rousing Muzak rendition of "See You in September" (gag, the students mimed) coming over the intercom. Then followed a steady stream of rock schmaltz. Doors opened, and students ran not walked outside, where they began shopping for summer yummies across the tender and romantic setting of the school's bus-packed parking lot.

Killjoys that they were, a few teachers cruelly refused to participate. Celeste's history teacher was one such wet blanket. He insisted not only on holding his class but also on giving the final exam that day. He switched off the intercom and passed out the test, and although music still seeped in from the hallway, students had to turn their young minds from dreams of muscular bozos and fleshy bimbos to the major uprisings of the labor movement in twentieth-century industrial America.

Right.

So big surprise that most of the class multiple-guessed in a frenzy and bolted from their seats, leaving only a few studious virgins to ponder the subtleties between A, B, and C.

And leaving Celeste. Who was not so much studious as hopeful: maybe, she thought, the halls might be clear when she finished, allowing her, for the first time since she came to Lickalinney, to fly the coop without getting nipped by some rabid youth or youthess and therefore to start her summer off right.

And lo, when she finally handed in the test and left the room, the only activity in the hall was the sun shuffleboarding along the floor, as music blared from the speakers. She smiled at her luck and hastened toward the back door.

But wouldn't you know, on the way her bladder suddenly dialed 911. No time to wait for luck. She opened the lavatory door and stepped in.

A quick check revealed no ankles beneath the stalls. Good. Freedom's just another word for nobody else in the bathroom. The door closed behind her, blotting out the music. She forgot the sturm and drang outside and let herself relax, never dreaming that her private lessons were really just about to begin.

Hey, don't give me that. We were getting some CDs from Billy's locker. He went to drink some water, and he saw her. That was it, so fuck you. It wasn't like we planned it or nothing.

—Boris Butane, as told to author

Celeste set her books on a sink. On one wall was a tampon dispenser. Beside it, a condom dispenser. Beside *that*, a poster on

AIDS. The condoms had been flung onto the ceiling, where they hung like the soggy aftermath of a political convention.

She peed and flushed and returned to the sink.

As she was drying her hands, the bathroom door opened behind her. Music from the gym blew in. Feet shuffled into the room. The door closed, the music was silenced.

And the overhead light snapped off.

She spun around. *No shadows!*

A fear sizzled inside her.

She could hear breath. "You turned the light off," she said, cheerily.

More than one breather. Two, three. Maybe more.

"Hello?" she said, a bit less cheerily.

She didn't know what to do. She grabbed for the sink. Her books tumbled to the floor.

"Come here, pussy, pussy," a male voice said.

"Go away," she said.

"Where are you, pussy?"

She inched back until she was between the sink and the wall.

She could hear them moving forward, their sneakers squeaking on the floor. She held her breath.

She could smell them. Hot dogs and soda.

She tried to make herself small.

Then fingers closed around her wrists. "Let go!" she said.

"Bony," one whispered. His hands were cold.

"Leave me alone!" she said.

They wrenched her arms apart and clamped her wrists against the tile wall, her rings clattering as they struck.

"Get out of here!" she screamed.

"Pussy's doing well," a voice said. "Who threw her in?"

And then hands burrowed under her dress, rode up her thighs.

She had never been touched there. She kicked like a fury.

"Stop it!" she screamed.

111

Laughter.

More hands. On her ankles. She could not kick anymore.

Another pair of hands. Hooking onto her panties. Yanking them down with her tights.

And pressing a palm flat—cold!—against her groin.

"No hair. She's a freak."

Laughter.

"Let me go!"

Then a finger snaked down the crack in her crotch. And for a second it felt . . . almost . . . *good* . . .

But then the finger burrowed between her thighs, and the good vanished, and all that remained was scare.

Vomit rushed her throat. "No!" she screamed, and she tasted tears; she had started crying.

"Where's that light?" one voice said. "Turn that thing on."

"Right here."

Muffle of pockets emptying.

Squint! A light was in her eyes. She couldn't see.

It rolled off her face.

She followed it down. It was a flashlight beam, and it shone on Billy Butane. He was crouched before her, his hand between her legs. His shadow rose up underneath him. The colors inside looked like they were being smothered by toxic waste.

Then his finger pressed somewhere she could not see.

Her breath came out hard and trembling.

"Oh, she's tight," he said.

He shoved his finger at her, into her, and it hurt, it was a tearing open, she could feel herself break, feel him there, and she wanted to close her eyes and cry herself away, but her gaze stayed locked onto his shadow, and as his finger rose up inside her, his shadow started to . . . his colors started to change.

"What the—," he said.

"She on the rag?" another voice said.

Celeste stared: in his shadow, his rhythms froze.

"This is . . . really . . . weird," he muttered.

"What, man? What are you talking about?"

And then the toxic waste in the shadow began to recede. It rolled back like a wave, rolling away from the shore, taking the waste with it, riding it to the far boundaries of the shadow.

"Shit!"

He jerked his hand away and held it before him. He gaped at it and swallowed. He was breathing very loud.

"What happened?"

"I don't know, man." Another swallow. "Turn that off."

No one moved.

"Turn that fucking light off!"

Darkness. The hands let go of her wrists. The hands released her ankles. She hauled her tights up.

"Something fucking—some fucking weird shit, man. I don't—"

She bent down and felt beside her for her books.

"What do you mean?"

"Like an electric shock—no, like—"

"Like what?"

She found the books.

"Get a grip, Billy. A pussy's a pussy."

"I know, but I—"

She stood up. She couldn't see them.

"I don't know, it was like, it was weird, man—"

She ducked under the sink and came up on the other side and started running. No one blocked her path. She scrambled to the door and whipped it open. Music blasted down the sunny corridor. She flew past lockers and bulletin boards, doors racing by, her feet slapping on the tile, a drum banging in her head.

She threw herself into the first open classroom and slammed the door shut. Her heart was beating hard. She tried to force calm into her lungs. She found a stool and pushed it to the door. She was heaving so loud! She climbed onto the stool and peeked out the window in the door and tried to slow her breath.

A pack of Hip Boppers was sashaying down the hall. Celeste shrank back. Their chatter laughed till they hit the end of the hall and turned the corner.

Celeste took a deep breath and peered out again.

The hall was empty.

The lavatory door was opening.

And she heard:

"He'll be all right. Must be the flu."

"What flu? It's June, dude."

"Asshole! You think Billy's gonna pass out over nothing?"

Then they emerged: four boys carrying the mighty Billy Butane, strung between them like a wounded soldier. His eyes were staring ahead, mouth open, as if he was in shock. And beneath him, his shadow pulsed with brightness and vibrancy; it was a shadow quite unlike the one he'd had before.

She had done something to him. Something she didn't understand.

It was like she had a magic power.

Like she had an ace up her skirt.

She watched as they hauled the casualty down the hall, and for a moment she completely forgot to breathe.

She wasn't scared anymore.

She was amazed.

The Story of the Sea
Day Two Twilight

It is the second night of the ocean cruise. Edwina has not cleansed her pores in the sauna, tanned at the pool, or downed a Cruise Special in the Twinkle Bar.

What Edwina has done, aside from eat meals alone and nap on deck chairs alone, is talk to a stranger in a lifeboat.

This evening, Edwina skipped dinner and instead went to the ship's theater and watched a movie. She thought she enjoyed the flick, but now, as she hobbles along the deck to the nightclub where she is supposed to meet John, she realizes she can't remember the plot. All she can think about is the stranger in the lifeboat. Not because he was Cary Grant handsome. But because unlike the movie, and most other things in her life, he made her laugh.

Edwina enters the nightclub. The floor is crammed with dancing couples. She scans the room and locates her husband. He is satisfying his posing habit with a tango. His partner, a girl in stilettos and taffeta, has great legs.

Edwina sighs and looks about for a chair.

"Psst! Edwina!"

She swivels. Outside, sitting on the railing, is the stranger.

His outfit is the same. She does not recognize the cloth. He waves to her, and she smells the hug again.

She hobbles out. The sky is drenched in lavender and rose. A single star blinks along the horizon. "Who are you?" she asks.

"Please don't ask me that," he says.

"You know who I am. It's only fair."

"Wwwwellll," he says, "I have loads of names, but it's best if you don't know them. Maybe you can call me"—and he smiles, and the hug scent gets even stronger—"the Ultra-Other."

"The Ultra-Other? What kind of kooky name is that?"

"I thought you'd like it. I thought you liked originality."

"I do, but—well—are you a passenger? Do you work here?"

"No, no. I came here for you."

She pauses. "Sure," she says.

"I did. I know you feel unhappy."

"John bribed you to tease me? Is that it?"

"No. You've got me pegged all wrong." He jumps down from the railing and turns to the sea. "Get a load of what I can do," he says.

He inhales deeply and blows out a huge breath. Wind picks up over the water, and a mile off the starboard bow, the sea rises into a whirling cone, like a twister made of water.

"Now, could your husband's buddies do that?"

Edwina peers at the spinning water. Even though it is dusk, she can see snatches of rainbow colors inside the cone.

"What's that in there?" she asks.

"Life," he replies.

She stares at him.

"Pretty nifty, huh," he says.

She looks at the water and back at the stranger.

She turns and limps quickly toward the ballroom.

Coming
of
Age

Summertime, and the living was easy. No blues to cure. No more pencils, no more crooks. Just sunshine and lemonade and bevies of birds and leaves drunk on chlorophyll and the lake playing Gulliver to sunbathers.

Didi said, "We're so lucky to have the lake right across the street. Why don't you meet your friends over there and you can all go swimming?"

Didi, her head soapy from showers, had never fully grasped that Celeste didn't have human friends. Didi also hadn't caught on that Celeste had had a humdinger of a last day at school. Though to be fair to the pink puffball, Mo hadn't wised up about that afternoon, either. The only person who knew was Miss Kelly.

Right after the attack, Celeste called and spilled out the story. Miss Kelly *oh dear!*ed and *oh no!*ed throughout, but at the bombshell of Celeste's secret weapon, Miss Kelly fell speechless.

"Grandma?" Celeste asked. "Are you there?"

". . . It is . . . so curious."

"I know. But it feels kind of neat. What do you think's going on?"

They pondered this a good while, until finally Miss Kelly said, "Time untangles all mysteries. Let us be patient."

117

So Celeste returned to the attic, trying to be patient. She wound her way past stacks of snoozing boxes, crates of records, the jukebox chewing its cud, and flopped on her bed. The window was open. She leaned out and filled in her lake friends.

Jiminy Crickets! the leaves squalled. *You mean you gotta summon patience for a whole summer?*

"That's what my grandmother said."

Patience rots! It's boring as drought! What're you supposed to do while you wait?

"I don't know."

You gotta find something to do. Knitting, hopscotch. What about reading? You're lucky you can do shit like that; all we can do is hang up here waiting for a goddamn breeze—

Celeste took a second look at those boxes, and while the leaves griped away, she reached for a nearby carton and dumped it over. As she expected, it barfed out books. But unlike last time, when she simply boxed them up again, this time she gave them a good looking over. *Fanny Hill, Justine, Vox, Portnoy's Complaint, Delta of Venus, Tropic of Cancer.* She'd seen some of these in the Home but never read any. Now, flipping through, she saw nothing that might excite leaves but . . . a lot that excited *her.* A generous dose of, ahem, venereal language.

South of her navel, a mountain pass opened to great fanfare.

She upsided another box. This one had magazines: *Epicure, Playboy, Steamy Creamy, Big Balls, Hot Cross Buns.* She paged through. Lots of naked people. In amorous poses. Women. Men. Women and men. Men and men. Women and clarinets. Men and dogs. Fat, thin, black, white. And so on.

A lone Harley cruised onto the pristine mountain pass.

She closed the window on her lake buddies and in silence and solitude staggered over to other boxes and ripped through Mo's treasured mementos that she was supposed to find "a drag." Some drag. Stories of call girls. *Her hormones stuck out their thumb.* Lingerie catalogs. *Her hormones extended a stockinged leg.* Bawdy tales of English wenches. *The Harley pulled to the side of the road.* Double-entendre greeting cards. *Her hormones hopped on the back of the bike.* Underground comics. *They peeled out.* Sexual guides. *They hit sixty.* Sexual fantasies. *They hit eighty.*

She couldn't help it. Her hormones were hurtling down the road. *120 mph! The banana seat vibrated maniacally!* She leaned back and slipped her hand down her panties, and—*there?*

Uh *huh.*

They hit a ramp and catapulted into space.

What a rush! It was like healing, only more so—more so—*Bazhoom!*

And when the dust finally settled, she opened her dizzy eyes and gazed at Mo's erotic archives, giddy as a boy in a bordello, and felt, for the first time ever, that there had to be a God. How else could such *oo-la-la* be possible?

Or, if not a God, then one heck of a Devil.

And though she hated to remember it later, at that moment she shrugged: God? Devil? I don't care! Long as He brings me more O.

So the fifteenth summer of her life, Celeste vacationed from all other activities (including chatting with her lake pals, understanding the event with Billy Butane, and contemplating who's who in the cosmic order) and mastered the baits of adulthood. And did her first proof of the theorem your teachers told you: genius *is* ten percent inspiration and ninety percent perspiration. She perspired through the ins and outs of them all: The Wet Watusi. The Spazzing Bossa Nova. The Tuna Twist. The Slide Guitar. The Butterfly Stroke. The Tippy Canoe. The Tabasco Tutu. The Suds.

Which is to say, she became a typical teen.

And like a typical teen, she made her room take on the feel of another planet. This happened after she heard Michener play back her *aaa eee iii ohh ooo*s downstairs; she knew she needed some auditory precautions. She chose the barrier method: by closing the window and door and feeding records into the jukebox, she would make thick walls of sound that her moaning could not penetrate. Metal, British invasion, rap, Motown, punk, hip-hop, doo-wop, boogie-woogie, ska, rhythm and blues. She blasted that box day and night. It had a great beat. She could read to it.

CELESTE: My foster family had no clue. They'd only ever seen me at dinner, and that didn't change. Except now it was *my* choice. Dinner was the only time I took a break. I didn't even wear underwear anymore.

IAN: Surely you took breaks at other times. Perhaps when you saw misogynous images. Didn't that give you pause?

CELESTE: I gathered up everything that was offensive and put it out of my sight. Why waste my time?

IAN: I see. But what about when you came across spiritually ill shadows? Undoubtedly some of the models in those magazines were photographed with their shadows intact.

CELESTE: They turned me on.

IAN: You mean the shadows aroused you?

CELESTE: Yeah.

IAN: Given your earlier concern about this spiritual malaise and your knowledge that you were a healer, didn't your onanistic response trigger feelings of, perhaps, guilt?

CELESTE: No! I realized I was learning.

IAN: What were you learning? Aside from the obvious.

CELESTE: That I had a fine line between concern and lust.

IAN: Didn't you ever feel concern without lust? Like perhaps when you saw your foster parents' shadows?

CELESTE: I still felt lust. But the concern weighed heavier.

IAN: So did that put a crimp in your hobby?

CELESTE: No. The only thing that did was news from the Home.

News about my mother. *That* always stopped me cold. I
hated thinking about what my birth had done to her.

—Celeste, interview on National Public Radio

Since her re-life, Marina had not uttered a single phoneme. She
communicated yes and no with a shake of her head, and emotions
with her eyes, but ask her anything she didn't know, or that required
a garrulous response, and you got a blink.

She was big on giggling, though, and she smiled okay too. Particularly with Samson. He found the tickle zone on her feet. He
wrote tunes for her Silly Song Pop Chart. He ordered an inner tube
for rides down the creek. He held her throughout the night.

The most famous couple at the Home remained platonically cou-
pled. They were most often seen in the garden or greenhouse, Marina
finger painting, Sam breeding botanical wonders. He tested prototypes of his plants on her. She hugged his hugging huckleberry, let
his licking violets tongue her face purple. Any plant she didn't get
along with, Sam showed to the compost heap.

Between the garden and the greenhouse, Marina seemed happy.

Sam didn't consider adding the office to that list. Marina's first
year back, he'd walked her into the tiny room on the first floor where
she'd spent much of her original life, typing Miss Kelly's work.
Caboodle was running the office by then, but aside from having
replaced Marina's Remington with a spiffy Selectronic, Caboodle
had let the status quo stand. "This used to be your natural habitat,"
Sam had said as Marina sat at her old desk. She pushed old paper
clips around her old blotter. Then she flashed Sam her *I'm bored*
look. And that was that. In the years that followed, she peeked in
occasionally, searching for a lost ball or person, but the office meant
no more to her than the broom closet.

Which was why Samson was so unprepared for what happened.

After fifteen years, without even a death rattle, Caboodle's spiffy Selectronic went suddenly to that great carriage return in the sky. Died, like Elvis, while on a John. Caboodle sniffled at her half-finished orphan list; how would she finish her work *now*? Seeing her so despondent, Kit zoomed down to the basement, unearthed the old Remington, and brought it up to her. An elated Caboodle kissed Kit for his white knightus completus and told him to go reap his rewards at lunch, where she would meet him later, after she had cleaned up the machine.

Around this time, Marina and Samson ambled into the living room for the midday meal. They had just served themselves when, in the office on the edge of the first floor, Caboodle rolled a blank sheet into the Remington and clattered through a test run.

Marina lowered her fork.

"Hey, she can tell it sounds different," Kit noted.

"What does?" Sam asked.

"The Remington. That was Marina's original baby."

"I didn't know—"

But Marina was already running. Sam scrambled after her.

When he caught up she was in the office, kneeling reverently before the Remington. Caboodle stopped typing, and Marina inhaled the smell of the ink and stroked the metal body like a lover.

Then she turned and, seeing Sam, stood up and cried, "Look!"

If Sam had worn dentures, they would have fallen out.

More insistently: "Look!"

"I can't belie—oh, Marina, you have such a lovely voice!"

Stomping her foot. "Lllllook!"

"At what? Look at what?"

She pointed at the machine. "A-s-d-f-j-k-l-;!"

"What's she talking about?" Caboodle whispered.

"Can you get up and let her sit there?"

Caboodle rose, and Marina sat. A longhand list lay on the desk. Marina rolled a fresh sheet into the Remington. She fixed her gaze on the list, lowered her hands to the machine, tensed her face in Beethovenish concentration. Then she hit the keys typing. Her fingers moved like anemone on caffeine. Like Rick Wakeman on fast forward. As if all the words she hadn't uttered were erupting from her digits. It's a wonder her fingers hadn't been blue.

Dear Celeste,

Yes, indeed, we have hit a milestone. Since Edwina told you about it, Marina's fingers have flown so fiercely that she's typed up every last stitch of Caboodle's backlog. (Making Kit and Caboodle think, in fact, of going into the world at long last.) I hoped she would type what's in her mind, but only other people's words seem to cut it. So I try to keep her busy. New idea is to have her retype published books. Kerouac's the big hit so far.

But wait, there's more. All this typing seems to be loosening her speech from its shackles. Which caused which? Who knows? Who cares? She's got "look" down pat. Also can say: "okay," "pica," "stet," "shift," "semicolon." Has trouble with: "margin." (Don't we all, eh?) An excellent start, I'd say.

By the by, hear you've discovered rock 'n' roll in its many permutations. Being as my pop was a piano tuner, and I grew up on Misters Jerry Lee and Richard, them heart-beating rhythms form the backbeat of my soul. Haven't heard any in a while, though; I live here, so I abide by the rules. Miss it.

Miss you, too. Know Marina would agree, if she could.

Letting Those Good Times Roll,

Sam

SS:mk

• • •

Interesting, Celeste thought, but she had her own which-caused-which mystery to think about. For as the clit lit steamed her heater, and her heater creamed her motor, and the motor maneuvered her hand, puberty came to her body. Her titties sprang out of bed. Her hips erected additions. Tiny hairs question-marked her pubes. And the more her body grew, the more she studied her erotica.

Mo watched in silence as every night a shapelier Celeste breezed barefoot down to dinner. He had heard that some boys grew into basketball uniforms in a single summer, so maybe some girls grew into Playboy bunny costumes as well. Could be. All he knew was that when she lowered the gently sloping curve of her hand-cuppable bottom onto the chair, an *oh mama!* flashbacked through his spine. He hadn't felt that since the days of make love not war. He basked in the feeling until his cock started to throb the opening to "Foxey Lady." Then he had to drink something cold and remind himself that this va-va-va-voom was—gulp!—his foster daughter.

Didi watched Celeste too. The child was certainly blossoming. A little quickly, if you asked Didi, but you wouldn't. *Didi* didn't ask Didi. All she asked herself was all she said, which was, "And how are we today?"—the same question she'd used when Celeste dragged her long face to dinner during the school year. Those days, Celeste had replied, "Not too good," and so Didi had spent the time serving up heaping portions of her own school experiences to console. But now a beaming Celeste said, "Great," so Didi couldn't think of anything to serve up.

Especially because Mo would immediately plunge in—which he'd never done before—and gush over the music Celeste was playing on the jukebox. Then he and Celeste would talk about band genealogies and great hooks. Stuff Didi didn't dig, as Mo would say. So Didi spent her meals with one smile on her family, both ears on her bird, and her heart waiting for the paramedics.

For her part, Celeste rediscovered conversation. She used to converse at the Home and had forgotten how much fun it could be.

However, she wasn't crazy about watching Didi edge from center field to sidelines to nosebleed seats, so sometimes Celeste would ask Didi, "And what do *you* think about Megadeth?" or some such, but Didi would invariably reply, "I think they're very sweet." *Everything* was very sweet. Except, probably, her husband ogling their foster daughter. Celeste didn't know how to change that. She doubted she could.

And so boiled away summer in the healthy Wolfly household.

Now, puberty in girls is famous for one thing, and the more voluptuous Celeste's body became, the more Celeste expected that red carpet to roll out. Particularly after her belly developed a nice little roundness and her breasts worked their way up to a C cup. "It could happen any day now," said Miss Kelly, who knew about Celeste's growth surge but not her avid hobby (Celeste, in her first cut of the apron strings, told her grandmother only that she was "doing a lot of reading"). So Celeste remained poised to haul out her box of o.b. at a scent's notice, and waited for that any day to happen.

Only, when her body struck the appointed age, she was taken by surprise. Not just because of the timing—it was Labor Day, which was the day before her scheduled return to Hell and therefore the day she had set aside to gird herself for the inevitable resumption of hostilities. She had not been anticipating a menstrual imposition.

But also because what arrived between her legs that day was not blood. In fact, it was nothing that stained.

It was something that spoke.

What she got that day was voices.

I was in the shower when I felt something. I thought, Hallelujah, maybe I'm finally going to menstruate. But then I realized I wasn't feeling the way the books described it; I was feeling a kind of vibrating in my genitals, and I was hearing something too. It took a minute to figure out: there were voices between my legs. The vibrating was because they were echoing.

I stepped out of the spray and listened. They were all male, and they were singing, their voices overlapping and harmonizing. They sounded like a Gregorian chant extruded through an AM radio. They were singing, *Celeste Celeste bo beleste banana fanna fo feleste fee fi mo meleste, Celeste.*

I said, "What?"

They stopped singing and said, *Good. You're listening. We need to tell you something. Ixnay the aitway.*

"Huh?"

Nix the wait. You've got no eggs. Your oven's never going to be getting any buns.

"Can you be a little clearer?"

They sighed and said, *You are never going to menstruate.*

This took a minute to absorb. "So toss the o.b.?" I asked.

Yup.

"Great!" I said, because I hadn't been thrilled by the prospect of enslaving myself to the tampon industry. But once I'd savored that, I figured I'd better find out who they were.

We are you are he are she are they are us, oh baby, baby.

"Must you speak in riddles?"

Must you be so impatient?

"I'm not," I said. "It's just that with you turning on the reverb in my private parts, I thought I should know who—"

You are interrupting our message.

"I thought I'd already heard it."

You only heard the A side. The B side's more immediately relevant and twice as likely to be a hit.

"Okay," I said. "I'm all ears."

They cleared their throat(s?) and said, *You will have your very own coming of age. You will hear secret sounds, you will smell secret smells. Your shadow will show none of your secrets, and your hair will be a crown of the world.*

"What does that mean?" I asked, but the vibrating had stopped. All I heard was the shower, and I knew they were gone.

I toweled off in a daze—if unbalanced people hear voices in their heads, what about someone who hears voices in her crotch? But before the morning was up, the prophecy of the "B" message came true. So I quickly accepted that the voices had to be real, which meant both that I wasn't nuts and that I'd never menstruate. And by the way, I still haven't menstruated, not to this very day.

—Celeste, letter to publisher of *The Sexual Bible*

That morning, Mo came up from the basement just as Celeste left the bathroom, and they almost collided in the hall. She apologized and then noticed strange sounds, as if his body were broadcasting music, and unusual scents, as if he had splashed on a complicated cologne. But before she could ask anything, Mo reached for her curls and said, "Groovy! Why didn't you tell me you were planning to color your hair?"

"Color my *what*?"

"Looks like you put some highlights in those little curls."

Celeste lifted her hair off her shoulder and peered at it. The curls were still black, but when the light struck at certain angles, colors did indeed leap to the surface. And not just red, like Marina's. Celeste's highlights were of every pigment. As if Technicolor were hiding in her curls. As if she'd conditioned her hair with mother-of-pearl. As if her shadow was so limitless, its colors were coming out of her head.

"Wow! Far out!" Mo said, and threw his arms around her.

Inside his hug, the sounds got louder. She closed her eyes and listened. The sounds were . . . a song. *My brown-eyed girl, but she's*

127

your daughter, asshole!, till Death do us Didi, oh god oh shit oh no harmonized to make the jitteriest ditty she'd ever heard. It was the Song of Mo, and it emanated from his body.

She held on and became ever more aware of the smell. Oreo cookies, audio tape, Bud, lard. And underneath it all—what was that? She'd smelled it before. Yes, she recognized it: tears.

At that moment, Didi skipped into the hall, bringing with her a new set of sounds and smells. But before Celeste had time to analyze, Didi's song crashed into a gasp, and Celeste could guess why: Didi had seen Mo's face, gooey and mooning. "Oh. Sorry," Didi said, and as she backed down the hall, her song became a high scream of one word: Don't! Didi's smells were Chanel, bird feed, soap, feminine deodorant spray. And again, below it all: tears.

Didi rounded the corner, and Celeste stepped away from Mo. His song pounded. His smells mushroomed. "I have to go upstairs now," Celeste said, and bolted down the hall.

She turned the corner and found Didi beside the door to the attic. "I highlight my hair too," Didi said, though Celeste knew Didi's subsong wailed like a person falling from a great height.

But Celeste decided to play dumb. "Do you like how it looks?"

"It's very . . . sweet," Didi said, and, further denying what her heart was moaning inside, flashed Celeste a smile. Sweetly.

It was too much truth to know. And the day before school, yet. *Thanks, voices.* Celeste ran upstairs, overwhelmed and sweating with confusion. And to top it all off, on the stairs she saw that her shadow had changed. It now revealed only serenity and normalcy, with edges as clearly defined as anyone's. In shock, she dived into her room, slamming the door shut behind her.

Well, ain't this too much—a slut that's never bled?
What more do you need—bitch got colors on her head.

You talking to her? She hears what you ain't said.
You know you took a shower, but she sniffs like infrared.
I'll say it now, say it again, say it ten times more:
If God's what you want and God's what you need,
Why bow down to a whore?
Well, she ain't no God, no angel, no saint.
God'd never x-ray you like this hag.
She's a flimflamming, fame-digging, AC-DC tramp.
What I say—she's the Devil in drag.

—"Devil in Drag," rap group Die N' Ice

Celeste cranked up the jukebox, hoping the music would run roughshod over her thoughts. Though from Golden Oldies to Red Hot Hits, the volume only served to amplify everything in her mind. She was sorry for Mo. She was sorry for Didi. She was scared and pissed and pooped and puzzled. But throughout the morning, one thought emerged as the loudest and most important, and that was:

No way was she going to return to Dodge City High School. She hadn't thought much about it since last spring's ambush, ducking the distasteful until the calendar forced a confrontation. But now the calendar was chiming, and for her blissful forgetfulness she'd been rewarded with the bod of a saloon tart and iridescent hair and more senses than she knew what to do with. She could imagine the Butanes, riding back into school with vows of revenge in their eyes and new and improved weapons in their arsenal, and herself, standing out like a peacock on the prairie. Of course, Celeste realized she wasn't doing so badly in the arms race department herself. Her new senses upgraded her standard-issue five-shooter to at least a six or a seven, allowing her (most likely) to smell or hear an attack before it was upon her. And she did have the secret weapon (whatever it was) that had so effectively disabled Billy Butane in June.

But those *most likely*s and *whatever it was*'s haunted her. Sure, she'd been reoutfitted, but she hadn't been given the instruction manual. So go back? She might as well volunteer for target practice. Heck, she didn't even want to go downstairs.

All day, Celeste sat on her bed, recoiling from tomorrow. What can I do? What can I do? she mantraed, and while she was at it added, And why am I so different? But her Gregorian friends did not respond, and her shadow stayed calm and quiet.

At noon, steeped in despair, she opened the window and called out her questions to her forgotten buddies at the lake. The leaves joined the lake and birds in offering her the unanimous advice: *Damned if we know!*

She stared out the window, fretting and weeping, and might have sobbed thus till morning. But blessedly, when dusk splashed across the sky, a familiar vibration began between Celeste's legs. "You're back!" she cried, sitting up, and the voices faded in.

You've got it, yeah baby, you've got it, they sang.

"Where have you been?" she said. "There's a lot I need to—"

Shush! This is an unscheduled visit, so we have to be quick about it. Now listen up.

They spoke and then were silent. So much for picking their brains. Or even for picking them out of a lineup. But at least they gave her a solution, and that's what mattered right now. She hauled her butt out of bed and got herself ready to practice.

FIDDLE WHILE YOU DIDDLE

Yes, you too can hear singing in your skivvies! Because now, thanks to pioneers in the exciting new field of condom research, you can buy the revolutionary (and patented!) new innovation the CELEST-A-LACTIC. This fruity-tasting rubber works just like normal latex, but when exposed to friction triggers a digital recording—embedded *in the walls of the condom!* So you and your partner can truly make music together. Order our catalog today.

—Ad by Zipless Zoo, mail order company

The next morning, a sunny Celeste departed for school on time but, as soon as she stepped outside, made herself invisible. Thus hidden, she waited in the yard as first Mo and then Didi drove off to work. Then she went back into the house and dialed the school.

Before last night, she hadn't disguised her voice in months, but after her practice session had no trouble pulling off a fifty-year-old-male-authority-figure baritone. "This is Celeste Wolfly's guardian," she said. "She's moving to another state."

"All right. What do you want us to do with the records?"

Can't let them stay, lest Mr. Beaks ever track her down.

"Hold on to them," she said.

Then, still invisible, she strolled on down to the school.

Classes had already begun when she arrived, so the halls were empty. Celeste walked unseen into the office. A secretary yawned at rule breakers like a bored prison guard. Celeste vaulted over the counter. Vice Principal Wesson sprayed saliva as he chewed out a quivering freshman. Principal Fleece dialed a phone sex line and twirled his mustache as he awaited the verbal massage.

When she reached the file room, she found the drawers blocked—darnation!—by a student lackey, who was picking absentmindedly at his zits. She'd have to come back later.

So she returned to the halls. There, passing classes in session, she watched shadows, listened to songs, smelled scents. Or, as she later called using her multiple abilities, synsensed.

Each individual seemed as complex as an entire world. Yet underneath everyone, from dominatrix debutante to snide old principal, lay tears. All the rest—the venom and ennui and fear—seemed to

131

float on top. As if deep inside each person was another self. An original self. Just like what Miss Kelly had said. Only now Celeste could smell that self, and she realized that in almost everyone, it was weeping. As if it was buried alive. And she realized it longed to be consoled and accepted, so it could come out and flush away all the junk—the symptoms of spiritual rot—and discover its special gift, and live.

But how to reach that inner self? She had no idea. And she found it hard to concentrate on, given how the shadows excited her.

Now, we know the Monday morning quarterbacks among you may want to brain her with the Dunce of the Century Award, but even after she saw the very odd sight of Billy Butane in a Home Ec class, wearing an apron and a healthy shadow and assisting a blind girl with measuring milk, Celeste still felt she had no clue.

Finally, the file room was left untended. Celeste snitched her file, slipped out a window, and chucked the papers in a Dumpster. She cartwheeled off into high noon, free at last, ready to start trying to understand how to heal this spiritual problem. Though how she'd do that, she knew not.

A few houses before she reached the Wolflys', while still invisible, Celeste came upon a man walking what appeared to be seven chihuahuas on leashes. She looked harder. They weren't dogs; they were pigs. Miniature Chubbucket pigs. The man towered over them, as tall and lean as Ichabod Crane. He wore a red-and-yellow scarf, his swine red-and-yellow collars. The latter broke formation and sniffed their porcine nostrils at Celeste's unseen body as she passed. "Stay in line," the man cautioned. Celeste almost laughed out loud. No, the joy comes from staying *out* of line, she thought.

And thus her formal education came to an end.

Our fury was unsurpassed when we traced her trail back and saw how many times she had slipped away from us. Fleece's bungling was unforgivable. Although he knew about the APB Beaks had put out, he never set foot beyond his office or even checked the computer for her, so he had no idea she was under his nose. This is an inherent problem with the Matrix: it is full of fools. The *nths* are much more competent, but they are not trained to be used for surveillance. Most unfortunate, that.

Years passed before we became aware of Fleece's ineptitude. Needless to say, then he paid. Needless to say, the penalty was quite dear.

—Gacy Guru, videotaped memoir,
And You Thought It Was Just Paranoia

No sooner had Celeste gotten home and become visible than the bell rang. Through the door she smelled vitamins, books, Vicks Formula 44, wool, tears—and pigs. This was no truant officer.

She opened the door. The man with the pigs stood before her, leashes in hand. Gray-haired, with crow's-feet and a Rudolphishly ruddy nose, he wore a brown jacket, brown trousers, and the red-and-yellow scarf. Hardly summer wear, but he wasn't perspiring.

"I, ah," the man began, and his inner song twanged, *Bellam puellam! Jove conserva me!*—words Celeste couldn't understand. "Ah, that is, one of my pigs just snapped his line and sprinted this way. I was hoping you'd spied him."

"Sorry. I've been inside. Haven't seen anything."

"Oh, terrible, terrible." His face reddened suddenly, and he launched into a coughing fit. As he whooped and wheezed, Celeste synsensed. No flu or asthma. Only tears. Sea-strength salty tears.

He was not ill physically—but what spiritual sickness! His shadow was positively *aaa eee iii ohh ooo* sexy.

Finally, he ahemed himself back to calm. "As I was saying, terrible. The pigs are Mother's. She'll be so distressed."

"I'll help you look," Celeste offered, and into the man's scent spurted a briny dash: the scent, which she'd whiffed on many a Jockey-shorted penile possessor, of maleness.

"That would be splend—I mean, if it's no onus."

"It's fine. I'm not busy." She stepped onto the porch.

"Oh, thank you. Incidentally, my name is Mr. Doloris."

She smiled. "You don't have to be so formal with me."

"Oh, yes I do. I have to be so formal with everyone. My first name *is* Mr. The abbreviated version. Mother prefers formality."

"Oh. Mother sounds rather—"

"Potent." He began to cough again. She waited for him to recover, then introduced herself.

"Celeste," he mused. "Such a mellifluous appellation."

They ambled to the driveway, small-talking. He was forty-six. He lived down the street with his mother. He hadn't seen Celeste in these parts previously. Had she just moved here?

"A few months ago. I . . . don't go out much."

In the garage, she climbed behind old drums while he poked through oilcans and rakes. "Does this pig have a name?"

"Mother named them after the Seven Deadly Sins, to provide me with a behavioral mnemonic. The missing one is, ah"—and he looked away—"Lust. But it's a misnomer. They've all been neutered."

Celeste bent to examine a snare drum and to break eye contact. "What do you do at home? Take care of Mother?"

"Mother doesn't need caring. No, I work there. I'm a translator. Classical languages. Latin and Greek."

So that explains the strange words in his song.

"And why are *you* home?" he asked.

A lie cut to the front of the line. "I'm unemployed."

"Ah. But aren't you a little young to be unemployed?"

"I'm eighteen." Fibs hit the jackpot. All that make-believe she'd done at the Home was paying off. "Graduated in June."

She buried her head in timpani. She was all confused. Here she had hoped to get down to the business of healing, and all she could think about was nooky. And truth was trapped in a corset.

For a while they searched in silence, the only noise the sound of one throat coughing. Then he spoke. "I, ah, have been admiring your hair."

"It's a special rinse," she called from behind a bass drum.

"It's very young. Oh dear, that sounds pejorative. I didn't mean for it to sound that way. I meant, well, that it signifies youth, with its bounty and rich palette of—"

"Here he is!" Pig nostrils pulsed from inside a tambourine.

She scooped up Lust and handed him over. "I am extremely grateful," Mr. Doloris said, stroking the little porker.

She climbed out of the rhythm section. "It was fun."

He watched her come close. She was so small. So open.

She stood before him, a breeze conjugating her gray dress, the overhead light ablative absoluting her rings. Pigs snorted softly beneath them. The moment felt like magic.

"I, ah . . ."

"Yes?"

"I, ah . . ."

Lust broke wind with a grin. Celeste laughed. Mr. Doloris lost his *ah*s. "I ought to be getting home now," he said.

He stumbled out of the garage, and as he hit the sun his coughs returned. "Allergic bronchitis," he informed her when he'd hacked through the phlegm. But she knew it wasn't that.

"So," he said, tugging at his Sins. "See you around."

"Wait." He looked up, his silvery locks glittering in the sun. The bags under his eyes sagged with a lifetime's supply of tears.

And as they stood staring at each other, she knew: if she wanted to understand healing, she could work on Mo and Didi, but only after she'd combed out her tangled dynamics with them. That could take a long time—maybe forever. Or she could try her hand on a clean slate, i.e., Mr. Doloris. Given that she was a lonely and frustrated adolescent, this had infinitely more appeal.

So she hiked up her spunk and said, "The pigs're so cute, and I've got so much time. Could I walk them with you? Now and then?"

"Ah . . ." Fear splashed across his shadow. Maleness dropped anchor in his scents. His song went bonkers. "Ah . . . all right."

So every morning, with my grandmother's blessing and my foster parents' ignorance, I left for school, turned invisible, waited for the house to empty, and went back inside. Mr. Doloris rang the bell at nine, noon, and three, and we went out together.

We walked the pigs along the road, hugging the fence that surrounded the lake, him talking, me itching to heal his cough—and his bursitis, colitis, tendinitis, ulcer, headaches, earaches, and eye tics. "Some part of me is always ailing," he told me. "Mother says they've taken so much blood, I'm more aware than anyone in America that I don't have AIDS." Of course, I'd already seen in his shadow that he didn't have AIDS. But I didn't know how to heal him.

But truth be told, I was in no hurry to figure out how. Not because he made my heart go pit-a-pat or inspired me to share all. In fact, I lied prolifically to him. (Although I did admit, when he asked obliquely, to being a virgin.)

It was just that in his presence, my genitals hit the high notes, and we all know how strong a pull that siren call can be.

—Celeste, oral history tape at Celeste Museum

● ● ●

It was his idea.

Indian summer. Warm. Muggy. The day she turned Sweet Sixteen. Nymphal Nineteen, he thought, but timidity prevented him
from purchasing any store-stocked extravagance to commemorate the
day. Instead, he contacted the owner of the lake and arranged for
the padlock key and thus access to trees and fresh air. He would
give Celeste the gift of a walk in a sylvan setting.

He picked her up at noon and was delighted when she adored
the idea. She was wearing a white dress instead of her usual gray,
and bare feet instead of her usual boots, and, instead of her usual
silver, rings of turquoise and malachite and garnet and citrine and
moonstone and lapis lazuli and opal. The gems complemented her
hair. And her face, which he had come to think could truly launch
a million ships, radiated mystery.

On the beach, he let the pigs loose. The Seven Deadly Sins
puttered to the water and frolicked in mud. Mr. Doloris and Celeste
strolled into the woods. Maybe it was Celeste's smile as they mo-
seyed along the path, maybe the wreath of leaves she braided for
his head, but he found himself telling her stories he had never
divulged before. How he had attended Oxford. How he had almost
wed. How, a week before the nuptials, he had visited his fiancée's
office and, behind the door, overheard a couple in carnal unity. One
voice was that of his fiancée, who was scolding, "Don't do it like
that. Doloris does it like that, and Doloris is a geek." How, at that
moment, he "stopped feeling like a man." How he terminated the
engagement and completed his Ph.D. at home. Where, ever since,
night had eagled down regularly on his life, tearing out his health
and his heart.

But Celeste, he added, made him feel the rosy fingers of dawn.
Indeed, she resembled Aurora; her tresses streamed like sunrise.

They walked on, he speaking so intently, she listening so com-

137

pletely, that they did not notice when a blustery turmoil began ruffling through the trees. Celeste's dress fluttered, but all she tuned
in to was a nice oxygenic lick between her legs. Soon the lake started
glissandoing gracefully in the breeze, and the leaves began to shake,
rattle, and roll. Still, Celeste didn't catch on.

Not until the couple neared the beach and Mr. Doloris said,
"Why, look at them," and pointed to his pigs, who were scuttling
across the sand toward picnic tables, did Celeste's static begin to
clear.

She glanced up. Black clouds were charging each other like
gladiators, spearing each other with lightning. Thunder was whip-
ping its way into the battle, spilling a flood.

Swans whooshed past them. *Take cover!* they screamed.

And the torrent began.

"Oh dear!" Mr. Doloris cried. "I was quite unprepared for this
possibility! What are we going to do?"

"I don't kn—," Celeste began.

Shelter's back that way, the lake interrupted in a whisper.

"Shelter's back this way," Celeste said, and turned from the
beach, and before Mr. Doloris could say Julius Caesar, she tore off
down the path, her prismatic mane flying. Mr. Doloris huffed after,
his wool scarf dragging. Rain pounded onto them. They hustled over
cedar chips, scrambled across pine needles. The path forked.
"Where are you going?" he wheezed. *Left!* some geese honked. She
dashed left. "Just follow me!" she replied, and he did, trusting, as
thunder boomed above.

At last, she rocketed into a clearing. Grass the deep green of
moss. Branches arching over like a leafy umbrella. Dry air. And in
the middle, the lake's promised pot of gold: a trellis.

Grapevines twined over the top. Roses shielded the sides.

It was a shelter as private and perfumed as a boudoir.

And suddenly Celeste understood how to heal.

She dived beneath the trellis and rolled onto her knees. Mr.

Doloris bounded over, smiling—she had never seen him smile this fully—and as he darted beneath the trellis he dropped to his knees, too, and reached out his arms toward her; she moved closer, and his hands gripped her shoulders, he pulled her to him, and they kissed.

The kiss was a thousand words, his song streaming into her, and she heard it and he heard it, it orbited them, the music of his soul; they kissed and his scent pillowed the air, and his song felt like colors, his scents like taste, and everything was touch touch touch —she could touch his breakfast, taste his maleness, ummm, hmmm, his lips so hard beneath her round ones. She swallowed and kissed again and her vulva swelled and she knew why she'd ditched school: it was for this trellis, her hands unwinding his scarf, her lips kissing his cheeks, his groin stiffening, her musk musking. "I don't want to rush you," he whispered. "Reach under my dress," she said, lying back. She moved his hands to her hem, and he gasped as he rode his fingers up her legs, over her fine thighs and, yes, no underwear, yes, just silky hair and mink-smooth skin beneath the cotton. When he touched her breasts, symphonies rose around them. She worked her hands beneath their lips, and she was unbuttoning, pushing off his jacket and shirt, and he pulled the dress up, his belt off—she knew this, it was all she had ever read or dreamed of doing—the dress over her head, his body climbing onto hers, and oh, his skin so hot, her breasts just the right cushion for his chest, her hands on his back, her clit clanging like cymbals, his thighs on her thighs, her legs spreading, her knees bending, coming up and ankles crossing over his back and he lowered himself and he was

in her

so much sound! so much color!

she was

his shadow

was she breathing?

Push ah push oh, the rain battering the leaves, his breath in her ear, his hair in her hands, and she beat up toward heaven, her hands swimming over his back, and Oh, he cried, and Yum, she said, and she was climbing up, coming near to peak, and he was looking into her eyes, deep but not seeing her, just seeing him, his smell all over them, her smell coaxing him; sweat

And then he closed his eyes, opened his mouth. Out came a shiver as he grabbed her close, her legs opening even wider, his hands pressing into her spine, and he went, Ohhhhh, rippling on and on like the sound of night dying. She clasped him to her and soared off the meter, doing the most *aaa eee iii ohh ooo* she had ever done, and he went off like a cannon inside her.

They started breathing slower. Quieter. Coming to rest.

Then . . . how much time passed? She didn't know. The rain was falling. She was stroking his head. He was perspiring. They were quiet. His hair was damp . . . so damp, and also . . . so soft.

She opened her eyes. The trellis seemed filled with light. She peered at him. His hair had lost its silver—he was brunette now. She blinked back her shock and studied his face. His nose was not red anymore. His crow's-feet seemed to have flown away.

She swallowed and, trying to hide her astonishment, brushed a dark curl off his forehead and whispered the question she knew he most wanted to hear. "So," she asked, "do I make you feel like a man?"

He blinked his eyes open and smiled at her. "No," he replied, as rain thumped onto the leaves and he gazed with the deepest affection into her eyes. "No. You make me feel like a boy."

The Story of the Sea
Day Two   Twilight-Take Two

"Shame about your legs," the stranger calls after Edwina.

She pauses. In front of her, dancers waltz across the ballroom floor. Behind her waits the stranger.

She turns. The funnel of water that lifted out of the ocean is gone. The stranger sits on the railing, his long coat settling as if a breeze has just died.

"What about my legs," she says.

He lowers himself to the deck. "Shame that your husband let the doctor do that to you. All because of a sledding accident."

"How do you know about my accident?"

"You hadn't wanted to go on that little trip to the mountains," he continues, "but it was your anniversary, after all, and if you didn't go, he'd go alone. So you finally gave in. And when you hit the tree on that snowy Sunday, you broke both your legs. And the doctor there was a quack; he wanted to substitute wood for your bone. Can you imagine? Wood for bone? But you were unconscious. You couldn't argue the cruelty of it, the absurdity of it. It was your husband, your till-death-do-us-part worser half, who took the liberty of saying yes."

Goose bumps rise on Edwina's skin. That is exactly what happened. She has been stuck with crippled legs ever since.

Edwina hobbles up to the stranger. He is smiling in the dusky light.

"Who are you?" she demands.

"Don't bother yourself with that," he tells her. "Just think about this. I have a deal you might be interested to hear."

Virtuosity

Celeste and Mr. Doloris lay beneath the trellis, gazing at each other. The storm had moved on. Above the consummated couple, leaves dozed in bliss. Beyond the trees, the lake hummed like a maiden toweling off after a bath. Light shimmered through the clearing. The air smelled of wetness and of sex.

Celeste closed her eyes to savor. As her lids met, however, she drifted not into the familiar darkness but into a small living room, crammed with bookcases and upholstered chairs. It seemed as if she was having a vision. She looked down at her visionary self. She was wearing red-and-yellow trousers and a Mets T-shirt, and she felt, inside the trousers, a tiny dangling something she had never felt before. As if she were in the body of a boy. "Mr.!" she heard, and looked to the voice. Across the room stood a stout woman holding an armful of piglets. The woman was glaring at a stray cat, which was hiding under a table. "A cat!" the woman screeched. "I *told* you to close the door! Why don't you ever listen?" Celeste ran to shoo the tomcat, and the tomcat hissed, and Celeste burst into tears. "I can't, Mama!" she cried. Only it wasn't Celeste's voice, and it wasn't a room she had ever seen or a woman she had ever known.

"Stop that crying!" the woman spat. "You're supposed to be the man around here!"

Celeste opened her eyes, the woman's voice ringing in her ears. Mr. Doloris lay grinning, eyes closed, in the quiet meadow. It *must* have been a vision; there was no stout woman here.

She shut her eyes again. This time a bald man sat working at a desk. Celeste, diapers encasing her bottom, toddled into the room, singing a song. The man glared at her. "Go," he said.

. . . And other visions chained in: hands packing a suitcase, the tearful pleadings of the woman, the bald man getting into a taxi, the taxi pulling into traffic, the woman hurling herself sobbing into Celeste's arms as the cab drove the man away . . .

Celeste pushed her eyes open.

Mr. Doloris was inhaling and exhaling with gusto.

"What are you doing?" she asked.

"I just—" He sat up. "Suddenly my lungs seem so clear!"

He tried to force phlegmatic verification of his bronchitis, but all that came out was a dry cough. He inhaled through his nose; the nasal passages were clear as a flute. Bursting into giggles, he combed his hands through his hair and cried out, "My bronchitis— I've had it for years! What's become of it?"

She knew—it was the old laying-on-of-hands routine—only just as she was deciding whether to come out of the closet about her healing skills, Mr. Doloris paused and remarked, "And—this is so strange—I feel as if I've become more hirsute!"

Celeste had never known the word "hirsute" before, but Mr. Doloris had learned "hirsute" in sixth grade, when his pituitary had spewed hair across his epidermis like Spartan soldiers and—*Epidermis? Pituitary?* Jupiter Pluvius! Entire dictionaries of new vocabulary were marching inside her: English. Latin. Greek. The feats of Hercules. The fiddling of Nero. That first exam at Oxford, monitored by meek old Professor Migglemuss—

And Celeste, suddenly struck with understanding, gasped:

Her visions were his *memories.* The eyes through which she saw them, the clothes she wore in them, the knowledge she gained from them, were *his.*

What happened, it seemed, was that as she had shared his body, she had shared his memories—*she knew everything he knew!*

But also, she realized with a swallow, she *felt* everything he *felt.* Because each memory came with strong emotions, and so she now felt a thick residue of pain, sludgy, sick, full of tears—the way his shadow always looked.

But his shadow no longer looked that way, she saw. It was now a textbook example of spiritual health.

He went on, babbling vigorously—"I can't feel my tendinitis!" "Where's the earache!"—little noticing how Celeste stared agog at him, her mind sprinting through logic. Somehow, she caught on, when she'd shared in his memories, all his emotional wounds had evacuated him and charged into her. So aside from knowing everything from his toilet training to last night's dinner, she'd also become a vessel for his deepest pains. They stung her as severely as they had once stung him.

Finally, his hypochondria made sense to her: his physical problems weren't physical at all but were spiritual problems masquerading as physical. Which was why he was flinging his arms into the air now, whooping it up like he'd won the World Series.

She sat back, shaking her head in wow, running her eyes up and down this fine specimen of a man.

That's when her very first impression finally sank in: "Did—didya l-l-look at yourself?" she stammered.

He peered down at his chest, which only a fornication before had been a silver-wisped concavity. Now the pectorals were taut and strong, the hairs brown and abundant. He touched himself.

"How do you feel?" Celeste asked.

His fingers continued down his body. No dishrag deltoids, no more abominable abdominals. Good-bye slight thighs, ta-ta cowardly calves. He felt as if he had died and gone to Jack LaLanne. "I feel twenty years old!" he exclaimed. "Or like I *might* have felt at twenty."

Then he was on his feet, stretching his new legs and arms.

"I feel great. I feel great!"

Naked, Mr. Doloris dashed out of the clearing. Celeste could see through the gaps between the trees; he ran to a small inlet and knelt before the water, examining his face.

Alone, without the *presto!* side of abracadabra to distract her, Celeste realized how miserable she felt, with the muck of his entire life dumped into her. She wondered how he had gotten by all these years. She wondered how *she* would get by from now on.

Well, she thought, too late to change that.

She rose to follow Mr. Doloris but, as she stood, felt some odd switch flip on inside her, and a wind began roaring in her ears. She grabbed the trellis to steady herself and realized:

There was a suck going on inside her. A giant suck.

It was vacuuming through those new memories, ferreting out all Mr. Doloris's grief and suffering. She held on as it cruised past the afternoon when Mr. handed Daddy a picture and Daddy laughed at how stupid it was. *Thpppt!* The suck nabbed the pain and bagged it. Then it roared through the days of Daddy leaving, of Mama asking her "little man" to keep her from crying, of Daddy refusing collect calls, of Mama saying "Wash the dishes," then rewashing them herself so Mr. would learn the "right" way. *Frrppt!* Into the grimy bag of anguishes. Through the months of headaches with no cause. Through the years of coughs with no cure. Through the decades of Mother saying, "You know I'll have a heart attack if you move out." Through the moment of the ex-fiancée stepping out of her office beside a smirking, rumple-haired undergraduate.

And then, when all the uglies had been dumped into the bag— *Pop!* The bag sucked itself up.

Leaving behind a startled and pain-free Celeste, alone in the clearing with his memories.

The water was still as a mirror, and when I saw my face without the frown lines, I felt as if my entire self, inside and out, had been renewed. Or to be more precise, I felt new.

I dived into the inlet and began to swim with broad, muscular strokes, marveling at every breath. The sexual encounter had surpassed any prior erotic experience, partially because of the intensity of the passion, partially because of how happy I had been throughout.

But as I crossed my previous threshold of physical capacity (a veritable Poseidon, I was!), it occurred to me that it was not happiness I now felt as much as love. Though, oddly, it was not a love for this woman. It was a love for myself.

Admittedly, I was slightly unnerved by the physical metamorphosis. I could easily chalk up the sanguine feelings to my afterglow, but afterglow does not cure one's ulcer, let alone make one's biceps bulge. I reached a log in the center of the water and held on while I thought. It was clearly impossible that her touch could have so altered my physical self. Impossible, that is, if she were a mere woman. Therefore, I had to consider the prospect—indeed, the likelihood—that she was no mere woman. Although I had been studying Olympians my entire life, the thought that I had just made love to a woman whose power equaled that of the classical gods was rather terrifying.

But just as fear began to swell in me, it crossed my mind that Mother was, at that very moment, staring with great consternation out the window, tapping her foot at the length of my absence. In the past, that thought alone would have brought me scurrying immediately back home. But now I realized I wanted to be here, and would stay awhile. More important, I saw there was nothing wrong with that and, contrary to Mother's predictable diatribe, nothing wrong with *me*. I kicked off from the log and floated freely through the water, feeling none of the shame or self-abnegation that previously would have infected such a moment. Indeed, my primary feeling was of peace within myself and forgiveness toward my mother, my ex-fiancée—all those in my past who had not been as I wanted them to be.

Thus I saw that Celeste had given me myself, and my joy over this vanquished any fear of her powers. I understand this did not occur with everyone. But fortunately, I had spent years in sympathy with the classical gods, so it did occur with me.

—Felix (né Mr.) Doloris, letter to author

Back in the clearing, Celeste released the trellis. The shimmery light that had danced upon the air had ebbed to the intensity of ordinary sun. She peered through the trees.

There was her lover, floating across the water. She watched him, this man with no wrinkles and no blues, and a thrill much greater than any she had ever known billowed up inside her:

She had healed his spirit! She had shared his memories! And she'd done it with *sex*! That great interlocker, that supreme reel and rocker, those in-and-out throes, those feverish hi-di-hos—the jam in the Trojan War! the true in the troubadour! the heat in the meteor! the carn in the carnivore! O frabjous day! Callooh! Callay! Hot diggety dog! Let's get some more!

Though not, she realized with a stop, in the arms of Mr. Doloris; his shadow was healthy! No more steamy spiritual illness to open her steamer trunk. True, he was better-looking. But Celeste, unlike some of us, didn't need a hunk to get her cockles cooking. All she needed was a shadow that cried Help. And Mr. Doloris's shadow was now a celebration of Health.

Which meant that if she wanted more whoopee, it couldn't be with him. Which meant they could not go on as before.

At the same time, interestingly enough, her lover was coming to the identical conclusion. Only, his reasons had nothing to do with Celeste; they rose from the new dreams he was making for himself, dreams that required his moving on alone.

Presently, he bounded back to the trellis. Celeste listened as he approached, and heard that he still held on to his memories but that deep down, massaged into the very essence of his being, were not the tears she herself had felt earlier, nor the nothing she felt now. Deep down was something new. Something like trust, or acceptance. Like the sense of being held.

When he reached her, he broke stride, and they stood before each other, naked in the afternoon sun. Their breath sang in two-part wonder, their eyes crooned a duet of glee.

Then, with a slip over here and a shirt over there, here a shoe, there a sock, everywhere a giggly kiss, they returned to the buckled and bodiced finery in which they had arrived. Then they rounded up the pigs and went home, discussing his new plan.

At her house they hugged tight, sighing the unique sigh that blends affection with good-bye. And when he opened his front door, and his mother greeted him with invectives, he said, "Mother, I have something to say." Then he sat down before her and took a deep breath and calmly uttered the words he had not let himself think for most of the past forty-six years.

After I lost my virginity, I tore upstairs and for the first time felt true exhilaration. This was great! I knew how to play baseball now! I knew how a male orgasm felt now! I could do a total scrub-up job on people with my body—and have a rip-roaring time to boot! Was this the kind of gift my grandmother always talked about? Had anyone else been given such a treat?

Then I heard: *Only youooo can make the world go round.* It was my Gregorian pals, back by popular demand.

"Hey, this sex stuff is even better than I'd hoped!" I said.

Bingo!

"Bingo?"

You bet. Because you are the Queen of the Unseen, the Princess of Caress, the Dame of the Lame, the Countess of Regress, Her Majesty of Nudity: Celeste, Celeste.

I asked them what they were talking about.

You are the sexual healer.

"You mean what just happened—that's sexual healing?"

In one of its many variants. But you get the idea.

"And I am *the* healer?"

Yes, indeed.

"Then who are you?"

You ask too much. You still have a lot to learn.

"Like I shouldn't ask who's mumbling in my undies?"

Like: Into every coronation a little complication must fall. Your first test awaits.

"Please, no more riddles! Can't you give me a hint?"

They whispered among themselves a minute. Then they chanted, *Celeste, Celestie, oh no, you'll have to go (yeah yeah yeah yeah yeah yeah).*

"What does that mean?" I asked. But of course, they chose that moment to exit. I was left sitting on my bed, with a question mark in my mind and a growl in my stomach.

Some coronation, eh? Nothing left to do but call my grandmother with the news and go get myself some lunch.

—Celeste, letter to publisher of *The Sexual Bible*

●　　●　　●

The afternoon Celeste popped her cherry, Mo arrived home at four-thirty and, as was his habit, made a beeline for the kitchen before he descended to his lair. As he strode, unbanding his ponytail, he noticed an uncharacteristic silence in the attic but figured it must be a pause between jukebox songs, or maybe Celeste was out doing some extracurricular. Therefore, he wasn't expecting to see his foster daughter eating a peach at the kitchen table. He froze in the door-way. She looked up. "I missed lunch," she said with a shrug, her face pouting and mysterious and somehow more hunga-hunga than ever. His dick suddenly volunteered for active duty. He'd felt this way many times, but never so, how you say, *hard.* He snatched his Pop-Tarts and scuttled down to his psychedelic sanctuary.

At the foot of the stairs, Mo turned off the unhip overhead bulb and flipped on the newly installed neato black lights. Rock stars rose out of the darkness in hallucinogenic glory. He sat at his drums and tried to let the Owsley ommm effect begin, but with Celeste's wet mouth biff-bam-booming in his mind, he just couldn't chill out. Her sex appeal seemed to have splashed beyond the border of her skin! It had ignited the air around her! Oxygen molecules must be humping themselves into polymeric reconfigurations of chain-reactive rapture when she was nearby! You could probably get off by doing a breath in the same room!

He started pacing. He had the perfect life, everything set up just right, except for these nagging unrequited hots for his daughter. *Shee-it.* If only he could snare her into his scene. Open a bag of gumdrops and find her grinning among the goodies. Turn a black light on her. What color would she be? Green tambourine? Mellow yellow? Crimson and clover? And what were the colors the boys at school saw in her? Couldn't be pom-pom blue and gold, not if their blood boiled near her the way his did. And you could bet your bippie it wasn't prom-night pink, either. It'd be—he paused and discharged droplets of bodily fluids from all the appropriate exits—cathouse red. *Oh, man!* Sweat and sperm trickled into his clothes. He could see her sashaying down the school hall, the chick with the pin-up bod and kaleidoscope hair, and all the snot-nose punks looking on, their eyes spinning like seventy-eights, their dicks belting the boner blues.

She should have an escort! A chaperon!

Then Mo wiped his head and recolored himself. Under black light he'd be the navy blue of a uniform, a drabness he'd wear at all times to defend her honor, buttons up his belly, billy club at the ready. He folded his arms and practiced a pig snarl.

But that wasn't what he wanted. He wanted to lead her to the basement, where he'd have on a CD of *In-A-Gadda-Da-Vida* and the black lights, and she'd sigh, *Far out,* as she beheld all the posters lit up like a swami's secrets, and he'd light some incense . . . and she'd gaze at him like a fawn . . . and it would be like . . . like . . . *the moon would move into the seventh house! and Jupiter would align with Mars! and peace would guide his bayonet!* And he would rip off her clothes.

Hmmm.

—Title of memoir by Mo Wolfly

A little later, when Didi was still at the perfume counter and Celeste was *hot damn!*ing in her diary to some hip-hop from the jukebox, there came a knock on her door. No one had ever visited her up here. But it was just Mo, she could smell, so she said, "Come in," before she bothered to synsense any more detail.

Her foster father stumbled in, waving a long, bluish-violet tube. "I thought maybe you'd be into having a black light."

Subtly, she listened to his inner song. *Let's just say hi,* it muttered, but the dank residue she smelled on his clothes prompted her to listen deeper, under the boardwalk of his consciousness, to where even his own thoughts don't shine.

There she heard a Jethro Tullish grunting about *eyeing little girls with bad intent* and *bungle in her jungle.* And thus she learned, before he even knew himself, what he was sort of, kind of, *fuck, man! if he only had the balls!* up to.

But she was not scared of his attacking her, not the way she'd been scared of the Butane Boys in June. No-ho, Daddy-o.

She was afraid of his shadow.

It undulated languidly as a Lava lamp. Turned off and tuned out, sexy as Mr. Doloris's shadow. And she realized that the more screwed up someone was, the more she'd want to—

She wrenched her eyes away from the floor. "What's a black light?" she asked, slipping her diary behind the bed.

He took a step closer. "Seriously groovy paraphernalia."

"What's it for?"

Another step. "It shows you things in a cooler way. Like"—he pointed to her with the tube—"it'd make that dress purple. Or the blanket: the green'd show, not the rest."

She riveted her gaze to his face. "Sounds interesting."

"I could put one up in here." He was beside the bed then. "You'd have the coolest pad." He sat on the bed. "It'd be a real funky hangout." He inched his butt closer.

She listened in the driveway, but no Didi. She should tell him to scram. Yes, she should. She had to. She must.

But . . . *just one more peek!*

Her eyes darted south.

His shadow stretched darkly across the blanket, purring with spiritual pain.

And her body warmed up for a quick doubleheader.

Thus did Celeste find herself in the position of many a young guy who has saluted the wrong person, place, or thing and had no recourse but to repeat the command *Down, boy!* until his body agreed with the setting. In this case, the man who was putting the ink in her mink was her *father.* And he was also Didi's *husband.* Though he was just a father in name, and the Wolfly marriage was a union not even Ann Landers could love.

But then all Miss Kelly's lessons on chivalry came rushing back, the importance of the knightly qualities of honor and fidelity, and Celeste knew: boffing this man would be wrong.

The weisenheimers among you are no doubt *what a bunch of baloney*ing Celeste at this very moment, knowing the road she'll walk as well as you do. So it behooves us to point out that she didn't decide this because she eschewed taboo. She did it because she realized Mo didn't crave spiritual health. He was deaf to how miserable he felt, blind to how his misery hurt others, and dumb, really dumb, about what was commonly called "unhealthy patterns." He was a no-problem kind of dude. Spiritual health? Right; all he wanted was a bang. And if she was going to be incestuous or adulterous, her knightly training exhorted her, it'd better be for something more noble than that.

"I don't think," she said, "I want the light."

"But I know you'd like it."

"Thanks, but the room's fine the way it is." She stood up. "So that's it, right?"

His face fell. Major league bummer! He looked away, and his eyes lit on her tiny toes, her slender ankles.

And at that moment he finally caught his own wavelength and surfed into the real reason why he was in the attic.

He blushed inside but decided, *Go for it.*

Looking into her eyes, he said, "I really want you."

Play ball! her body yelled.

"I know," her mouth said.

He stood up and stepped close.

"You're so hot," he said.

He was blocking the way to the door. He was a meaty, beaty, big and bouncy side of beef. A hulking tub of goo. Maybe she could make his fat melt. Maybe she could—

Stop it!

"And I thought we could, like, you know, become friends."

"I'm already your friend. Yours and Didi's."

"I mean, the Harvest Dance is coming up soon at school, and I don't know if you want any pointers on how to, you know, kiss."

Her lips got soft. "No."

"I'd like to teach you."

Her mouth grew moist. "But—"

"Please, let me show you."

"That's okay."

"But I want to."

"But I don't think you—"

Then, before he knew he was going to do it but after she did, his lips were on hers. He had a hard mouth and stubble and a jangly song with a feedback of fear and *I can't do this!* and *But you're in it now, jerk-off,* and she wanted this but not here! not with him! and then *boom!* she was down on the bed, underneath him, and his hands were all over her dress, and he was going, "Ohhh, ohhh," and she thought of Mr. Doloris and how easy that was, and she *could* just do it again, right here, with this ha-ha father of hers, she could, and she felt her legs—a mind of their own!—open like a fan, and *his knees eased her thighs open* but he weighed so much and she could barely breathe and his mouth tasted like Cracker Jacks and she didn't want the toy surprise inside even though she did and *what was that music around them?* and he groped at her chest and her nipples cheered and *no!* and *yes . . .* and he pinned her down, his tongue in her mouth—*way down inside, I'm gonna give you my love*—and his free hand moved lower to his belt (think of him moving back and forth with his drummer's rhythm) and she could feel his hardness inch out of his pants and his other hand moved down her dress and *what was that music? he smelled peach* and god if she did it he would get healed even if that wasn't right and then he was rocking his pelvis, his penis on her thighs, and *she was his daughter!* she had a conscience *she was a Layla!* she had a deed to do *Ruby Tuesday* satyr protégé *Sugar Magnolia* Bacchus in heat, and Mr. Doloris's semen was still warm inside her and what would another feel like—would it feel as good? were fucks as unique as fingerprints? were dicks as distinctive as snowflakes? and even against her thigh she could feel he was larger *and he wished he weren't so small* and her legs spread like butter and he lifted up the dress and she didn't know if she should shove him off or draw him in and the voices had said she'd have to go and Grandma had said she should be a knight and then he grabbed her thighs and her pubes came into view and his mouth came off hers and he said, "Oh God," and moved his cock higher, angling now for the final strike, and she tilted toward him, and the music was raging, and when the breath was beating wild and he was one second to contact he thought *what a great setup it'll be, Didi for the food, Celeste for the lewd,* and—

"No!" she cried. She heaved him off her.

Much to her surprise, the force propelled him into the air. High into the air. His trajectory took him on a quick tour of the room. He was as high as the rafters. He was an astronaut in the attic. He stared down, his mouth open, his pants at his ankles. No scream, just silence. His face was burning red. His eyes were bulging. Boxes passed below him like his life.

She looked at her hands. She had never been that strong.

Then, *kerpllunkk!*

He splashed down into a box, his descent broken by porn.

They stared at each other.

They both barely breathed.

Cars passed outside.

The air crackled with shame.

Then he said, "I'll go slower next time."

She fell out of her stare. "*Next* time?"

"Yeah, I mean, I'll take it easier."

For a moment, all sound ceased. The blood halted in her veins. It had been hard enough for her to fight *herself*—but to think she'd have to keep fighting *him*! How could she do that? It would be impossible! Constant turmoil. She looked away. She felt tears rising up. She swallowed them down, and as she did, the voices' hint slammed back into her head.

Could she? It was really impulsive. And rude.

But yeah. Sure she could.

She jumped to her feet and snatched up her shoulder bag.

"What are you . . . ?" Mo mumbled.

Then she went about the room, grabbing clothes.

"You're not *leaving*, are you?" He tried to rise but winced.

She glanced at his shadow. "Your ankle's broken," she said.

"How'd you know that?" He moved again. "Ow! Shit!"

She zipped up the bag.

"Wait!"

Then she was on the stairs. "But everything could be perfect!" She reached the living room. "Sorry!" She whipped open the front door. "But I promise I—" She heard him all the way down the block, but she just kept going. Michener would parrot it all to Didi. There was no reason to look back.

"She called the Home from a pay phone somewhere in Lickalinney. It was a big contrast from when she'd called earlier in the day— *overjoyed* about what happened with Doloris. But after the mess with her cousin, she fell off Cloud Nine and had to deal with reality, like where the hell she'd live. So I told Miss Kelly Celeste should come live with Kit and me."

"See, that was the day we were moving away to California, to a job we'd found near Death Valley. In fact, when Celeste called I was outside, packing up the cars for the trip west. We told Celeste to stay put, we'd send the Dodge to go get her. They could rendezvous that night."

"It was perfect timing, actually. Of all the cars, the Dodge— Loretta—had taken the move the hardest."

"What she means is, Loretta was pissed. My homemade fuel had given all our cars personalities, and Loretta was the prima donna. She didn't want to be herded west with the others. She didn't want to settle near Death Valley. For weeks, she hadn't budged out of Park. I'd tried to wheedle back into her favor by doing a makeover on her. I'd dug up hundreds of plastic toys from the cellar and glued them onto her body. It was so extravagant, it would put Bob Mackie to shame. But it hadn't achieved the goal; she still would not move."

"But since she always had a soft spot for Celeste, this seemed like a way we could get Loretta to California and help Celeste at the same time. And darned if that car didn't jump at the chance. She let us start her up, got all sweet—"

"She even took me to Mahoney Patchett's gas station so I could get her a map, which was amazing, because Loretta would never be caught dead in gas stations. So there we were. I parked under the PRAY WHILE YOU PUMP sign and was walking in when Reverend Patchett came out. He was chewing on something, and then he saw Loretta and his eyes almost popped out of his head. She was a sight: a toybox on wheels. He blasted back inside and came out with his wife. Good old Nurse Patchett. Last time I'd seen her was at Celeste's birth. They came over to check Loretta out, and while they were gawking, I reminded Nurse Patchett we'd met at Celeste's birth. She got all curious and asked if Celeste was still healing. I said funny she should ask, just that day we'd gotten a call from Celeste, and she was healing with *sex* now. Mahoney Patchett spit out what he was chewing and asked what that meant. I said I wasn't sure, except she'd made someone a lot happier by sleeping with him. 'Well, we all do that,' the minister said, shooting his wife an amorous glance. And I said, 'Yeah, but she also made this guy drop twenty years off his looks.' They reeled back, and then I remembered the whole Gravely Beaks thing and started kicking myself. I dashed in and got a map and left, too ashamed to tell Caboodle till we'd gotten to the Nevada border."

—Kit Lincoln and Caboodle Davis, *Lifeline*

At dawn, Celeste woke to the glorious spectacle of blazing headlights.

She had spent a shivering night on the loading dock at Licka-linney's abandoned hot dog factory, brooding over her impetuous departure. But the moment that Dodge minced onto the drive and batted her Chrysler whites down the long, empty lot, Celeste deep-sixed her troubles and whistled.

The Dodge homed in on the girl and paraded down the drive. And the closer that car got, the more astounding she looked.

Loretta was a doodad menagerie. From bumper to mascaraed headlights, whitewall to rooftop, she was adorned in vampires, drag-ons, leprechauns, ghosts, acrobats, clowns, dalmatians, toads, swans, sombreros, parasols, crowns, lion cages, hot-air balloons, merry-go-rounds. When she neared, she illuminated her overhauled interior. Celeste jumped close and peered in. Loretta had been reupholstered in Hawaiian shirt. The dashboard doubled as a soda fountain. Plastic flamingos danced on the sides. Feather boas hootchy-kootched on the ceiling. And dangling from the rearview, the requisite fuzzy dice and bongos.

"You like?" Loretta rasped in her husky voice.

"Like?" Celeste said. "You could knock Detroit's socks off."

"*Merci.* Would you mind spraying me with some Chanel? I keep a bottle in the glove compartment. Under my front fender and inside my wheel wells. Oooh. That's it. Yes. Ummm."

Celeste had perused the entire range of shtup, but never had she heard about juicing up a machine. She paused. "That should do," she said, and put the bottle away.

"Ahhh," Loretta murmured as Celeste slid into the front. "Sensation is so *magnifique*! I want it all the time."

"Me too."

"I wish I could locate a worthy partner, but Kit's auto sapiens are unadventurous dullards, and no other car is man enough for me. You can imagine my frustration! I even used to make passes at inanimate Porsches and Jaguars when I went to the movies, but of course none of them ever responded."

"You went to see *movies*?" Celeste asked, recalling Miss Kelly's admonition about media in their many forms. "Where?"

"Well . . . Can you keep a secret? I took clandestine trips to a drive-in, many towns away. As you know, art can be so cathartic for those of us who suffer from involuntary chastity."

"Uh, Loretta, I have a news flash."

"Yes?"

"I'm not suffering from involuntary chastity anymore."

"Excuse me?"

And there, in the hot dog factory parking lot, Celeste described her recent staggering discovery, and Loretta proved to be the most vicarious creature ever to roll off an assembly line. "More detail," she kept moaning. "More!" She gushed windshield fluid throughout the slow-building romance. At the climax, smoke rose from her hood.

"Oh, to have flesh," Loretta sighed. "To eat! Make love! This is the tragedy of Kit's formula. I'm a hot-blooded Bardot locked in a chastity belt of steel. Oh, Celeste, Celeste, if it were *my* gift, I'd make the most of it."

"I will. Once we get to Death Valley, that is."

Loretta paused. "I thought you said you could heal the spiritually ill."

"That's right."

"So tell me—where *are* the spiritually ill?"

"You name it, they're there."

"Well, I just assumed, since you're so eager to reach Death Valley, that the spiritually ill must be concentrated there."

"Oh no."

"Then why must we take up residence in that place?"

"I need to live somewhere, and I have friends there."

"You have a friend here."

"Mo is not my friend. And Didi sure isn't by now."

"I mean *me*."

"You'll be living there too. We'll all be together."

"No. I mean you could live with *me*. *In* me."

Celeste laughed. "Don't be ridiculous."

"I'm not. Life on the road! *Rainman. It Happened One Night. Thelma and Louise.* We could have a marvelous time!"

"Live in a *car*?"

"I beg your— Hear me out." And then Loretta proposed the idea she'd sparked around her engine all night. "We could travel. I could drive, and you could heal. Your . . . sexual healing. Yes. You see? All I need is Kit's special fuel, and I know the formula. And thanks to his mechanical wizardry, I can hit sixty in five and one fifty in ten. I am patient, kind, and eager to hear your tales. And I have Highway Hi-Fi."

There was a silence. It *could* be lots of fun. Traveling with a buddy, staying free of Gravely Beaks, reveling in purpose and adventure and totally bitchen *oo-la-la*.

Celeste mulled. Last night, while on her way to this safe haven, she had scooted past many a house and synsensed all hominids within range, and it had wrung her heart. So many were grimacing at the sufferings of yesterday. So many were wishing they could wince away tomorrow.

It was a sexy battle, and someone had to fight it.

"Charge!" Celeste clarion-called.

With a giggle of "*Vive la sensualité!*" Loretta lurched into gear, and then the healer and her trusty steed sallied forth onto the spiritual back highways of America.

Dear Box 1032:

I was the kind of asshole who'd cheat on my girl but throw fits if she looked at other guys, or who'd pound the wall in the mail room when my boss dicked me. One day at work, I had it out with this witch lawyer upstairs. And surprise—at lunch I got my walking papers. I phoned my girl and started raving and she said enough already and hung up, just like that. I almost started crying right in the mail room, first time since I was a kid, but I held it in and went to say bye to a few people. One was this new temp. Some of the guys had a thing for her, me included. It was her figure, her tight dresses—and her eyes changed color! Anyhow, I went to her. She said I looked like I needed a pal, she'd take a break with me and I could talk. Fine. We got on the elevator and it was empty. The doors closed and she hugged me and I gave up the act and started crying into her shoulder and then she hit the Stop button and kissed me. I mean *kissed.* I hit boiling like that. We balled on the elevator floor. I fucked my whole life out in my head—that had never happened. It was great! I wanted to see her again, but she quit later that day. But I got right to work cleaning up my act. It was easy, I could see the other guy's side for a change. Not like I'd think everyone's cool. I just didn't let them get to me anymore.

Luke Bonaparte Jackson

Dear Box 1032:

I was a college student at the time. One day a professor wouldn't give me an extension on a paper I needed to keep my 4.0 GPA. I went to the student center all freaked and ordered french fries. French fries were my best friend, a fact I cursed every bikini season, when I'd have to wear a tent dress on the beach.

While I was moping, Celeste sat beside me. She was in jeans and a T-shirt, so I thought she was a student, and she didn't correct me. She said she lived off campus. In the next few weeks we did some intensive hanging out. She had a great laugh and listened well. One night it hit me that I'd fallen in love.

I'd had relationships with other women, so this was no shock. But I wasn't sure how she felt until that night. She came by, and it was like she read my mind. We got together. It was amazing, all emotions and sensations and memories. Somehow the sex made me slim too, which made her seem even more wonderful in my eyes.

I can't say every moment has been perfect since that night— problems come up in every life (problems more real than a GPA). But I have a perspective and confidence I didn't have before. Also, everyone I've slept with since then has come to feel the same way. It's as if she gave me a contagious calm.

Maria Bonito

Dear Box 1032:

When I was a kid I had a fall at the mill where I worked and lost an arm. My folks said it was God's revenge for my telling lies about our priest, and I believed them. After I got older, I quit school and became a bartender. I started solo parachuting off cliffs, hang gliding—loner stuff. And then I quit church. My folks couldn't abide that. They stopped talking to me.

I knew a tower you could parachute off, 800 feet up. One day I'm trekking over a field to it, and this girl appears out of nowhere.

It's illegal to jump off towers, but there was something about her that made me not worry. Maybe it was that cops don't wear minis or say they like climbing towers. Or that her face seemed open. Whatever. We climbed together. Two hours straight up, a slow climb because of my single arm. She let me say what I wanted, didn't push like most people. At the top it was windy. I wanted to kiss her. I did. It was like music. She said Let's do it here. I thought Wild. So I unzipped and sat down. She lowered herself and we went at it.

First I felt wind slapping me. Then I realized it was my butt being slapped and I was a baby. I was reliving my life. Six and getting whipped for saying goddamn, ten and catching the priest sneaking a smoke. I felt layers coming off, like whenever I'd start feeling the old stifling, it would just peel away.

When I came I started crying, it was all so much. Then I remembered what I'd heard about the Devil. With that sex so weird, suddenly I was scared she was it. She laughed when I said so. She told me she didn't believe in any devil. She helped me down to my car. I was so spooked I took off right away.

I went to bed and when I woke up, my missing arm had grown back! Right down to the fingernails. I went to my doctor. He said he couldn't figure it out, and what's more, there was this strange thing in my blood he'd never seen. He asked how I felt. I said pretty good, which was actually true for a change.

I still don't talk to my folks, but I still feel good. Only one thing bugged me for a long time, and that was the blood mystery. The doc said don't worry, and the only difference I felt was better. But it scared the living hell out of me.

Wendell Ellenbogen

Dear Box 1032:
I had been up all night helping my husband practice a talk for work. In the morning, so he could nap, I took the children to breakfast.

There wasn't any money around except what I'd set aside for my next haircut, so that's what I had to use, despite the moplike state of my hair. Afterward, I brought the children to a Castle of Values and let them watch the TVs while I rested on a mannequin pedestal nearby. But instead of relaxing, I berated myself for not being a better mother and wife.

A few minutes later, a young woman in sweats sat beside me, saying she'd just brought her son to day care and was she ever tired. I told her I was too, and I wished we could afford day care. "I had to use my own haircut money to take them to IHOP," I said. She said, "What luck—I'm a hairdresser. I could trim you." All she needed was scissors, and since we were in a store and she wanted a new pair anyway, she could just buy some.

So we went to a park and she cut my hair while the children played. Whenever she touched my scalp, I felt something flow into me, something like self-esteem. But frankly I've never thought about any female sexually, and I didn't with her, either.

She finished up and we said bye. That was it. It wasn't a revolution of the self (as some magazine called it when she went "all the way"). It was more that, with this taste of self-esteem, I realized something was awry in my life. This prompted me to make a lot of changes, the most obvious of which was family counseling. Soon things started to improve.

Barb Dwyer

And so Celeste healed. For three years she healed.

During those years, her fame was limited to the status of urban myth, as oft-mentioned but unprovable as the one about the lady who, after a rainy walk, microwaved her schnauzer to dry him and ended up cooking poor Rover, or the one about the anchorman who, after a party-down kind of night, had to hustle himself into an emer-

gency room so a gerbil could be extracted from his tuchis. Celeste
and Loretta were just one more of *those*, gossamer truths that people
sometimes wondered about but no one printed up and no one whole-
heartedly believed.

Since we're at the point in the story where questions always fly
thick and fast, it seems prudent to quell all queries before proceed-
ing with our tale. Hence, a brief pause for:

The Seven Most Asked Questions About Celeste
(At This Time in Her Career)

1. How did Celeste choose whom to sexually heal?

Wishing to adhere to some standard of fairness, she followed
this set of rules:

For starters, she looked only at those ready to be healed. That
is, spiritually ill folks who'd caught on—maybe years before, maybe
moments earlier—that *Holy shit! There's a problem in how I deal
with the world!* (Though she didn't know it, this necessarily booted
the Gacy Guru's students from the pool.)

Next, she narrowed it to those oriented to make love with a
woman, i.e., most guys and any ladies south of the heterosexual
absolute.

Then, she dismissed all parties who would have, as the pulpit-
ically correct expression went, strong moral objections.

And finally, she looked for that chemical *click*.

2. What was Celeste's MO?

Each incident was unique. She and Loretta would roll into some
new town, and while Loretta settled into a secure hiding space,
Celeste would prowl about, guided by whim. Sometimes she zoomed
in on a quarry instantly; sometimes she took days.

She always used her real name but a false biography (and some-times a disguised voice) in order to "be" whatever nonthreatening persona the individual needed. She was a student, a sculptor, a stockbroker, a maid, a mother, a magician, a hash slinger, an atta-ché. The deception was a cinch to pull off, as each episode fattened up her knowledge and thus fortified her lies.

Once she got said quarry in the sack, she knew it all: when to tease her squeezes and speed her tweezes; how to intuition a new position and match it to calm the memory's bitchin'; where to 2/4, to 3/4, to 4/4, to 5/8; to segue, to slow down, to rest, to accelerate (*andante! on presto! on prestissimo! on Vixen! on your back! on my knees! on our sides! ah, friction!*). Not till the finale did Celeste allow her lover—and then herself—to do the Big Bang. But since anything inside her set her come clock to ticking, she had to sneak herself a few little o's on the way to ease the itching. It was either those well-timed relief valves or lose her concentration. She chose the baby o's every time, without any hesitation.

3. Did she have any difficulty attracting people?

It wasn't that, as some revisionists believe, her mere presence sent genitals athrobbing. Sure, her face and figure harmonized fetch-ingly. So did her personality, an ensemble of openness, innocence, mystery, and that tom-tomming newcomer, exhilaration. But most important, since Celeste could hear whatever people were, on some level, thinking at any moment, she could revise herself to fit their wants. And when we find the personification of our dreams, it can make the stiffest grinches among us want to get off our leaden asses and dance.

Sometimes, though, orientation or AIDSphobia made sex a no-go proposition. Then Celeste resorted to nonsexual touch—teaching dance, cutting hair—which she knew from the memories. Nonsexual touch helped, but its effects tended to be lower voltage than those of a good roll in the hay.

4. Speaking of AIDS, though it's now a concern only to historians, how did she handle it?

She could spot AIDS as quickly as any illness and heal it as thoroughly. As for her partners, she used condoms when asked, but her healing powers defied latex with an ease most viruses would surrender their buccaneering enzymes to learn. In other words, rubbers couldn't stop her gift.

5. Then did things *never* go wrong? At this time, that is.

Given her many abilities, she could detect problems before they'd nosed out of the gate and make a quick getaway, invisible if necessary. (Once, in a pinch, Loretta revealed she shared that talent. "I had to learn *some* trick to slink out for my celluloid fix," she explained as they roared off unseen.) The few times Celeste was surprised by a fist or a glandular goon, her Supermannish strength came to her rescue.

She did have one vulnerable point, though: the phone. Over the fiber optics, her synsensing abilities failed her utterly. But this did not impede her healing, as she used the phone only once a week, and then just to call Miss Kelly.

6. What did Celeste know about the Gacy Guru?

Zilch. In one of those bizarre accidents of history, neither Matricists nor *nths* ever happened to think about the Guru when they were within Celeste's synsensing distance. A few times, she saw people reading shadows and heard them think *Matrix* and guessed that, since they were shadow readers, they had something in common with Beaks—but then, having no more info, she botched her guess by assuming this Matrix was a secret organization roughly similar to the Masons. About the *nths* she had *no* guess; being more furtive, they eluded her radar entirely.

At the same time, however, she came to recognize that spiritual health could be thwarted by forces she could do nothing about—

forces that so bolted out of the blue, oppressed, tranquilized, or otherwise fucked you over that many people simply decided Life Sucks And Then You Die and gave themselves up to spiritual illness. According to her observations, the Four Major Fuck-You Groups were:

a) Natural disasters. Think you've had all you can take? Whammo. Here's a shit pie in the face for you. Flash flood. Volcano. Cancer. AIDS. Feel worse now? Good.

b) The media, especially the boob tube. Promising fun but delivering sedation. Had a tough day at life? Well, just sit yourself down right here and let us do the embalming.

c) Politicians and business folk, who reward the haves while screwing the have-nots. Looking to get ahead? Too bad. It's our bat, so it's our rules, and if we don't like you, you're out.

d) Killers with no conscience. Looming around the corner, sneaking into your house, ready to bump you off with no apparent motive. Feeling safe, are we? It's only an illusion.

Given our hindsight, any first grader knows that when you put these Four Fuck-You Groups together, the result is a seriously rancid status quo. But Celeste didn't put them together; she fretted over each Fuck-You Group individually, never considering that a larger system was at work or that a single grand pooh-bah might be stirring up the whole thing.

Incidentally, the Guru's minions didn't tune in to Celeste, either. Beaks's APB had described a girl with a nebulous shadow; Celeste was an adult with an inconspicuous, everywoman shadow, and besides, she didn't watch TV. So the Matrix didn't catch up with her. Nor did the *nths,* though that was to be expected, as their role didn't include surveillance anyway.

And so they went on, Celeste and the Gacy Guru, each unaware of the other, shadows passing in the night.

7. So how did she feel about her gift?

She was a sucker for *aaa eee iii ohh ooo.* Give her a person's memory, and she'd lick its knots and whorls for days. She delighted in the chance encounter; she basked in brightly packaged lies. Life was an amusement park of mind, spirit, and body. A splendid time, she felt, could not be more guaranteed.

Indeed, it could be said she came into herself during these years. She discovered she had a way with deviant birds; using fowl language, she invited sick, surly, and spacy feathered misfits to hitch rides with her to their migratory destinations. Brief, intimate relationships ensued as the birds boarded the cages dangling from Loretta's ceiling, and then car, girl, and winged dropouts entertained each other with Hollywood, jukebox, and progressive ornithological tunes. Celeste also discovered a taste for card games—and for creaming her opponent. Daily she challenged Loretta, the Dodge tsk-tsking the girl's competitive streak and obligingly propping the cards in her steering wheel, and then head to dashboard they went at it, birds placing their wagers and squawking for their favorite, Celeste chewing gum (Bazooka only), Loretta steaming up: "Dole 'em out!" "Lay 'em down!" "Cut a kiss!" "Raise you one!" "Hit me!" "Wild card!" "Banco!" "Blackjack!"—squealing so voluminously from the recesses of the doohickeyed jalopy that passing motorists swerved to avoid these no-doubt—*Hey! Did you hear that, Mommy? They said Gin!*—drunks. And more: Celeste developed a tea tooth, chugging tangy brew as they sped down the highways. She took up barefoot running, thrilling to the endorphin *whee!* of an aerobically powered ride. She screeched up at garage sales, hunting for new rings (which often went unworn, given the fashion demands of her vocation), then strung the jewelry from Loretta's ceiling to make colored stars among the birdcages. She taped *Calvin and Hobbes* strips to rest room walls. She wrote copiously in her journal.

But occasionally, after a tryst, before the cards had been dealt or the tea poured or Loretta was ready to roll, Celeste, still floating in afterglow, would gaze out the windshield. There sat the world: Aqua-raincoated children scampering off to school. Flouncy-skirted girls trading romantic dreams on front stoops. Testosterone-tanked boys shooting baskets at school courts. Thick-waisted families barbecuing hamburgers in backyards. Cotton-haired retirees ambling hand in hand down country lanes.

And sometimes—more often than she liked to believe—these everyday scenes would deflate her afterglow with a quick hiss, and Celeste would sit, stripped suddenly of existential validation, and she would think:

She could learn about regular people, and act like regular people, but given her responsibility to use her gift, she could never *be* regular people. She would never live in a house, or spend a lazy Sunday doing nothing, or go to football games with buddies she'd known for years. She would never be able to drop the lies. She would never have a love of her own.

Then she would look away from the window, blinking back the thought, and ask Loretta to move on.

"Grandma, why am I the way I am?"

"Why is any of us the way we are? It could be a dollop of nature. It could be a wallop of nurture. Who can say?"

"It's just that sometimes I wish I were normal. I mean, my shadow says I'm normal, but I know that's not true."

"Did King Arthur wish he were normal? Don Quixote?"

"No. But it's hard sometimes."

"Who ever said being a knight would be easy? You can perform unprecedented miracles! Consider yourself lucky."

"I do."

"And just go on."

"I will, Grandma. I will."

—Tape recording

In the beginning, some say, was the shopping mall.

The Coalbelch shopping mall, fifty miles outside Fossilfink Falls. There, a supermarket, a pizzeria, a video store, and a Castle of Values ringed a sprawling parking lot. In the middle of this parking lot stood a raised platform, which variously served as a high jump for aeronautically inclined skateboarders and a stage on which extra-facialed terrestrials from defunct soap operas touched down to bestow autographs on spiritually famished fans.

But one dusky spring evening, three years after Celeste had begun her tour of America, the platform was festooned with roses, rainbow-colored banners, and baskets of pamphlets, and onto the steps climbed the two Patchetts, Nurse Regina and her spouse, Mahoney, wearing their Sunday best. A small crowd of passersby and invited friends clustered about the base of the stage. Among the latter was the entire congregation of Reverend Patchett's church, and the hair-happy Nurse Bee and a gaggle of her gossipettes. One guest was noticeably absent: Mahoney Patchett's drinking buddy, the green-suited mayor, Gravely Beaks.

Weeks before, when the invitations had gone out, Beaks told the Patchetts he would "be therrre with bells on"—but could he first be clued in on what was up? "It's top secret," Reverend Patchett had said, sucking on his bullet. "Let me put it to you this way: we've been working it out a long time."

But Beaks bah-humbugged the concept of patience and arranged enough here's-to-good-friends tequila sessions with Mahoney that at last, a mere twenty hours before the shopping mall speech—ho ho!—Beaks fermented Mahoney's silence into talk. Well, it was more like Beaks watered it down; Patchett did not actually pour forth 100% proof yap, but he did pass the mayor the written speech, the speech that the Patchetts were delivering right now.

"I have never done this before," the nurse began, a breeze peeking up her hem, the Castle of Values spewing shoppers in the distance, "but I have discovered something so . . . *divine* that after much inner conflict, I have decided I must tell the world."

She turned to Mahoney, who slipped her the long-distilled piece of paper. Then, in angelic soprano, she began to read.

Gravely Beaks had choked on his tequila when he'd seen the speech the night before. "Arrre you *surrre*?" he'd asked Mahoney.

"Haven't spoke to the girl myself," Mahoney replied, "but the kicker was, my wife was visiting an aunt in New Jersey and met this lady, a Ms. Placenta Doloris, and she told Regina how her son had it all done to him. He deflowered the girl, in fact."

Beaks gakked at the speech in his hand. Could it be that all along—fuck that cloudy night!—he had been on the trail of Something Huge?!

"Nineteen years ago," the speech read, "in the health clinic at Fossilfink Falls, I helped deliver a child under the most extraordinary circumstances. . . . During her childhood, Celeste displayed a talent for laying on hands, but at puberty she began to heal in a more unique way. Now, when this young woman has sex with a person, that person is cured of all his illnesses, as well as his age. Cancer-stricken men become well. Forty-year-old men become twenty. Woe becomes joy. And then this woman moves on."

Beaks glared at Mahoney, nostrils dilating. This was *his* job! *He* should've been the one to find out! With a mighty inhale, he sucked his nostrils back to size. "So wherrre is Celeste?"

"Traveling around. Got wheels somehow."

"Fancy that. Ourrr little Celeste. Um, does she still have that long hairrr?"

"Yes. Only now it's full of colors."

"It's *wha?* Eh, how do you know all this?"

"That Ms. Doloris. Her son hears from Celeste now and then."

"The son told you?"

"Hell, no. The mom told him if he packed up, she'd broadcast it. And he did pack up, so she's broadcasting. What else you want to know?"

On the Q & A went, and with each A, Beaks's voice quavered more with humiliation. He'd been on the case, but herrre he'd been one-upped by this dumbshit minister and his drainpipe of a wife! Unfair! They weren't even in the Matrix. Grotesque! Incontrovertible evidence that there is no justice in the univ—

Ah, but what! If he skedaddled to contact the Temporary Zero-Zero, then perhaps he could redeem himself. Perhaps the Gacy Guru did not know. Ho ho! Perhaps he, Gravely Beaks, would be handed the reins, given the go-ahead, told with no uncertain urgency that his one, his only, his exclusive purpose in life was to pull out all the stops, to Monitor her down to the finest detail, to find out what was up, locate her, deliver her, and await his final, his glorious, his *dripping in power* reward . . . and become as powerful a man as— *dare he think it!*—the Gacy Guru.

He bolted (politely) from Mahoney, blasted back home. There, to the squall of the television, he dived under his bed and seized his Matrix box and, with a few quick spins, did the combination. The lid sprang open.

No time for gushing over the slice of shadow that lay within. No time for gloating over his yellow belt. He just grabbed the Crystal Cup and huffed over to the blaring TV.

Then he was in place: mouth pressed to one end of the Crystal Cup, TV screen to the other, headphones on. He looked closely at the dots that made up the picture. Greens, reds, and blues lit up like Chinese lanterns. But he knew how to see between them. He knew how to hear the others. He knew when the moment was right to enter the flow. He timed it: One, two—

Now!

And then his voice was in the Gacy Guru's eyes, and he was telling everything he had found out and apologizing—but not too much! the Gacy Guru does not like apologies!—and he could hear the Gacy Guru pause and he could hear the Matricists chattering away, not hearing Beaks, and then the Gacy Guru answered in his slow, controlled fashion that it all fit into place now, and Beaks had done well to report this, and he should know he was a special component of the Matrix and vital to the resolution of this incident (not person; incident: that's what he said), and yes, they *could* use the Phone Snooper, but before that eventuality—before that—would Beaks be so kind as to assume the position of Voice—that is, because the Gacy Guru could not?

Voice? What does that mean?

Because she is mobile, we cannot easily Monitor her. We therefore must resort to the hackneyed but effective approach of incantation. And for that, we need a Voice.

The Guru had never held a seminar in incanting. "You saying you want me to place a spell?" Beaks asked. The idea seemed pretty wacked.

Not exactly place one. We cannot lay one spell on top of another. Nor can we remove a preexisting spell. But we can modify it. You can modify it. We need your voice.

And then—curtail that curiosity! spells might seem a bit metaphysical for the Gacy Guru, the king bee of technological manipulation, but the man *was* a genius, who did a lot no one understood, including having a shadow that made no sense to even white belts in Shadow Reading, so ask no questions!—Beaks listened to the strange words and memorized them. But he was not to incant right away. He was to wait. Until he could be where she had come into life. Until the sun was low in the sky.

And so, while much of the town of Fossilfink Falls was standing in the shopping mall parking lot that evening, and unassuming consumers were absorbing the first publicly spoken reports of Celeste Kipplebaum Runetoon Kelly, and the Patchetts were announcing the formation of a crusade they had christened the Spiritual Nudity Movement, Gravely Beaks was letting himself into the vacant clinic and padding toward the room, rehearsing the words in a whisper, reviewing how he was to go to the spot where Celeste had embarked on consciousness, hold his left foot in his right hand, and recite the incantation. The room loomed ahead, door ajar. He wiped his sweating brow with a gloved hand and entered. The window saluted him darkly; daylight had just finished its striptease. He scuttled to the bull's-eye, reached back and grabbed his foot and opened his mouth, and just as his voice uncoiled, he remembered the cryptic last words the Gacy Guru had uttered when they signed off, and for a single, gizzard-clutching moment Gravely Beaks wondered what the ding-dong, dangblast, foolafucking hell they could mean:

Good, the Gacy Guru had croaked in his deliberate fashion. *Good. We will lift the veil, Student Beaks, lift the veil, and then we will let the fun begin.*

The Story of the Sea

Day Two   Twilight—Take Three

Dance tunes drift onto the deck from the ballroom. Edwina scrutinizes the stranger who has just offered her a deal. A deal? What does he mean, a deal? "Are you a salesman?"

Her legs hurt. She backs up to a deck chair and lowers herself onto it.

The stranger shuffles over and sits down, except beneath him is no chair. "If that's what you want to believe."

She stares at the empty space between his body and the deck. He's even got his feet up as though he's on a lounge chair. No part of him touches the ground.

She looks back to his eyes. Inside, far in the center, she thinks she sees colors, flickering like flames.

"What are you selling?" she asks.

He smiles. "What if you could feel better?"

"What do you mean?"

"What if you could feel joy? If this darkness was washed away from your life?"

She sighs. "I want that more than anything."

"Good. Now you know what I'm selling."

She gazes down. "But I have nothing to pay."

He smiles again. "That's not really true," he says.

Monkey

A rubber-balled sun rolled into a new day. In an East Coast college town, Little Susies woke up to face their reputations, Casey Joneses woke up to face their hangovers, Miss Grundies steeped red pen tea. Pigeons pontificated from the library roof. Janitors shuffled from office to office, unlocking. And in a tiny garret four stories above the alarm clocks, a solitary figure hunched over a desk, reached for her machine, and pressed Record.

Iambia Teneye, former Kelly Home orphan and current college professor, was taping recollections. At midnight, she'd bolted awake, struck by the shrapnel of a memory long buried and suddenly exploding. Now she was yammering into the machine, telling about the boy, his flutes, the doughy aroma of his yeast. But for hours she'd been too stunned to stagger deskward; her clarity of thought kept getting Rosemary Wooded by the nagging question: *How the* [expletive deleted] *could I have forgotten?*

An hour later, the sun yawned above the buffalo grass of the Plains. While jackrabbits ducked for cover and prairie grouse strutted the King Tut, Broomcorn Jerry, in a farmhouse beside freshly plowed fields, ignored his chores. He had wrenched out of dream last night, sweating with memory. *There'd been a boy at the Home.*

With dark hair. Who never wore shoes. And this boy had loved to sculpt bread. He'd whipped up rye pterodactyls, pumpernickel pianos. When Marina was pregnant, she'd played his sourdough flutes. Now Broomcorn poured his daughters some juice and ambled onto the porch, scratching his head, asking himself: *Have I just woken from a sleep I didn't know I was in?*

And an hour after that, in a room above an auto shop on the pine-flecked Sierra Nevada, Kit and Caboodle dazed in bed, sharing, for the umpteenth encore, their simultaneous recollections.

Caboodle: "The boy's name was Monkey McCoy. He was sixteen. He wasn't at the Home long. He liked Marina—he got her to dance once. On her seventeenth birthday. I was there. He coaxed her (that stoic with the braid and wild dreams) from the office with the smell of his bread. In the kitchen, he gave her a buttered slice of whole-wheat horse. Then he took her hand and kicked the back door open and waltzed her to the songs of the birds. Everyone laughed. Even Marina. Marina laughed. *How could I have forgotten that?*"

But it was Kit who had the super-unleaded memory. It was months later, after Marina was in the family way and no one had fessed up to being the One. "A misty night. I was working under my Chevy and heard a couple whispering. I peered over, and saw clogs and bare feet, and knew right off it was Marina and Monk. When they passed, I stuck my head out. They were walking hand in hand toward the giant path. I wheeled back under the Chevy, thinking, *So that's the dad. I shoulda known, with Monk giving her those sourdough flutes all the time.* It made me smile.

"Then, a little later that same night, I was washing up in the back when I heard them again. I peeked out front. Monk was kissing Marina's fingers like he was making love to her hands. I'd never seen anything like it. Then Marina went inside. Monk headed to the garden, and when he traipsed behind a rosebush, I figured he was picking her flowers. But after a while, no Monk emerged on the other side. I thought he'd caught on I was there and was trying to hide from me, so I shuffled over to tell him to come out already. Only behind the bush there was nothing but roses. I looked around. Holly. Hyacinth. Moonlight. Mist.

"No Monkey."

And at that moment something had gone dark in Kit, like a corner of his head got short-circuited, and suddenly he couldn't remember why he was in the garden. He went back to his cars. A hair ribbon lay on the ground. It looked like Marina's. *What's that doing here?* he thought. *Marina never goes near the cars.*

The next morning, Marina went to the clinic and died.

But by then Monkey had been erased from everyone's mind. It was as if the boy had never existed. And with his bread all eaten, any physical evidence was gone. No—one trace remained.

The baby.

━━

Dear K&C,

Mighty odd, all these calls we've been getting—orphans far and wide who haven't touched base in years. Everyone's flummoxed. Count me in on the ponder. I've scoured my med books, and group amnesia doesn't even rate a footnote.

Miss Kelly didn't let on when you rang, but when she remembered she got seriously agitated. Spent two days combing through Home records, all in vain. Nothing was writ on that boy, or if it was, it's gone now. Since then all the no-nonsense she used to muster at will keeps failing her. She spaces a lot when you're talking. At night, I hear her sometimes in her room. Can't make out the words, but the tone cracks like anger.

I want to tell you about Marina—that fuddles me more than anything. You know how when we spoke about your Monkey memories I had to drop the phone to check on some high-speed typing? Well, on my quick zip to the office I reasoned this recollection renovation must have got to Marina too, and what I was hearing was the sweet rattle of full-throttle recall. I burst into the office. She whipped a sheet out of the Remington. With quivering phalanges, I snatched it, thinking, *Yada yada, our day has come!*

In a pig's eye. Here, reproduced for you, is the first line:

qzq rgea of ft$v ng kae oz ngf qusg kog x*ll qh hiok td gkf
of uqf getq f#s oftk iq xslx ho zlu qf uhs qfa%

And the thing is, comparable gibberish springs from her digits every waking minute. She's filled half a ream already. I ask her what it is, and she says, "Look!" I look, but all I see is mess. So tell me, eagle-eyed folk: what do you make of this?

Sam

Dear Sam,
Beats us.

Kit and Caboodle

It beat Celeste too.

She found out about her paternal roots beside a roaring river in Utah, when she made her weekly call to Miss Kelly from a pay phone.

Immediately, bewilderment pinballed into Celeste, lighting up images of herself—not how *she* saw herself (she *didn't* see herself, not really), but how some of her lovers saw her. There they'd be, in flagrante delicto, and *kerpow!* it'd flit through their minds that this lady had to be something . . . different—no, something . . . and snatching for a quick label, they would rip open long-locked mental drawers until they hit the one for Supernatural. Yes, she had to be supernatural! Then, rummaging through, they'd seize on: *Angel* (a wingless cherub with divine eyes)! Or *Demon* (a sexy succubus with hidden horns)! *Fairy! Witch!* Yes! She had to be! She had to be! And then they'd pause, and think, Omigod! I just did it with a $\overline{\text{[supernatural being]}}$, and then they'd swallow a huge gulp and get . . . *real . . . scared.*

She'd always pooh-poohed such fears. Okay, she could *almost* feature how her do-goodery could make her seem on the harp-and-holy side of the supernatural fence. But more reasonable, given that her do-good did best in bed, was that she belonged on the fire-and-brimstone side, from whence carnal activity, according to every preacher, originated. If she *had* to be supernatural, well, then, from the wrong side of the fence she must be.

But she didn't buy that, no, ma'am, not one drop. After all, *she*'d never seen supernatural creatures. Perhaps *some* people had, but if so, those folks must not need healing, or must not be healable, so Celeste had never screwed a memory of the King of Kings or the Satanic Majesty, et al., and therefore laughed at the very idea. Besides, once when her Gregorian buddies were passing through, she asked them point-blank if there was any truth to the stories of such beings. *Scant little,* they'd chanted. So that clinched it for her: the whole supernatural business was hokum.

But then how do you explain the forgotten father . . . ?

Miss Kelly could console Celeste, Miss Kelly could speculate with her, Miss Kelly could hold her telephone as visions of Lotus Eaters danced in their heads. But Miss Kelly could not explain a forgotten father. And Celeste accepted that.

Now you smart-asses out there, quit rolling your eyes. Look at it from her place and time: to Celeste, it was so mysterious, it broke the bounds of mystery, rocketed beyond puzzle and enigma, splashed through the far reaches of conundrum, and lodged itself in the realm of random weirdness. What the hell choice did she have? Either obsess over the unknowable, or forget it and go on. And she chose go on.

So: Oh, well, Celeste sighed, hanging up the phone with a shrug. It can't mean anything. It's not like *I* feel different. It's just odd, that's all. Nothing has changed.

But as even a mountain hermit can tell you to this day, with that call much more had changed than she could know.

We had just instructed Student Beaks on using the Phone Snooper to Monitor the phone, when she made that call home from Utah, thus allowing us to fix her location exactly. Buoyant with discovery, he urged us to seize the opportunity to "bag her now."

We informed him, however, that it was acceptable—nay, desirable—to allow her mobility. Now that we had located her, the goal was not to catch but to needle. To encourage a body to squirm until it shoots itself in the foot.

He did not ask for an explanation. We like that in a student. No need to compound incompetence with overinquisitiveness. Supposedly he had learned from what happened with Student Fleece, who, when told he had overlooked Celeste at his school in Licka-linney, *asked us questions,* thereby forcing us to alter our sentence from mere demotion to decapitation. (A slipped window.) Student Beaks was more obedient. When we explained we had a plan for Celeste and described his role, he complied. No questions asked at all.

—Gacy Guru, videotaped memoir,
And You Thought It Was Just Paranoia

The day after Celeste called home, impurely by coincidence, the public myth about her began metamorphosing into fact.

That morning, a producer at UBC-TV proposed that a segment

of the top-rated show *Miracles, Madness, and Moonmen* be devoted to an obscure husband-wife pair from Fossilfink Falls, Pennsylvania. These folks, he pitched, warranted a story not simply because they were making the standard claim of knowing the Messiah but because they were asserting that the Messiah was a—well, they didn't have the noun, but the producer sure did—nympho. In the executive suite, the idea caught on like measles, and the following week, after a little prodding from their local mayor, the Reverend Mahoney Patchett and Nurse Regina Patchett debuted on national TV. Wearing their Sunday best and speaking in down-home voices, they told the interviewer all they knew about Celeste: how she looked, what she drove, what she did. Mr. Doloris refused to appear, but his PO'd mom, who still couldn't accept his moving out on his own, flaunted Before and After pictures. Also, a bowling captain from Toledo related his assignation with Celeste, and a septuagenarian barbershop quartet (some of whom looked forty now) serenaded the audience with a self-penned round titled "The Night of the Seventies Swoon."

Some viewers turned their backs on the whole idea, but many let themselves be lassoed in, as evidenced by the number of calls that immediately herded into the Patchetts' I'm O.K. If She's What You Say corral, the Spiritual Nudity Movement.

A slight digression for a history lesson. At that time, self-awareness groups flourished around the country. The most genuinely helpful ones held that each person could feel better by embracing a buried self, but only with the assistance of a Higher Power, which each individual defined for him- or herself. Your Higher Power could be the Lord, or a redwood tree, or your dead Uncle Marvin —whatever you wanted. The rub was that some people dismissed this Higher Power stuff as mumbo-jumbo and, as a result, refused to sample these groups. In private, however, such skeptical people often admitted to secretly craving evidence: If you *prove* to me there's a Higher Power, *maybe* I'll come around.

At the same time, there were other people who equally dismissed conventional religion. With its sacred list of Thou Shalt Nots, religion seemed, to these sideliners, to squelch individuality and therefore to prevent them from knowing or liking themselves. They *believed* in some form of God, but they wanted to live their lives with God as companion rather than, as they felt religion demanded, dictator.

Now, the Patchetts, clever bumpkins that they were, had spent three years stumbling through amateur market research and emerged on the other side with the insight that there was a vast array of people out there: those in pursuit of self who wanted a tangible Higher Power, those who had a Higher Power but were in pursuit of self, and—Gravely Beaks's last-minute addition—the horny bastards who didn't give a shit about either. If we could unite these groups in the state of Holy Recovery, the Patchetts reasoned, we would do a great thing—and make a mint too, Gravely Beaks pointed out, if you charge $49.95 for membership. (The money didn't appeal to Regina, but Mahoney's wallet went erect with the mere thought, as Beaks knew it would.)

Loosely based on self-awareness groups, the Spiritual Nudity Movement postulated a specific Higher Power: the unwitting Celeste. (Hold the Kipplebaum Runetoon Kelly; only the first name was used.) Believers were supposed to be empowered by the proof that She was out there. They were encouraged not to chase after her but to "feel her in your body." Movement meetings consisted of sharing one's deepest darkest and, "so that we may open ourselves most fully," were conducted in the buff. Hanky-panky was frowned upon—there was a sexually transmitted epidemic raging, after all —but some blockheads eventually took it upon themselves to imitate Celeste as their Christian brethren imitated Christ. But we get ahead of ourselves.

The day the television show aired, membership in the Movement ballooned from nineteen to five thousand. An updated segment ran a month later, and by summer solstice the Patchetts were renting infomercial space on late-night TV, on which they dumped the eye-witness approach and instead featured inspirational sermons and meetings, both presented, no kidding, in the nude.

Celeste became aware of this slowly. The first twinge of *What's going on?* occurred when she waved hello to a forklift operator and heard him think: *Well, if it ain't* her. But after she got to know him better, as the linguistically challenged Patchetts so politely described her activities, it turned out he'd simply heard some talk about a "rainbow-haired babe." The next few lovers knew zip, but when a clerk at a fruit and nut store blurted out, "Celeste!" she got wise that something was up. Grabbing her cashews, she took a swift synsense and learned about the Spiritual Nudity Movement.

The fame—only a decibel above myth at that point—made things both more frabjous and less so. More, because when she came on to someone who'd heard of her, the wheels of seduction were already pregreased. Less, because she had to dodge passes from not-ready-for-healing rogues and because, if she thought it was tough feeling normal before, how about knowing that some spiritually forlorn wretches out there believed she was the Messiah? Several times she strolled back to Loretta and was met by autograph hounds. Once, she saw a tabloid story on "Celeste sightings"; like a flying saucer, she was supposedly luminescent.

Consequently, this was the time when Celeste and Loretta and the passenger birds began traveling under cover of invisibility. No trace, no fuss. You don't gotta slink in and you don't gotta skedaddle out. Just leave Loretta in some pastoral privacy ("In order of preference, *s'il vous plait,* a drive-in, a racetrack, a field of my own"), let the birds out to shoot craps with the fuzzy dice, and mosey on into town. Then, Hello, big boy; Whatcha doing, little girl. (With hair bunned up and contacts on, in case this quarry needed time to come around.)

You might think Celeste resented the Patchetts for forcing her into this shady existence, but after the first few days, seeing she relished descending out of nowhere like Mary Poppins when some suffering soul was in need, Celeste scrubbed the Patchetts from her mind. Clarity of mission prevailed; her only thoughts were of healing and her after-healing frivolities. Indeed, she was untroubled enough to cultivate a new after-healing frivolity, the one that, unbeknownst to her, would eventually get her into some serious deep shit.

She'd always found journal writing to be a joy. Only now, after an encounter, after she'd ally-ally-all's-in-free'd to the birds, climbed back into Loretta and kicked off her shoes and slipped on a dozen rings from her ceiling stash and opened her journal, Celeste didn't just pen your stock *Today was a nice day* entry. Instead, she made her words read like stories—like tales of healing. From scout-out to bed-down to memory-minuet. She crafted the openings. She honed the structure. She made the language sing. In utter concentration, she conducted these recording sessions, pen jiggering like a hyperactive baton, tongue protruding with thought, as she ignored the raucous return of the birds, blocked out sweet Loretta Chrysler wishing she was a woman but wailing that she was just a car, shooed off the feathered friends poking beaks and the horny Dodge sneaking peeks at the unfolding, no-holds-barring story—until at last Celeste decided the entry was done, and—Take it from the top—read the tale out loud to her eager audience, who whistled and sighed along with the author every word of her healing way.

It all sounds halcyon, and Celeste thought it was, but there was one little wrinkle. A sporadic snafu. There she'd be, reading with gusto, Loretta creaming her gas tank, the birds heavy breathing like casino groupies, ecstasy dancing in Papermate blue before them— and suddenly it would hit.

"What's wrong?" Loretta would ask.

"Let's play cards instead," Celeste would reply.

And then she'd slam the notebook shut and whip out the deck, but sometimes, even as she was immersed in a flashy shuffle, even during a high-stakes hand, the realization would swoop once more through her like a bat, shrieking, ripping across her spirit, then blast into the darkness and be gone: She knew real life. She fucked real life. But her own life was less real life than a tease.

This is the map wherrre I trrracked herrr. One pin for each call Home. You see how she often stayed in one generrral vicinity forrr weeks at a time? Ho ho! It was perrrfect. She'd hop frrrom suburrrb to suburrrb, then enterrr the nearrrby city, loop thrrrough neigh-borrrhoods therrre, then move on.

It was the Gacy Gurrru who noted this. *We can use it to our advantage,* he told me on the Crrrystal Cup, and then instrrructed me to turrrn to Channel 12. I did. It was a cooking show. *Watch this,* he said. *Learn it so well you could do it any place at any time. This is part of the plan. We will want it later.*

—Gravely Beaks in Broadway production
The Baffle or the Bust

In the fall, as whispers about her grew louder and the Spiritual Nudity Movement launched a direct mail campaign and Celeste went on, oblivious of Gravely Beaks's Monitoring her every call home, the invisible knight excursioned into the Virginia mountains. In a valley where autumn leaves were throwing their retirement parties, Celeste and Loretta passed a billboard for a Renaissance fair. Though they didn't know what that was, they liked the phrase *Live a fantasy for a day.* So they swept through the hills until they came to the high walls ringing the fair. Loretta parked then, and the healer proceeded on foot.

At a Tudor inn beside the entrance gate, Celeste paid her admission and learned that the fair was living theater. That is, it was a re-created Renaissance town filled with actors in period costume. "They won't break character, no matter what you do," the peasantly attired ticket girl said. She also mentioned that Celeste could rent a costume. Celeste darted into the inn and, a moment later, emerged in a violet tunic and steeple headdress. With hair inside hat and contacts in and so many other visitors equally Renaissanced up, she looked like everyone else. She smiled a smile of grateful anonymity and passed through the entrance gate into a fairy tale world.

The fair was indeed a complete town, with dirt streets and thatch-roofed huts. Celeste meandered about, letting herself fall into the fantasy. In shops, blacksmiths shod horses, spinners spun wool, alchemists mixed potions, glassblowers blew glass. Merchants sold Merlin-esque magic wands and gypsy dresses, jewelry, perfume, spices. Chickens ran free. Village idiots spouted sounds and furies from their benches, buxom wives chewed out peg-leg husbands on front porches, and next to pubs, merry drunks sang beer songs with drool and bad harmony. Horses passed, hauling wagons of visitors. Flags flew from the tops of walls. The air was thick with the vocabulary of another time. Any silence was filled by a minstrel.

In her costume, Celeste could indulge in sensation and experience the same as anyone else. She savored tea with the king, gobbled Knave of Hearts' tarts, inhaled perfumers' oils, lost herself in a lute, shambled on a camel, struggled to juggle, hurrahed at archery, giggled at debauchery. This, she thought, is life consummated. This is life without tease.

And so the morning spun by swiftly.

At noon, she became weary. She found a small grove and there, on an inviting log, drifted toward a Renaissance nap.

But she never got there. Just as REM was heralding its arrival with a parade of half-dreams, a fake British drawl barked into the grove: "Ah! A wench in my domain!"

She opened her eyes. Two men were scrambling through the trees. The dark-haired one wore a prissy yellow cloak and white hose. The other, whose hair was a cyclone of red and whose beard a tumbleweed of the same color, wore a plain waistcoat with trousers. And both were brandishing swords.

She sat up.

"She is a *lady!*" Redhead retorted in the same piss-poor accent, the last word bending off-center like a blue note. "And this is public domain! You make me chortle, swine!"

"Do not question me, commoner!"

"Don't boss me around, prawnhead."

"You have insulted me the final time!" Prissy Cloak declared. "I challenge you to a duel!"

"My trousers tremble with trepidation, wanker face!"

They saluted each other in mock rage, thrust themselves in the *on guard* position, and as they ad-libbed momentarily while a crowd gathered, Redhead turned to Celeste and announced, "Fear not, my lady, your honor shall be defended."

Then the opponents launched themselves at each other. "Dastardly brute!" Prissy Cloak maligned, lunging. "Brute!" Redhead parried. "At least I'm no wart pus!" Prissy Cloak thrust back: "Lowbred scoundrel!" Redhead riposted: "Coddled toad!" Crash, clatter, clank, curse. The crowd thickened. The swords gleamed like sneers in the sun. Celeste sat in the middle, unable to bolt, tee-heeing with participant-observer glee. "Lily-livered miscreant!" "Impotent cur!" They swashed, they buckled, they somersaulted away from blades, they vaulted onto logs. Prissy Cloak kept tangling his intricate apparel, a klutz on all twos. Redhead ducked and charged, a perpetual percolating maniac. "I shall not be defeated!" "Take a bath, ungulate thunder mug!"

At some point Redhead tumbled onto the log near Celeste. She glanced down to mentally snapshot her defender.

The prevailing wind ruled his hair. The colors of fire ruled his beard. His eyes were blue orbs of laughter.

He winked at her.

And some chord in her nether regions went *twang*.

Then he was on his feet, flying back into battle. She watched more alertly now, hot to spot his shadow. One quick glimpse of steamy misery and she could start concocting her moves. Even a trystworthy wistfulness would do.

But much to her stupefaction, when she scanned his shadow, she saw that rarity, that exception, that Hope of all Diamonds: health. As polyrhythmic and polyhued as an infant's, as vigorous and vivid. Her jaw dropped. His shadow was *healthy*! So his shit must be together! But—but—then *how* could she be sizzling with those old familiar hots? She always got stoked by shadow, never by mere presence!

It felt very strange.

It felt very . . . normal.

She yoked her gaze to him. He leaped about, burly and mischievous, wagging his furry eyebrows at the spectators, spewing creative monikers at his rival. Hair bucked off his head like a wild horse. *Aha!*s exploded from his throat. Celeste was as dizzy with curiosity as she was fizzy with desire. What might occur if she followed her libido and boinked a healthy man? *Could* she snag someone who was healthy? Was that *right*?

Such questions chased their tails in her mind until at last Prissy Cloak lost his weapon and Redhead cornered him, sword to chin. "Mercy can be yours," he said, "if you say, 'Leonardo da Vinci was reincarnated as Blind Lemon Jefferson.' "

Prissy Cloak glared an unscripted *What?* at his rival.

"Say it!"

"Le-Le-Leonardo da Vinci was reincarnated as (who?)—as Blind Lemon Jefferson."

Redhead removed his sword, and the loser dusted himself off.

Then Redhead strode over to Celeste, saying, "You are safe, my lady," and bowed theatrically before her.

She peered at him, and when their eyes locked, something happened. Without a blink, without a word, their eyes opened like cameras, and they exposed themselves to each other. *One second . . . two seconds . . .* He penetrated her negative. She entered his positive. *Three seconds . . .* Their sprockets overlapped. *Four . . .* She could hear some birds above her; she couldn't make them out. *Five . . .* It felt like the famous look across the crowded room. *Six . . .* The feeling she felt in others' memories. The magic she knew from others' lives. *Seven . . .*

And then the defeated jouster whistled. Redhead shook his Miles Standish tresses, broke his blue eyes away. The photo session was over.

"Excuse . . . I mean . . ." He stood up. She could still smell their connection. It smelled like moonlight. He gripped his sword. "That is . . . Farewell, my lady!" He saluted with a grin and ran off.

She burned to pursue, but she could not justify it. The guy didn't need healing. But for the rest of the day, as the fair grew more and more packed and Celeste began prowling to heal, she kept dropping her attention back on that groove. Yes: their eyes had held hands. Lust had become trust. Such a thing had never happened before—in *her own memory.* She wanted to drape herself in that memory. She wanted to wash her spirit in it. She felt petals opening from its heat.

The worst of it is, she has never heard the meaning of affection! Here we need to be promoting family values, and instead we have this violent, sleazy little piece of—well, it rhymes with crass. This is no role model for American kids.

> —Vice President Stinkweed, sound bite from speech
> before Suburbanites for the Status Quo

•   •   •

And when the first firework shot high in the air that night, the cobweb-haired man Celeste had spent the rest of the day with pressed himself to her back. He was a sixty-four-year-old file room clerk, a man who smelled of Post-its and paper cuts and who lived a life of quiet procrastination, taking ten weeks to fill orders, his wizened figure auraed by bitterness as he shuffled to the front counter at the office, logged in the request slips, and popped them in the Fuck Off bin on his return to his shoe catalogs. He sucked on toothpicks. His socks never stayed up. And his nephew was Senator Perkodan, the stalwart scam scum from Oklahoma. Which meant this cobwebbed gonzo was Celeste's first politically connected quarry. Dust-colored and mole-eyed, white strands fuzzing his scalp, the clerk wore a suit that was too large for him, as if he'd once expected it would house a more formidable person and found too late that it was just him, after all. Celeste met him at a tumbling demonstration. He'd been sweating there in the afternoon sun but kept his suit jacket on. That morning, his wife had casually nailed him with the grievance she'd stifled for three decades: that he was as dull as the back of a bus. He'd slunk off to work, then passed work and kept driving, and a few hours later he came upon the fair. Only, once inside, his scalp kept beading in the heat, and the outdoors were giving him buggers in his nose, and so it was tough to concentrate on this Renaissance stuff, however undull it might be. He drifted around in discomfort. Sudden thirsts kept sending him to the water fountain. It was there that he initially spied the girl in the violet dress. She was looking through an astrologer's telescope across the way. Later he wandered into the gymnast area. There was the girl again. They began talking. He wasn't sure how. Oh yes. He'd dropped his hankie after patting his forehead. She'd picked it up and handed it to him. She had an easy smile and a quick laugh and straw sandals. She was a student at his own alma mater—how's that for coincidence: he'd just been thinking about college. *Do you know Professor Wherefore?* Yes, she did. They sat in some shade. His sweat surged; since his nephew had become senator, no impropriety was allowed, not even on the outer banks of the familial pond. Too bad she was so lip-smackin' good. He spent hours with her. Actually, he said bye twice but all roads kept leading back to the girl, and every time, a joyous reunion. He thought he should phone his wife, but he did not. He thought he should leave the fair, but he did not. The girl ate corn on the cob at dinner. She had a beautiful instep. She touched his socks. Then night fell with a thud. Fireworks! the girl squealed after a peasant told them to go to the north pasture. The man enjoyed her enthusiasm. He'd been like that as a kid, he remembered: so happy he could squeal. What had caused such happiness? He couldn't recall. She gamboled toward the north pasture. He followed. Everyone was standing; it was that crowded. They laced through the throng until they could go no farther. Two vertical bodies in the midst of hundreds, she in front of him. He admired her figure. He wished they could go to a hotel. He tried to ask. He chickened out. Then Henry VIII lit a firework. It shot up. All heads angled skyward. The girl turned her back to him, lowered her steeple headdress veil over her face, pressed herself into him. The crack in her rear ran down the zipper of his pants. He almost backed away. She switched her hips left, then right. His impropriety hardened. The flaming St. George in the sky fizzled and fell. She reached behind her. Another firework blasted up. At the burst into sparks, he felt her hands on his pants. She was undoing his fly. Right there in the crowd. The sparkles faded. She whispered back, Time it right and no one will know. Then she took his hand and placed it under her long skirt. She wore no panties. He filed away a sigh. Her skin was smooth. He stroked. The back of her neck seemed to glow beneath the veil. She shifted her legs. He'd fit her like a shoe tree. Okay, she whispered. A rocket zoomed heavenward. *Scccrackle!* It opened. Oooh, the crowd replied. Oh, the girl and the man went. And they moved slow, holding their motion between displays, rocking together during, her hands reaching back for his ass, his hands fixed on her hips, pumping and pausing, pumping and pausing, timing it right so no one could know, not even a passing senator, but the truth was, it was hard to care, hard to pay attention, because the man was not fully present, he was somewhere else in time, and the girl told him, Relax; let me do all the work, so he left himself in her hands, and then all his worry went away.

I healed him like I healed anyone, but what I learned that night was unlike any other time, and deeply terrifying.

Between the twists in his failed football tryouts and the turns in his job at Wardock, Inc., he'd become a senator's uncle and in that capacity had learned a secret. Well, part of one. He'd been at his nephew's victory party, getting his wife hors d'oeuvres, when he overheard two men who were sampling the bacon florets, one a government official, one a pharmaceutical CEO. They were winking at everyone, looking at everyone, commenting on shadows—which seemed very odd to the file clerk—while elbowing each other and gloating about a toxic dump they'd avoided cleaning up. And between the bacon breath and the champagne chaser, they gushed over some strange word. Something that prompted them to chuckle with jubilation. Something they called the "Matrix."

The nephew, Senator Perkodan, had kept a flat face when the file clerk asked him about it. But over the years, whenever the clerk attended an inner-loop gala, he listened, and eventually he pieced this together: The Matrix was an extensive, elite organization to which many top business leaders and politicians belonged. Where they met and what they did he couldn't tell, but this much he learned: It was how things really got done (or didn't get done, he once thought). It was how business and government colluded. It was how innovative newcomers got crushed, whistle-blowers got gagged, undesirables got locked out of promotion, dolts got in executive suites, unneeded bombs got built, much-needed bills got ignored. In short, it was the powerful thumbing its nose at the powerless; it was the Friend in the Right Place.

And—the Matrix had a pyramidal structure, on top of which was some mysterious character, some head honcho he'd never seen, who moved around, instructing "students" in secret arts, and who went by the ludicrous name the Gacy Guru. And who somehow communicated by television.

This was all too much and too frightening—I thought I'd gotten everything down, and suddenly I learned there was some large, secret network pulling all the strings. I was so freaked I lost concentration and had a whopping orgasm instead of one of my smaller ones—but it was not pleasurable, not at all—and then of course the man lost *his* concentration and came. Usually I comforted them then, but this time I bolted right away. I did *not* want to know about this Matrix! I just wanted to be like everyone else! At my car, I flung off the steeple hat and dived into the front seat, riling the birds, telling Loretta to floor it, and as the fair grew small in the rearview, I wondered how the hell I was supposed to heal this Matrix, and I felt more alone than ever before.

—Celeste, interview, *Galaxy*

For hours, Celeste and Loretta looped through the hills, reeling in revelation, rocking through shock, babbling as aimlessly as their route. "Dear, dear. How does one combat such machinations?" Loretta asked. "I can't think about that," Celeste muttered. "I can't even . . ." *complete my sentence,* she would have said, if she could. But she could not. She could not even muster the oomph to put on her rings or write in her journal or change out of her rented tunic, which, in her rush to leave, she'd neglected to return. So they drove, Celeste slipping in and out of syntax, Loretta gliding around conversational potholes, the birds speaking only when spoken to.

At some point it began to rain, which was the final blow for poor Celeste. Think of it: when you've reached the brink of overwhelm and the sky starts to piss on you, there's nothing left to do but cry. Celeste cried. Loretta attempted to engage her friend in a bracing rendition of "Singin' in the Rain," but even with birds taking the brass and string parts, it was to no avail; Celeste needed the kind of reassurance only human touch can bring, and that was the one thing her pals could never give. Soon all fell silent. The only sounds were Loretta's wipers and Celeste's deep soul sighs. And thus would the night have continued, and perhaps her whole life, a bottomless whimper out of which she would never have climbed, and this book wouldn't have rated even a gleam in the author's dark eyes, and you'd still be toting condoms and maybe also handguns whenever you went out into the world—had Loretta not spied an all-night diner glowing neonically on a rise.

"Celeste?" The Dodge nudged the dazed girl. "*Excusez-moi,* but I simply must rest my windshield. Perhaps you should consider pampering yourself with some tea?"

Celeste glanced up. Ribbed aluminum with jukebox windows and lipstick-red roof, the place looked like a Chuck Berry guitar lick. "Fine," she mumbled. Loretta pulled into the lot and Celeste got out, still dressed up in her Renaissance finery.

Inside, booth after booth sat empty. Save for a waitress doing a crossword in the corner and a customer under a baseball cap at the counter, the diner was bare. *Thank God—or Matrix—or whatever,* Celeste mused, and then shook her head quickly, trying to whip out the thought.

She slid into a booth. The vinyl felt comforting, the laminated menu soothing. *Normalcy, thy name is diner.* The waitress took the order: club sandwich and tea. Celeste didn't bother to synsense.

Why? What good were any of her powers, if they hadn't shown her the Matrix? The drink came fast; she sipped the tannic warmth. Her head hurt. She rubbed her temples with both hands. In a world of sick spirits whose ruts were dug by a cabal, her gift was pitifully dinky, a spitball at a stealth bomber. Yet she had to do what she could, didn't she? Only, when she did, she felt so alone. It was too much. She was lost. She didn't know what to think. She reached back for her cup—

And realized the customer at the counter was peering at her.

She started.

Once because he was looking.

Twice because of who he was.

It was the man with the red hair.

He grinned, quick and easy, his beard puffy as an orange cumulus, and across the row of empty booths he said in an American accent, "My lady! Will luck never cease astounding."

Celeste blinked. His voice still had that blue-note tone every few words. He wore no shirt, just a vest, allowing his not-too-hot, not-too-cold, just-right muscles to get some dineresque fluorescence. A harmonica peeped out of the vest pocket. He also wore a bandanna around his neck, a Guatemalan braided bracelet around his wrist, and colored pencils behind each ear. On the counter sat a drawing of a house.

Bad timing! She couldn't do anything with him *now.* No, correct that: she couldn't *ever;* the dude needed no healing.

He gestured to the window. "Isn't it beautiful here? Stunningly cowabunga. Everywhere else feels a warm-up act."

She looked. Mountains and rain and fog.

"So, my lady, be these your stomping grounds?"

She shook her head.

"Mine, neither. I just needed to see a friend about a horse and stayed on for the caffeine. Finest in the land, you know."

She nodded.

He paused, and she could see thinking roll into his smile, and he then said, "Pardon me, but is something distressing you?"

She cranked up a half grin, and the *Nah* was virtually dialogue—her lips fully parted to launch the *n*, tongue curled for the *ah*—when she found herself bursting into tears.

"Oh, Alex," he mumbled to himself, "you misspoke again!"

Wanging sob. Tears running rivers, salting her lips. Her face crumpling like used paper. Where were her tissues? Out in Loretta. Celeste wiped her face with her hands.

Then she felt something brush her arm. She opened her eyes.

He was standing beside her, offering his bandanna. "Here."

She pressed the cloth to her face.

"Must have been the dogdud of all nights."

Ordinarily she would have listened inside him, but now it was all she could do to calm down.

He slid into her booth. The waitress delivered the sandwich and returned to her puzzle. The man remained silent.

Finally, Celeste composed herself. She made to hand back the bandanna and then stopped. "I can't give you this," she said. "It's all soggy. Let me pay you for a new one."

"Surely you jest."

"No, I'm serious. They probably don't have washing machines at the fair, so you'd have to find a laundromat just for—"

"Wait. I'm not a regular there. I only did the gig this once."

She sniffed. "Then how'd you know the lines?"

"Simple. Except for the accent, that's how I truly converse," he said. "The rest was spontaneous blatheration."

"The fencing couldn't have been spontaneous."

"It's cake. I've been fencing since I was a tot."

"You looked like a pro."

"Ah, she makes my ego palpitate. No, fencing's but a hobby. For pro I do architecture. Recycled houses, specifically."

"What does that mean?"

"Houses built from old objects. Like this one I'm drawing here"—he pointed to the counter—"worn-out stoves, sinks, and shower curtains. My own residence is a dome of glass bottles. You can play flute by blowing on the walls." He grabbed an almost empty ketchup bottle from the counter and demonstrated.

She smiled.

"And she cracks the smile barrier! The crowd goes wild!"

She smiled higher.

"By the by, the name's Alex. Alex Popoverovitch." He tipped his cap.

"I'm Celeste."

"Celeste! Quick—backward that's . . . Etselec. Bleh, sounds like baby formula, and you may be a babe but you're no formula. What about an anagram? An anagram is . . . ah, time for the Scrabble tiles. Three things I always carry: change for a call, Band-Aid for cuts, and Scrabble tiles for . . . here we go, we got *Select e,* but that stinks, let's see if we can do better. . . ."

She looked him over as he babbled. His vest stretched across a grope-perfect chest, his hair waved thick as bison mane. Once again, her blood sent a dit-dot-dit direct to her private parts, but just as she tried to imagine him à la natural, she remembered the file clerk at the fair, and thus the Matrix, and the sprinklers turned on in her eyes all over again.

"Hey," Alex said, "if you're needing company, I'm bunking down till the rain gives up, so I would blissfully enlist."

She tried to resurrect her smile. It was all so normal. Just like she was anyone else. Only she wasn't.

"Thanks, but I should go."

He did a mock grimace and clutched his heart.

"Really," she said, rising. "I'd make for bad company."

"Balderdash! Crying doesn't make for bad company; it makes for bad driving."

"Well, I don't actually do the dr—"

"Oh, please tarry with me. I'd like it. I would. With the storm and the dark, only talk might redeem this mangy evening, and somehow I bet you could go as long as Scheherazade. Am I right? Who are you anyway, Miss Celeste? What do you do?"

She eyed him. Could he be with this Matrix? She glanced to their shadows. He was not reading hers, so count him out of the Matrix. Whew. What about a Spiritual Nudist? She burrowed her hearing inside him. There she heard the clatter of rapiers, the hammer of nails, the choo-choo of a harmonica—and nothing about her. The guy didn't know her from Eve. Whew times two.

But big patooties. Because the real score was: the fellow didn't need healing. She had no business spending a single extra nanosecond with him.

His eyes had that feed-me-your-reply look. "I'm . . . ," she began, and then the lies that usually flew so trippingly off her tongue got snarled in her throat, and the words that swerved past them, that stunned her as much as any contrived coincidence had ever stunned her lovers, was the very true "I'm different."

"One of a kind, eh? That's the *best* kind."

She didn't know how to respond to that.

He said, "See that booth in the back? It could be our oasis. I'd tie my ears to your words. Ever do a heart-to-heart at two A.M. with someone you just met? It can take the only out of lonely, and then you're halfway back to life. Whaddya say?"

She closed her eyes. She'd had too much to think tonight. The door was a yard away. Loretta could scoot her off like that.

She opened her eyes, and this man, this puckish, loquacious, redheaded man, smiled. And it was no One Size Fits All smile. It was a smile tailored just for her. A half-tuck, affectionate, you-got-nothing-to-fear, crinkle-of-a-wink kind of smile.

He said, "Or you can be quiet. We can just watch the rain."

She looked out to the road.

She looked back to him.

He needed no healing, but . . . maybe that was okay.

Maybe it was time to get some healing for herself.

She said, "If we sit all the way in the back."

And all the way in the back they went, where they watched the rain sparkle like beaded curtains and the fog spread like genie smoke and the moon do the Dance of the Seven Veils, and at some point after the seat had grown warm, Celeste did indeed feel the only drop away from her lonely, and she told him, this Alex Popov-erovitch, something she'd never told anyone: that she had this . . . *gift*. "Whoo-ey!" he said, shaking his head, and then he asked questions. But not about her gift. He asked what she loved. He asked what she feared. He asked what she wanted in life.

Only later, after Loretta followed them to his glass-bottle dome in a Washington suburb, with its green and amber light streaming down on his hat collection and harmonicas and blueprints and basketballs, his swords and Persian rugs and Scrabble tiles and one electric guitar strung up and plugged in and waiting like art in the corner, did Alex and Celeste lie down on his futon and let themselves modulate from talk into touch. Before that, they had sat up all night in the diner, speaking, and when the rain broke they had gone outside and he had serenaded her with his harmonica and she had made up lyrics and they'd climbed into his Volvo and driven to a field of golden flowers and gotten out to find a bush of wild berries and picked the berries for each other and sat down under a tree and watched the sun rise. By the time they pulled up to his house, Celeste was wide awake and eager to embrace a healthy shadow, and she finally knew firsthand how it felt to fall in love.

The stranger is being a fool. Edwina's in no position to make a deal. "I don't have any money," she says.

The stranger waves his hand. "This debt can be handled on a long-term basis," he says. "And I don't want money."

"Then what do you want?"

He points to her belly. "Life you can help me create."

She studies his face, trying to remember what little she knows about folktales, about religion.

"You can give me your offspring," he says.

"Who are you?"

"I told you," he says. "Call me the Ultra-Other."

He stands up, brushes lint off his coat with his hand.

Edwina hasn't thought of children for so long, the idea enters her like a stutter. "C-c-can I raise the child?"

"Absolutely. Though I did say offspring."

"You'll leave us alone?"

"Completely. You'll never see me again."

The idea is too new. She cannot think straight.

He says, "Kick it around. I'll find you in the morning."

Then he hoists himself over the railing. She hears the water hiss below, and gets up and goes to her stateroom.

She changes into her nightie and lies in her bed. She can't see what she has to lose. If she and the child are left alone, she can raise it the way she feels a child should be raised. And if, in return, she gets joy again in her life—well, there seems no reason not to say yes. Edwina has not felt joy since she got married. She has wasted her life. This is her second chance. A miracle. A gift given to her. She is so lucky.

That night, Edwina, alone in the ship's double bed, has a dream. In the dream, she is in a desert. All around is white sand, and the heat is unbearable. The sky above her is just as white, but also wavy. She squints up and realizes that's because it's alive: a thousand seagulls are circling above.

She wakes in a sweat.

The stranger could be God, she realizes. But God never makes deals. Only his counterpart makes deals. She gulps. He could be the Devil.

She lies awake all night.

In the morning, she fills the bathtub and climbs in. As she is reaching for a washcloth, she glances up.

The stranger stands above her in his coat, his black curls growing tighter with the steam in the room.

"What are you?" she asks.

"Don't ask me such questions," he says. "I cannot give you answers. That would defeat the purpose."

She thinks of returning—to her marriage, her job, her life.

"I can keep the child?" she asks again.

"Yes," he says. "That is not how I operate."

He presses his finger to her forehead. She feels hot inside. He runs his finger down the middle of her face.

"I'll do it," she says.

Love

Of course, Celeste learned in Alex's house that with love, sex is no ordinary lay. During her rapture under the bottle dome, she didn't *become* his shadow; they *shared* each other's shadows. Which meant that in the throes of the jimjam rolls, his memories didn't do a magic carpet ride into her, nor did his pain. It was touch that sailed in and curled around her insides. And emotion that billowed up, sweeping into her back corners. So sex didn't bring his grief into her—so what. Here was a man who listened to *her* instead of her just listening to *him*. Who asked questions about things she'd never hooked a ? onto. Who wouldn't let her tweedle his dum without deedling her twee. Screw slipping in her controlled baby orgasms along the way; she could Big Bang whenever she damn well pleased. What had been fascinating was now transcendent; what had been exciting was now profound.

"Tell me more about yourself," Celeste actually had to say (*say!*) that first morning. They were lying on his futon. The emerald and topaz light of 5,896 jam jars and juice bottles gave the single room a watery glow. With that and the baptismal fire of love, she felt as if she were reclining in a mythical cave, where the inhabitant was not a salivating ogre with oversize canines and bloodshot eyes, but a dynamic and enthralling prince.

In fact, the inhabitant *was* a prince.

"My sister, Olga, and I are twenty-third and twenty-fourth in line to assume rule in the tiny nation of Accordia," Alex told her as he poured tea, his red hair typhooning on his calm head.

"Last month I healed a cartographer, but I don't remember seeing any Accordia in his memories."

"Like I said, a mite. A mere scintilla of a nation." He retrieved a globe from his headboard. There it was—Accordia—embedded in the folds of Europe. "My old man spent his life prepping to ascend to glory. So, too, did he raise his hapless progeny." Alex did a mannered *sniff!*

"In Accordia?"

"In Cleveland. In a standard subdivision split-level. To outsiders we were a photo-perfect family, but enter that door and you entered aberration. The interior was nouveau medieval: wooden wainscoting, coats of arms, stiff chairs, four-poster beds, Olga and me in our imperial robes. 'Twas absurd; who saw us there anyway? Only Mother and Dad. They never went out; we subsisted off his royal allowance. We were to act charitable to our peasant neighbors but in private to carp snootily. Dad carried a sword at home, in case he ever needed to ward off the proles."

"So that's how you know fencing."

"And polo, and how to say cheese from a coach, and how to gather intelligence to detect burgeoning rebellions."

"But *you're* not snooty."

"I never bought that genes-is-destiny, scepter-in-your-blood folderol. I used to sneak out to shoot baskets, go to blues clubs. I coveted facial hair. . . . All very unprincely. Olga lapped up the royalty rap, and I witnessed the consequences. Always wearing those Accordian robes—"

"With swords?"

"With accordions. That's where they come from. Traditional royal regalia consisted of an imperial mantle with capelet, cordon, and full-size squeeze box strapped to the front. We may not have won any wars, but our nobility sure could play a mean polka. Anyhows, Olga capitulated entirely. She still resides at home, still wears that doofus-assed regalia."

"What does she do?"

"A lot of glowering from the window. Sometimes she yells at neighborhood kids."

"So you made the decision to walk away from your title and become an architect?"

"No. I said to myself, 'Alex, you'd better learn to like yourself for *you*, rather than what you *do* or *will be* or are *told* you are.' *That* was the decision. Then I pursued my whim and came to architecture. But someday maybe I'll do something else."

"So you don't see yourself as an architect?"

"Perish the thought!"

"An ex-prince? A Scrabble buff?"

"Alex—that's how I see myself. Alex, impure and unsure, warts and all. Now, that's enough of this. You like the blues?"

"You bet."

He nodded toward the electric guitar that was strapped high up inside the dome. "Mississippi Delta blues, Memphis blues, Chicago blues, boogie woogie, R and B, or British blues?"

"You really know your blues! Umm—how about a hybrid?"

He leaned toward the carpet and found a stray sneaker, which he hook-shot toward the red sunburst Telecaster. With a *bloing!* the shoe bounced off the middle pickup, and then the strings began twanging themselves. A kick-your-piss-off blues belted into the room, a cross between B.B. King and John Mayall.

"Player guitar. Acquired in a blues club on a trade for my accordion. Where you hit determines the tune."

"The instructions said to throw a *shoe?*"

"Instructions? Hearty har-har. Give Alex instructions and you give him the key, but this had nothing in writing. I had to do the old try and error, which led to the whack-it approach."

One more dive to the bedside. This time he fished out his harmonica and began playing along. She grinned. With his free hand, he drew her ringed fingers near. She stroked the vibrating metal, felt his breath blasting out. Then he parted her legs and aimed his solo into her. His beard blustered up; her inner thighs trilled. She lay back. Her knee bumped the globe; the globe rolled to the floor. This man knew more than the blues. This man knew the cure.

"Grandma! I've fallen in love!"

"Oh, wonderful! Magnificent!"

"All this time I've been giving and giving. Now finally the one-way street is two-way. I'm so happy!"

"He is a good man?"

"Yes. And funny and curious and spirited and passionate."

"I have hoped for such a moment! Congratulations! Every day must feel like a celebration! But—I need to ask you—does he know about your gift?"

"Well, sure."

"Do you still plan to use it?"

"Yeah."

"He does not mind?"

"He's not ecstatic about it, but he says if I feel good about it, that's what counts."

"So will you keep traveling about?"

"Sort of. I'll keep coming back to his house."

"My. He sounds like a very special man."

"He is. He comes from this amazing background—and you

know, it's made me wonder about myself. I realized I don't know much. For starters, what was my grandfather like?"

"Your who? Why do you ask?"

"I know so little about my family history. Who was he?"

"That time is over. This is the time to talk about you."

"I *am* talking about me. My grandfather is part of me. I want to know about him. You and him."

"He passed through my life, zoom-zoom. Nice while he was here, and then he was gone. Now what makes me feel good is the Home. That and you, my little peppercorn, seeing you do so much. I need no more to feel good. Now, back to your man—"

"Hold on."

"Hold on for what? What more is there to say?"

"A lot. What did he look like? What did he do?"

"It is not important."

"But it is to me."

"I do not wish to go into it."

"Why?"

"I berate myself enough already."

"Did he treat you badly?"

"No."

"Was he married?"

"No!"

"Then what was wrong?"

"Some things are better left unsaid."

"*What* things?"

"Let us speak of other matters now."

"But what was his name? What was he like? How long were—"

"I cannot—"

"Grandma, please. Just a little?"

"I must get off this phone now."

"Right *now?*"

"Yes. Kim has just fallen off her bike. May this man be as good

Rachel Simon

in the future as he is at this moment. I kiss you over the phone—
mmwah! I must go. I am sorry. Very sorry. Call me soon."

—Tape recording

One month spilled into another, and another. Celeste took "business trips" from Alex that lasted a day, a week—great spasms of
healing that she wrote up in her journals as Loretta found their way
back to the familiar suburban Washington main drag, cruised past
corporate centers and condominiums, shopping malls and schools,
until they reached the incongruous, blink-and-you'll-miss-it dirt
road that snaked off the suburban strip into a patch of woods. Yes,
Loretta, there really can be woods in the suburbs. A quick swerve
into oak and walnut, a quick return to visibility, and a quarter mile
later, in a clearing far from the road, they pulled up to the glass-
bottle house, where a top-hatted Alex shot baskets near the front
porch, his player guitar wailing inside, and Celeste closed her journal and bolted from the car, and into his house they went, onto his
futon, lighting candles and sipping tea and yakking up the who,
what, when, where, how, and then of her new adventures, until they
set aside the words to make love.

Alex enjoyed her stories (let's face it: you can't listen to a hard-
driving hosanna of pump and heal without feeling a little tweak in
your trousers), but he was later to get in a lather over whether he'd
made an error at this time. He'd told her he wasn't gaga over her
dedication to her gift, but he'd told her only ½ of why, which was
—big surprise, green-eyed readers—that her dedication sometimes
set the pointer surging on his jealousy scales. But the other ½ he'd
censored out: that it was a bit, well, obsessive. Celeste defined herself by her gift—it was how she, in her words, "justified" her existence. She was not *Celeste* but *Celestesexualhealer.* How would she
cope, Alex stewed, if age, or AIDSphobia, or whatever, made her

212

sexual allure lose potency? He fidgeted at the idea of her becoming a sexual-healer version of his dad and sis, a Miss Havisham of seduction, scrabbling at a rigor mortised self-image because she'd never learned to like herself for just being *her,* as distinct from what she *did*—which meant (and here he did an arctic *brrr*) as distinct from the way she'd been conditioned to think at the umbilicus of her highest esteem, the Home. Sometimes he wondered if she'd learned its lessons too well and if the day would come when she'd reinspect them and find her own doubt coating its *shoulds.*

But knowing no one introspects before her time, Alex told himself to keep his trap shut. Instead, he tried the subtle strategy of urging Celeste to develop other aspects of herself—and of *them.* They built an aviary in his house for the birds, stripped each other bare in poker, learned to cut gems for her rings, jogged around his property, played matchmaker between Loretta and his Volvo. He even tried to learn invisibility (though had to measure his success in fingers, he was so inept at it).

Mostly, however, he simply encouraged her to talk. About the Home, about her thoughts, about her sexventures. And being more curious than jealous, he'd want whole tales, A to Z. If she casually referenced some ear-wiggling car mechanic in Tulsa, for instance, Alex would inquire away until he'd scarfed up every how and memory—and then ask if she'd had any other jaunts with similarly afflicted individuals.

"You bet," she'd usually reply, and skip out to Loretta's trunk, wherein were stashed many journals of postcoital musings. Back to the house she'd run, and read Alex entries aloud. They were like nothing he'd ever heard, informative and arousing at the same time, and often he'd get so caught up and she so giddy that she'd read more and more and they'd make love and read more and she would postpone her next adventure until tomorrow.

One day, when he perched one of his Stetsons on her head, she was reminded of a cowboy she'd duked in Texas. "Can you dig him up?" Alex asked, and from the entry learned how to lasso a dogie, brand a bovine, find *some*thing to like in country-and-western music, and do a Flapjack Fanny, an esoteric sexual move.

"What would you think," he asked after Celeste returned the notebook to Loretta's trunk, "of setting these tales in print?"

"You serious?"

"Educational erotica! They'd make for sublime reading."

"They would?"

"Plus, they're already composed. It's an author's fondest paradise! All that's needed is a stint at the typewriter!"

"No one would publish these things."

"What? Did I hear no? Well, I happen to have a buddy who runs a small press out in Boulder. Yellow Brick Press. Next you're out there, you could investigate the phone book and see."

Celeste paused. Put her words between covers? It was a boffo suggestion. Imagine: her fairy tales might wake millions from their sleep! (Or at least give them a hardback aphrodisiac.) But the snag was, her life finally felt *normal*—the maximal normal she was likely to get—and *positively* more normal than if she published her sexual goings and comings.

"Nah," she said. "My life's perfect just the way it is."

Alex could have let it pass. He was going to—he knew we don't see anything till we're ready to polish our opera glasses—but for some reason he let his trap crack open. He said, "*Is* it? Or is your life the way your grandmother told you it *should* be?"

"What's *that* supposed to mean?" Her tone stung like ice, and he realized too late that he'd just launched their first spat.

"I mean, maybe it's perfect, but maybe there are many perfects—you know? She doesn't have a monopoly on perfect."

Celeste glared at him.

He stammered, "I mean, you don't have to do what Edwina s—"

"You'd better stop attacking my grandmother."

"I wasn't. I simply thought you might—" He flicked his gaze

away from her, and bowed out of her blind spot while the bowing was still good. "Beg pardon," he said. "I misspoke myself, as I do from time to time. No disrespect intended."

The apology proved to be an instant elixir; as soon as he uttered the words, her glare un-Jekylled and sweetness dawned again in her face. "Okay." She nodded. Then she leaned forward and delivered a kiss. Alex was taken by surprise, but tasting no bygones in her pucker, he set aside the quarrel himself, and the lovers cut loose in a naked improvisation of rhythm and lead.

Thus were publication and grandma forgotten, and thus dissolved their only fight. Which was exactly, wouldn't you know, the way Celeste wanted it. Her life had at last achieved happily ever after. She wasn't about to let anything nix it.

But unbeknownst to her, and to her redheaded prince, there was a force much greater than any romantic tiff that was raring to nix it but good. The Gacy Guru was waging a war, and if triumph meant Celeste lost her pleasant existence, tough titties. They'd *all* lose their pleasant existences if he won. Besides, Celeste was the trump card he'd been hoping for; the bomb he would make implode. *Thank you, my brother!* he chuckled as he drew up his three-point plan in the Temporary Zero-Zero. After so many millennia—*Fuck us dead!*—finally victory was near.

And so the Gacy Gurrru sent me to Washington. To a bakerrry. He said, *They'll put you up. You can work in the kitchen until.* Until what, I want to ask, but this is one guy I don't ask anything. I just pack my bag, and off I go.

—Gravely Beaks, in Broadway production
The Baffle or the Bust

• • •

Throughout most of his forty-nine years of life, Vice President Stinkweed had revered his potty breaks. Everywhere he'd lived, every job he took, he thought of the bathroom as one would a place of worship. At regular hours, he took polite leave of his company and entered this sanctum sanctorum, hands empty but for the rosary of a newspaper, lips sealed for silent prayer. He was never to be disturbed, even if the President had one foot on the banana peel. Family and colleagues waited patiently, calculating the problem was alimentary, my dear Watson: he was simply a bit more anally discreet than most of us. But in truth the quirk had nothing to do with the end products of mastication and everything to do with another, more humiliating, matter.

With his breezeproof hair and skin just the right shade of white and blue eyes that twinkled sweet nothings, Vice President Jefferson Stinkweed ("Buck" to his friends) was attractive in that blandsome politician way. When it came to vision, he trod the fine line between vehemence and vacillation. Indeed, this varsity fullback, high school prez, average IQ scorer, distinguished military sycophant, party-line senator, zealous Hooterville fan, and happy family man had worked so hard at being "one of us" that nobody, not even his wife (the only soul who knew he sucked his thumb in his sleep), guessed that he carried a secret, a malfunction of body that had begun with his first political lie and ever since had filled him with shame and self-loathing and made him cherish the john more than anything in the world.

Because in the john, after he set aside the newspaper prop, removed his belt, unfolded the hidden seal in the back, and withdrew his oral hygiene kit (the one his mother, rest her soul, had had specially made when she'd discovered there was no remedy), he could go at it: shear off the newly sprung whiskers that taunted him from the glistening mucous membrane of his gums and the insides of his cheeks and his tongue and the dangling pendulum of his uvula. How he hated it! Why couldn't he have greasy palms, like normal politicians? Or something the pharmacological conglomerates had found cures for, like dandruff? No: *he* had to have the heartbreak of mouth hair; he could barely make it through an hour without a trim. And if he left it a whole day? Hair would wiggle through his teeth, pour out of his mouth, cascade down his lips, gush onto his chin—until his mouth resembled a frothing armpit or, dare he admit it, that other hairy hub of bodily functions—and then his words would get trapped in the thicket, and his party would drop even lower in the polls (if that was remotely possible), and he would be vilified from coast to coast, wouldn't even be able to go out and buy a goddamn newspaper without evoking guffaws, and would be left to decay, alone with his floss and his tweezers. Forever persecuted for not taking it off, taking it all off. So Stinkweed had been forced to acquire the habit of continually rubbing his hand across his mouth to check for stubs, which he did so expertly it looked as if he were brushing his fingers over his lips in thought. He didn't enjoy this habit—it was hardly presidential—but at least it kept him safe from discovery.

Years ago, Stinkweed learned to make the most of his private prunings by having a TV installed beside the can. This enabled him to stay plugged into the heartburn of America as well as, once he'd been recruited by a high-placed Matricist, to reach out and touch the Gacy Guru. The TV was also the way the Gacy Guru knew about Stinkweed, but Stinkweed was not aware of that. Like all good Matricists, he'd chortled when he'd learned that members of the Matrix spoke to each other, and their fearless leader, over the television— but like all good Matricists, Stinkweed had no idea that TV was used to keep an eye on *him*. On *everyone*. He thought contact was initiated by sound, not sight, and besides, as far as he knew, the Gacy Guru was on the Matrix's side. How could Stinkweed have guessed the Gacy Guru had only one side to be on. Which was not the Matrix, not the *nths* (which Stinkweed didn't even know about). The only side the Gacy Guru was on was the Gacy Guru's.

But to return to our program. On a dreary, gray morning, six months into Celeste's love life, Stinkweed was in the private throne room off his White House office, shaving a nasty snarl that had just erupted on the inside of his lip, watching Arnold the Pig give Oliver conniptions, when he heard the Guru High Whine.

Stinkweed lowered his razor. The High Whine. Screeching from the TV like Edith screeching for Archie. Audible only to those with Matrix training. It was one of the two TV sounds that demanded, *Listen up!* The Low Whine meant a group conference. But this was the High Whine. That meant a personal message.

Instantly, Stinkweed snatched his Crystal Cup from a secret compartment inside the TV and clamped on the mouthpiece. Then he adjusted his vision to Channel Zero. Most TV viewers didn't know Channel Zero existed, but it was readily accessible, after one took a lesson in seeing between the two hundred fifty thousand spots of color that made up the TV picture. Stinkweed peered at the box, swishing and spitting away the last stubs of oral beard. Arnold the Pig faded, and the Gacy Guru came on.

There he was. The Head Honcho. The one who created the Matrix. Bigger than 86's Chief, the Angels' Charlie, the Prisoner's Number 1. Bigger even than the President himself.

"Yes?" Stinkweed said, focusing on the TVs in the Guru's eyes.

We have found something, the Gacy Guru said in that voice that always seemed overcontrolled. *Something that might benefit us both.* And then the Gacy Guru explained about Celeste.

Euphoria ejaculated into Stinkweed's veins as his leader elaborated. This was it! A hooker who'd been mascoted by some lunatic, quasi-religious fringe! Exactly the kind of scapegoat his speechwriters had been searching for! It could be his party's answers to its political woes! Yabba dabba doo!

"Well," Stinkweed said when the Gacy Guru finished, "I think we can arrange something."

Today, the Gacy Guru added, in his halting fashion. *There will not be much competing news today. Strike now.*

How the Gacy Guru could predict this would be a meager news day, Stinkweed didn't know, but the guy had a spotless record for such details. This was one of the main reasons he was so respected—and feared. He was a man of superhuman qualities.

So Stinkweed returned to his office and, as the Gacy Guru had urged, buzzed the speechwriters, and later that day, while addressing a meeting of Suburbanites for the Status Quo, the Vice President shot off the first volley. "It's all about values," he sound-bited, "moral values. What kind of country is this when some Happy Hooker becomes the centerpiece of a new religion?"

He went on, raging about the "new immorality" and how it was responsible for AIDS, crime, and the deterioration of the faces on Mount Rushmore. But it was the Happy Hooker line that clinched it, and when nothing happened in America that day besides the usual 49 murders, 126 rapes, 35 cases of AIDS, 133 car deaths, and 3,000 new teenage smokers, the TV news gave the speech their lead slot. With Stinkweed in one corner decrying Celeste's morals, and the Patchetts in the other extolling her virtues, Celeste was pounded into controversy and so hauled into the Up from Relative Obscurity to Household Name Hall of Fame.

Alex and Celeste learned about the brouhaha the next day. Alex drove to the store to pick up a newspaper and returned home with more than a dozen. "Well, ain't life grand," he said, flinging them on the table. Celeste glanced at the headline of the paper on top: SLUT GODDESS AMONG US. She gaped at the words, and her tea grew cold in her hand.

My dad. Wouldn't let us play with Erector sets or watch the boob tube. Nope, merriment in the Popoverovitch house meant mastering Accordian spying. Codes, infiltration, surveillance. "Vee royalty zhould know effery dirty trick," he told us, "so vee can nip any coup in zhe bud." By seven, I could peek unseen from behind a portrait; by ten, decipher Caesar's renowned code alphabet; by thirteen, jiggle open a multitumbler lock.

When Stinkweed's harangue hit the fan, Celeste banged the table and said, "That's it. Time to learn about my enemy," and told me she wanted to gather intelligence on the Matrix. Could we infiltrate some gathering, weasel our way into their circle? Sure, my lady, but since she wanted to do it invisible—*and* have me along—we had a small plight, because despite her instructions, I'd been downright doltish at invisibility.

But serendipity came to the rescue! Horseradish Smith-Smith, the fifth-richest fart in America, was throwing a Halloween shindig, A-list only, which meant there'd likely be slews of Matricists. For the first time since I was a kid, I exploited my royalty and just like that wangled an invitation.

So we didn't need invisibility. We could simply go, as Loretta put it, *en masque* and hope it worked out from there.

—Alex Popoverovitch, as told to author

A hotel near the White House. Fountains and marble steps sweeping up to an elegant portico garnished with doormen in quasi-Beefeater uniforms; glass vestibule gilded in classical motifs; red-carpeted lobby, soft light above, *GQ*- and *Lear's*ly-attired loungers below; crystal decanters of Perrier and brandy. The wide corridor. The Ming vases. Then: the Grand Ballroom. The bobbing of the moneyed on the dance floor, a band uncovering Moldy Oldies, and everywhere: sprays of feathers, flashes of glitter, hairpieces, masks, taffeta, velvet, silk, lace, perfume costly enough to feed a family for a year, jewelry that could pay for college tuition, power and money and greed and power.

Celeste and Alex gumshoed into the crowd, she in marigold-colored harem pants and bikini top, with black Egyptian wig to hide her prismatic hair; he in harlequin costume with jester hat. Both wore masks. *"Tres bien!"* Loretta had proclaimed before they took off in Alex's Volvo. In the ballroom, Celeste and Alex stayed close, rubbernecking to match faces with pictures they'd seen in the papers—"Look! There's Senator Perkodan!" "And over there, Governor Quissoff!" Senators shook hands with oil magnates who shook hands with cola manufacturers who shook hands with TV network owners. The backs were so well patted they shone. Above, the chandelier, as many-necked as a plague of serpents, showered bright light over the room, baring all shadows—which virtually everyone, Celeste told Alex, was reading.

"Everyone?"

"Not spouses. Most of them have no idea this is going on."

After one circumnavigation, they broke apart, hoping solo snooping would net more dirt. Alex tried to hob his way into a nob of ITEL chairpersons, only to get snared by a swizzle-sticked lobbyist who tried to cajole him into posing for a liquor ad.

Celeste, meanwhile, wound through the whirl of chiffon and gloves and masks and sequins, straining to hear inside nearby bodies. But with the wangbong*whatareyousaying*dingblat*myhusband-thinks*biffting*andthedow* din in the room, she couldn't penetrate the subtleties of internal thought. And given the barrage of perfumes, her olfactory skills were just as useless.

She roamed about awhile, thwarted and blue, until, at the culmination of her frustration, she did a time-out. Near the kitchen she sat, at a lonely table. She adjusted her wig. She'd *have* to scrap the synsensing to powwow face-to-face, and this was hardly an easy task.

Think about it: she was a nobody with an average shadow. Why should Mr. and Ms. Big blab to her about secrets a nobody can't know? She was just about to select a curse to mutter over her breath about this very dilemma when a scowl-mouthed waiter swung by with an almost empty tray. "Caviar canapé?" he asked, offering the remaining nibble.

She deselected her curse and took the nibble. Without smile or eye contact, the waiter gave his head a horse toss to throw back his dark hair, then strode to the kitchen, his walk a cocky lean-to. More to test her hearing than to probe the waiter, Celeste lackadaisically listened inside him—and so almost burst her bra when, droning beneath the polyphony of *Fuck that boss/Better do at least a fifty tonight/*Love Boat *on at break,* she heard two words like moaning eels: "Gaaacccy willlinnnggg."

Her caviar fell splat on the floor.

Moments later, the waiter butted back out of the kitchen, bearing a tray of wineglasses, and stalked into the costumed crowd. This was her only lead. She crept after him.

The waiter paused at a trio of faux Scrooges and offered the wine. He was young and petite, with a Ren & Stimpy earring and a heavy-lidded glare and pursed lips and—

And he was *not* reading any shadows!

Impossible! He knew the Guru, and the Guru did Shadow Reading! So why didn't *he*? But—but—how could a *waiter* be in the Matrix anyway? Hadn't that clerk at the fair, that file clerk who knew about the Matrix—hadn't he learned that Matrix members were on the in side of influential? And what waiter's influential?

Then something happened that took Celeste's tizzy and raised it to vertigo: as Scowl Boy ambled about, offering the bubbly, he leaned too close to some of the biggest Mr. Bigs, and lickety-split, and with detect-defying dexterity, he—he—*he picked their pockets!*

A Matricist ripping off his own kind? No way! But there it was. A fifty from Mrs. Gordon Knot. Two hundred from Mr. Smith-Smith himself. And every victim fully unwitting, because though the waiter's shadow was as fouled as the worst of them, no one deigned to glance at his; after all, he was only a waiter.

So when Scowl Boy took his break, you know Celeste followed.

He shambled down the lawn to a fountain, sat, and pulled something from his pocket. Removing her mask, Celeste stormed after him, huffing, "It's such bullshit in there! Such pomposity!" and plunked herself hyperbolically beside him.

He was watching *The Love Boat* on a Watchman. He glanced up.

"I'm sorry," she said, her voice steeped in character. "You're a waiter here, aren't you? I interrupted your break."

"Yeah," he said. He returned to his show. Gopher was stumbling over a bikinied cliché. The laugh track activated.

Celeste said, "I'm a guest here and I can't stand it, but you must *really* hate it. Rich people pretending to have fun."

He turned his head her way. His name was in white script on his uniform. George.

"Did you get to try any of the food, George?"

"No perks," he said. "It sucks."

She said, "Yeah, but when the night ends, you get to go home. *I* have to keep up the farce. My daddy's *just* so rich."

His heavy lids did a Richard Simmons push-up. He eyed all of her suddenly, breasts to toe. "But bucks ease the pain."

"That's true." She zeroed her hearing inside him. He was babbling about her jugs and knocking down the bank of her V.

It was a frenetic, familiar sound—the falsetto of hopped-up hormones—but she could listen till the cows came home and not advance her Matrix education one credit unless George thought, on some level, about the Gacy Guru. And unless he obliged randomly (possible but so far no cigar), or she queried him outright (*sure!*), the only way she'd get info was—

Except, George was light-years away from healing. But probably everyone in the Matrix was. And, Celeste decided, if she didn't ditch her nicey-nice rules in order to yentz somebody knowledgeable, she'd have to do a lot of cloak-and-dagger work to learn even the most rudimentary info.

"How long's your break?" she asked.

He looked at her with $EXed-up eyes. "Half hour."

She lifted his hand off the Watchman and set it down in a different place.

"Great," she said. "That's long enough."

Tonight, the Gacy Gurrru told me, and then descrrribed wherrre to find the carrr. I wrrrapped up the figurrres I'd baked and made my way to the glass house.

Maybe that Dodge was animated, but you'd neverrr guess. It just sat, quiet as can be, while I did what I had to do to it.

—Gravely Beaks, in Broadway production
The Baffle or the Bust

Canned goods crammed to the ceiling, smell of Danish, of bread in wicker baskets, radio playing at the register but no customers today so I run upstairs and Uncle Jocko's in black and Pop's in tears and "Your mother's dead, George," and now what is little Georgie going to do? Come learn Parcheesi, Georgie. Come learn the cash register. (Whisper: Why can't the boy learn?) *Why can't you learn, stupid?* Jonny Quest, Winky-Dink. First grade twice. The bruiser in third grade shoving my head in tuna salad till I hand up the change. The girl in fifth grade not kissing me at Spin the Bottle and me showing her what for. George of the Jungle, they call me. I can crunch Coke cans in one fist, see? Can hock Good & Plenty. Can hock leather coats. Ninja Turtles, MTV. My pitbull, Bob. My knife, Fred. A prick in the bush is worth two in the hand. The shooter salesguy. My first semi. Kills bugs dead. The drive to Chicago. Hotel register, fake name. The jewelry store, walk in, owner goes white when I pull out my machine. I'm dumping out the drawer when UPS guy comes in. Piss timing. One bang and he's down. I stand over. Blood out his eye. Then—the alarm! Heart pounding, snot streaming, frantic, sweat, claw through street, next block, over fence, down alley, leaping over trash, bums, onto roof. Huh—huh —slip into my hotel. Hide. Here. Never find me here. Good. Sit down. Put on tube. *Gilligan's Island.* Good. But then—suddenly it's not Ginger. It's a guy in a brown polyester blazer, Class A couch potato, staring out the tube. Some asshole ad, huh? Only he says, *Hello, George.* I almost shit! He's pudgy, bald, your average Sears shopper type, except for two things. One's his skin's blue, faint, like he's cold. Two's his eyes. They're dark, and the deeper you look, the less color you see. Instead, you see TVs, maybe a hundred, reflecting in his eyes, each playing a different show. I grab the remote. *No need,* he says. *We're on every channel.* I flip through. Sure as shit. I throw the remote. I shake. He smiles this smile that's calm and fierce at once and says, *Our name is the Gacy Guru, and we will get you off the hook if you come to work for us.*

I say, "Fuck off."

He laughs. *We have been watching you, George Goode.*

"How do you know my name?"

His smile tastes like bad fish. He says, *We have our ways.*

"Go watch someone else."

Hear our proposal first.

Outside, squad cars screaming. Not screaming for me, I hope. Couldn't be. Better not be.

He says, *We want you to come work for us. To become an* nth.

"What the hell is that?"

It stands for the indefinite number that changes every equation it's added to.

"Fuck math. I flunked math."

It is not math. It is what we call individuals who . . . how shall we put it—he pauses, blinks his TV eyes—*throw a wrench into the quaint notion of law and order.*

The cars are getting closer. Must've got my number!

Nths *are the criminal element no one expects. The mugger on the subway, the rapist from the hedges, the robber in your house, the killer with no motive*—

"I'm not doing no one in."

You already have, Georgie Porgie. But as you wish. If we play our cards right, they will do themselves in anyway.

Some of this makes sense, some don't. Outside, cars wailing up the street. I say, "What's in it for me?"

He says, *Lessons. Power. Money.* Cop radio going outside in the parking lot. I try not to move. He adds, *And protection.*

They're here for me. I know it.

Say yes and we'll remove them.

I go to window. Four squad cars. Cop talks on radio—"Suspect in UPS shooting in Mermaid Hotel. Heading in now."

This is it. I go to the bed, grab my semi. I could wait right here. I might get one—but they'll get me. No doubt. Not a single doubt. Stupidfuck me. It's an easy choice. He stares out from the TV. Cops charging inside. Shouts on the stairs.

"Yeah," I tell him.

Cop radio suddenly says, "Suspect in UPS shooting found dead in store. Hold off pursuit. You've got the wrong man."

Cops stop, hobo takes the rap, and I got jewelry in my pocket. And left on the screen: an invitation. To the lessons he talked about. In a store across town. After hours.

That night I go. It's one of them Castle of Values places; they look like papier-mâché castles but inside are like Kmart. Only, at night here it's Crime College. He teaches tricks you'd never guess.

Shows how to do it and not get caught. Classmates pop up later in the paper: the Dweeb Stalker, Mack the Hacker. He says we got just this once to learn, then we're on our own—cut loose from him and from each other too. We may all be called *nths*, but we ain't no organized group. He tells us he watches us on TV, that's how he knew about each of us. Can see anywhere, anytime. Surveillance on the world. Thanks to the grace of Gacy—he teaches us to say that. He teaches us a lot. When class is over, I go to shake his hand. The other guys are waiting to leave, and he takes hold of my hand. His fingers are cold as my mother's corpse, but I don't say that, I say the one thing I've been wondering, I say, "Hey, who do you work for?"

We do not work for anyone.

"But you always talk about 'we.' "

That is because we are so numerous now.

"Well, you seem kind of familiar."

We love knowing our reputation has preceded us.

"What reputation? I never heard of no Gacy Guru."

Perhaps you know our other names.

"What are they?"

Well, we are often referred to as Lucifer—

!#$(#)*#%(*(*$#%&@&^!@(&$(*#%(+!@(*#(*$(*$#(@_*!_
!@*#(*$(*#!

"*W*hat're you doing?"

Celeste is disengaging their bodies. She's hauling on her pants. She's kicking open the limo door. George's up on his elbows, shouting, screaming, "Hey! What're you doing?!"

She's bolting through the parking lot.

"No one runs out on George!"

She runs.

"You bitch! You fucking bitch!"

Alex was lounging in the ballroom, munching celery near the piano, when he spied Celeste. She was hailing him from the doorway, and as he scrambled toward her he sensed from the strain in her face that serious business was afoot.

She seized his hand, and they ducked into a linen closet, and there, with the sheets as their audience and hyperventilation as her backup band, Celeste blurted out the freaky truth.

"Whoa! The *Devil?* Horns and everything?"

"He doesn't look like that. But that's who he is."

"Truly? How can you be certain?"

"He told this George guy his name was Lucifer."

"I never fancied old Beelzebub was for real."

"Me neither. But there he is."

"Which means the Matrix is run by the Devil?"

"Yeah! But that's only one of his games. The Matrix is just for the guys in power. He has a whole other operation for lowlife. The *nths.* That's what this waiter was trained as. *Nths* do crime—vile crime. Like serial murder."

"So the Matrix is in league with Mack the Hacker?"

"No. The two groups don't know about each other. Actually, the *nths* aren't even a *group.* They may get trained as a group, but after graduation they never talk to each other—or their leader—again. They just skulk around as individuals, bashing innocent people."

"Do the *nths* know who the Gacy Guru really is?"

"Not most of them, and not *any* of the Matricists. They just see him the way they see everyone—as a tool. Give the Guru devotion and you get what you want. That's all they care about."

Alex shook his head in a stun. " 'Tis incredible."

" 'Tis screwed up!"

He took her in his arms, and for a long moment, a moment of jolt settling in, and dread swelling out, and images of the forked-tail one flitting through their minds, neither prince nor healer could speak.

Finally, she whispered, "I wish I didn't know this."

"Amen," he added.

But then she appended a statement he couldn't amen. One she'd hinted at the night they met in the diner.

She said, "I hate this gift."

He loosened his hug and looked into her eyes.

She went on. "I hate it. I hate what it's shown me. I don't *want* to know there's a Devil. I don't *want* to know there's spiritual illness. I want to be like everyone else."

Alex paused before responding, the memory of their one and only spat flashing DANGER in his head. He calculated rapidly. Yeah, she'd hit the ceiling that time, but this was different. Number one: They'd made up. Number two: She was gouging at herself only because her discovery was too hot to face. Number three: She wouldn't get hung up on this shit when the real enemy'd just raised its pointed little head. So betake yourself to speak, he told himself; it's safe this time to reply.

All you goodhearted Charlies out there, hold your tongues. We sympathize with your wanting to whoop *Don't do it!* at the page. But alack, lads and lasses, Alex can't hear you; this story's already become history. What good will it do to remind him that ourself is our most sensitive topic—press that button and *anything* can happen. Because, as we know, anything *did.*

Alex said, "Celeste, it's not a life necessity that you keep being a sexual healer. You could abdicate your dedication."

"No." Celeste sighed. "I couldn't."

"Certainly you could. It's a splendid gift, but a full life would be possible without it."

"No. I *couldn't*."

"Why not?"

"I'm to be a knight of the world."

"Is that so? Or are you to be Celeste?"

She blinked. "Are you saying you want me to stop?"

"Only if you wish to."

Ice coating every word: "But you'd like me to."

"Honestly? Indeed I would, but that's not the point."

Arms crossed over chest. "So you admit you're jealous."

"You've known that. But what I'm addressing here is—"

"I *can't* stop!"

"I see it that you don't *want* to. Which is okay. I just—"

"Not want! *Can't!*"

"You have many facets. We all do. And you can choose to focus on another one. You know what they say—overspecialization leads to Chapter Eleven."

No laugh. "I wouldn't be able to face myself if I stopped."

"But you just declared that you hate it."

"It's who I am!"

"No. It's what you *do*."

Defensiveness flooded her face. Defensiveness, Alex suddenly caught on, directed at himself, not the Gacy Guru.

"Look," he said, fumbling quickly for damage control, "fighting tonight is not my goal. My only point is, if you need to take a break, take a break. That's all I'm saying."

Silence. She narrowed her eyes at him.

"Celeste, it really doesn't matter to me. I love you no matter what you're doing." Her face remained tight, and in his haste to squash the quarrel, he found himself veering away from wisdom and sense, careening onto that tricky road marked Keep Talking, Stupid, and skidding into the spectacularly insensitive question: "But what I can't help wondering is, do *you* love you?"

A stunned hurt rose in her eyes, then immediately chilled into anger. She made to respond but, too outraged to speak, spun around and whipped open the door.

It was turning out to be a very bad day for our beloved Celeste. Poor girl. Turmoil and misdirected fury filled her to the brim. She scampered back alone to her lover's house in tears. Tears! Doesn't your heart just bleed.

But hold the hankies. One more mine still lies in wait. By midnight, target should step on mine, and if you felt this day was bad, just stay tuned: it's about to get infinitely worse.

—Gacy Guru, videotaped memoir,
And You Thought It Was Just Paranoia

She'd leave town. That's it. Pack up Loretta and vamoose. Then there'd be no facing Alex, no nonsense to answer. Him and his idealism. What did he know. She had to get out. Maybe for a day. Maybe a month. She wouldn't heal, no; no more of that. She'd contemplate, that's right. Hash it out with Loretta, with the Gregorian voices if they happened by. Or the leaves. She'd cogitate and ruminate and let this storm die inside her, think it over, write it over, see where the drifts came to sit.

The metro and a brisk run transported Celeste to the glass dome before the Volvo had delivered Alex. She scrambled across the lawn, thinking about what to pack. Loretta sat visible in the drive. "Taking off in ten," Celeste called out to the Dodge, and reached behind the porch steps for Alex's extra keys.

"*Pardon,*" Loretta replied, "but Celeste?"

"What?"

"I had a visitor."

Celeste paused.

"He carried a box of toys. He put some on me."

Celeste froze. "Who? Who was he?"

Loretta said, "A dwarf."

The keys clattered to the ground.

"He's gone now."

Celeste ripped down the drive. "Are you all right?"

"Perfectly fine."

"Did he leave them on you?"

"Oui."

"Show me."

Loretta turned on her lights.

Celeste peered at the thingamajiggy jungle, inventorying the familiar creatures. The frogs, the werewolves, the tigers, the spiders, the griffins, the goblins, the gas lights, the gliders—

And then she spotted the newcomers. By the windshield.

She stepped closer.

Half a dozen new figures: red men with horns and pitchforks grinned up at her, snake-tongue tails merrily erect.

They were a platoon of devils.

"He's taunting me," Celeste said, and then saw they were somehow unlike the other toys. She bent lower, and even with the colored glazes, she could make out that these dolls were porous.

They looked as if they had texture.

They looked as if they were made of bread.

And that's when she saw, in the center of all the others, the one exception. It was glazed bread, but it was not a devil. It was a replica of a bridal sculpture, the kind that decorates a wedding cake. A short woman in a bridal gown and, beside her, a groom. Only, there *was* no groom. It was simply a cloak; no body was inside.

Celeste leaned over the hood, zooming in for a closer look—

And jumped back.

The face on the bride was Miss Kelly's.

"What is this?"

"What is what, my little caraway seed?"

"This thing I found on my car!"

"What are you talking about?"

"On my car. On Loretta. Gravely Beaks came by my house— *Alex*'s house—and glued some toys on her, toys made out of bread, like what Monkey used to make, the guy who's my *father?* And one of the toys was a wedding cake decoration—you know, the couple on top of the cake. And guess what, Grandma? The bride is you."

"Me? Well, that's . . . flattering."

"But what about this? Explain this: the groom has no body."

"He what?"

"He's a coat with no body! And all the other dolls were little devils. What is this? What does all this mean?"

"I—"

"Don't walk away from this! *I* can't walk away. Tell me."

"You don't want to know, Celeste."

"I want to know."

"No. I feel such shame."

"Why?"

"No."

"Tell me, or I'll never call you again."

"Don't do that. Never bargain with love."

"Tell me!"

"Celeste, it is terrible to make bargains."

"Do it. Now."

". . . Celeste. It was when I was on a cruise. On a vacation. That is what the sculpture refers to. How he knew about that, I don't—"

"Knew about what?"

"The man! The man!"

"My grandfather."

"Forgive me, Celeste. I had nothing."

"What did you do? What happened?"

"He came to me, he came, he was nice and funny, and on a ship in the middle of an ocean anything can happen, anything at all."

"What did he look like?"

"He was tall, Celeste. Brown hair. Dark eyes."

"And what happened?"

"Celeste, Celeste, I am not strong. I would have traded anything to taste life, to feel joy once again. I would have said yes to any bargain—"

"What did you bargain?"

"I didn't mean—"

"What did you bargain!"

"I didn't know what he was! Don't think the worst. I didn't know if he was good or evil, but when he asked what I would give to feel joy again—Celeste, his name was the Ultra-Other. Is that the name of God, Celeste? Is it the name of the Devil?"

"What did you give him? What did you trade to feel joy?"

"I traded *you*, Celeste."

"What?!"

"He said, 'The debt can be handled on a long-term basis.' But when nothing happened to Marina, I forgot about it. Then she died and you brought her back and then I saw he was collecting—"

"You traded *me?*"

"Yes."

"You traded my *life?!*"

"I didn't know what it would mean!"

"How could you? You always looked down on selfishness!"

"Celeste, you must understand."

"You taught me—all of us—to surrender our lives to others, discover ourselves for others! But—here you did the most selfish thing you could have done! You gave me to the Devil!"

"I didn't believe in the Devil! I didn't—"

"But I just saw him! He's running the entire world!"

"Celeste, I'm sorry. Maybe it was not him! Maybe it was the other one, the better one—"

"Sure. Only the Devil makes deals, Grandma. Only the Devil would give the gift of sex."

"Forgive me, Celeste. I didn't know—"

"It all makes sense now."

"Maybe you are jumping to conclusions. Maybe—"

"How could you? How could you!"

"I didn't mean to! I'm so sorry. I—"

(*Line disconnected.*)

—Tape recording

No packing a suitcase.

No retrieving her birds.

No penning a note.

Just rage and horror and confusion and hurt.

She dove into her car.

They shot down the drive.

She sobbed and she seethed.

And then she went berserk.

The Story of the Sea

Day Three   Dawn

In the steaming bathroom on the cruise ship, the stranger smiles at Edwina. She lies naked in the bathtub, knowing he can see all of her, even her misshapen legs. But she is not afraid.

"You will not be sorry you said yes," the stranger tells Edwina. "I will make new nations come from you."

Then he hurls off his long coat. It dissolves into light, brightening the room as it arcs through the air.

His body is beautiful. She can see each muscle and sinew.

He climbs into the bath. When his leg touches the water, the water begins to bubble.

She throws back her head. Seagulls watch from the ceiling.

He kneels above her body and whispers, "Just one more thing. Beware the voices of the air."

She looks quizzically at him.

"Stay far away from them. Then you will be safe."

"I don't understand."

He kisses her in the boiling water. His kiss is exotic, spicy, rich—and with it she knows what he means.

She loses herself in a love she has never known. He lies fully on top of her, and in the middle of a kiss he enters her. Heat fills her body, and they begin to move.

She goes to brace herself, and her hand slices through air.

The porcelain has become dry.

The water has boiled away.

The
Rampage

Early that November, a naked man was found wandering along the Shenandoah River near Funnel Mountain, Virginia. Beside the old factories and boarded-up warehouses, he stumbled like a d.t.'d drunk, eyes dazed and confused, hair askew as a dump of hay. The two nine-year-old boys who came upon him while out fishing crouched behind a weed and watched him shuffle parabolas beside the bank. "He saying something?" they whispered. Weed to weed they crept, dew dotting their shirts and sneakers, till they could hear the naked man's mumbles in the crisp autumn air.

"Oh, oh, oh, oh," he wailed like a mourning dove. "I'm s-s-so sssorrrrry. Never again. No more, no, oh, oh, oh."

They retreated before he discovered them, and skedaddled back to town. The police taking the report thought the guy must be one of those homeless types, except they usually wore clothes. That, or else a camper gone bonkers, which happened all the time. But at that spot? No campers there before; it was too industrial to tempt even the bozos. Four cops hustled to the site, ready with Mace, rope, nightsticks, and loaded rifles. Turned out they were way overarmed. The naked man, on seeing them, simply came toward them, hands out to be cuffed, saying, "I'll do my time, I will, I know what to 'xpect there." They wrapped a coat around him and charged him with indecent etcetera. He was one of their most compliant arrests, easy as a white-collar criminal, sitting quiet in his cell, saying "please" and "thank you" like he was visiting his Aunt Tilly—which was why it was so inconceivable they'd done his fingerprints right. According to the records, these particular swirls and whorls belonged to Joe "Tenderloin" Nelson, the notorious chop-shop baron who'd masterminded the sixfold increase in car thefts in the D.C. area within the last year. "Couldn't be," the Funnel Mountain police declared, but when the D.C. detective who'd been on the case came to town, she took one look at the docile puppy behind the bars and positively ID'd the long-sought-after sucker.

But what was Tenderloin Nelson doing in the hinterlands of Virginia? And *naked*, no less? What could possibly have happened to the six-foot bad-ass who'd so effectively thumbed his nose at police that he'd ordered the theft of *their* cars? No one could figure it, and Tenderloin wasn't saying, not even to his own attorney. "We plead guilty to all counts," the lawyer told the judge. They put Tenderloin away for fifteen, eight with good behavior, and immediately, and much to the authorities' and his wife's bafflement, he established himself as a model prisoner. So model that within a month of his incarceration he was in the prison morgue, victim of a stab wound to the butt, the latest in-house punishment to all presumed brown-nosers.

A few days after Tenderloin turned up on the Shenandoah, another incoherent naked man was found, this time in Macungie, Tennessee. He was sitting astride the copper statue of a historically significant horse in the town square, staring with apparent remorse at morning joggers. A compassionate dog walker, recognizing the man as State Representative Pinkley Beauright, helped him down in an attempt to spare his remaining dignity. Notoriously crotchety, widely rumored to have kept his lock on his job through voter fraud and graft, Beauright played Etch-A-Sketch quietly under an afghan in the dog walker's living room until a clerk came to shuttle him home. Word leaked out, and later that day, Beauright's office issued the statement that the representative was retiring. The official reason was a stroke, though when, the following week, he sold all his belongings for a lump sum, took a bus to the very impoverished area where voting machines chronically broke on Election Day, and personally handed out hundred-dollar bills to the inhabitants—and *then* took up water painting—some wondered if this was actually the case.

The stories of the Virginia crook and the Tennessee politico received media coverage, though if a connection was made at all, it was that they were a rather odd coincidence.

But it became less coincidental as more naked people began popping up. In New Orleans: Fifi Blue, madam extraordinaire, who serviced the Short Dong Silvers of the business sector. In Pudding Patch, Missouri: Clay Lee Jones, local rapist, who'd terrorized the blondes in town. In Margaret, Kansas: the three owners of Americans Against Leukemia, a fake charity, which had bilked well-intentioned donors out of millions. In Aspen, Colorado: Ken Glut, Hollywood producer of slasher flicks.

Over and over, they were found, naked, babbling, confused. Over and over, they would not tell what had happened to them, and instead apologized to those they'd hurt in the past, and set about living a life to make Pollyanna proud.

It was the Patchetts who first publicly voiced what others had wondered. On their cable TV show (Stinkweed's harangue having increased interest in Celeste and thus their viewership, they had graduated from infomercial to their Very Own Show), they pointed out that there had been no sightings of Celeste in ages, and that though these incidents did not follow her MO, all these naked people had been *healed*. Look: a gangster bankrolled a widows' pension fund; a pyromaniac joined Habitat for Humanity. One could only conclude that Celeste was doing this.

The Survivors of Sudden Nudity (as they were called) had never given explanations for their transformations, so the Patchetts urged their followers to be on the lookout. "Perhaps if one of us is the first to assist a survivor, we'll be able to ask the question directly." In other words (given a yes-no proposition instead of the much vaguer *What happened*), a newly created birthday suiter just might cough up the truth.

Finally, the scenario played itself out: Frank Fox, deadbeat dad to seven ragamuffins in three states, was sitting naked on a curb in Nebraska when a fanatic Spiritual Nudist spied him from her window. The Nudist scrambled outside, and while Fox cuddled a stray cat, the inquisitor posed the burning question: Was it Celeste did this to you?

Mr. Fox's "Yes" resounded from coast to coast, prompting a few of the reformed naked babblers to 'fess up as well, and the Patchetts' show, which had moved to cable only a few weeks before, was snatched up by a major network. Because (and even the numskulls among you can dig this) it's one thing to claim that your god heals blundering stumblebums, doleful screwups, repentant boors, aching victims: the folks ready to ask for help. It's another thing altogether to claim that your god takes on the snot of society, the termites of life, the shysters, the swine, the sleazeballs, the wicked—and brings them to their knees.

The Patchetts basked in what they saw as their vindication. They finally built their Pocono getaway, diversified into their own newspaper (*SNM Today*), plated Mahoney's bullets in gold.

As for why Celeste had changed her targets? A god doesn't need to explain herself, the Patchetts preached. But the truth, obvious enough to us now, was that they didn't have a clue. In the whole U.S.A., only one man came close to a clue. That was the harmonica virtuoso and former prince, Alex Popoverovitch.

Since the night when he returned from the party and found no Loretta and no Celeste and only the birds to tattle an incomprehensible (to him) tale, Alex had moped about in his house, unhatted, despondent over losing his love, blaming himself for spawning her flight. Insomnia blossomed. Blueprints grew gray. Then he read about Tenderloin Nelson in the paper, and a solar cell went off in Alex's head. *Could it be . . . ? Yes! It had to!* He tacked the article to a bulletin board, and with each subsequent sighting of a naked person, his theory hardened more firmly into belief.

Celeste, he reasoned, was simply after anyone connected to the Gacy Guru—who was, it seemed, the root of all misery, or at least the more systematic misery. This must be her new MO: she would come upon Matricists or *nths,* and rather than dismiss them for being unhealable, turn on the juice (not hard, given how readily sick shadows got her britches itching). Hotel? Fine. Side road? Take me, I'm yours. But with her synsenses and herculean strength, the trick waited to be turned. At first, she would seem like an easy conquest, young, submissive, her prey unzipping and going at it, she so expertly, so exactly, fitting their every dream, until, just when they thought she was in their power, *just* when they thought she was theirs—womp! Down on your tush, buddy, I control the horizontal around here. Then they'd fall down the rabbit hole of their memories, claw and gasp as they relived all they wanted to forget, all they'd spent their lives making others pay for, and they wouldn't want to be there, but she'd give them no quarter—yet always cooing warm things, stroking them gently: madonna and whore balled up in one. And in the tumble and bramble of memories, these cons and cads would see the error of their ways—and then they would come, exhausted, shocked, ashamed, and she would roll off and leave them alone.

It was a reasonable theory—right on the money, as we know now. But as Alex pinned more articles to his bulletin board, he came to feel jangled; something didn't add up. Not that Celeste was using the gift she claimed to hate—he figured she was so hot and bothered from their fight that she was simply hurtling herself at her work. No, what bugged him was that Celeste wasn't being very *kind.* She was attacking those not ready, abandoning them without compassion or undies, so bombshelled by the transformation that they couldn't walk straight or, sometimes, even utter a monosyllable, and often remained unable to sound off about what happened, so foolish did they feel for needing a good fuck to set them straight. It was as if Celeste was determined to be thoughtless—maybe even cruel. Which wasn't like her.

But if, Alex continued thinking, she *was,* for some bizarre reason, determined to be cruel, there was one eentsy-weentsy glitch: everyone she touched became, if not spanking new, at least substantially better. She may have wanted to be a torpedo, but instead of devastation, she wreaked revivification. She was the bazooka that blew *together* the spirit, the supersonic that planted youth. And one thing more—something she hadn't known—which science had just uncovered. *How,* Alex agonized and fretted, kicking the wall, could she possibly be ignoring this?

ANTI-VIRUS IDENTIFIED

A virus has been identified in the blood of 24 patients who had sexual contact with controversial healer Celeste Kelly, which appears to both overpower and immunize against AIDS, researchers announced yesterday.

"Not one of our patients has AIDS, including those who did previously," stated Dr. Inez Guerrero at a Harlem Hospital news conference. "The virus seems to act as an antibody against AIDS, neutralizing it in those already infected and shielding all carriers from future infection."

Researchers also have evidence that these patients have been spreading the so-called Anti-Virus into the population at large via sexual contact, inoculating the healthy as well as eliminating the disease in both AIDS and H.I.V. sufferers.

"We have no idea how it works," Dr. Guerrero told the astonished crowd, "but in truth, our patients could care less."

—*The New York Times*

At the end of every *nth* or Matrix seminar, the Gacy Guru bade farewell to his evil beavers and shuffled back to the television department, brooding. He had miscalculated real bad. Instead of imploding upon learning Edwina's secret, as he'd anticipated, Celeste was lashing out—healing his cronies to disarm him. Worse, by getting so much media attention (this Anti-Virus was humongous news), she was boomeranging his own weapons at him. Not that she *appeared* on the tube or the radio or granted interviews; she remained unknown. But that was worse[2] because his minions couldn't play kickball with her image. There was no embarrassing video to make her into a laughingstock; no faux pas to expose some hidden bitchiness; no product affiliation to reveal any hypocrisy. There was just the facts—she drove around invisible in a wacko car, smelling and listening inside people; fucked them, healed them, dumped them—*never, dammit, using the phone, let alone watching the tube!*—so he couldn't keep track of her.

These thoughts tormented the Guru as he ambled down the Castle of Values aisle, his stocky figure reflecting, along with the red Exit light, in the treadproof linoleum. *Be patient. We need patience.* Humiliation pustulating, he browsed in Men's Suits for tomorrow's outfit and slung it over his arm. *Patience has always worked in the past.* Then he strode into Furniture, seized a La-Z-Boy. *Just go about our business, and things will take care of themselves.* In the TV department, he hung the new outfit from a Sony sign. Then he pushed the La-Z-Boy to the center of the room, threw open the trunk that

245

contained his precious media-manipulating devices, set up the devices on TV trays, and videotaped another brief, up-to-the-minute installment of his memoir. That done, he unzipped his fly, wiggled out of his brown polyester pants, tossed off his Fruit of the Looms, and lowered himself, bare-bottomed, to the leather cushion of his La-Z-Boy recliner—and *then,* and *only* then, after all his work was done and he had nothing left to do but indulge, did he truly, *really* believe it would be fine, that like TV, *Celeste will ultimately work to our advantage.*

How he had progressed! To think that not long ago he'd lived in darkness and resembled a cross between man and beast, with hoofed feet and pointy ears and billy-goat whiskers. Which was one step up from serpent, but still totally foo yuk. But what could he do? He was cursed with looking the way he felt deep inside. When he'd felt like a slippery, sneaky, wind-around-people's-minds-and-strangle-their-will kind of guy, he'd found himself a snake. When he'd felt like a stinking, filthy, eat-any-speck-of-life-until-nothing's-left-but-death kind of guy, a goat-man he became. It had been repulsive, first slithering in dust, then having goat breath all the time. *Yech!* he thought now, remembering it. *Ech! Ptooie!* As for his powers? Nothing but wienie-wuss! Okay, so he could do natural disaster. Big fucking deal. All the rest was Wimp City. Traipsing around until he *happened* to run into some angry victim who was eager to sell out his human heritage, graduate from wounded to scoundrel. Pissant bullshit, because—damn, damn, damn!—he could corrupt only one-on-one! He had to spend so much fucking time just getting *around* that even after he'd founded the Matrix and the *nths,* he *still* missed many opportunities to assist aspiring assholes. *This was no way to win a war! Fuck this! Fuck it! FUCK IT!*

Ah, but then Phyllis Bombay came along.

Good old hairpin and four-eyes. Phyllis Bombay. Who, ticked off over her seventy-four cents to every male dollar, quit her job and moved into her Minneapolis garage, where she invented a cornucopia of subversive devices. Among them: the Crystal Cup, an ear-mouth-and-screen contraption that enabled users to speak *into* the TV, using the broadcast bands for party lines; the Telephone Snooper, an abacus-looking gizmo that could tap any phone line in the world; and, most spectacular of all, the Pirate Box. Shaped like a captain's hook, the Pirate Box was the magic wand of media manipulation. Set the Pirate Box before your TV, and on your screen you could see anyone in the world who was, at that moment, watching the plug-in drug (in America, 43 percent of the population during prime time). There they'd be, picking their noses in their living rooms, drooling cereal in their kitchens. It was much better than Orwell's Big Brother, who everyone knew was watching; with the Pirate Box, *no one* knew. But there's more! The Pirate Box could *also* toggle from Input to Output—that is, change from receiver to broadcast camera. So that let's say you wanted to preempt your friend Jim's favorite news show. Znap! There you'd be, waving hallo on his screen. Or let's say you wanted to appear on *everyone*'s favorite news show! Just crank the Pirate Box to Full Steam Ahead. *And* what's even *better,* you could choose to broadcast yourself either so *everyone* could see you or "between the dots," so only the specially trained could make you out! Which meant that while whole families were guffawing through *Married . . . with Children,* the trained viewer could actually, unbeknownst to anyone in the room, be watching a different, parallel, network.

—And that's not all! Phyllis Bombay crescendoed before the Patent officials. It can also make a High Whine come over the—

That's enough, the Patent officials quipped. Go back to your bonbons and delusions, honey, and see if you can get some help.

The Guru and Bombay met up that rainy afternoon, when Bombay was staggering, widgets tucked under her arms, *Defective* stamped across her shadow, toward her car. A hairpiece plopped swiftly over his horns, a dash across the Patent parking lot, some charm oozing out of his mouth—and the Devil got shown the goods.

He had been aware of TV, but before Phyllis Bombay sat him down in her hotel room with the prototypes and a nineteen-inch Zenith, he hadn't fully tuned in. She switched on her machines. She switched on the set. And the Devil's great love affair began.

TV was beautiful. Its breastplate of laminated plastic, its bejeweled circuitry, its deep, illuminated dials—and that face! Those red, green, and blue freckles! Ever sunny! Ever ravishing! But, also, ever wondrous: even *without* Bombay's inventions, TV could etherize the viewer, seducing the most driven into not-think and don't-do. A better path to spiritual illness he'd never seen! Give it a few years and he would win, hands down!

And so, with Phyllis Bombay safely booted off a bridge, the Devil immersed himself in the world of sitcoms and miniseries, lost his goatee, horns, and bad breath, and metamorphosed into a porky, pasty, middle-aged schlump, as visually charismatic as Cremora, the kind of guy you roll your cart past at the Super Fresh and don't even see. There was still enough death in his heart that his skin bore a Ty-D-Bol-blue tinge, and still enough animal that he retained his skinny tail, but no one questioned him on the skin, and no one saw the tail. Thus normalized in appearance, the Devil became the Gacy Guru. (Name lifted from your friendly neighborhood serial killer, but no one questioned him on *that*, either, dunderbrains.) He set up camp in the TV department of the popular bargain store Castle of Values, moving from one location to another to give seminars in corruption and mayhem. With the layout identical in each of six thousand branches, he followed the same routine every night: holding a seminar, saying adieu, pushing a La-Z-Boy into the TV area, recording his memoirs, dropping his drawers, and fucking away till dawn at his luscious electronic lovers.

The phraseology is barely an exaggeration. The Gacy Guru hadn't had a great screw in centuries. He needed to behold anger or power games to get turned on—but since his very presence tended to inspire fear, and fear tended to obliterate anger and power games, his opportunities for arousal had dropped to zilch.

But with TV, all that had changed. Now, every night after he fastidiously removed his trousers and drawers and sat his body down, he flicked the Pirate Box to Input and, spying into reality, let the screens do the stimulating. Before his eyes, spouses would get walloped in their beds, children would get *You're so stupid*ed in their dens—and his satanic pecker would begin to bone up. *Ahhh*—the anguish of child abuse. *Ohhh*—the despair of domestic violence. With each cruelty, he grew harder. Soon he would uncurl his tail from beneath him and coil it snakelike about the shaft. Then slowly he would massage himself, up and down, up and down, eyes glued to the tragedy and turmoil that were molding the same fucked-up bastards who would, someday, come seeking his assistance. *Yesss. Mmmm.* He kept his face expressionless, arms free, torso clothed, in case Matricists called on their Crystal Cups, which they often did. But no one knew that during conferences he would be stroking, beating, thrusting toward fury and agony, working himself into a hellish frenzy, until, after many a *Shut up!* many a *Swack!* he would spazz out over the top and jizzle his way to true bliss.

Thank you, brother, he often thought, as he wiped his demon semen from the armrests, *for creating the tube!* It was the one gold star he would concede to his brother, his dim-witted bro, who kept begetting weapons only to lose them to the Guru. *That's because we're smarter,* mused the Guru. He could usurp any weapon that came his way. TV was a Poppin' Fresh example.

But perhaps, the Gacy Guru thought one night, when he tuned into *UBC Late News* while in the midst of his own dong show and learned something that so startled—so *thrilled!*—him that his tail halted mid-wank . . . perhaps Celeste was an even better weapon.

Because her sexual guerrilla tactics, he learned that night, were inspiring *copycats*—most unimmunized by her Anti-Virus. Flouting the safety of condoms, plunging relentlessly into promiscuity, these jackasses were spreading AIDS like wildfire.

Magnificent! The patience had paid off! Oh, how well this served his purposes! It would slaughter large segments of the population; arouse fear, bigotry, and prudery in the rest! End result: death. Physical *and* spiritual—with her, he'd get both! He didn't need to brood, after all! His brother had blown it again! And brother thought he was so smart. Ha!

But then the Guru paused, and a worry warp-speeded through him, a worry he had never considered before.

What if—what if sexual guerrilla wasn't enough for her? What if she tried to publicize who he was?

Pah! *He* controlled virtually every media outlet. It could never happen. *Don't worry, be happy,* the Guru thought, pumping up the volume, and he returned to varnishing his pole with vigor.

Dear Alex,

I'm writing to extend my gratitude for your pointing your old girl-friend toward Yellow Brick Press. She stopped by yesterday with a book she'd written, a variation on the one you'd urged her to write. I told her we're too small for her (our biggest seller has been a book of poems about yogurt), but she said she wanted to be far from the mainstream. She called it "safer."

In addition to the healing tales she used to read to you, her book exposes this Gacy Guru nut. I told her I thought this was noble of her; after all, Satan might not be very forgiving. She said, "It's not noble. It's revenge." (Whatever that means.) She said that's why she's calling it *The Sexual Bible.*

I'll be sending announcements to the media in a few days, but first wanted to let you know. Please excuse my not calling; she asked me to avoid phones until the press reports are out.

Oh, and by the way, she said to tell you hi.

—A. Colin Backslash, editor of *The Sexual Bible*

Bathed in the recycled light of his house, Alex read the letter from his old buddy and got goose bumps under his beard when he hit the word "revenge." Maybe, he thought, gazing at his bulletin board, *something* hadn't added up because he'd lacked the whole equation. He sat at his table, slide-ruling through his information. Light turned to night, and the moon arced above his dome, and by morning he knew there was no better place to start the equation than the beginning. So he popped on his Sherlock Holmes hat, packed up his Volvo, and drove as fast as its wheels would carry him up twisting northern roads to the Kelly Home.

When he finally pulled up to the entrance, it felt—after all that time of hearing about the place—like he'd discovered Atlantis. Those gates arching toward the sky, the kids dressed like extras from a Fellini movie, all the dogs . . . He didn't even need to ring the bell. The dogs barked, the kids came out, and the leader of the pack was a tall gentle man in overalls.

"Much pleased to meet you," Sam said, letting Alex in. "We've been wondering who the love bug could be."

Alex kicked the lawn. "Love bug. I haven't seen her in months. We had an altercation, and she blew the coop. And ever since . . . You been reading the papers? That's why I came here."

"When was the fight?"

Alex knew the date better than his own birthday.

"Shoo-ee," Sam said, shaking his head, fret rattling around his brain. "Your fight's not why she disappeared."

"You weren't present. She was spitting mad."

251

"No, but I was here, and not much could be as big a whopper as what happened here. It's why Miss Kelly's inside now instead of out here greeting you. She hasn't left her room since that night, she's so despaired."

"That makes two."

"Well, tell me your side of things, and I'll tell you ours."

They walked to the garden and sat beneath a ginkgo. Then they traded their narratives about the fateful night, Alex describing Celeste's discovery of the Guru's identity, Sam describing Celeste's fight with Miss Kelly—which he'd overheard while lying in bed. The mutual revelations caused the prince's mouth to fall like a drawbridge, the nurse's eyes to open wide enough to say *ah*, and when both finished, the two sat in stereo stun, so quiet they could hear the garden grow.

"So," Alex said finally, "that explains the revenge stuff."

"I wonder," Sam said, "if it explains the typing too."

"You mean the book? Yeah, it *does* sort of sound like *Granddaddy Dearest.*"

"No. Marina's typing. The morning everyone remembered Celeste's father, Marina began typing crazy nonsense. She still does it, hours a day, always telling me 'Look!' Now I'm wondering if maybe they're missives from you-know-where. Written in devil-tongue or something." He pulled a folded sheet from his overalls. "We've got so many around, I use 'em for scrap."

Alex took one quick scan at the paper and said, "I don't know about any devil-tongue, but that's a code."

"Boing! But wait—Marina wouldn't write in code. She *wants* to communicate."

"Well, I know codes, and that's a code."

"What's it saying?"

"I don't know, not instantly. It's virgin code to me."

"You know how to take codes apart?"

"I'm rusty, but"—and Alex reached into his pocket and scooped out a fistful of Scrabble tiles—"with these little babies I might be able to crack this."

"Really? No kidding?" Samson said, as Marina stepped out front to wave him in for lunch, and in her eyes Sam felt he saw, as he often did, twenty years of locked-up thoughts, a veritable hieroglyphic opus for which no Rosetta stone had been found. He waved back. "That would be great," he said, something catching in his throat. He swallowed. "That would be truly great."

CELESTE TO PUBLISH TELL-ALL BOOK

—Headline, *SNM Today*

Who knew about this? the Gacy Guru roared on a hastily called Matrix conference, displaying the newspaper on Channel Zero, his voice not remotely as controlled as usual.

"Not me," Vice President Stinkweed said.

"Nor I," the owner of a newspaper conglomerate added.

"That's not one of ourrr paperrrs," Gravely Beaks said. "It's that rrrag put out by those Spirrritual Nudist jerrrks."

Where did they get their information? Why didn't we know?

"Says therrre," Gravely Beaks said, "that Celeste herrrself contacted them."

Not by phone, she didn't! We'd have known that!

"Says they got a letterrr from herrr, and then the publisherrr confirrrmed the news."

Who's the publisher?

"Some small press," the newspaper emperor observed.

Who? Who! Which one of you?

"None of us," Gravely Beaks noted, reading down the page.

"Some podunk prrress in Colorrrado. Not a Matrrrix operrration."

"Shit," Stinkweed said. "Look at the fifth paragraph."

Thousands of Matrix eyes snap-crackle-popped down their screens, where they saw, bold as the tide, blacker than black, the one word none of them ever thought they'd see in print:

M a t r i x

A shudder rippled from the governor's mansion in Maine to the President's hotel room in Honolulu as the entire membership of the Matrix foresaw that its private party was about to get busted.

"Readers may not know what the Matrix is now," the article read, "but according to the publisher, they will after reading this book, and it'll 'make their heads spin.' "

Gravely Beaks: "They can't publish that!"

The newspaper emperor: "Who does she think she is!"

The governor of Maine: "We have to stop it!"

"We can't stop it," said the Vice President, who was a quicker picker-upper. "See? Paragraph seven: the copies are already printed. We'll have to choke them off at distribution."

For minutes, they squabbled over what to do. The Gacy Guru remained silent. If she was exposing the Matrix, well, obviously she'd expose *him*, and what the hell good is a decognitoed devil? He'd be out of business! Washed up! Totally kablooeyed!

Unthinkable. It was time to can the patience and round the bitch up—that was it. That was the answer. An easy one too. Because if she was this vengeful, he knew exactly how to do it.

There is only one certain solution, interjected the Gacy Guru, now back in control. *We must get her to renounce it.*

"How're we going to do that?" a tobacco impresario asked.

Student Stinkweed, beef up the morality crusade. You others assist, but let Stinkweed be the front man. Network heads, cover his every word. All we need do is bait her, and we'll reel her in.

"We'll never net her," the tobacco impresario said.

Certainly we will. She'll come to us.

"How can you be so sure?" the impresario said.

We are sure.

"But she hasn't come to us yet. Why should she now—"

In a white, plantation-era estate in South Carolina, a television suddenly exploded in the bedroom of the local tobacco impresario. The room immediately burst into flames, and the man, an outstanding member of the Matrix and an upstanding citizen, was immolated down to his dental records.

Do not question us, the Gacy Guru said. *We are always sure.*

${\rm A}$nd, wouldn't you know, two weeks later:

Good work, Student Stinkweed. She's back in Washington.

"What has she done?"

"Who" is the proper interrogative pronoun. He was a demented serial killer. The Tap-dancing Terminator, he's called.

"Where was this?"

Not far from the White House. We believe she'll be coming for you next, or the President. Tomorrow, probably.

"We'll be ready."

Good, Student Stinkweed. We need to count on you.

${\rm C}$eleste jettisoned the healed tap dancer in the alley. Then she and Loretta drove the four miles to the estates, hedges, and security guards part of town, the ritzoid district, where they pinpointed the Stinkweed mansion and waited the night out in front.

Loretta did not like it there. "Call it intuition," she whispered huskily. "I just don't feel comfortable."

"But we're invisible."

"We should depart."

"I need to get this done first."

"That's what James Bond always needs. But then he spends too much time and finds himself in a perilous cul-de-sac."

"*I* won't."

"If you're certain . . ."

The next morning, when the security gate swung open and a limousine egressed, an invisible Celeste slipped onto the drive. *"Au revoir!"* Loretta whispered. "My motor will be running!" Celeste waved back, and the gate closed behind her.

Inside, she perused her options. A guard knitted a sweater near the gate. A maid Windexed inside a parlor. A gardener planted orchids at the far edge of the lawn.

All small change.

She traipsed up the drive. Past bushes bearing Asian fruit, topiaries of former VPs; past the leaded glass of Stinkweed's home office—empty, she confirmed, peering through the window; past the side porch, the kitchen with the cook humming inside. No. Go for broke. Up the slate walk, past the tennis court. Onto the terra-cotta tile. Across to the pool.

There.

Beside the shimmering chlorine, a slim young woman sunbathed in a chaise longue. Clearly her daddy's daughter. Trudy Stinkweed. The girl rumored to be her papa's greatest political liability. The girl who had spent his tenure being bounced from school to camp to Europe. The girl who was a dyed-in-the-pull femme, a leg-of-labia kind of gal, a champion wet-nose, a lesbian.

And, as far as Celeste was concerned, pay dirt.

Mr. Stinkweed never called home, but that day he did. He asked me to tell him what everyone was doing at that very moment. I said,

"Why, Mrs. Stinkweed is at her lucid dreaming class, and Tad's of course at polo camp, and Trudy, she and that girl just asked me to bring them up some lunch. I'm setting the tray as we speak. You know, it's so nice for Trudy to get a visitor now and—"

And he cuts in and says, "Girl? What girl?"

And I say, "Your secretary's daughter? You know, the one you sent over to talk to Trudy about what college to pick? They've been in Trudy's suite all day. Holed up like the two best buddies in the world."

—Housekeeper Lilac Dimple, as told to author

*S*ttmmpshuffle.

> "What's that?"
>
> "I don't know. Come back to bed."

"Open the door."

"It's locked, sir."

> "Omigod! It's my father!"

"I said *open the door!*"

BLAM!

Ten men, all in suits, crash open the door.

Two women, both in their altogether, spring up in bed.

The room is a carnival of stars. Light trapezes along the ceiling, ferris-wheels in the corners. Light loop-de-loops down the wall, snake-charms across the sheets, swan-dives onto the floor. Light surfs along the carpet like a phosphorescent sea.

And these men, so well trained for terrorists, so inured to Mata Haris, so bench-pressed for combat, frazzle in the dazzle.

They can see the two lady lovers on the bed, sheets up to their necks, bodies scrunched in the corner, but the men cannot move.

Not with that light all around them. Not with the iridescent hair flashing like leopard fur. Not with the stun of *So this is the bitch that can ball your brains out.* Not with that music—where is it? Someone stash a calliope in here?

Eyes lock. Bodies freeze. Stinkweed thinks Celeste must be calculating some maneuver, but Celeste isn't thinking at all. She's so tingly from her Big Banged orgasm, so inflamed from Trudy's memories, that all she can do is wait for the dustbust of her afterglow suck. In other words, Celeste's "calculated maneuver" is nothing more than post-lust pooped-out.

It's Trudy who excavates her wherewithal first. "Daddy," she says, "leave me alone."

The music fades, a steam whistle losing its steam.

Trudy sits up taller. "Daddy, this is my lover. Get out."

The light in the room begins to go flat. Celeste makes to rise, but her battery still needs recharging. Trudy looks to her lover. The men look to their leader. Stinkweed nods to the baddest Bluto in the group.

And the man lunges.

Celeste kicks out, her legs whacking up through the sheets.

Fwock! In the eye. "Ooof!" And he's sprawling back.

Ah! So even exhausted she can muster some—

And the nine remaining palookas pounce. She leaps up, naked, aiming to kick-box but only kicking, Trudy's smacking the men, the light's pulling up stakes, Stinkweed's seizing his daughter, his daughter's biting his hand, Celeste's swatting his head, the light's clearing out of town, the men are clamping down on her arms, the men are hoisting her off the bed, she's bucking like a banshee, screaming like a meemie—

(it should be no big deal, should be just another escape, but all the tight spots she's ever wiggled out of always came *before* healing, not after, not when she was one hundred percent sapped, not when there were this many Blutos, all pumped up and programmed, all deltoid and docile, all lucky enough to raid her at her most vulnerable nadir)

    —which is to say, they got her.

The Story of the Sea
Day Three   Coming to Dock

A banging on the stateroom door wakes Edwina.

"Missus! Missus!"

She is lying in the dry bathtub. The stranger is gone.

"Missus!"

No sign of birds. But she knows she has just been with a man; she can feel it between her legs.

"Emergency on deck!"

She grabs a robe.

"Missus!"

She unlocks the cabin door. The steward stands in the hall, panting and terrified. "Come to deck. A terrible accident."

"What? What happened?"

He will not say. She limps down the corridor, up the stairs, and sees the crew running about frantically. She pushes through a thicket of people.

Her husband lies on his back, his body crisp and charred.

She recoils.

A deckhand peers up from the body. "Hit by a lightning bolt. Just a minute ago. Strangest thing I ever saw."

"But the sky is clear!" Edwina says.

"That's what I've been telling them all," he replies. "It's the work of the Devil. Leaving you a widow like this."

She kneels to the body. John Kelly looks like a wooden Indian that was used in a fireplace.

"This is horrible," she says, and she means it, but what she really feels is freedom.

The
Truth
Comes
Out

The Secret Service sometimes cahooted with the police and sometimes worked alone, and this time was one of the latter. Agents had rented a store-it-yourself unit, the kind of sumptuous steel shed where transients, tossed-out spouses, and college students deposit personal effects when in effect they have no place personal. A corrugated-metal crypt as sprawling as a laundry room, this particular unit contained one vinyl sofa, one desk, one chair, one lamp, and Celeste, and her interrogator.

Celeste had screwed into many memories of TV detective shows with their bull pens and pokeys, but this joint was a far cry from them. Besides the garage ambience, the main distinction between this dump and TV was that on TV, the guy snarling the questions was your basic boy in blue, whereas here he was a member of the executive branch of the U.S. federal government.

"We do not appreciate your tactics," Vice President Stinkweed said. He was sitting at the desk, hands folded.

"*We?*" Celeste said from the sofa. "You mean the Matrix."

He flashed his famous closed-mouth grin at her.

She said, "So you admit it."

"As if you needed verification."

"It's always nice to get the truth from the horse's mouth."

He skimmed his hand over his grin in a thoughtful fashion. "As I was saying, we are not happy with your battle plan."

She winced, as she did whenever a Matricist used that battlefield metaphor. Remember, folks, this is the girl whose grandma used to refer to the world as a battlefield. Before her rampage, Celeste figured the phrase was just a handy orphan motivator, but since she'd learned about her genesis, she gagged every time she heard it. "What battle plan?" she said.

"Don't play coy. This is not a game."

"It's not a plan, either."

"Come now."

"Is that what you want? Okay, but you might not be able to face yourself in the morning."

He glared, wiped his mouth again. "We know you've got the whole thing mapped out. The first volley is the random—mmm—*heal*ing." The term prompted a derisive shudder. "The second is that book. Here is our offer. Withdraw the book from publication and cease the healing crap."

"Fat chance."

"I'm not done. And go on national TV to denounce the Spiritual Nudity Movement."

"Ha! No TV for me; that's your tool."

"*And* renounce your own activities. That is our offer."

"That's no offer. What do *I* get for it?"

"Your life, of course."

"You'd *kill* me?"

"That has not been decided." He grinned again. "Why don't you think it over."

She sat back, and as she watched tiny licks of hair peep out from between his lips and tried to formulate a response, it occurred to her—the same *it* that had rattled through her mind as her dress had been yanked onto her body and her rings yanked off her fingers and she had been pitched into the van and the van doors had slammed shut and she had sat in the windowless vehicle, hands cuffed, cuffs chained to the floor, and the truck had floored it over roads she couldn't smell through the walls, finally screeching into this parking lot, and she was marshaled into the shed, unchained, uncuffed, presented to a grinning Stinkweed, and trapped by the steel door clanging down behind her and armed guards on the other side: that the Gacy Guru was a total fool. Here he'd knocked up Edwina Kelly, picked a doozy of a gift to bestow, sat tight for two generations—only to have his progeny paddle her own canoe rather than sign up for first mate on her papa's ship. Here he'd reckoned that genes would be destiny and then discovered—just like a gazillion other boneheads before him—that his kid wasn't playing aye-aye to any of his biological imperatives.

Like, whoop-de-do, couldn't any basic parenting text have set his expectations straight? But no, *he* had to learn the hard way. So now he was losing his shit, throwing tantrums, *making her walk the plank!*—with the same vehemence and manipulatory rock and hard place that Alex's parents had used on him—

Hmmm . . . Alex . . .

Stinkweed sat photogenic and smug before her—slightly antsy (she could hear) about his sprouting mouth beard, now curling like scrubbing bubbles down his lower lip, but otherwise quite tickled with himself and pantingly ready to receive a promotion.

"I am waiting for your answer," Stinkweed said.

She had no doubt that these demands were just the beginning. The Gacy Guru wouldn't stop with a mere cease and desist. He'd beg, bargain, and cheat until he netted her body and soul; until she swore to live out her destiny; until she—of course, what else could it be?—took up arms alongside him.

She tried to imagine it. Slipping onto a throne next to His Satanic Majesty in the Temporary Zero-Zero, apprenticing herself with lessons on secret arts, mirroring his moves, echoing his goals, until she graduated to partner and, side by side, they blitzed this imperfect creature that mortals call humanity, *rah-rah*ing misery, *bravo*ing pain, *toro! toro!*ing spiritual illness with such vim and ubiquity that humanity would come crashing down like one mighty putrid carcass—and, all the while, never being able to heal, never being able to touch, never being able to . . . *love.*

Right. She could see that about as readily as she could see Alex strapping on some accordion to march in a royal procession. It just wasn't in her to be whole-hog cruel, not unless she stomped down, corked up, and freeze-dried her inner self.

—But isn't that, you may ask, basically what she'd been doing throughout her rampage: screwing people who had no interest in getting well, leaving them naked and scared—being *cruel?*

—Yeah, that's what she'd been doing. And finally, there in that luxury storage shed, her self-sight defrosted, and she beheld her own cruelty standing stark and hideous before her—and also, beyond it, the bigger picture, the landscape on which her cruelty had been able to dig deep and grow:

That all she'd done for months—no, Celeste saw, her entire life—was chart her course by someone else's map. When she'd trusted Edwina, it was Follow the Leader. When she'd felt devastated by Edwina—and the Gacy Guru—it was Fight the Leader. She never did what *she* wanted. She never *knew* what she wanted. Her inner self was as stifled as anyone else's.

She sat up. "Shove your offer," she said.

Stinkweed fumblingly loaded his retort. "W-w-what?"

"I'll only stop what *I* want to stop."

"Now, think this through very careful—"

"If I want to publish the book, I will. If I want to keep healing, I'll do that too."

He stared at her, and his face began a subtle boil, as if a nuclear bomb had just detonated under his skin.

"Are you *sure?*" he asked.

She crossed her arms. "Yup."

Color rolled across his face—raspberry red, lemon yellow, orange orange—and finally, around the time his eyes took on an Alka-Seltzer fizz, she wised up that she'd better eavesdrop on his thoughts, but just as she dove in for a listen—

"*Rape!*" he exploded.

"Rape?" she repeated.

He bolted from his desk and pounded on the steel door for the guards. "*Rape! Rape!*"

"You're such a jerk, Stinkweed," she said.

But when the Secret Service hauled up the door and Stinkweed babbled, "She—she—came over to me, and—and—she tried to— she almost— Oh, it was awful! Just awful! I feel so victimized!" Celeste could only sit, mouth agape.

Then Stinkweed pointed a finger at her. "Arrest that bitch!"

So they did.

TRUMPET INTRODUCTION: *Theme song, "Good Evening, UBC"*
Lou Magoo at desk

LOU

The world is still reeling from the events of this morning. As you probably know by now, when Vice President Stinkweed went home for lunch today, he was allegedly accosted on his own grounds by the mysterious and controversial Celeste. He claims he directed her to his office, where he tried to enlist her assistance in governmental matters. She claims he tried only to suppress her upcoming book. He claims she then attempted to rape him. She denies this. Whatever happened, Celeste Kipplebaum Runetoon Kelly has been charged with attempted rape, and thousands of people have converged on the plaza around the jail. Barbie Bikini reports live.

CUT TO: *Barbie outside*

BARBIE

As soon as word spread, the crowds began massing on the plaza, turning this normally quiet street into a zoo.

SERIES OF QUICK IMAGES: *Banjo player, girl walking sheep, posters, vendors, people in various states of undress, etc.*

NAKED WOMAN WITH BIG EARRINGS

I mean, how do you rape a man? Tell me that.

MAN WITH WHITE BEARD

Stinkweed has a reputation to keep—unlike some people. Whose word are you going to take—his or some slut's?

BARBIE

And on the debate goes. As for Celeste, bail was set for an astronomical hundred million dollars, so she's expected to be here all night. This is quite a change from what we understand her regular lifestyle to be. But she has gotten some support. A few moments ago, her famous car delivered two visitors, an African American man and a white woman—family members, I'm told. They'll get a few minutes with her, and then tomorrow she'll be arraigned. In the meantime, those who've lived in fear of being ambushed by Celeste can rest easy tonight. UBC will stay posted should there be some new development, so keep your TV up and running. Till then, back to you, Lou.

—UBC News

Late afternoon. In the private visitation room usually reserved for high-profile yardbirds, Sam and Marina waited, quiet and contemplative, at a table. On the table sat the sheaf of papers Sam had cleared with security, and beside the papers rested a pair of hands, dark clasping pale in shared worry.

The door opened. In shuffled a guard and Celeste. Decked out in chains and cuffs, the prisoner was a clanking ad for S-M equipment, hands locked to legs locked to back locked to waist: a slave bracelet over her entire body. The guard chained her to the table and departed, and Celeste looked over at her visitors.

The hair at Sam's temples resembled dandelions gone to seed. Marina showed no gray, but her auburn had lost its luster. Had that much time passed? Yes, it had. Celeste scanned their shadows. Marina's still teemed with other shadows—thousands, maybe millions. A throng of voices prattled and yammered inside her—not speaking *to* each other, just *speaking*—and over by the margins, floating free of the others, was Marina's voice: no words, just a strand of beaded sighs. Celeste inhaled. Typewriter ribbons, she smelled. Finger paint. Tiddlywinks. Begonias. Sam.

Celeste turned to the nurse. Except for some sadness, Sam's shadow was as spiritually robust as Alex's. Celeste hadn't clued into this before, but hey, the last time she'd seen Sam, she hadn't yet conceived of the notion of spiritual health. Nor had she been able to synsense. Now she smelled—roses, iodine, Marina. She listened. Sentences heaped on sentences like leaves waiting to be jumped in. Babble about mothers and fathers and some ocean or somethi—

And what was that? Another voice, it sounded like—not Sam, not Marina—and it seemed to be beside her. She glanced that way, but it slipped off; an echo that ran back to Mama. Then there was no aroma to be sniffed. Must have been only herself.

All this happened in a second. Now she blinked away her synsensing and addressed her visitors with a sheepish "Hi."

Sam said, "It's a damn treat to see you, Celeste, even under these circumstances. We know you've been through a lot lately."

"Yeah, getting arrested's no fun."

"Actually, what I mean is, Miss Kelly—"

"She sent you?"

"No. But for months she's been bluer than gloom."

"Good. Serves her right."

"I don't think you understand it all."

"And you do?"

"Let's just say this visit's about more than hello. We came on a mission." He turned to Marina. "You do it, honey."

The silent woman slid the stack of papers toward Celeste.

Celeste glanced at the top sheet. It read: *At a dock in New York City, on a glorious sapphire morning, an ocean liner hauls up its gangplank.* She looked up. "What is this?"

"Remember how Marina began typing gibberish? The morning everyone unamnesiaed your dad? That's it."

"This is not gibberish."

"That's right. Thanks to a visit from your friend Alex."

Celeste's heart did a backflip. "Alex went to the Home?"

"He wanted to get help finding you."

"Why?" She girded up her attitude. "To give me more grief?"

"To remind you you had a friend."

"Gee," she muttered, attitude falling away forgotten.

"Anyhow, when he arrived, I showed him Marina's gibberish, and he jumped on it pronto and told me it was a code."

"Well, how about that." Her heart backflipped again. "Those Accordian skills came in handy, after all."

"Right. So he began decoding. It took a while of camping out in the living room, but finally we got that Marina's alphabet resequenced the regular ABC's in the order of a keyboard. So *a* equals *q*, *b* equals *w*. There were a few nulls and some jumbling, but once he caught on, we decoded the whole shebang. Which ran an acre of paper, believe me."

"And what was she writing?"

"Other people's stories."

"What does *that* mean?"

"Seems Marina's got many people inside her. You know all the shadows you spied inside her years ago? That was other people's lives she was picking up. It's like she knows what anyone's seeing —what anyone's *thinking*. Like something inside her and inside the rest of us is the same. That's why she does finger paintings of places she's never seen."

"I don't get it."

"She can see through anyone's eyes. Even yours." Sam flipped through the papers and extracted a clipped few. They began: *A man tap-dances in the shadow of a church, click-clacking off the minutes as he waits in the sticky night air.*

Celeste peered up. "Could this be the Tap-dancing Terminator? I healed him in Washington just last night."

"I know," Sam said.

Celeste looked at him, then at Marina.

"Like I said, we've got reams of the stuff. It's about people all over the world, and not just from now, either; she types up things that happened in the past too. Those first sheets you saw, they're about Miss Kelly—and your grandfather."

Celeste raised her eyebrows.

"Read them," he said. "I call them 'The Story of the Sea.'"

Slowly, Celeste bent her head, set her eyes to the words, and, shushing the throbbing pump organ in her ears, read about the central event of her life, an event for which she had not even been present. She learned about John Kelly—a man she'd never known —and the stranger: a man who was not a man. About the events on the ship. About emptiness and desire. About being so desperate you would do anything.

And about making love to someone who never said who he was.

Her pump organ seemed to cease pumping. Air intake occurred exclusively by gasps. She could feel herself under her skin.

Finally, she finished. "So my grandmother really *didn't* know," Celeste mumbled. "But if it's the gift of healing . . ."

Then a kind of understanding rang the doorbell inside her, and just as she was opening the latch, a choir began to sing from across the table—a choir that sounded like the Beach Boys on liturgic acid. Could it be . . . her Gregorian friends? But they hadn't stopped by for ages! Celeste glanced toward their voices and saw, to the tune of the excellent vibrations that Nurse Samson seemed unable to hear, Marina's shadow starting to shift and dazzle, and then, like spectra threading back through a prism, coalesce from ROYGBIV into a shockingly white light. It was as if Marina's colored others were melting into one crazy diamond—no, into a champagne sunrise— no, into a—a—*multigalactic, spherospiral supernova!* It twirled about the room, making Celeste's ordinary sex-induced carnival of stars look like a four-watt Mickey Mouse night-light. This was a Mardi Gras of illumination, an Olympic Games of brilliant white. So radiant, in fact, that Celeste had to turn away.

"What's wrong?" Sam asked.

"Her shadow," Celeste said, gaze still averted.

Being shadow illiterate, like most folks, Sam said, "Huh?"

Celeste held up her hand, trying to block some of the light. "It's unbelievable," she shouted, the better to be heard over the choir, but then realized the choir had faded out. She squinted back to Marina—and saw in her mother's eyes a knowing that hadn't been there before. Not a knowing that had just woken up. This was a knowing that had just moved in.

And in a voice more playful than she had possessed in this life, Marina asked, "So do you get it now?"

Sam whipped around. "Marina!" he cried.

"No," Marina said. "Marina's just my amplifier right now."

Celeste said, "Who are *you*?"

"Oh, you know. The crown of creation. The dream you dreamed

one afternoon long ago. Your grandfather and your father, the Ultra-Other, the King of Kings . . . uh, God."

Celeste covered her mouth with her hand.

Sam burst into a sweat.

"Yeah," Marina/God went on, "it sounds corny. But what can I do? I am who I am."

Celeste felt like she'd been thwacked with a two-by-four. Constellations orbited her head, or maybe it was just that shadow; she couldn't tell. She synsensed to get her bearings. Listened: a thousand civilizations in infinophonic sound. Smelled: a river of spirits in polyodorous scents. She splashed in it all, synsensing through Cro-Magnon caves and Roman courts, African markets and Chinese temples, Mayan tombs and European glooms and Arabian dunes and American saloons, smell adding to smell, voice adding to voice, until at last she surfaced into clarity.

She said, "So Marina and I are the daughters of God?"

"By George, I think she's got it."

Celeste nodded, but the anger she'd cocooned for months prevented a joyous reunion. "Then why did you do *this* to us?"

"Time was not on my side. My brother was winning."

"Your brother—is that the Gacy Guru?"

"Such is his latest alias."

Sam asked, "And you're saying you two are brothers?"

Marina/God sighed. "It all comes down to that old wrinkle of sibling rivalry. See, all humans are born with a bit of me inside. So at any time I can see from your eyes—or anyone's—because we are you are he are she are they are us, oh baby, baby. But my bro lacks this ability. He has almost no abilities at all—can't even control his appearance, poor bastard. And a long time ago he got so peeved over this, he declared war. We've been at it for millennia, duking it out on the battlefield of humanity. At first, I managed all by my lonesome, never needed a helping hand. But it's gotten so solo's a no go, a wipeout, a guaranteed lose, which means lately I've been singing the Help Me, Rhonda, I Need An Ally In Here Right Now Blues."

"So you made me a sexual healer to help."

"Bingo."

"Hey, the last time someone said Bingo to me was those voices in my, you know. Was that you?"

"Bingo again. I knew he wouldn't overhear them there."

"But once I asked them if there was any truth to tales of super-natural beings, and they—*you*—said no."

"There *isn't*—not the stories you usually hear. My brother distorted them. Once they were accurate, but alas, no longer."

"Fine, okay, but why didn't you make me a regular healer? Why *sex*? That's half of why I thought *he* was my father."

"You thought lust came from the Devil?"

"Sure."

"You bought into that nonsense?"

"What do you mean?"

"Sex is about frolic and vivacity and trust and love. God is about frolic and vivacity and trust and—" Marina/God cleared their throat. "Let's put it this way. I am life, ergo I am energy, merriment, and freedom, and you can feel me through lollipops, shady trees, music, toboggans—you get the idea. But my bro is death: numbness, fear, restraint. You can feel him through guns, disease, the green-house effect, Muzak—anything that bumps you off physically or spiritually. Think of humanity as a giant battlefield, with me fighting to encourage life, my brother to encourage death. Every mind that's anesthetized, dream that's gagged, punch that's thrown, scores him points. Every mind that shakes off stupor, dream that do-re-mi's, punch that opens into a handshake, scores me points.

"I'm always devising new tactics to coax people my way, and he's always trying to sabotage my plans. I launch new religions to spread love; he uses his wiles to pervert them, so instead of leading to the family of humanity, they lead to *us*es and *them*s and hatred and war. I design the ideal genetic makeup and upbringing to cultivate great leaders; he uses his cageyness to corrupt, embitter, or, when all else fails, assassinate them. I bestow on every person the possibility of connection through love and sexuality; he bombards you with viruses to make intimacy deadly."

"Then where do I fit in?"

"You are my secret weapon. I've had other, not-so-secret ones —Socrates, Jesus, Lincoln, Gandhi, King, Lennon—but he so successfully shot each down that this time I decided to be *top* top secret. I'd use a *second* generation and make all who knew your dad forget him. Thus you'd either foil my brother entirely or, at least, get a running start before he picked up your trail."

"But why the gift of sex?"

"I tried words, but words don't stop him. So why sex instead of, say, flamenco dancing? Because thanks to bro, sex is now the front line of the battle. It was bad enough when he lobbed nastiness and anger into the sexual experience. But now that two people can't even cuddle up close without dreading death, and those who *are* dying get dumped on by the self-righteous living—well, it doesn't get any worse than that. I needed to torpedo him with an Anti-Virus. Plus, people listen to sex talk more than all other tongues combined."

"Why'd you make me female?"

"It was high time to give women a crack at saving humanity."

Celeste shook her head. "But why *me*? Why my *grandmother*?"

"I selected Edwina because her philosophy matched mine. And because she already had an aversion to the voices of the air . . . uh, that is, the media. I knew bro had found ways to appropriate the media's power—television, especially—so I needed a helper who would avoid exposure to it. And Edwina, with her hall-of-mirrors beliefs, would. But I also chose her because she'd had a run-in with an *nth* and hadn't caved in to bitterness."

"What run-in?"

"That charlatan who ruined her legs. He was an *nth*. Had an M.D. on his wall and an evil wasteland for his heart."

"But what do you mean, she didn't cave in to bitterness? She gave away her offspring!"

"Only after much inner wrestling. I promised her joy, you see, and so she decided that if she was feeling that joy, she could raise our child up right. And she did."

"What about Marina? She didn't get anything from the deal."

"Sure she did. In her first life, she had an uncommon inner serenity and intricate collages of dreams. You see, she had as many souls available to her eyes as I, but in her first life she just heard herself and saw those other lives only in her sleep."

"But then she died."

"Unfortunate but necessary. I had to keep her from spilling any beans about your father. She wasn't supposed to be reborn, but when you were placed on her and she returned to life, I had to make her silent to preserve the secret. So her own self became quiet and small, and inside her the other lives were able to pump up the jam."

"But if you wanted me secret, why the Cloud Lady?"

"FYI—for *your* information. My brother didn't find out about it for years. It was a rather localized phenomenon."

Sam asked, "Can you explain Marina's typing?"

"Sure. When my brother realized who Celeste was, he lashed out at me by hurting those involved. He began by delivering an incantation that lifted any veil I had drawn, and *voilà!* everyone remembered your father. Marina could have returned fully to life then, since I no longer needed her silence, but vindictive dirtbag that he is, he cursed her with being unable to make herself understood. So she could see all I can see—and *know* she was seeing it —but communicate it only in a twisted way. It was a game, you see, to get back at yours truly. And then he had Beaks glue the wedding cake couple to your car, just to make you believe falsely that Monkey was the Devil—just to make you self-destruct. In other words, just to demobilize my secret weapon. People are never the issue, get it? It's all just to one-up me."

Celeste asked, "Will Marina now be restored to herself?"

"Not till he retracts the curse." Marina/God paused. "Or he himself is retracted. And that is not something I can do."

"Who can?"

Marina/God smiled again and began to sing, as the Gregorian voices had once sung, "Only you."

Celeste glanced at Sam as the doo wopped on. The nurse's eyes were wet with tears, his brow crinkled in concentration and pain. At the song, he'd laughed, and now his gaze met Celeste's, and they shook their heads. "This is nuts," Sam said, and then they turned back to Marina. Only now her eyes were closed.

"Dad? I mean, God? What am I supposed to call you anyway?"

Marina/God said nothing.

"I have to ask about this retraction thing. I mean, if I'm supposed to do it, *how* am I supposed to do it?"

More silence.

Celeste shot a nervous look at Sam but then realized that beneath them, around them, Marina's shadow was sucking into itself, contracting, shrinking to the shape of the woman's body, and, as it did, shifting from the white light back to Marina's everyday kaleidoscopic layers. It was as if her shadow had just pirouetted in front of a miniature prism. As if the light orgy had wedged itself into a three-sizes-too-small gown. As if it had gotten liposuction and a makeover by Munsell.

And when the shadow was back to its crowded colors, Marina opened her eyes, and in them was her normal childlike gaze.

"Marina?" Sam asked.

Marina nodded.

"Is it just you?"

Again, a nod.

Celeste shook her head and uttered the thought that had been bonging in her head since Marina's shadow fanned open: "Wow. Have *I* been an idiot."

Sam said, "You didn't know," and took hold of Marina's hand.

"But what should I do now?" Celeste said, as Sam and Marina hugged each other. "I have to do something. Make amends, or at least try to free Marina. But how? I'm stuck in prison."

"I don't know," Sam said, stroking Marina's face, then turning to Celeste. "But I'd guess the answer will come to you."

"Sure," Celeste said.

And then it was Time's Up. Hugs and good-bye, and Celeste was led back down the labyrinthine corridors to the room she'd been checked into earlier: her very own solitary cell. Windowless, except for a slot in the door. Dark, except for the single overhead light. There, she was locked to the wall, locked to the floor, locked to the bed, and left alone.

Thus fettered, the healer pounded the floor in frustration. We know, we know, she had the strength of Hercules, but the chains that bound her were reinforced to resist snapping—and locked to boot. Try though she might (and she did; this is not a lady who pounds floors without good reason), she couldn't bust the damn things open. Dinner came and the nocturnal shift came, and in those hours she snapped nothing except the rhetorical question "What am I going to do?" And *that*, she snapped at herself incessantly.

As you know, Celeste was not a crackerjack professor. She'd tried tutoring me in invisibility, but I kept botching it. Not till my decoding visit to the Home did some orphans reveal the few nifty—and essential—tips she'd spaced on telling me, and in less than a trice I went from bumbling to able.

The day of her arrest was akin to my exam. I snuck into the prison on Sam's heels, hovered in the corner during the visit, and accompanied her back to her cell when it ended. All without her knowledge. Obviously, a passing grade for this boy!

Shortly after lights-out, she lay down, and I removed my invisible straw hat and lowered it onto her head. She reached up, perhaps thinking it was a draft, then slowly realized it *wasn't* a draft—something was indeed sitting atop her hair. "A straw hat!" she mumbled, grin building on her face, and then she burst out, "Alex! You're here!"

I said, "My lady, here'll become there in the time it takes for tea," and started picking the locks on her chains.

—Alex Popoverovitch, as told to author

Invisible, the reunited couple slipped out the prison doors when the guard waddled through for her midnight check. They were beyond the front gates when the unlocked chains were discovered in the cell. They were climbing into an invisible Loretta when the prison sounded its alarm. They were peeling off into the wild black yonder when the warden dialed the Gacy Guru on his Crystal Cup. *We'll retrieve her*, the Guru reassured, *no sweat*. Because as far as he was concerned, Celeste *couldn't* find him now, not in his new location.

But little did he know what Marina had scribbled before her departure: an address in code—a code Celeste could now *de*code—for a Castle of Values near the Maryland shore. A fake-stone department store, which that day was hosting specials on women's shoes, flannel sheets, pet supplies, and something more, something that was not merchandise, something less tangible than merchandise—but far more powerful. It was something every Castle of Values hosted at one point or another. It moved from store to store, concealing itself in the manager's office during the day, thriving in the TV department at night. It was clean and quiet and had made

Castle of Values the top schlock shop in the country. It was a moving boardroom, a roving command post that relocated every few days, and now it had touched down here, in this particular store, bringing the managers contacts and influence and untold piles of dough. It was the Mobile Capitol of the Matrix. The Training Grounds of the *nths.* The place where Celeste knew she had to go. The Temporary Zero-Zero.

The
Fuck
to the
Finish

The Gacy Guru was lecturing to his students in the TV department. On the screens flickered every program shown at that hour: *Doogie Howser, The Simpsons, Star Trek, Studs, Sesame Street, NBA Basketball,* and an assorted ninety others. The freshmen, only blue belts in Shadow Reading, were learning how to hear the many Matrix voices that crackled across every TV broadcast, wheeling and dealing at high speed. *This is how we keep in touch with our world,* the Guru explained. *This is how we keep our world where we want it.* The students chuckled a we're-in-on-this-together chuckle. But of course, since the Guru had omitted telling them he could see *through* screens, that he trained serial killers, that he was, in fact, the Satanic Majesty, he was doing the only true chuckling around here.

Outside, Loretta pulled invisibly into the back lot.

Alex said to Celeste, "Let me come. I'll set picks for you, be your power forward—whatever you want. Just let me help."

Celeste said, "I don't think you should."

"Oh, Celeste, take the *monsieur*," Loretta purred.

"Right. Take the *monsieur*. You shouldn't do this alone."

"Sure I should."

"But what if you need assistance?"

"Listen to him, Celeste. Rhett Butler isn't as gracious."

Celeste sighed. "If you come, who'll keep watch?"

"*Moi*," Loretta said. "I'll honk if there's trouble."

Alex said, "Besides, the real ado is in there."

"Okay," Celeste conceded, "but stay out of sight. And if things go crazy—run. I don't want your butt on the line."

Alex tossed up his hat with glee.

The couple slunk into a side entrance and wound through the employee rooms of the Castle of Values. Desks, johns, lockers, stock, tissue paper, foam packing peanuts, credit card forms, mannequin parts, coffee mugs. They stepped around it all, maintaining their quiet, bracing themselves for a sudden *Boo!*, senses cocked and ready, invisibility turned up to full blast.

At last they emerged. There, before them: the single football-field-sized room of the store.

"Cover me from the side," Celeste whispered, and Alex whizzed off the linoleum to the carpeted area and followed along, darting from rack to rack. He knew that no one but Celeste could see him but reasoned this would put him in the proper mood.

Celeste strode silently, peering down aisles. Women's Dresses, empty, resembled a Tupperware party for scarecrows. Men's Suits, empty, resembled a convention of Headless Horsemen. Past them. Past Shoes in their turnouts. Past Kiddie Clothes, Perfumes, Housewares, Furniture, Greeting Cards, Sporting Goods.

Then there. In the back. Bleating like a luminous herd.

The televisions. Arranged in a semicircle amphitheater-style. Floor to ceiling like wallpaper. Star-studded, high-produced, fast-flashed, laugh-tracked.

She inched closer. Voices hailed *Thanks!* from the rear. Up on tiptoes she went, and then she saw a dozen students loitering by the exit, some lighting cigarettes, others waving bye-bye.

And in the aisle: a small, potbellied man, with a bald head and used-car-salesman attire and tar-black eyes.

Yup. It had to be.

Him.

She crept closer as he saw his students off. Except for those eyes, the Gacy Guru looked like any middle-aged Joe on the street. Though the shadow was peculiar. Whereas her dad's had been a frothing orgasmaverse of light, the Devil's was a complete void. It was the blackest sludge she'd ever seen—no color, no undulations, no backbeat. And X-tra, X-tra, *X-tra* Small size.

It was the sickest, sexiest shadow the healer had ever seen.

She calmed herself and stepped close enough to listen inside him. *Sssssss,* she heard. Like white noise. Empty of words. Vacant of thought. The sound of a cemetery on a rainy winter day.

She sniffed. *Wwwwew!* The stench of ancient rot skanked up her nostrils, worse than a casserole exhumed from the back of a thousand-year-old fridge. That squelched the turn-on but good. She whipped her head away, promising herself to shut off her olfactory valve and not to look at his shadow again.

Finally, the last student departed. The Gacy Guru secured the back door and shuffled toward Men's Suits.

This is it. Strike while the surprise is hot.

She calculated his velocity and direction, ran ahead to an intercept location, planted herself on a square of linoleum at the juncture between Men's Suits and Furniture, scrunched her face into a scowl, locked her hands on her hips, and when he was two inches from her face, his trajectory about to collide with her fixed point, she took a deep breath and materialized.

He reeled back with a cry, white noise lurching into wheeze.

What are you—, he began, then contained himself. *So,* he continued, straightening his polyester duds, *you have come to us.*

"I *am* my father's daughter."

So unfortunate, that, he said. *You could have helped us so.* He reached out and stroked her cheek with one fat finger.

She grabbed his wrist and held his hand.

You think you're so strong.

"You think you run the world."

No, we think we will *run the world. We* know *we will.* His inner wheeze settled back to white noise.

"My father says," she said, releasing his hand and circling him, "you two are brothers."

That is true.

"He said you're fighting a war. That you're playing out your conflict on the battlefield of humanity."

Ah, him and his purple prose. Yes, it is a battlefield. Though we think of it as a feast. Humanity is laid out before us, waiting to be consumed, and we are relishing every morsel.

She stopped circling. They faced each other, arms akimbo. "Well," she said, "the feast is over."

He snickered. *You think it's that easy?*

"I don't care if it is or it isn't. I want my mother restored. And I want you to pay for all the quote unquote morsels you've eaten over the years."

He snickered again, then turned and ambled into the furniture department, his white noise hissing louder.

Celeste looked about and saw Alex, waving his straw hat from behind a display of Snoopy quilts. The Guru selected a La-Z-Boy and pushed it to the TV department. There, he lowered himself to the chair, rummaged through some videotapes and peculiar devices in a trunk beside him, extracted a hook-shaped machine from said trunk, and pressed one of its buttons.

The programs on the televisions went mute.

The Gacy Guru lay back, opening the recliner. *Fine,* he said, folding his hands behind his head, a hundred TV shows blathering soundlessly before him. *We'll work it this way. We will agree to walk away from the feast, including Matrix and nths, leave you our videotaped memoirs, and disappear. If.*

"If what?"

If you can ask a question that we cannot answer.

"Somehow this sounds too simple."

Perhaps. Though we are quite knowledgeable. As knowledgeable as our brother, but in somewhat different fields.

"Like what fields?"

You have three tries.

"I said, What fields?"

Are you game?

She paused. "Yes." (Why did she agree so quickly? you may ask. Well, she probably figured, how could she lose? Or, as psychohistorians see it, she'd played so much poker that when it came to most any challenge, she was just a gal who can't say no.)

Excellent. We shall call the scorekeeper. Then the Gacy Guru threw his head back and let loose the most grating, screechy *Eeeyyyaaahhh!* she'd ever heard. It sounded like a stampede of tape fragments ripping at incredible speed; an operatic mosquito.

And from Sporting Goods, she heard: "You rrrang?"

Celeste glanced across the floor. Into smelling, hearing, and seeing range padded a grinning, green-suited dwarf.

Student Beaks, you have an assignment.

The Gacy Guru gestured, and Beaks turned.

"Hello, Mayor Beaks," Celeste said. "Fancy seeing you here."

Beaks smiled, and Celeste listened inside him. Trrriumph! he was tittering to himself. He'd *known* his efforts would get the little wench herrre! And to think—the firrrst night he everrr spent in the Temporrrarrry Zerrro-Zerrro, she appearrrs! Ho ho! Vindication! Jubilation! A rrrush even betterrr than masturrrba—

"Hello, Celeste dearrr," he said, holding out a gloved hand.

The Gacy Guru said, *Student Beaks, we are about to engage in riddle combat. Celeste will be asking us three questions. If we cannot answer any one of them, then we will . . .*

"Will what?" Celeste asked.

Destroy the Matrix.

"WHAT?!" Beaks belched, dropping his unshaken hand. This was the first he had heard of any such bizarre notion.

"And," Celeste prodded.

"AND?" Beaks what-squared.

And eliminate our other holdings.

"OTHERRR HOLDINGS? WHAT OTHERRR HOLDINGS?"

Do not concern yourself. You were called out so that you might officiate.

Yes. Ahem. Let's not fuck up *now*. The Guru's probably just bluffing to throw the bitch off. Beaks adjusted his green velvet suit. "Rrright." He nodded militarily.

Go over there.

Beaks followed the wave and seated himself atop a console.

Now, are we ready?

"Yes."

Your first question?

Celeste cleared her throat. She listened in Gravely Beaks for a clue, but got none. She listened in the Gacy Guru but heard only the hiss of a corporate headquarters. She'd have to go it alone. What should she ask? What? Okay, she thought, seizing an idea. Here's a question that has gummed up papal conventions from time immemorial. It's stymied kings and popes. It should stymie him.

She said, "How many angels *can* dance on the head of a pin?"

Gravely Beaks got a *What the fuck?* twist on his dwarf face and shot a look at his boss.

The Gacy Guru blew out a laugh. He sounded like the Michelin Man with asbestosis. *Five hundred thirty-seven,* he replied with utter confidence.

"I'm supposed to simply accept that?"

Argue if you'd like. Though we have in our possession documentary footage of this very phenomenon. Student Beaks? Prepare for a video demonstration.

Gravely Beaks wiped his confusion off his face and nodded. Then, leaping from the console, he grabbed a cart upon which rested a VCR and TV and pushed it over to them.

The Gacy Guru said, *Now, insert the tape marked "Answers, volume LXXIV," and play starting from index 4567.*

The dwarf rummaged in the Guru's trunk, found the tape, did as instructed—and sure enough, on the screen appeared five hundred thirty-seven angels, each clearly numbered like a football player, winging their way through clouds and pink sunbeams toward an ordinary little straight pin. One by one, they alighted on the tiny metal head. When all were comfortably settled, a trio of angels on an adjacent cloud strapped on electric guitars and struck up a bouncy surf song, and on the pinhead, every one of the heavenly hosts had just enough room to watusi.

The evidence was irrefutable. "No argument," Celeste capitulated, hanging her head. Beaks stopped the tape.

One down, two to go.

Celeste cracked her knuckles. Better leave Classic Questions behind and move on to a query that hadn't been in such heavy rotation.

"Okay," she said. "Next question is, Who wrote the Bible?"

Gravely Beaks flashed a look of desperate perplexion.

The Guru laughed again. *God and four hundred ghost writers.*

"Oh, yeah, I bet."

We expected you to doubt us, but it just so happens that we filched the original item. Student Beaks, fetch the book. He gestured toward the trunk.

Gingerly (No questions! Spurn that lust for knowledge!), Gravely Beaks stepped over to the maw of the Guru's hope chest and extracted a leather-bound, dog-eared, gold-leafed tome with the words "Holy Bible" engraved on the cover. Each of the letters appeared to have the depth of infinity, as if the words themselves were windows to the far end of the universe, telescopes into the beyond.

"Let me see that," Celeste said, hoping it was a fake. But when Gravely Beaks lugged the book over to her, staggering beneath the weight of the pages, and set it down on the console, Celeste opened the cover to find the words "First edition," written by hand—and to find all the text inside written by the same hand. And every loop and vertical and flourish of the script, all the pressure and tilt and shading—even the latitude on which the dots had been dotted—were exactly like her own. No doubt about it: this had to be her father's writing.

And what's more, the Gacy Guru said, *it is a signed copy.*

Celeste turned to the flyleaf. There, beneath the inscription "Best wishes," she found four hundred and one signatures. With the top one unmistakably her father's.

Ipso facto, we have won the second question.

Celeste nodded with an irked shrug.

Behind the console, sweat had begun marching up Gravely Beaks's legs like an army of fire ants. What the hell was this about? Some joke about the Spirrritual Nudity Movement? She a stool pigeon forrr the Pope? What *is* this—a showdown between the Big Cheese and the Little Cunt, orrr a theological dialectic?

He waited to see the Guru guffaw, to elaborate, to do something—*anything!*—but the Guru merely said, *Last question.*

The sweat army on Gravely Beaks's legs suddenly slid up his spine as up a backward banister, invaded his brain, and gave him a thought he didn't like at all.

Celeste wouldn't have asked these things, and the Guru wouldn't have had this evidence, unless . . . *unless* . . .

He glared back and forth between the combatants.

That would explain his weird shadow!

The Gacy Guru sat smugly quiet, waiting.

Celeste ran her hand through her hair. She paced down the corridor, past camping gear and barbecue equipment. She had to find a question he had no evidence for. Something so personal . . . She screwed up her eyebrows. So arcane . . . She hummed the opening bars of "Only You." So unanswerable . . .

She marched back.

Last question.

She looked down at the Guru in his recliner.

"If you and my father are brothers"—Gravely Beaks let loose a snort—"and he is God and you are the Devil"—Beaks made a sound like a garbage disposal—"then who, I'd like to ask, are *your* parents?"

The Guru's eyes popped open. His mouth dropped down. His inner hiss sizzled to a halt.

Th-th-that is not a fair question!

"It's fair," Celeste said, grinning. "And I see from your response that you can't answer it!"

The Guru bolted up, white noise puffing in small bursts. *No, it was not fair. Did you think it was fair, Student Beaks?*

Gravely Beaks was staring, bewildered, at his gloves. Had he been toiling for the Devil all this time? Yikes! Beaks may not have had any scruples, but Satan was a little low even for him! Shit! Bamboozled by the Devil! Hoodwinked by the master! Here he'd found his one true friend, only to learn that he'd been used to swab the deck! Disgusting! After all this—the pandering and the sneaking and the it's-not-nice-to-fool-with-Father-Matrix attitude—there was nothing to be gained! Nothing! Not even power! Climb to the top of the heap and what do you get? A belly flop to Hell! That's all! That's it! That's—but what should he say *now*?

What do you think, Student Beaks?

Gravely Beaks peered at Celeste, then back at his heretofore respected boss, and mumbled, "Absolutely fairrr."

The Gacy Guru glared at his student. *Silence!* he roared.

Gravely Beaks leaped behind the console, hyperventilating so hysterically he could barely hear what was happening.

Celeste danced a little jig. "I won! I won!"

The Gacy Guru glowered at Celeste. *You will not get us!*

"I already have."

He stomped, à la Rumpelstiltskin—once, twice, three times—and bent as if he were bowing. Then he charged, head rod-straight before him, body a battering ram. *Nooooo!* he bellowed—

And *splsshh!* slammed into her.

And combat commenced. As Alex peeked from behind a stereo and Gravely Beaks from behind the console, the Devil and God's daughter battled it out. Fists, kicks, spits; the choke hold, the strangle mold, the punch to the jaw, the flip over the back, the crack to the noggin, the chop on the chest, the scratch to the cheek, the elbow in the eye—each dishing it out, but each taking it (he might look like a couch potato, but he still had a passion for bashin' and he still had the muscle for tussle; she might look like a nice little lady, but could she punch out some lights! and had she memoried into some fights!—judo, karate, kick boxing, family feud, sumo, kung fu, jujitsu, South Bronx attitude), so she caught fists like pop flies, he blocked kicks with his thigh, they were a tangle of dog-and-cat, a mangle of tit-for-tat, a frenzy of fit-and-fat, a free-for-all melee. And so well matched. *Too* well matched. In Camping Goods, he Frisbeed lanterns; she punched them off one by one. In Sporting Goods, she heaved barbells; he snapped them right in two. He slung a ski pole; she dodged it. She fired a crossbow; he caught the arrow. Knives were thrown and broken; rings were whipped and crushed; glass was hurled and smashed; hoses were sprayed and knotted. *Spplattt!* sounded everywhere. *Fwack!* A china set over his head! A jump rope around her neck! Nails and teeth and knuckles and knees—

Until the edge of Furniture, where, arms gripping arms, they faced each other, panting, hatred flaring in their eyes.

"Neither of us will win," she said.

But one of us must.

Arms twined and straining, sweat pouring down their faces, they growled like animals, muscle matched by muscle.

And suddenly she glanced down at his shadow, and she knew: "There is only one way."

What?

"A fuck to the finish."

Gravely Beaks, still behind the console, peed his pants.

Alex, rummaging through a trunk to find some helpful weapon, shuddered. Oh, my lady! You *would* think of something like that!

The Gacy Guru said, *Define yourself.*

"You get the basic gist," she grunted as she struggled against his grip. "And whoever gives up first wins."

Either that, he added through his sweat and strain, *or whoever comes first loses.*

Dismissing her need for the occasional baby orgasm while climbing toward the Big Bang, Celeste boasted, "I can hold off."

And the Gacy Guru, so used to teasing his beef for hours before popping off, boasted back, *As can we, little darling.*

"So we're on?"

We're on.

With a mutual *oomph!* they freed each other, as revolted as if suddenly emerging from a cesspool.

"But how can I trust you?" she panted, wiping her face.

You want trust?

"I must have some assurance you'll keep your word."

You Godly characters are so tiring.

"I want witnesses."

We have Mayor Beaks.

"Why should I trust *him*? I need more."

That's unfortunate. There are no more.

"I beg to differ!" they heard from beyond the flung hatchets and shredded pool nets and dismembered food processors, from way over by the TVs. There, surrounded by muted TV shows, stood Alex, waving a Pirate Box like a victory flag. "Use this!"

What's he doing here?

"Oh, come off it, Guru, you've got a helper too."

Gravely Beaks gasped as Alex scrambled toward them. "This gizmo will turn his surveillance cameras backward," Alex said.

Put that down!

Alex went on. "Instead of you being able to see everyone with a TV, *this* can make everyone with a TV see *you*."

"How do you know?" Celeste asked.

"Give Alex instructions and you give him the key. I read the blueprints. They were in the trunk where he keeps his toys."

Celeste glanced at the contraption.

"That's it, Guru," she said. "We'll play it out on TV."

You cannot be serious!

"Sure I can. It'll be a worldwide TV special."

But—

"If you win, my father and I will become your slaves. I'll get him to do a group amnesia thing so no one will remember having seen the show, and you can take over the world."

And if we lose?

"Then they all remember, and you surrender." She smiled. "So. What'll it be?"

The Gacy Guru paused. His inner song, which had hooted and honked throughout the fight, now ceased entirely.

Gravely Beaks stopped trying to dry his wet pants with towels from the White Sale. He froze, waiting.

Alex held his breath. The idea of Celeste doing this raised a tornado in his spirit, but if she had to, well, he'd be there for her. He loved her, and that's all there was to it.

"Well?" Celeste asked.

The Gacy Guru looked hither and yon, and then a slow smile leaked over his pasty face.

We accept the challenge.

"Great."

Celeste glanced at Alex, and they exchanged one of those epic lover looks, the kind, unfathomable to anyone else, that are a sweetheart odyssey through the past, present, and future of Us, as intricate as a whale's cry, as deep as the sea.

The Guru marched over to Gravely Beaks, snatched away the towel, and yanked the dwarf over. *You will be our second.*

"And I will be Celeste's," Alex said, breaking their look.

Hastily, he scrambled up a plastic jungle gym to set the Pirate Box in a bracket reserved for a security camera. On the floor below, Gravely Beaks tried to calm his rat-a-tat-tating heart, and the combatants had a moment alone with their thoughts.

But only a moment. Because soon Alex called down, "Ready?"

"Rreeaaddyy," the duelists replied in double track.

"Okay." He threw the switch and jumped to the floor.

And all across America—all across the world—in the middle of a Doogie hormonal crisis, a Bart Simpson "Ay, caramba," a "Beam me up" Scotch and coda, a Cookie Monster snack attack, a Michael Jordan liftoff, a Spiritual Nudity nude-in . . . a shriek, and then—the picture gone! . . . and just snow! *What's wrong?* four billion viewers mumbled to their sofa companions, reaching for antennae, fiddling with remotes, dialing cable companies, getting up (finally!) to pee, cursing . . .

And then the distortion cleared. How do you spell relief! They settled back in their seats, returned their nachos to their laps . . . but wait—*what the hell's this?* Some other show was on! They snatched their remotes and flipped through the channels, but on every network, the same four people stood in a department store aisle: a Joe Average, a dwarf, a woman with long hair, a redheaded man in a straw hat. Staring right into the camera. Taking over!

Then the woman said, "My name is Celeste Kelly," and jaws fell earthward everywhere. "And this is my second." The redheaded man took off his hat and bowed.

As if that wasn't enough, then Mr. Average said, *Our name is Lucifer, and this is* our *second,* and across the world, toupees hit the ceiling, face-lifts collapsed, bowels bow-wowed.

Those viewers who could tugged at their vocal cords and hollered to the next room. You could hear it rolling over the land like a fireball: "Get in here! You won't believe this!"

Celeste babbled some brief explanation, which no one listened to, and then dwarf and redhead stepped back, and Celeste and Lucifer, in the age-old style of duelists, faced each other.

"A fuck to the finish," she said.

A fuck to the finish, he agreed.

"Oh no!" squealed Polly Prudes all over the world, clapping hands over their own and children's ears. "Let me listen!" the kids yelled, seizing the volume control. A slight struggle, but then all stopped. Because then, with one swat, Lucifer and Celeste tore the clothes off each other. *Whhmmmpp!* They stood, naked, panting, snarling. Who could turn away from *that*?

And who could turn away from *this:*

Potbellied Lucifer with a whanging hard-on, tail switching behind him; lithe-bodied Celeste with erect breasts, hair flashing colors.

And then—

Boom! Down on a sofa in the furniture department! Side by side, they went at it, banging like the wind against an outhouse door, jigging and jagging like a fiddler's elbows, hammer and tong, ping and pong—grunting and hating into each other's eyes, switching positions—leg over leg, ankle to shoulder, missionary, dog—"Look at that! Is *that* how you do it?" kids cried, and their mommies said, "Gee, *I*'ve never done it that way, but maybe I *should*," because oh my, it sure did look likely to bull's-eye their favorite target—never detaching, appendages tangled and beating, sweating and flying, Pirate Box following right along, broadcasting the rage, the grunts, the hair, the bodies, pumping like the fuck to end all fucks, like no way could they keep from coming like A-bombs, like a televised catalog of the good old *Kama Sutra*, like making Hugh Hefner take notes in his bed.

They tumbled to the floor, him on top of her, her on top of him, shagging like a rattlesnake. In his mind—in her mind—in *their* mind—he was a pissed-off little boy devil—*Oh no! Not that Job shit all over again! Not dinner with the pharaoh! And—fuck us dead!—isn't that Nero? We'd recognize that fiddle anywh— Fuck! Argh! Caligula! Attila! We don't* want *to remember! Don't* want *to! Fuck! What is she doing to us?*—and she kept going, a hump-and-jam tour of human history, living in the Devil's skin as he hunted and pecked out the losers, the spoiled, the angry, offered them the candy of evil—*How're you doing, Genghis? Can we stay for dinner?*—and it was a horror beyond all horrors, his dark canceling out her light—*Good day, Señor Pizarro! Could we interest you in some greed?*—but somewhere around Ivan the Terrible, Celeste realized she was fizzing up but good—how'd that happen?! she was way too turned on!—oh no! she'd forgotten about her little baby o's! No! She couldn't give herself one, not now, not with the agreed-upon rules—but wowee! her seat belt was fastened and she was ready for takeoff, already taxiing down the runway—

"To the finish!" she shouted aloud, thus tuning down her turn-on—but also inadvertently tuning down *his*—and unlike any who'd come before him, he could relive his own memories *and* diddle her at the same time, and so, with his life raging like a hurricane, they threw themselves to the floor, each trying to do the other first—

bump, grind, in, out, up, down—spinning across a dining room table, whirling onto an ottoman, flying into a grandfather clock—
rolling over the splinters, up against a fireplace—Bricks into your
back—*No!*—Bricks into *your* back!—swing your partner onto the
bed!—dos-à-dos under the table—and all the while—*slave traders!
Robespierre! Napoleon!*—trying to keep her head straight. Every
fuck she'd ever had, every holding-off ruse she'd ever used, she
dredged them all up: the sailor tricks and hooker habits, philanderer
flair and nympho bravura, mercenary sobriety and four-star sagacity
and contortionist elasticity and Celestine electricity. Don't look at
his shadow! Okay, done. Just keep yourself going! But it feels so
oo-la-la!

(Don't let it!)

"Wow, Mommy! Look at tha—"

And *into* the perfume counter, *on top of* the half-price shoe
bin—searching deeper than his memories (*Vlad the Impaler! Jack
the Ripper!*) to find strength, to find solutions—he wrapped his tail
around, wagged its tongue tip at just the right spot—oooh, that felt
good; she shoved him back, got a mannequin to butt-fuck him—
Yow! he grunted, then *oooh*—was that it? Could he be getting
close—his breath quickening, his moan moaning, his memories
twentieth centurying—down deeper, keep going, don't let anything
stop you, don't be fooled, go, go, go—

And then in the imported rug area she found it, something she'd
always known but never admitted, something she'd floated around,
kicked around, *spread* around, but never thought about deep enough
to see, to know, to *feel*. She was beneath him on a Turkish rug, and
she felt it, at last. She had something inside her. Something she
transmitted by touch. It was the virus she put in people's blood. It
was the power her father gave her in the dream. It was the light she
exuded during love. It was God's little helper, God's twist and shout,
the be-all and the end-all, the magic we call . . . life.

Now, with death inside her—*Stalin! Hitler! Mussolini!*—she

could feel it, a power swirling in her womb, vast, potent, colorful as the creation of the universe. And she knew that if she held off long enough, she could fuck it all into him—and maybe it would wipe away his cruelty, negate his death, turn him helpless—oh, fuck all that—as long as it *made him come!!!*

But what if—what if that meant she might not heal again? Might not *live*? Could she do it? Should she? What about—

Shit! He'd found the ravishing rhythm! the devastating angle! Here they were up to Pol Pot, and she was on the conveyor belt to orgasm! Oh no! Slow down! But no matter what she did, she was on a fast track to *aaa eee iii ohh ooo* and there was no time to think, just his memories in her mind and light shooting out of her pores and his shadow blackening her light and resolve thundering in her crotch: Do it! Do it! Do it!

. . . She closed her eyes. She focused. She used every memory she knew. She shifted her legs.

And she fucked the most metamorphosic fuck of all time.

She could feel it right away. He was writhing, clawing, screaming. She turned her head and looked in his eyes and saw—

Green eyes, blue eyes, black eyes, brown. A high forehead, a low forehead, a pompadour falling down! He was shifting shape! Right in her arms, copulatingly connected, he was flickering form as fast as flame changes! He was a montage of bodies, skin colors, hair textures, noses—all while his memories blitzkrieged away! One after another after another, his appearances howled and rasped and squirmed and grasped—each fighting the suck, each bucking the rise, each vavooming past the crest, each soaring into bazhoom— and then staying there—until he was one long spazzing climax, body after body, identities changing faster than she could see, faster than you could name, and they were no one she'd ever met, no one she'd ever known, but so much a part of his scheme that they were who he'd become inside, who he felt like deep in his heart:

J. R. Ewing with his smarmy grin; Sam Malone with his graying temples; Alex Keaton with his junk-bond hair; Max Headroom with his dark sunglasses; Al Bundy, grimacing in disgust; Archie Bunker, mugging in distrust; chunky George Jefferson; rotund Cliff Huxtable; pug-nosed Tatoo; mealy-mouthed Major Healey; Sonny Crockett; Fred Sanford; Perry Mason; Reuben Kincaid; gangly Hawkeye; skinny Felix; duck-tailed Fonz; stone-jawed bionic man; Magnum, all mustache and wink; Mork, all talk and twink; Greg Brady, all teeth and sophomore; Gilligan, all hat and no more; Colonel Hogan; Major Dad; Captain Kirk; Sergeant Bilko; Hill Street hustlers; Mayberry morons; Ponderosa punchers; Twilight Zone turkeys; Dr. Kildare; Dr. Smith; Dr. Fleischman; Dr. Who; Mr. Drysdale; Mr. French; Mr. Eddie's Father; Mr. Grant; Uncle Martin; Uncle Charlie; Grandpa Walton; Cousin Itt—and faster now, faster—that Family Value Icon Jim Anderson, all cardiganed up for wisdom; that Family Devalue Ralph Kramden, all bus-drivered out for rage; Ricky Ricardo; Rob Petrie; Darrin Stephens; Herman Munster; Ted Baxter; Jim Ignatowski; Barnabas Collins; Maxwell Smart—on and on they went, slipping into commercial—Mr. Whipple, the Isuzu liar, Frito Bandito, the Marlboro Man—and then, as if he was regressing—he did seem to be shrinking! his darkness losing ground to her light, his memories wailing like saturation bombing! George Jetson, Archie Andrews, Daffy Duck, Speed Racer, Boris Badenov, Fred Flintstone, Magilla Gorilla, Scooby Doo, Alvin, Beanie, Yogi, Casper, Top Cat, Beavis, He-Man, Mr. Magoo—and she held on as his body twitched and spluttered and thrashed and rocked, and he cried, *Noooooo!* his voice jolting with each new body, sliding from Miles Drentell into Illya Kuryakin into I can't believe I ate the whole thing into Deputy Dawg—and it was so hard to keep going, it took all her spit and spirit to stay through this machine gun metamorphosis, but she gritted her teeth, fucked through her disbelief, as he gasped and screamed and commercialed and cartooned and came and came and came and

then

it was silent

no memories

just light

and breathing—

   her breathing

and somewhere, far off, the whimper of a child . . .

She had stopped moving.

Cautiously, she reached out, feeling for the Guru—

And her hands touched . . .

A baby.

A child lay between her legs. Small. Maybe a year old. Gazing up at her with wide, human eyes.

She tried to listen, but all she heard was the rubber-ducky quack of an infant's mind. She tried to smell, but all she inhaled was the sweet scent of milk.

She sat up. The child sucked his thumb. His shadow looked . . . his shadow looked . . . polyrhythmic and polyhued . . . dancing and colorful . . . simple . . . light . . . like a baby.

By the time she cleared out her confusion enough to find the words, Alex was kneeling beside her.

"How . . . how did this kid get here?" she asked.

"That's him," Alex said.

Celeste examined the boy before her. She *had* fucked the Guru to the finish; her life had pulverized his death. This was all that was left of the Devil.

She touched the child. His skin was soft, his body warm. She leaned forward and wrapped her arms around him and inhaled his lovely baby smell. A child. All tiny fingers and chubby knees, long eyelashes and huge eyes. She hugged him, and he hugged back.

Alex knelt beside them and brushed Celeste's hair off her damp forehead.

"What should we say to the viewers?" she whispered.

"I don't know," he replied, "but I bet it doesn't matter."

And he was right. For in the months to come, Celeste would grant hundreds of interviews that would explain it, but right then no one could hear; most viewers had seen more than they could process, and at least two billion had fainted. Besides, the camera had stopped focusing on the heroine. It had aimed itself at Gravely Beaks, who was now staggering down the flotsamed corridor, scratching his head in awe at what he'd just seen, shedding his white gloves behind him.

And
So . . .

In Fossilfink Falls, Pennsylvania, the first rays of morning were always heralded by blackbirds, as blackbirds had for generations been the only kind of bird in town. A notably small one kept a perch outside the coffee shop, where for years it had greeted all A.M. caffeine guzzlers with its familiar *sweet sweet sweet what-cheer what-cheer*, and this particular morning was no exception.

Inside the coffee shop, Gluper Flugel rubbed his eyes and watched the singing fowl. Glupe, a Fossilfink Falls native and long-time coffee shop fixture, had watched that bird many a morning, but usually not with such fatigue. Three-thirty, he'd been up till three-damn-thirty the night before, holding smelling salts under the wife's nose and fielding questions from his offspring. It'd been quite a scene: popcorn all over the living room, the dog yapping at the pandemonium—and of course that duel on the TV. Now Glupe took a swig of the liquid beneath him and tried not to listen to the conversation at the counter, where several townspeople were musing over the unscheduled program that had kept them up till the wee hours too. Glupe wasn't feeling up to handling talk. He'd taken his usual two-sugar sleep quencher and slid off by himself to a booth, and there he would stay, gazing out at the black mountains of the town and that bird he knew so well, until he felt good and ready to face it all.

Glupe glanced up from his sip. *Sweet sweet sweet,* the bird went, and then a gust of wind came up, ruffling the creature's feathers. A nice gust, Glupe thought, a lovely little breeze—but then he realized that the wind had to be way fiercer than it seemed: red splotches were rising up from beneath the black feathers, as if the wind were pummeling the varmint, peeling off his hide, stripping him down to his very blood. Though, would you get this, the bird kept on singing like nothing was happening, even as more and more of the black was blowing away, and more and more of the red sparkling through. And suddenly Glupe caught on that the blackbird that had sere-naded the Fossilfink Falls Coffee Shop for years wasn't a blackbird at all! It was a *cardinal,* all gussied up in showgirl scarlet. The black must have been an accident of environment, a shroud made from the same coal dust that coated the mountains of the valley. It had settled onto the critter, tainting the red feathers mourning black, making it seem what it wasn't, concealing the real bird inside.

But the cardinal wasn't the only bird to get such treatment, no siree. Out across the street, Glupe saw, dozens of other birds were zipping around—oriole oranges, thrush blues, canary yellows, war-bler greens—and hey!—seagull whites! Glupe always thought the only winged species that inhabited these parts was the blackbird. Now he saw a whopping big otherwise.

"Hey, check this ou—," he began, but then spied something far more important than a bunch of pretty birds.

Cruising down the pass between the black mountains, twining down Route 55, bumping across the small bridge spanning Hee-cheemonkee Creek, and coasting into town, was the four-wheeled object of myth and song, Celeste's famous Dodge, now as visible as day—and inside her, three equally apparent passengers.

Gluper Flugel and the other customers in the coffee shop gaped as the car strutted into town, glittering regally. "Guess she don't need to be invisible no more," Glupe muttered. "Guess them folks inside don't, neither"—and then he remembered he'd said something very much like that to himself this morning. He'd woken with the same old blues he always had but, for some reason not immediately clear, found new thoughts popping off in his head like firecrackers, leading him to remark out loud, before he'd turned on the lights, before his wife was even awake, a statement that had never crossed his synapses before: "Hey, I don't *need* to feel this shitty no more. Damn right! And I don't think I will."

And now, watching as the car passed the coffee shop, every person in the place remembered thinking the same thing.

The Dodge tooled past the coffee shop and continued down Main Street. In the plate-glass windows of the bankrupt stores, Loretta could see herself, buxom and ornate. She paused in front of the old hardware store, the vacant apothecary's, the deceased Arthur Murray dance studio, admiring her exquisitely adorned body. "I do cut a superb figure, *n'est-ce pas?*" she commented to her three passengers. The two in the back seat drifted up from their private huddle and shared a glance at Loretta's reflection. "*Oui*," Celeste replied. "Indeed," Alex said.

As for the passenger in the front, maybe he concurred, maybe not. It was hard to tell, seeing as he was a kid—a prelanguage toddler, to be exact—and all he could say was, "Oofa moofa boof." But he said it with enthusiasm, as he jiggled Loretta's soda fountain dashboard and batted her fuzzy dice and bongos. Obviously, he thought Loretta was just great. Clearly, he thought everything was just great. He was a giggly, what-is-it? I'll-play-with-it kind of guy. No one peeking into this car, not even the coffee shop gawkers who'd seen it all last night in beautiful living color, could possibly have guessed that for thousands of years this little guy had been the Devil.

Loretta and her cargo sailed out of Fossilfink Falls, leaving behind the black mountains and boarded-up houses and stunned coffee drinkers. Before her windshield spread the fields of weeds. There was the zombie grass, and there the Dracula creeper, and beside it the phantom fungus—same as they ever were.

Celeste could count the minutes now. "We're almost there, Tommy," she called to the boy in the front. The boy, who didn't know what "there" was, let alone "we're" and "almost," giggled in reply, as he reached for the Milky Way of dangling rings and Loretta teased him with her feather boas.

At the gate to the Kelly Home, the Dodge retracted her boas and shifted into Park. Before them, beyond the iron railing, lay the Oz-emerald lawn, the Through the Looking Glass garden, the Bazooka-pink building.

"Home," Celeste said.

The three passengers decarred. Celeste lifted Tommy up and carried him to the front gate, and the new child rang the bell.

On all quarters of the property, dogs and orphans pricked up their ears at the sound. The canines dashed fastest; they bolted from the giant path and house before the *dong!* had fully reached the orphans' eardrums. But soon the youngsters wised up, and a great rush of children spilled down the drive toward the gate.

In the garden, Sam and Marina heard the hullabaloo. "What could that be?" Sam mumbled. The two stood on a rock to see, but before the physical evidence was in view, Marina shouted, "They're here!" The night before, her voice had suddenly flowered, burst full-grown out of her larynx like a princess snapped out of a spell. All night she had reveled in reclaimed communication. She'd seized Sam by the hand and run with him to the garden, and there they had stayed, Marina chattering at a steady 135 words per minute, Sam savoring her every syllable, as the moon had arced across the sky and the sun had slogged its fat ass above the horizon and the birds had struck up a symphony. She told him all about being gagged and bound inside her own mind, knowing others' lives but never living her own—and now she would live her own, at last she would, she and Sam, she told him, hugging him to her, taking his face in her hands, and kissing him, for the first time. Ah, and what a kiss! Even Cupid couldn't have made a better one to order.

And then they had gazed at each other, and she squeezed his hand and said, "Let's write about it."

"About what?" Sam had asked. A bullfrog was croaking across the garden, and the shadows were long with dawn. "About you?"

"I'm just one part of it. Let's write a book. A history. A *mystery*. We'll tell the whole story."

Sam mulled it over. They *did* have the inside track on this narrative, and it *was* one of the more monumental events in human history. How it would affect the world, he didn't know, nor could he have foreseen. The Anti-Virus hadn't yet been subjected to the scrutiny that, in a few months, would reveal it to be not just an AIDS antibody but a misery antibody; in other words, a virus that spread spiritual vitality or, as one of Celeste's partners called it, a "contagious calm." Nor had the stores yet received Celeste's book, which would, in a month, expose the complexities and identities of the Matrix and the *nths;* nor had, in the few weeks prior to publication, hordes of Matrix members resigned from their prestigious positions and masses of *nths* turned themselves in. And maybe most important, people hadn't yet begun speaking among themselves. It would take a few days before the world comprehended that many—maybe most: no one's ever been sure—folks woke the morning after what's become known as the Celestial Cataclysm and realized that what they'd thought was a fit and fine inner state was actually a long-tolerated spiritual malaise. Moreover, many saw that morning, they didn't have to stay that way if they didn't want to.

But Sam didn't know this was to happen. All he knew was how the Cataclysm came to occur and that he had one fine partner to write it up with.

"You're on," he told Marina.

"You were there, so you should write it," she said. "Besides, my dad's a mega music fan, and so are you, which is all the more reason." She smiled. "I'll type it."

He agreed with another kiss, and that afternoon they sat down and began to pen the book you are completing right now.

And so as Celeste and Alex and Tommy strolled inside the gates that morning, surrounded by barking mutts and babbling orphans, we stood up in the garden, Marina and I. We climbed on a rock and waved to the homecoming and called out "Hallo!" and "Welcome!" In a few minutes we would learn that Celeste and Alex had returned for good to the Home, where they were going to explore *all* their gifts while raising their boy as if he were just a child, which, now stripped of his death and his evil, is in fact all he was. It seemed we hadn't witnessed a Second Coming nearly as much as a Second Chance. But as we raised ourselves on tiptoe that morning, I couldn't concentrate on the boy, or the future of the world, or anything even the tiniest bit mystical. Miss Kelly had hobbled onto the lawn, and Celeste had stepped tentatively toward her grandmother, and crimson apprehension was on both faces. They had reached the edges of each other's shadows and locked their eyes together, and as I watched, they silently but visibly traded accusations and answers and apologies back and forth, crissing and crossing, a tangled look picked at by each and then handed back, more tangled, then more ordered, more tangled, more ordered, until grandmother and granddaughter blinked, both at once, anchoring the latticed look not with the one or the other but *between* them, suspended like a cat's cradle, like a game with no winners and no losers, just *these are the facts, yes, this is what happened, and let us go on from here.* They each took a step closer. Clouds frolicked on the horizon, and Tommy sat down and picked buttercups, and as the two women reached for each other on the sunlit lawn that morning, their shadows touching, their shadows overlapping, I knew the world had just watched the grandest battle ever fought, the one humanity had waited for and forsoothed and cringed in fear of, and I could see rainbows forming in the sky, signs of a new promise, and the air smelled sweeter than ever and the blackbirds in town had all turned color and I knew I'd just learned the truth about sex and God, I knew all this, but right then none of that could compete with what was happening before my eyes: forgiving smiles and a hug that sealed those smiles. The kind of hug you lose yourself in. The kind of hug where both sides promise trust. Cosmic battles may be exciting and earth-shattering, I thought, as I watched them embrace on the lawn that sunny morning, but this is the only way that the war can stay won.

for

bertha—helper in the dream

and

mr. h—court jester
master speller
wise & warm imblabafon